Matthew gently pulled Gyneth closer, and she closed her eyes. All the taboos of the past came rushing into her consciousness, telling her that it was wrong to have sex with a black man, regardless of the fact that he was her best friend's lover.

Yet neither the taboos nor the betrayal could stop her now. It had been so long since she had felt a man's hands on her, especially hands as confident and skillful as Matthew's.

"Yes, yes, don't stop, don't ever stop," she panted, sobbing with the release of pent-up desire, as she gave herself entirely to mounting waves of erotic pleasure.

Then the front door opened. Carolyn stood poised on the threshold, frozen in shock. "Gyneth, is that you? I can't believe it. Matthew? No, I won't believe it. It can't be true."

**But it *was* true. Undeniably true. And the friendship between Gyneth and Carolyn that had withstood all that the world could do to destroy it was now imperiled by passion gone out of control and an act that could never be erased—**

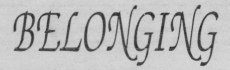

*BELONGING*

# Belonging

## LARRAINE SEGIL

A SIGNET BOOK

SIGNET
Published by the Penguin Group
Penguin Books USA Inc., 375 Hudson Street,
New York, New York 10014, U.S.A.
Penguin Books Ltd, 27 Wrights Lane,
London W8 5TZ, England
Penguin Books Australia Ltd, Ringwood,
Victoria, Australia
Penguin Books Canada Ltd, 10 Alcorn Avenue
Toronto, Ontario, Canada M4V 3B2
Penguin Books (N.Z.) Ltd, 182–190 Wairau Road,
Auckland 10, New Zealand

Penguin Books Ltd, Registered Offices:
Harmondsworth, Middlesex, England

First published by Signet, an imprint of Dutton Signet, a division of Penguin
Books USA Inc.

First Printing, July, 1994
10  9  8  7  6  5  4  3  2  1

PUBLISHER'S NOTE
This is a work of fiction. Names, characters, places, and incidents either are the
product of the author's imagination or are used fictitiously, and any resemblance
to actual persons, living or dead, events, or locales is entirely coincidental.

This book is dedicated to my parents,
Norma and Jack Wolfowitz,
whose lives were my inspiration,
and to the children I didn't have.

# ACKNOWLEDGMENTS

My thanks go first to my beloved husband Clive, and son, James, whose encouragement, love, and input has supported me throughout the years this book was in development; and to my sister Pamela Goldberg whose love and companionship I cherish greatly; to Sharleen Cooper Cohen for her advice and generosity in introducing me to Sandi Gelles-Cole, who has given me the guidance and direction for which I am forever grateful; to Bronya Pereira Galef, who early in the process, brought Ken Sherman, a constant and caring supporter, into my life; to my business partner, Emilio Fontana, who has been an interested supporter; to Jackie Nach for her insights and perceptions; and a very special thanks to Flo Dunagan, for her continual, professional, and efficient input; finally, to the many people who have touched my life and enabled me to delve deeply into the wondrous emotions and relationships that were the material from which this book was developed.

# PART I

# BASUTOLAND 1955

# Chapter 1

Martha stretched her young arms up toward the ceiling of the thatched hut. If she peeked through her fingers and held them apart in a V, she could frame the neatly woven rafters of dry veld grasses that formed the secure roof covering of her round family home. Her home was just like the others in her village—neat triangles of thatch and wood covering a collection of mud walls perched on the mountaintops. The peaks soared eleven thousand feet above sea level in her home country, the tiny mountain kingdom of Basutoland, an inland enclave in the inhospitable country of South Africa.

She yawned. It was almost time to get up. Her mother would expect her to fetch the water from the creek and start the fire under the big iron pot that would fill with white bubbling porridge, enough to feed the whole family of eight children. They were only good for working in the fields, her father grumbled, and since they ate so much he had to be sure that they worked hard so that the family had enough *mielies* to eat. There was always enough fish, but Martha didn't like the way the fish eyes looked at her, sort of bulbous and accusing, as if to protest the fact of being caught at all. Her strong legs jumped nimbly down the mountainside as she bounced the pot on her head, holding onto it with both hands. The trip back up again would be graceful and steady, as she adopted the rock-steady stance her mother had taught her, her legs moving but her upper body immobile. She sang the songs of her Southern Sotho people, with click sounds and rhythms impossible for the white tongue to master.

Life in Basutoland in 1955 was simple, a life of farming, fishing, playing, and doing household chores. Martha, her mother and sisters took care of the household and the growing of the grain, while her father and brothers did the fishing and cared for the pony and few cattle. They lived on the side of the imposing mountain that overlooked the town of Maseru. Her father was the only man in the little village, the *kgoro,* who chose to have just one wife, her mother. He was one of the older members of the small community but was still agile and energetic. Their lives were built around raising enough food to feed the family, but sometimes they would listen wide eyed to tales about the cities in the south, Cape Town, Durban, and Johannesburg. There seemed to be so many riches in those great cities; the ones who went to work there came back again laden with material things beyond all imagination, which made Martha feel as if her destiny was in those places, not pulling water from the creek and squabbling with her brothers and sisters.

She wrapped the brightly colored blanket that was the trademark of her people around her slim body as she waited for the water in the pot to boil. The little pony, playmate of the children but workhorse of the family, whinnied softly for some grain. She grabbed a handful and scampered to throw it beneath his inquisitive nose. She was pleased to be able to ride him on the return journey up the mountain whenever she went down to the town with her parents to sell vegetables and grain, since mountain trails were tiring for a little girl who'd been jumping around all day talking to the tradesmen and their children.

Unlike her brothers and sisters, Martha always went with her parents on market day to the town of Maseru. She was invigorated by the sights and sounds of the town, intrigued by the sophistication of the children she met there, and chattered endlessly about how she'd soon go to school and visit faraway places.

Finally her parents agreed to allow her to stay with her friend, Mary, and attend the convent school in Maseru. Though the town had a population of less than eight thousand people, to Martha it was a metropolis. She settled right into the routine of the school day, wearing one of Mary's old uniforms, and started learning with great enthusiasm. Her life became an adventure. She loved the privacy of having just Mary around, and not a whole crowd of curious and inquisitive brothers and sisters. Going home every few weeks was an opportunity to show off her newfound reading skills, and on the holidays, she took books home to demonstrate the rightness of her parents' decision. She was equally keen to go back to the town, to join her new friends and life. Now her ambitions were greater. She longed to visit a real city, like the one in the south, Johannesburg, the City of Gold.

It was the young man Daniel who helped her to realize that dream. But, as often happens with dreams, not in quite the way she had imagined it.

She met him at market day, during the summer vacation of her thirteenth year, as she dutifully helped her father sell his corn. Daniel's body glistened with perspiration, the heat of the day shimmering around him, but all Martha could see were his well-defined muscles and bulging tight shorts. Daniel looked appreciatively at her budding young breasts. Martha could almost feel his heat as the young man paid for his purchase. He pointed to the corn roasting on the embers of a small coal fire in a cast-iron drum. The smell was delicious.

"How much are those?" he inquired, his voice reverberating in Martha's ears.

"Two for a penny," she said, trembling slightly.

"What is your name?" Daniel asked.

"Martha," she answered.

"*Kundjani,*" he said, greeting her in the old-fashioned Sotho way. Martha dropped her eyes and smiled, rather shyly.

Daniel slid over and off the bicycle on which he'd carelessly been sitting and leaned it against the nearby tree trunk. He squatted down on his haunches and viewed Martha slowly from the top of her head to her toes. Martha flushed with embarrassment.

"I have never been on one of those," she said, trying to deflect his eyes from her body as she pointed to the rusty two-wheeler. He offered to show her how to ride. Martha looked at her father who was negotiating loudly, using many hand movements with two women who were suspiciously eyeing the quality of his corn. He wouldn't even miss her.

She mounted the bicycle awkwardly and immediately fell off.

"Here, let me show you how," Daniel said, and he jumped on and swung around her in a circle. She clapped her hands together in gleeful excitement and he flushed with pleasure.

Daniel lifted her onto the bike and held her firmly while they went for a short and rather wobbly ride.

So their friendship began. For the next three market days Daniel biked up to the corn stand and they spent the rest of the day together. Martha finally learned to sit on the crossbar of the bicycle, even though it bit into her buttocks, as Daniel pedaled laboriously along the sand road. He held her hand with one of his, and she thrilled to his touch.

Martha asked about his family. He told her that they lived in one of the small villages outside Maseru and his father had four wives and twenty children. Daniel explained that he had left them as soon as he could with little regret. They'd hardly miss him in the confusion of family members. He'd taken any job he could find, cleaning or garbage hauling. Now he worked as a waiter in one of the hotel restaurants in the town. Daniel spoke at length of the big cities in South Africa and how he was not going to do the expected, take a wife and stay in Maseru forever. In fact, Daniel stated emphatically, he had no intention of getting married until he'd made his fortune in the City of Gold. Martha could almost imagine herself walking there beside him as Daniel described his one and only visit to Johannesburg, where gold could buy things like a bike, fancy clothes, and a radio.

The third weekend after they met, Daniel took Martha to a special place away from the town, a woodsy area only he knew of. It was deep amongst the trees and the cool earth was soft with the footprints of little deer hooves and the marks of other small animals. It looked as if no human hand had ever touched the foliage as it drew its cool leafy protection over the little sunken close. Daniel beckoned to Martha. She followed him. He bent low beneath the tree branches and suddenly they were there together in the sand and Martha felt his strong arms enfolding her. He was hard and rippling with muscular strength and she gasped as the heat ran through her body and made her sigh and open her legs, welcoming him to her. Martha let her instincts guide her and she moved her body against Daniel's, enjoying the feel of his muscles, the hardness that was now between her legs. Then Daniel started to remove her thin underpants and soon her light summer dress was pulled over her breasts. She struggled to free herself from the material, not knowing that the consequence of her wriggling under Daniel was to inflame him out of control. She could hardly catch her breath as his weight pumped down on her and a hard weapon between her legs pierced into her body.

"It hurts, hurts, stop now, it hurts me," Martha tried to say to Daniel, but along with the hurt was the pleasure and the desire for more of the now exciting movements inside her. Martha started panting, thrusting, meeting Daniel's pumping movements with wild and uncontrolled spasms as her body reached orgasm and Daniel exploded inside her. Then all of a sudden he was quiet and together their bodies relaxed, their panting subsided and they lay quietly together, overwhelmed by passion.

Martha was in love. The next weeks were filled with new sensations as she hungrily explored Daniel's strong young body. Day after day, as she lay gasping in his arms, his thick penis piercing her body, Martha's own evolving needs exploded into jerking, grasping, heated coupling, and her desire for his manhood became difficult to satisfy.

But two months of lovemaking and elaborate lies to her parents were soon reduced to stark reality, unwanted but inevitable. One morning Martha could not get out of bed. Tired and sick, she realized that she was pregnant. As soon as she had dispensed with her daily chores, she ran desperately down the mountain, frantic to elicit Daniel's help. But he was resentful, unwilling to face the truth, and told Martha she was imagining her symptoms. He had his own dreams to fulfill, and Martha was not part of them. To her horror, he withdrew, becoming distant, unavailable.

Martha tried to go about her normal duties, caring

for her siblings, hauling corn and fish to the market, but the days marched inexorably onward, and she knew, with the certainty learned from her mother's interminable childbearing, that the baby would come. She had one last card to play. Trembling with fear, she began the long, lonely trek up the mountain. Her only hope for reprieve lay with the *inyanga,* the witch doctor.

The mountain peak was rocky, with little foliage. It was here that the witch doctor would jump and dance, ranting incantations in a high shrill voice, which sometimes in the cool mountain air reached all the way across to Martha's village.

Slowly and with beating heart, Martha approached the mud hut. Long strings of beads clinked against each other in the breeze and created a frond over the entrance to the hut. Martha wanted only to run down the hill as fast as she could, but a wave of nausea reminded her of the urgency of her need. Then she heard the low moaning. It permeated her body, invading her with deep sounds and she stood completely frozen with fear.

"Come closer," the voice rumbled.

A long fingered hand came slowly through the beaded curtain, reaching for the young black girl. It stopped just an inch away from her arm. The finger curled, beckoning.

"Come to me," the eerie voice repeated.

Martha moved uncertainly forward, unable to do anything but obey. The voice continued, becoming slower, more hypnotic as Martha felt herself drawn inside the dark interior.

Her eyes widened in fear as she saw the bones, the skulls, the cans filled with evil-smelling potions. Then nausea hit her again, and she hiccuped and managed with difficulty to hold down the acid rising in her throat.

Slowly her eyes became accustomed to the dark and she looked fearfully at the woman on her haunches in the corner of the hut. She was thin with very long legs. Martha had seen her once loping through the town in the shadows of the early evening looking like a bony-legged springbok deer, hopping, then running, sometimes fast, then slowly creeping around corners only to speed up again. Now she could see her clearly. Her one arm was twisted with the hand turned inward like a giant claw. Her nails were very long and her eyes glistened yellow in the dim light.

"You have the sickness of the unborn child," she crooned, "sickness that will last five more months . . ."

Martha's lips trembled as she tried to speak.

"He is young and tall and strong and thick," the witch doctor said in the same crooning tone, motioning her hand slowly upward from her groin in an obscene phallic movement.

"Yes . . . yes," Martha whispered in awe, filled with shame at the thought the witch doctor had seen everything. "Please take away the baby," she pleaded, forcing the words out of the trembling lips.

The witch doctor looked with shrewd eyes at the full breasts of the young girl. This one would have to carry the child, she was too far gone. "A baby, a baby . . . mmmmm," the woman crooned softly.

"I don't want it—my parents—they don't know about me and Daniel," Martha stammered. "Please w-will you help me?"

There was no response, just the rhythmic, low humming as the witch doctor rocked back and forth on her heels. It was as if the woman had not heard her. She continued to rock back and forth, back and forth.

Then suddenly she leapt up into the air, almost

touching the high rafters of the ceiling of her hut. Martha shrieked in panic and turned blindly, groping for the hut's entrance, desperate to save herself from the furor of the *inyanga*. But before she could, she felt the long nails digging into her soft arm, pulling her backward onto the rocky floor. Then she was pinned under that terrible claw, unable to move.

"You will have this child in five months' time, and you will go far to the golden place to bear it. The child has many tasks before it—you must not keep it from the future. It is your duty to bear this offspring and your time is short here, so young, so young . . ." The grip loosened on Martha's arm and then she was free.

Martha slid away, running, slipping, scraping her arms and legs as she half fell down the sharp incline, desperate to escape from the foreboding, dark presence that lurked in the hut. Tears streamed down her face mixed with dirt as she ran sobbing and trembling until, in relief from her narrow escape, she found a sunny spot and sank to the dry earth.

Martha laid her head on her hands and wept, hiccuping and coughing as her nose swelled up and her eyes streamed with tears. There was no disobeying the *inyanga*. Witch doctors were all-powerful and if their advice went unheeded, they'd send the boogeyman, the *tokoloshe,* to do terrible things to people while they slept. There was no decision to make. Martha had to have the child. But where was the golden place? Then she knew. The City of Gold. Her heart began to hammer with growing excitement. She was to go with Daniel to Johannesburg, the City of Gold, to have the baby. Her spirits lifted dramatically as she ran to tell Daniel.

He was less than enthusiastic. "This is not in my plan. I am not ready to leave. I want to make more money, to journey to the city in the new year. Anyway I don't want to marry yet. I am too young. Look, I'm busy now. Go to your other boyfriends, they'll help you." He closed the door in her face.

Martha stared at the paint peeling off the wooden door of the small quarters in which Daniel lived with three other young men. She could hear them laughing inside, probably mocking her innocence. The tears ran down her face, tracing rivulets of dust. Other boyfriends . . . she had no other boyfriends, surely he knew that. Then with the clarity derived from pain, she realized that he would not help her, not now, not ever. She was alone in her plight. And now, unless she traveled to the City of Gold, her parents were forever doomed to be haunted by the *tokoloshe,* as she would be, if she did not do the bidding of the *inyanga.*

Martha trudged back up the hill. Her brothers and sisters were squabbling as usual, but this time she looked at them with affection as she grabbed one after the other, hugging and holding them as they scrambled impatiently out of her grasp, anxious to continue their game. She prepared her blanket, filled like a sack with the possessions she could not bear to be without, and then, as she left the hut, she hugged her mother, squirming as she told her one last lie.

"There is a party for the class at Mary's house tonight. I will stay over there and return on the weekend, Mama. I'll see you then." Martha's mother was distracted. Her pregnancy, the tenth in almost so many years, was exhausting and her concentration was poor. She noticed that Martha seemed tearful, and made a mental note to find out if things were well with her and the young man she had seen her with. It was time for the young woman to marry anyway, enough of the freedoms the school had given her.

Martha had one last stop to make. She returned to Daniel's quarters. The party inside had now reached the level of loud singing and drunken joke telling.

Martha padded silently around the modest building. She ducked under the open window, lest any of the revelers inside hear or recognize her. An empty bottle came sailing out, narrowly missing her. She held her breath and stood absolutely still. Then Martha saw what she was looking for. Quietly, she slipped onto the bicycle on which they'd spent happy days together and pedaled carefully away. Daniel would help her get to the City of Gold despite himself.

# Chapter 2

Martha's heart pounded and her hands were clammy with nerves. She was to begin her first job, as a laundry maid, in Johannesburg that very day. She stood in front of the imposing gates of the red brick, ivy-covered mansion, the home of the white family called Amron, in the exclusive northern suburb of Hyde Park. The Amrons' first child, a little girl, Gyneth, was a year old, and the washing and ironing were increasing daily. A message had been passed around the neighborhood that the Amrons needed a full time laundry maid. It was the perfect opportunity for Martha and now she stood nervously pulling at her sweater on the threshold of her new life.

For over a year she had lived with a gentle elderly couple, Matthias and Ouma, in Soweto, the sprawling black township on the outskirts of Johannesburg. Matthias had found her at the side of the road from Basutoland to the Transvaal. She was suffering from heat and dehydration, and her bicycle had been stolen. He had taken her to his wife in their modest Soweto house. Ouma, her children grown and her life empty, had welcomed the teenager into her home. The older woman taught Martha most of what she needed to know to work as a laundry maid as they waited out her pregnancy together. Martha was a quick learner and grateful for the lessons. She accompanied Ouma to the large white homes in the suburbs and carried the baskets of soiled linens. She stood quietly as Ouma's iron swept back and forth, whipping under collars and over frills, flattening the broad expanses of sheets and tablecloths. During that year, Martha observed how carefully Ouma spoke to white people and their servants. The young girl stammered when spoken to, not knowing how to use the iron, her fingers trembling as she smoothed the fine fabrics and laces. The languages of the city were foreign to her, English, Zulu, Xhosa, and rarely her familiar Sotho. Many times she longed for the familiarity of her mother's protective arms and even the irritations her energetic brothers and sisters brought into her life. At home she had been the confident and talkative one, the leader of the group.

Matthias had told her about the City of Gold on their journey there in his battered truck.

"Buildings," he'd said, "are taller than the hills of your hometown. They shine on warm days as the sun lights up their windows." Martha had hung on Matthias's every word.

"I arrived in the City twenty years ago when it was mostly a place where people came to find work on the mines."

Matthias paused and sighed. "It was far from the cornfields of my home. Johannesburg is a place of hard, strange shapes and machines; iron, glass, trains, carriages. As a young person, like you, I was in awe at the thought of such grandness, eager to learn to become part of the new world." The old truck clanked along the roads into the dusty Transvaal.

"Then, as the years passed, I found out that hunger was always just a day away. You see, child," he said, looking away from the long straight road and focusing intently on the wide-eyed young girl next to him, "cornfields may be dull, but the land gives comfort and food, not the smoke, dirt, and pain of the city."

Martha had listened without really understanding.

Matthias and Ouma had been the first people Martha had met who didn't know her family or friends. And Martha realized as she entered Soweto, huge with pot-holed sand streets and small dilapidated houses, that she knew no one there. A pall of smoke hung over the place, obscuring the blue sky and making the day dull.

"I have never seen daylight this color." Martha had searched the skies for an impending storm.

"It is from the coal stoves that burn in Soweto. The houses have no electricity here," Matthias explained.

Martha remembered with a sharp sense of loss her home in Basutoland, a collection of small huts in a clearing, clean, under clear skies filled with the bustle and activity of a community.

The birth of Martha's baby was a wrenching experience, made even more difficult without her mother's presence. She was grateful for Ouma's assistance. Twenty hours of ever-increasing pains and a wet sheet clamped between her teeth belied the stories Martha had heard about the old days, when the women in the fields had squatted to give birth and then continued with their work. A baby girl slid out at last, and Ouma caught the child deftly and bit off the umbilical cord as she wrapped her in a blanket. She placed the squealing infant on Martha's belly.

"Her name will be Carolyn," the young mother whispered, "after my favorite sister." She touched the small bundle gently. The tears poured down her exhausted face, already wet with perspiration. She was no longer alone.

The next few months were a time for loving discovery. Martha reveled in the sense of well-being that she had with the child in her arms, a little person perfect in every way, dependent on her for everything. She knew her time at home with Carolyn was short. She had to find a job.

Ouma, now striken with arthritis, was unable to continue working as a laundry maid and had to replace that income by taking care of three other children whose mothers had live-in jobs in the white suburbs. Carolyn would be one of those children cared for, and Martha's income would help support the household.

Now Martha was about to enter the world of white people, praying she would not stammer the unfamiliar English words she had struggled to learn. Her tears were not far from the surface as she thought of the little person she had left in Ouma's care.

Matthias parked his truck carefully at the tradesmen's entrance of the Amrons' home, then joined Martha and her sack full of possessions at the side gate. Martha stumbled slightly as she pushed open the door, and all of a sudden she was in a big courtyard, filled with activity. A large woman was pinning sheets on two long lines that stretched from corner to corner of the square.

"That is Anna, the head maid. The thin older man," Matthias said in a soft voice, "is the cook, David." He had a white chef's hat on his head, and sat on an upturned orange crate puffing on a cigarette.

Leaning nonchalantly on the side wall shading his eyes from the bright sunlight was a distinguished-looking man with a handlebar mustache. "His name is Armindo. He's the butler," Matthias added in a final whisper.

Martha's knees started shaking. How could she ever fit in with these sophisticated people! Matthias gave her a little shove forward. Then Anna saw them.

"Ah, Matthias," she called, a big warm smile on her

face, "you have the new young one." She dropped the rest of the clothespins into the washing basket and nimbly stepped over it, to welcome Martha.

They walked into the small house at the end of the courtyard. Next to the coal fireplace and stove sat a younger man holding a mug of tea in his hands. He stood up as Anna entered.

"This is Andrew, he is the head gardener, and," Anna pointed into the adjoining room where a man was ironing a shirt, dressed in black pants with suspenders hanging down, "there is Austen, the chauffeur. You met the others outside."

Martha swallowed hard. It was difficult to remember everyone's names. They all looked like city folk to her. Andrew had the kindest eyes, and she saw that he understood how she felt. She looked around for Matthias's familiar face. He was standing near the doorway, chatting with Armindo. He glanced up, saw Martha's beseeching look, and came over to her.

"I must go, my dear," he said kindly. "You are in good hands here and I know you will be fine. We will see you on your off day on Thursday, is that right, Anna?"

Anna nodded and Matthias solemnly shook Martha's hand, then he was gone. Martha took a deep breath. The feeling of not belonging was all around her. She was on her own again. She felt the tears welling in her eyes and she blinked furiously in order not to have to wipe them away.

"It's time for you to meet the family," Anna announced. "Come with me."

Martha clasped her hands together tightly so they would not tremble. What if they didn't like her? She hadn't spoken to white people before, other than the nuns in Maseru.

Anna walked through the courtyard, beckoning Mar-

tha to follow her. Together they climbed the steps that
took them into the main house. The kitchen was large
with rooms leading off it. She stopped and stared.

"One room is for serving, the other is for the
freezers, and the last one is for plates and cups and cut-
lery," Anna said brusquely.

Overwhelmed, Martha was not sure where to look
first, but she had little time to explore because Anna
started walking through the swinging kitchen door and
all of a sudden they were in a carpeted hallway with
subdued lighting and artwork on the wall. They walked
the length of the whole house and stopped outside a
richly paneled door that was partially open. Martha
could hear the light tones of a young woman's voice
from behind the door.

Anna knocked softly. The woman called, "Who is
it?"

"It is Anna, madam, with the new washing girl."

"I'll be just a minute," the woman said. A few seconds later the door opened, and Martha saw her new
mistress, Estelle Amron, for the fist time. She was
slender and delicate with light brown hair and beautiful
blue-green eyes. Her skin was pure and unblemished,
and she smelled of the sweet smells of springtime.
Her green blouse over cotton trousers offset her eyes
and skin. Martha had never seen a more beautiful person and lowered her eyes and head respectfully. Estelle
smiled gently, thinking how charming the young girl
was. She reached out her hand and shook Martha's.

"I am very glad to meet you, Martha. Anna has
much work for you and I know that you will do well.
We have a new baby, you see." Estelle's eyes shone as
she spoke of her child, and Martha's eyes filled with
unexpected tears as she remembered her own baby, so
far away. She kept her eyes down deferentially. Then

the phone rang and Estelle waved a dismissal to Anna and her new assistant as she picked it up.

Anna hustled Martha out of the room.

"Dr. Amron is not home at the moment. He is a very busy person," she explained in a low voice. "It is possible that you will not see him for days. But," she warned, "it is very important that his shirts are ironed perfectly."

As they made their way across the hall, Anna added, as an afterthought, "you could lose your job if the shirts are no good."

Despite this stern admonition Martha felt herself beginning to relax. Certainly the madam of the house was no ogre, compared to some of those about which Ouma had spoken.

Anna headed up a long elegant staircase covered by a thick carpet, and Martha gasped at the beauty of the rooms they passed. The first was the baby's. It was all in pink with white lace, ribbons, and little paper animals on mobiles suspended from the ceiling. There were stars and moons in glitter and gold. Stuffed animals and dolls filled a loveseat, and a small dressing table was covered with powders and lotions in pastel colors. Anna put her head into the room and seeing no one there, whispered, "They must be in the playroom." The next room, she explained softly, belonged to Emily, the English governess.

Then they heard gurgling and cooing, and Martha's heart skipped a beat. It sounded just like Carolyn. For a wild moment she hoped that a miracle had happened and that her child was here after all, but then a stringy grim woman stepped out of the last room off the passage, carrying the most beautiful little girl Martha had ever seen. The child was all pink and gold, with curly rings of blond hair all over her head. Martha longed to take her in her arms; her heart yearned for her own baby. But Emily was rigid and unbending and she cradled her arms around the infant protectively as Martha swayed forward to get a closer look. Martha drew back, sensing the hostility of the woman, and Anna flashed her a warning look.

"This is Gyneth, the new baby," Anna announced. "Miss Emily—this is Martha, the new washing girl." Emily nodded dismissively and pushed past the two of them as she made her way back to the baby's room. Martha was confused. This was the first unwelcoming person she had met so far.

"She is always like that," Anna whispered at the first opportunity. "You just stay away from that nanny—she is a bad one. You will not get to see Gyneth while she is around. When she has her day off, we can hold the child. Now remember, the child's name is pronounced *J-i-n-e-t-h*, Mrs. Amron is very particular that we say it right."

Martha nodded, grateful for the warnings.

Then it was time for her to see her room. They made their way down the stairs and through the spacious house into the large sunny courtyard once again. They crossed to the other side and walked up two flights of outside stairs into a large building. On each level there were three bedrooms with a bathroom on each floor.

Anna threw open a door. "This is where you'll live."

"It's wonderful!" Martha gasped. "Is it all my own?" Anna smiled at her enthusiasm. She was so young.

"It's all yours. See you downstairs."

Martha was thrilled. The room had a bed and a dresser with a little table, a lamp and cheerful curtains on the small window. She was delighted at the room's size and the fact that she didn't have to share with anyone. The young woman carefully placed the few possessions she had on the windowsill and bedside table and then walked down the stairs to start the day's work.

Her new life had begun.

Martha took the first basket of soiled clothing that Anna showed her and sang softly to herself as she washed and scrubbed the clothes on the ribbed washing board in the sink. The rhythm of the movement allowed her to escape to the mountaintops of Basutoland and the days, not so very long ago, of her childhood. She felt proud of herself. She had traveled many miles, had a baby, and got her first job. She was one of the people that her family would talk about with awe. Soon she would send things home for them, and they would know she was successful and safe.

A week later, the young woman made the tedious journey to Soweto in the foul-smelling green buses marked clearly NON-WHITES ONLY. On the first leg of the journey she had to stand. Holding on to a ragged strap, she swayed precariously as the bus rolled and jerked along the main road. Martha bent her head at an uncomfortable angle in order to look through dirty windows past the stony faces of the black passengers. The homes that flew by were large, their second stories visible above high walls and gates. The passing scene of white suburbs, endless in their opulence, was finally replaced by tall office buildings, larger than any Martha had ever seen in Basutoland. The lights of Johannesburg were on and she felt a thrill of excitement at being part of the City of Gold.

Forty minutes later, she had to change buses. Anxious to know where to find her connecting ride, she stumbled and fell for a moment to her knees while stepping onto the rough pavement. Pushed and shoved as masses of people forced their way past her, Martha scrambled to regain her balance, trying to move aside out of the path of those behind her. With knees burn-

ing, scraped by the gravel, she pulled herself to her
feet. No buses could be seen over the heads of those in
front of her.

"Please, can you help me? Where can I find the bus
to Soweto?" Martha clasped the arm of an older
woman, moving slower than the rest. The woman
paused, surprised.

"Everyone is going the same way, to Soweto. Just
follow them."

"Everyone?" Martha gathered her few belongings
and forced herself into the throng, pushing along with
the thousands moving toward a long line of buses
belching black diesel fumes. After an hour of shuffling
her feet an inch at a time, it was her turn and Martha
struggled to find a seat on the bus. Finally, elbowing
her way forward as she'd seen others do, she sank onto
a hard bench, joining once again the black backbone of
the white country, moving up and down the highways
to service the industries and homes of the whites.
Lulled by the rocking of the bus, Martha half dozed,
her head knocking against the window of the dusty bus
as it bumped along the potholed streets to the township.

Martha slowly opened the door of the small Soweto
home, in order not to frighten the old people.

"Child, it is good to see you again." Ouma's arms
outstretched in welcome and Martha returned her hug
warmly. Matthias immediately poured a glass of milk,
Martha's favorite drink, and the young woman tapped
her hands together softly with respect as she took it.
Ouma nodded appreciatively, remembering the girl
who just over a year ago had entered her home unkempt and pregnant. It had been clear even then that
she had been taught good manners and respect for her
elders. Matthias was also filled with pleasure at the
sight of Martha. He took out his pipe and sat on the

narrow porch as was his habit, puffing contentedly. It was good to have noise and activity in the house again. It felt like earlier days when their children ran in and out, and the smell of rich stew and *mieliepap* filled his nostrils.

As Ouma bustled around, readying the extra bed, talking constantly about Carolyn and her escapades, Martha reached into the small cot to pull her child into her arms. The delicate sleeping body was warm, sweet-smelling. Carolyn grasped her mother's hand tightly in tiny fingers, settling into the familiar embrace without opening her eyes. Martha sat carefully in a sagging upholstered chair and rested her chin gently on the soft skin. Ouma chattered on but only now did Martha feel at peace. The pain she'd felt all week was suddenly dulled. She held on to Carolyn as if each moment were her last.

# Chapter 3

The dawn yawned like any other. Black South Africa stirred while the sky was still dark. The white country slept for another hour. In Soweto, the township smoke hung over the sprawled mass of government housing and illegal shanties. The city within a city crept nearer to the downtown area of Johannesburg as the work force that was the life's blood of South Africa made its presence felt through the buses and trains which clogged the arterial road to the industrial areas in the early-morning light. Streaming in dark subdued waves of humanity, the black workers moved into the city and out into the residential areas to service the thriving economy that was South Africa in 1959.

In Hyde Park, dawn came slowly to the blacks who lived and worked in the white homes. There was activity in the servants' quarters of the Amron estate as the staff of men and women who kept it operating smoothly began another day of activity. Martha stoked the stove. She had been part of the Amron staff for over three years now, and she tried to rise earlier than the others to get the fire going for them. They sat around the warm stove drinking from large enamel mugs of milky sweet tea and eating thick slabs of coarse bread with whole fruit jam spread liberally on the surface. Today was a special day, Gyneth's fourth birthday. The family were all at home and many guests were expected.

The cook, David, was first to put down his mug and straighten up. Martha looked at him and wondered if this was going to be a good or bad day for him. When he was grumpy, she knew to stay out of the kitchen as much as possible.

David's wrinkled features contorted as he massaged his hand on his back. *"Einaaa,"* he said, sighing, "this weather is no good for my back." He thought longingly of his perennially humid hometown, Lourenço Marques, the Venice of Portuguese East Africa. Some days, the ache in his back was a sharp reminder of the distance between him and his homeland.

The head gardener, Andrew, gave Martha a friendly salute of thanks for preparing the fire and hot tea as, with his normal bright disposition, he hastened the two junior gardeners from their seats by the fire to place the chairs by the pool, on the patio, and at the tennis court. The lawn had to be mowed, errant flower beds trimmed, the traditional English rose garden tidied, and the Japanese walkway swept to be sure all was perfect.

As Martha quickly rinsed off the large mugs, she noticed that Amos, the stable hand, had walked back to the stables with his mug. He was always up earlier than everyone else since the horses snorted and pawed the hay in the stables next to his room. Amos was generally in better spirits in the morning, since there were chores to be done, keeping him from the mournful depression that overtook him as the day waned. Martha's heart went out to him, since she recognized the sadness in him as the same she sometimes saw in herself. He missed the green, damp terrain, the miles of sugar cane groves of his hometown in Natal, and had never become accustomed to the dry stark landscape of the

Transvaal. Some months before, Martha had discovered his secret. She'd wandered down to the stables as
darkness fell, and knocked on Amos's door.

"Can I feed the horses some carrots?" she asked
softly, not knowing if he were sleeping.

There was no reply.

Martha pushed the door open.

Four cartons of government-issued Bantu beer lay
empty on the floor and Amos was stretched out next to
them.

"Easier ... when home thoughts and beer come together, beer wins," Amos had muttered as Martha tried
to put the cushion beneath his head. She'd covered him
with the blanket and left him alone. The beer deadened
the senses. He was not alone in choosing this course.
On her weekly trip back to Soweto, she saw many
drunk men and women in the streets of the township.
After that, Martha began to understand what Matthias
had said to her about the City of Gold.

Anna heaved her large frame off the chair. Martha
had learned on her first day not to take Anna's seat.
She was, after all, as maid to the household, the mother
to them all. Her sharp wit and mimicry of the various
white members of the family kept everyone amused in
the after hours of their long days. Anna's favorite was
Gyneth, so her mockery was often directed at the English nanny, Emily, who with starched uniform and attitude guarded the child like a terrier, snapping at
anyone who came too close. Soon after Martha arrived,
she discovered how Anna bypassed Emily and her
rigid rules.

On Emily's off day, Martha saw her leaving the
house. The governess walked to the corner and was
joined by another white woman.

"Another starched friend. They are two of the same
kind." Anna chuckled. As soon as Emily was out of

sight, Anna beckoned to Martha. "Come, the child is ours for the day!"

Together they peeked into Gyneth's room. She was awake and playing in her bed. Anna lifted her up high in her strong arms.

"Anna loves you here and here, here and there." Anna tickled Gyneth with gentle fingers and the child's giggles filled the Amron house for the rest of the day. Martha played happily with the little girl, singing and carrying her on her back.

Now Martha watched Anna as she teased Armindo, the butler. She envied them their relaxed friendship. Armindo was tall, elegant, and suave in his daytime white uniform with red sash, or evening tuxedo or tails. He was well educated, having graduated from high school in Lourenço Marques, a considerable accomplishment in his village. He'd traveled to the city, on foot, over a period of three months, through the game parks, sleeping in the trees during the day and walking at night, determined to reach the affluent cities of South Africa. Jacob Amron had hired Armindo, impressed by his intelligence and bearing, and had trained him to become a first-class butler, arranging flowers, crystal, and silver embossed with the family crest on the dining table nightly, decanting wine from the Amron cellar, and serving with flair and discretion. Armindo also became Jacob's personal valet.

The sun's rays warmed the Johannesburg landscape as the city rumbled into the day's business life. The smell of diesel fuel filled the air of the downtown streets as the buses from the southern suburbs disgorged the black work force and the Mercedes, Rovers, and Jaguars, some of them chauffeur driven, with the white elite coming from the north drove into parking lots of office buildings and hospitals.

Dr. Jacob Amron lit the first of forty cigarettes he'd

smoke that day and walked to his dressing room, where Armindo had laid out his suit, shirt, and tie for the day. He looked appreciatively at the crisp collar on his shirt. That new washing girl did a good job. She was such a shy little thing, obviously fresh from the countryside. He'd met her only once and she curtesied low as she was introduced. He liked her work, he must tell Anna to praise her. His shoes were neatly placed beside his chair, his gold cuff links on the dresser. He dressed rapidly. He had two hospitals to visit, at least fifteen patients to see, and a number of calls to make before coming home in time for Gyneth's party and puppet show. He'd arranged a surprise, a Shetland pony for the children to ride, on a lead rein of course, and he wanted to be sure that Amos was still sober and able to control the excited children around the horses. His face beamed with anticipated delight at Gyneth's expected reaction. He knew she'd run to him with arms outstretched to give one of her famous "daddyhugs."

Estelle was still in bed, giving Anna instructions on the various outfits she needed ironed and prepared for the upcoming week. Their social calendar was, as always, heavily booked.

"Gyneth will wear her new party dress today. Could you see that she puts it on only at the last minute? Then please ask David to come up. We have people for dinner twice this week and we have to go over the menus."

Since Estelle's dreams of many children filling the house with their games and laughter were yet to be fulfilled, she had consoled herself by becoming the most accomplished hostess in Johannesburg. Her dinners and table settings were the envy of her friends. Estelle's guest lists varied from doctors and their wives who were supporters of Jacob's large surgical practice to the traditional family Friday night sabbath dinner.

Estelle's parents, Jewish immigrants from the east side of London, had moved to South Africa when she was two years old. Her father had created an empire as the first furniture manufacturer in the country, building a national chain of retail furniture stores. Estelle's privileged lifestyle had prepared her well for her role as Jacob's wife, and elegant entertaining came easily to her. Jacob's family, immigrants who had fled the pogroms of Eastern Europe, had also done well. Their butchery had been the key meeting place of all the religious Jews in the city, and his mother, a pianist, had given recitals with his older sister, who sang opera, throughout the community. But when his father had died from a stroke a year after Jacob's bar mitzvah, the young man had assumed the mantle of family responsibility. Finances became his concern, and as the family business dwindled, he had entered medical school, determined to take care of his mother and sister as his father would have wanted. Instead of filling his days with the creativity that was so much part of his home, he used his considerable musical talent as an interim means to supplement his family's income while he was plowing through the arduous training to become a surgeon. He played piano, drums, and trumpet in nightclubs all over town, organizing two dance bands, and using the extra money to put himself and his sister through college.

During these years of struggle, Jacob developed a drive for success that could not be satisfied.

His place as the fulcrum of the family stayed sacrosanct. Friday night dinners were always at his house, and he reveled in his role as paterfamilias, seated at the head of a table laden with the rich and filling Lithuanian food that he loved and which contributed to his ever-present struggle to lose twenty pounds. Estelle was happy to host the weekly event. However, as the years went by, her sister-in-law gave birth to three children before Estelle's first pregnancy. Although she tried to ignore the conversation about baby carriages and such things, she had been filled with a sense of personal failure until Gyneth had arrived. Only then had the pain faded.

Estelle pulled herself back to the realities of the day, and smiled gratefully at Anna, who was still waiting to hear whether Estelle had any further instructions.

"You are a wonderful help to me Anna, thank you." Anna nodded. Mrs. Amron was gentle and courteous, a pleasure to work for. Nothing like the governess. Anna grimaced as she left the room.

Estelle frowned, trying to remember all the things she was sure she had forgotten. She was adding items to her long list as Jacob appeared at the door and blew her a kiss.

"I'm off now. See you soon, in time for the party, of course!"

Jacob walked swiftly down the elegant stairway in the energetic manner that was his trademark. Every week he led his entourage of doctors, nurses, and students on Grand Rounds at the University Hospital, where he was chief of surgical staff, and his brisk trot kept even the fittest puffing after him.

"No time for breakfast today," he called to Armindo, who was about to pour his strong-mixed blend of coffee. "Have Austen bring around the car, please, I'm late already!" The word went out to the chauffeur that the doctor was ready to leave and as Dr. Amron opened the front door Austen pulled up in a black Rover.

They drew away from the house as Gyneth awoke and lay in her bed singing to herself. "It's my birthday, Emily," she called out, "it's today!" Emily sighed as she heard Gyneth's voice. It was going to be a long, tiresome day.

Martha had begun her morning chores. As she did, she remembered that today, Gyneth's birthday, was also the birthday of her own little girl, Carolyn. But for her there would be no large family gathering, no party with gaily colored balloons and cakes, no puppet show or gifts, in fact nothing at all. Carolyn was still living with Ouma in Soweto, but now the house was filled with sadness.

Some months before, on a routine visit to see Carolyn, Martha had noticed that Matthias was coughing. "Do you want me to take you to the clinic?" she'd asked. Matthias was shivering with fever.

"No, child, I just need some rest. By the time you visit next week I'll be better."

But the next week he was gone. Martha had attended his funeral, but the grief and loss continued long afterward. The warm hug Matthias had always given on her weekly visit, his calming influence on Ouma, who was crotchety with arthritis pain, the smell of his pipe, all these memories lay heavy on her heart.

Now there were ten children in Ouma's house, offspring of young mothers working in the city. Martha gave most of her wages to feed and clothe Carolyn but even though her baby was cared for, her heart ached to hold her more often. Being near Gyneth made her yearn for her own child. The pain was sharp and penetrated Martha's thoughts, so she grabbed the first basket of shirts and began to set up the ironing board in the laundry room, placing it in the sunlight, hoping to lift her spirits.

In the poorest part of Soweto, the day was already tiresome as Ouma wearily moved the youngest child away from the coal stove. She was heating porridge for the ten youngsters crowding into the room that served as bedroom and kitchen for her and her wards. The events of the past year had aged her prematurely. The metal cups jangled as the children chanted, *"mielie meal, mielie meal,"* reaching for their portions. Carolyn took her special place near the stove and held her cup quietly, wanting to be noticed.

The day Matthias died had been so confusing for Carolyn. Ouma had been wailing, and strangers had come in and out of the house until late at night. Carolyn stayed in the corner of the room, terrified, ignored by people and events, as Matthias lay in Ouma's arms. Finally, someone said he was dead. Carolyn thought maybe it was her fault because no one spoke to her. She withdrew into her corner, trembling, hoping someone would tell her what to do. Eventually Ouma came to her, held her tight and let her cry.

Everything changed then. There were more children to feed and Ouma was cross all the time. Her mother's visits were the happiest times of her week and she counted the days between them.

She had become very well behaved after that, waiting patiently for her cup of sweet thick milky porridge. The powdered milk was routinely given to mothers with children suffering from dehydration and malnutrition who came into the emergency room of the large Baragwanath Hospital at the entrance to the Soweto Township. Ouma knew a kind nurse who would give her a couple of cans a week, but she had to go and fetch it. The walk from her narrow street to the hospital clinic took an hour over dusty roads. Her arthritis was worsening, and the lack of rest and nutrition didn't help her depressed condition. Today she just did not have the strength to make the effort.

Ouma sat down on a wooden chair. The children were eating, licking their spoons between bites and wiping the bottom of their cups with their fingers. The noise of the spoons clanking against the cups rang loudly with a dissonant rhythm.

Ouma closed her eyes and dreamed of the days when she was young and fleet of foot, when she would run through the cornfields, dodging her lover Matthias. She could hardly believe that he was gone, and could still feel him in her arms. His last struggles for breath and the blue tinge of his face would never leave her. She moaned softly. They should never have lived in the city. Perhaps if they had stayed in the pure air of the countryside, Matthias wouldn't have caught influenza and would still be alive to this day. The tears ran quietly down her cheeks. Matthias really had not done well in Soweto. For the twenty years they had lived in the city, he had made a meager living as a chimney sweep. The children all grew up with tar and sand in their noses instead of the clean African air and spacious veld with springbok running around their village.

So many years of struggle—and for what? She did not even have the comfort of her children near her. After Matthias's death, the family had splintered even further. Her married daughter was now living apart from her husband in an apartment, taking care of an old lady with strange eccentric habits. Her oldest son was in Ladysmith, so far away that she never saw him or his wife and children. And her youngest son—where was he? He'd left his job in Pretoria after Matthias's death and took to tinkering with broken-down cars and drinking all day long.

Chaos reigned in the room as the children danced around the hot stove and beat out their cry, "more, more, more." Carolyn joined in the dance, giggling with the others. Ouma pulled herself up and shouted, "Enough, go out and play, out, out, out" as she waved her arms and the ten children between two and four years old ran out the front door.

She swung around in frustration and grabbed the can behind her, thinking it was the reconstituted milk. The liquid sloshed onto her loose-fitting dress and soaked it with foul-smelling kerosene. "Oh no!" she moaned cursing her absent son and the obsession he had with cars and the smelly tools and oily liquid he left around the house.

The stove coals settled, a spark flew out, and in seconds she was on fire. She batted the flames on her body with her twisted arthritic hands, but the fire moved instantaneously to totally engulf her. She was burning all over, screaming, in her last moments running wildly as she staggered to the front door and lost consciousness in a tortured mass of scorching flesh and fabric.

The house turned into an inferno of flames.

Carolyn heard the screaming. Not understanding, she turned in the direction of the noise. She stopped breathing as she saw that her home was burning. The sparks leapt high into the sky, and the noise of exploding and crackling deafened her. Then a figure appeared in the door framed by a ring of fire, and she watched as, with flailing arms, it spun slowly around in a half circle, then fell to the ground.

Could that person be her Ouma, the one who held her tight every day? Carolyn ran closer, afraid of the heat, but driven by the need to know, to somehow stop the fire. The burning smell made her retch with nausea. The heat forced her back, preventing her from approaching the terrible apparition. She stood on the edge of mortal danger, quivering with fear, knowing with a wisdom beyond her years that the smell and fire were one and the same, a horror burned indelibly into her mind.

The rest of the children ran screaming down the narrow street as the elderly people who populated Soweto

during the workday gathered in horror with outstretched hands and watched the burning house collapse and fall, burying the woman beneath its fiery
timbers. A neighbor saw Carolyn choking from the
smoke, staring with horrified eyes. She grabbed the little girl and covered her with a sweater. But even
though they covered Carolyn's vision, she would always see that monstrous figure in her nightmares.

Estelle Amron was excited and full of anticipation.
She could hardly believe that it was Gyneth's fourth
birthday. She was looking forward to the fact that
Jacob had promised to spend all day with them, together, as a family should be. So often she had entertained alone after the phone rang and with apologies
and an excited air her husband would leave the house
to tend to a patient at the hospital. Surgery was a tough
rival. The excitement of the affair with another surgical
challenge, and the resulting ego boost and exhilaration
she saw reflected in her husband's face was something
that she couldn't provide. She had to accept it, smile,
and play a secondary role.

Today would be different. He had promised her he'd
be home in time for the party, for Gyneth. Estelle felt
blessed to have such a child—so sweet, loving, and
happy with the world. She only wished that she could
preserve Gyneth's innocence forever.

Estelle held out her hand to Gyneth as she ran into
her dressing room in her new green party dress, Emily
in tow.

"Oh, Mummy, can I see your powder?" she cried as
she plopped herself down on the little footstool. Estelle
gave her a powder puff to tickle her nose as she
sneezed and giggled and sneezed again. Estelle continued to make up her face with extra care, while giving
Emily instructions.

"Tell David I will be down to confirm the menu with him and be sure that Andrew has the chairs out and tables laid for forty adults and twenty-five children. They'll be here in an hour."

Emily stalked out, not pleased to be delivering messages. "I'm the governess," she grumbled under her breath, "not the intercom."

Estelle placed the final touches to her makeup. She looked at her flawless skin and clear green eyes and ran the comb over her fine eyebrows to smooth them into place. Her light brown hair curled gently away from her face and her figure was youthful and lithe from years of horseback riding and tennis. She was pleased with her appearance. "Come on, then," she said to Gyneth as they swept their way to the staircase. Gyneth's blond curls bounced as she ran next to her mother and tried to keep up with her long strides, chattering all the time. They reached the bottom of the stairs and the telephone rang. Estelle answered, praying that it wasn't Jacob telling her that he would, once again, be late.

"Hello?"

"Madam, is this Dr. Amron's residence? Excuse me, madam, can I speak to the doctor?"

Estelle didn't recognize the voice, but the accent was Zulu.

"He's not home," she said. "Can I help, is something wrong?"

"Oh yes, madam. Something is very wrong." The man's voice became agitated and his words tumbled out, burning into Estelle's ear as she realized the horror of his tale. "The grandmother, she is dead, burned in a fire. The children are loose. There is no house, madam, no one. The child Carolyn, she has nowhere to go. Please, madam, you must help and take Martha's child. She needs to be with the mother. There is no one else to care for her."

The man paused. Estelle waited for him to continue. The man regained his composure. He spoke quietly and slowly.

"I am very sorry, madam. I am the cousin of the child Meli, one of the children in the house with Carolyn. Please, madam, you will take the child?"

Estelle gripped the phone tightly. She felt quite ill at the thought of the woman dying such a horrible death. It was too dreadful to contemplate. She sighed. A decision had to be made immediately. She felt some resentment at the fact that it was the same old situation—when things happened at home, Jacob was never around. Well, he'd just have to agree. They could take the child in for a short time while other arrangements were made. It would be a *mitzvah,* a good deed. But it would disrupt Martha and the whole household.

"Yes, we will take her, but just for a short time, you hear. I will tell Martha. When will you bring the child?"

"Today, madam, thank you, madam, may God bless you, madam."

"Mummy, Mummy, come and see the balloons." Gyneth came flying over the Persian rug and nearly careened into the antique table in the hallway where Estelle was standing.

"Be careful, child. Emily, where are you and why is Gyneth running wild? Gyneth, you need to go with Emily now and play quietly on the swing. Emily, where are you?"

Estelle left Gyneth flying from table to table touching the decorations, the balloons, the governess flying after her and Goldie, her spaniel, jumping up and down in the dog run, barking frantically. She entered the

laundry room, where Martha was listening to qwela
music, swaying her body and ironing with gusto.

"Ow, madam." She squirmed in embarrassment as
she saw Estelle enter the room. "Excuse me, madam,
the music is too loud, I'm sorry, madam. I'll make it
lower, madam, so sorry, madam."

"It's fine, Martha" Estelle said, "but can we turn it
off for a moment? I want to talk to you."

Martha's heart sank. She just knew she was going to
be fired. Dr. Amron didn't like the way she ironed the
shirts. Maybe they had found someone else, maybe . . .

"I have some bad news. Your grandmother has died.
A man called, he is Meli's cousin. He is bringing
Carolyn here to you. You will have to take care of her
for a time while you look for someone else for her to
live with. I am very sorry about your grandmother. I
will call Anna. She will help you. Then I'll talk to the
doctor when he returns home, about Carolyn, I mean."

Martha gripped the side of the ironing board. She
felt dizzy and faint, relieved about her job but filled
with grief for Ouma.

Estelle called worriedly for Anna, who came up the
stairs puffing. "Yes, madam?" Estelle explained the situation and Anna put her ample arms around the young
girl's shoulders. Martha held her face in her hands,
confused and shocked.

Later that afternoon, while Jacob observed Amos
walking the pony continuously around the paddock and
the puppeteer entertained the children, the adults ate
cucumber sandwiches accompanied by delicate bread
fingers covered with smoked salmon and sipped champagne. Carolyn arrived at the servants' entrance.

Her serious brown eyes stared as she looked at the
red brick mansion with its stately driveway. The two
stories of the servants' quarters loomed larger than the
biggest buildings in Soweto and she hid behind the tall

thin man who led her kindly through the gate into Martha's waiting arms.

Carolyn saw her mother and ran to her, clasping her arms tightly around her legs.

"Mama, Mama," she sobbed, keeping her eyes wide open, as if to be sure that her mother was truly there.

The man accompanying Carolyn took off his hat and shook Martha's hand formally. Martha swung the child up into her arms.

"It is all all right now. You are with me and we are safe together. All the bad things are over now, you are safe."

Carolyn buried her face in her mother's neck and tried to block out the horrible scene that kept repeating itself over and over in her mind.

Every time she closed her eyes she saw the same dreadful reality—her Ouma burning, spinning. The people in the street, the children, the world seemed to be screaming, and no one did anything to stop it all, to make the horror go away. Carolyn opened her eyes again with a shudder and shook with panic.

"Ouma was burning, I smelled her burning, I saw it all." The little girl spoke clearly. "No one came to save her."

"It was too quick." The man was speaking softly, over Carolyn's voice. "Thank God we saw the child standing there. The neighbor says Carolyn wanted to go back into the house."

Martha shuddered at the thought that her baby could have been caught in the same inferno.

"She has hardly slept since this happened yesterday," the man said. "She saw it all—all the children did, you know. It was so terrible. Thank God the children had left the house and were playing outside. It is a miracle they are all alive. Carolyn kept calling for you. She needs you so much, she will not rest at all. I felt it was best that she stay with you. Anyway, we have no place for her in Soweto, our place is already too crowded."

"I need her, too," said Martha softly. "We'll be fine. Thank you." He left, in a hurry to return to the township before dark. Martha carried the exhausted child gently into her new home.

As soon as Carolyn opened her eyes the next morning, panic rose in her chest; she lay completely still in the folding bed that had been hastily set up for her the previous evening. There was someone breathing in the bed next to hers. The shapes in the room began to appear as her eyes adjusted to the darkness. She turned and saw that the person in the nearby bed was her mother.

Her heart was still beating wildly even though there was no fire here, no burning. The bed felt big and long, and her feet were lost somewhere under the covers. She longed to climb over into her mother's bed, to be held and loved, the way she used to climb into Matthias's bed and wake him up in the early morning.

Since Matthias had gone, she'd longed to be with her mother.

Carolyn glanced again at the woman covered with a brightly colored Basuto blanket. She had rarely seen her without her head scarf on. Martha's tightly curled, short-cropped hair made her look like a young man. Carolyn turned onto her side to gaze squarely into her mother's face. That was better. Now Martha looked like Mama again. It was very quiet. All Carolyn could hear was the noise of her mother's rhythmic breathing and the clock ticking in the corner. It was so different from Soweto, where the early-morning noises were loud and jarring. Then a faint clacking of trains far away in the distance echoed through the clear early-morning air. The noises soothed Carolyn. She snuggled down farther into the bed and drifted into a light sleep.

All of a sudden it was morning, the sun was shining through the window above her bed and her mother was shaking her, saying, "Time to get up. We have to do the ironing. You must learn to help me so that the madam will let us stay here together."

Carolyn quickly splashed cold water on her face. She looked at her image in the small bathroom mirror. Her small head was covered in tight curls framing her narrow face with big brown eyes. She pulled her short dress straight and, having dispensed with her bathroom duties, tiptoed downstairs and toward the voices in the living area of the servants' quarters. Then shyness overcame her, so she stood outside the door not venturing in, twisting herself into as little space as possible, with one leg crossed over the other, until Anna saw her, took her hand and pulled the serious little girl into the group. Andrew smiled kindly at the shy child and Armindo patted her head gently. Then the moment of softness passed as David massaged his back and stood.

Another day had begun.

# *Chapter 4*

Upstairs in her bedroom suite Gyneth awoke as Emily drew the draperies. The little girl stretched out her arms for a morning hug.

Emily brusquely lifted Gyneth off the bed and pulled her to the bathroom. This part of the morning routine always seemed to take the longest time. Then it was over and Emily dressed the child in a white dress with a teddy bear embroidered on the bodice. Gyneth ran her fingers tenderly over the bear's face, then clattered down the stairs, out the French doors onto the red-paved patio that ran the length of the house, relieved to be able to leave Emily's presence. Gyneth peered over the balcony into the window of the laundry room. Martha was listening to kwela music and the swaying rhythms wafted softly up to the patio with the honeysuckle scent that surrounded the house. Gyneth loved the music and the way that Martha would dance in slow, smooth, repetitious patterns, clicking her tongue and singing along. Gyneth enjoyed the sound and no matter how hard she tried, she could not imitate it.

But now Gyneth had to plan her strategy to be sure Emily did not see her as she made a dash for the warmth of the laundry room. Emily didn't want her to go into the servants' quarters at all. That made the opportunity even more tantalizing.

She picked up a doll and eyed Emily. The nanny had her glasses on and was reading the newspaper. Gyneth tiptoed over to the steps and ran quickly to the servants' area and laundry room.

"Martha, Martha!" she called as she entered the room.

Martha was standing with her back to the door, swaying and singing to the music. In front of the ironing board was a little girl, not any taller than Gyneth, dipping her knees and swaying just like Martha.

The two children looked at each other uncertainly for a few moments, and then the little black girl ran behind her mother's knees. Martha saw Gyneth.

"Hello, missie . . . here is my baba," she said. "Carolyn, this is Miss Gyneth, this is the young madam."

Carolyn came out slowly from behind her mother's legs. Having lived in the township all her life, she had never seen a white girl her size. This child had hair that was golden, smooth, with loose curls. Her skin was fair, her eyes green and Carolyn was intrigued. Gyneth took a small step forward and offered her doll to Carolyn.

Carolyn stretched out her hand, took it and tentatively touched Gyneth's hair. They stared at each other, then Gyneth giggled and sat on the floor in the sunlight, beckoning to Carolyn to join her.

Gyneth loved having company. She was constantly asking Estelle to invite children to visit. Finding Carolyn right there in her own home was a treat she had not expected and she was thrilled to have a playmate. Carolyn was in awe of this person who had so much to say and chatted away to the doll, all the time including Carolyn in the three-way conversation. The morning sun filled the small room with light, and the music played as Martha ironed shirts, the children close by.

Gyneth put her arm around Carolyn's shoulders. "You are my friend," she stated firmly.

The music beat rhythmically and the little girls danced.

Then Gyneth pulled her new playmate into the garden and across the patio. "Here is the pool and the garden. That over there is the tennis court." She was skipping along, beckoning her new friend to follow. Carolyn's head was reeling. There was so much new information. The area of the house and garden was vast, larger than whole city blocks in Soweto. She had many questions, but shyness kept her from interrupting Gyneth's constant chatter.

Then she saw the horses.

Amos smiled as he saw the children with eager faces trying to climb up on the paddock fence, then snorted as he spotted Emily in starched white uniform puffing down the hill past the fruit trees. He drew two pieces of sugar out of his pocket.

"Now little madam, you hold out the hand like so." He held out his rough fingers straight like a board and uncurled her little white fingers. Sugar, the large bay gelding, flapped his upper lip as he gently flipped the sugar into his mouth. Carolyn copied what Gyneth had done. Sugar obliged in the same way.

Carolyn threw back her head and laughed and Gyneth joined her. All of a sudden the world of Soweto, the burning, the smell and the pain was far away, and everything became simple and clean in the joy of a horse, the children and two lumps of sugar.

Emily arrived in a huff. "Now don't start getting all dirty, Gyneth. It's time for lunch anyway. Come along, up to the house."

Reluctantly the children left the stables and made their way up the path behind the thatched little summer house near the tennis courts. Just as Emily was about to shoo Carolyn over to the servants' quarters, Jacob stepped onto the balcony of the house. He gave a long whistle, which Gyneth recognized immediately with glee.

"It's my daddy!" Gyneth cried, dragging Carolyn by the hand.

Jacob appeared at the top of the patio stairs, and Gyneth pulled Carolyn after her. Carolyn looked wide-eyed at the man with an imposing presence but twinkling friendly eyes. Jacob solemnly took Carolyn's little hand in his.

"How do you do, young lady," he said. "Your mother has told us a lot about you. She is very proud of you, you know."

Carolyn was overcome with shyness and unable to speak.

"Say 'How do you do,' child," said Emily, trying to make a good impression. Carolyn felt fear again as she saw the grim face of the nanny.

"Is it time for lunch?" asked Jacob, smiling.

"The Bantu child was just going to her mother, and Gyneth will be at the table in two minutes, sir." Emily hustled Carolyn in the direction of the servants' quarters as Gyneth waved to her, then turned and went inside the house with her father. Carolyn ran to the warmth of Martha's arms. She was confused about Jacob.

That night after dinner, when Martha was tucking her into bed, Carolyn sat up and held on to her mother's hand.

"Mama, was Matthias my father?"

Martha took a deep breath. It was time that she explained about fathers.

"No, he wasn't. You have a father, of course. His name is Daniel. He went away and I don't know where he is. Maybe one day he will come back to be with us again. I know he would be very proud to know what a good girl you are."

Carolyn thought for a moment, her little forehead wrinkling with concentration. Then her face brightened.

"Can Gyneth's father be my father since Matty is gone and we don't know where my real father is?" she asked, pleased at her solution to this confusing problem.

Martha dismissed Carolyn's question by clicking her tongue and shaking her head in the Sotho manner.

"No, silly. First of all he is white. Second, you already have a father. He is just not here, that's all."

She stood up and pulled the covers firmly, almost roughly, over Carolyn, impatient to end the difficult conversation. "It is time for sleeping anyway. Good night, my girl."

Carolyn lay in the bed. She did not understand anything about fathers, but talk of them obviously upset her mother. She nevertheless did have a wonderful feeling about her new friend. They could play again tomorrow. She pulled the doll lovingly under the blankets with her. Together they lay side by side in the bed as Carolyn fell into a dreamless sleep.

That was the first of many wonderful days together. During the long summer months the children played all day. Carolyn adored Gyneth's spaniel, Goldie, and the feelings were mutual. She learned to swim using one of Gyneth's old swimsuits and taught Gyneth songs that her Ouma used to sing.

Both children loved music. The harmonies of the township became blended with the songs of childhood—Ba, ba black sheep, Ring around the roses, Pat a cake, and even a song Gyneth said came from a far away place called France, "Frère Jacques"—all the tunes that Gyneth sang out in her high clear voice, and that Carolyn learned to pitch, in rich contrasting tones. Then during the days when Gyneth was playing at the houses of other white children, Carolyn would sing away her loneliness, the clear notes rising and falling as she made up songs to amuse herself.

Some days they ate their lunch sandwiches together under the large oak tree, but if other children were there, Carolyn ate with the staff while Gyneth sat at the breakfast table, her little back straight and Emily's eyes following her every move.

Carolyn learned to be extra careful around Emily. She watched how her mother stood in a deferential position when addressing her as Miss Emily and how different it was when she was alone with Gyneth.

The subject of fathers still concerned Carolyn. She watched enviously as Gyneth and Jacob played together.

"Up, up, and over," Carolyn could hear Jacob's deep baritone mingled with Gyneth's squeals of glee as he picked Gyneth up and swung her around, high in the air. In the swimming pool he would let her ride on his shoulders, and sometimes he would jump up, above the water throwing her off in an arc. By standing on her tiptoes, Carolyn could watch them from the highest stair of the servants' quarters. She longed to be part of the game.

Martha saw the envy on her little girl's face. "Carolyn, you have to understand, when the family is together like this, you are not permitted to join them."

"But why, Mama? I know how to swim."

"Because that is the way it is." To Martha, the subject was closed. But Carolyn was not satisfied with her reply.

One Sunday, Gyneth came to find Carolyn and together they played on the patio while Estelle and Jacob
sat, talking quietly about the events of the week. Jacob
stood up and yawned.

"What a wonderful restful day we've had," he said,
kissing Estelle gently on the cheek. It had been exactly
the kind of Sunday he loved, horseback riding in the
morning, swimming in the afternoon. He wandered up
to the house, and soon piano notes were heard from the
living room.

"It's Daddy—he is playing the piano. Come,
Carolyn, Daddy will play and we can sing," Gyneth
cried.

The children ran up the stairs onto the patio and saw
Jacob sitting at the Bechstein concert piano, while his
fingers sent rippling arpeggios into the air. Carolyn followed Gyneth uncertainly into the living room. This
room was off bounds for her. She looked in awe at the
crystal chandeliers, the fine antique wooden furniture.
Then Jacob started to play one of the songs that she
and Gyneth sang together. Carolyn's heart filled with
joy as the music dispelled her hesitancy; she opened
her mouth and out came the purest, clearest sounds
Jacob had ever heard. Estelle stood quietly at the open
doorway, and Jacob's eyes caught hers as the little
black girl, with uplifted face, lost herself in the melo-
dious sounds.

Gyneth's little voice chimed along as she sang happily, oblivious to the effect that Carolyn was having on
her parents.

Jacob ended the song by beginning another and the
children clapped wildly as they recognized the melody.
Jacob explored more complicated pieces until Gyneth
fell silent and all that could be heard was Carolyn's
soprano, flowing up and down effortlessly as she harmonized without even thinking about it.

Then Jacob stopped. Carolyn looked around in surprise. Armindo, Anna, Martha, and Estelle stood at the doorway. Gyneth sat snuggled up against her father on the piano stool. Only Carolyn stood alone, apart, suddenly empty and silent.

"Well, I think it is time for all little girls to take a bath," said Estelle breathlessly. It was clear that Carolyn had an incredible talent.

Jacob stood up and gently patted Gyneth on the head. "Off you go," he said. "I'll be up to read you a story after your bath."

Gyneth went off, giving Carolyn a wave.

Jacob turned to Carolyn who was shyly trying to slip away behind Martha's skirt. "You have a very good voice, Carolyn," he said. He paused, as if to say something more, perhaps about his joy in music, then he, too, turned away.

Martha grabbed Carolyn and pulled her off to the servants' quarters. "What were you doing there in the living room?" she whispered. "You know that on the weekends you must leave the family alone. That is not the place for you. Anyway, it is time to help me with the ironing."

Carolyn's logical mind could not make sense of the situation, but she obeyed her mother. Everyone else seemed to understand and accept the way it was.

Within a few minutes the staff and family at the Amron house slipped effortlessly back into their normal routine, and, as quickly as it had happened, Carolyn's moment of glory had passed.

All too soon, the summer was over.

Gyneth started preschool three mornings a week. Carolyn saw her getting dressed and watched as Estelle and Gyneth left in the large black car with Austen, the driver.

Carolyn wanted to go with her.

Martha explained. "This is not for you. You must learn what I do and stay home with me."

"Why, Mama?" Carolyn asked.

"Because the white school is not for our people. Soon you'll go to the school in Soweto. I must find somewhere for you to live, and I don't know where that will be now. So if you are good, the madam will let you stay here until then."

Carolyn did not understand why Gyneth went to school and she didn't. But she accepted what her mother told her, the same way as she accepted that she slept in a different place from Gyneth, never ate dinner with her, and only sometimes ate lunch together.

Anyway she liked her lunch better than Gyneth's. She saw David making things with lettuce and green vegetables while she ate a delicious rich tomato stew with *mieliepap*. Sometimes Anna would hold her close, dip the pap that she had molded into a round soft ball into the tangy sauce of the tomatoes and meat, and feed her. Gyneth loved that, too. On Emily's day off, the children would eat their lunch this way, but in the kitchen of the big house rather than in the servants' quarters.

Carolyn waited patiently for Gyneth to return from school.

"What did you do there?" she would ask, envious of Gyneth's colorful picture books. Gyneth smoothed her dress carefully as she sat down, mindful of Emily's wrath. She then proceeded to show Carolyn what she had learned.

In this way, as Gyneth started to read, so did Carolyn, dreaming all the time of the day they'd go to school together.

The Amron staff became Carolyn's extended family. They, in turn, saw the little girl as a welcome part of their evening relaxation when they all gathered around the stove, to smoke and talk. The child stayed away from the heat and never sat facing the sparkling embers, as if afraid to see terrifying images from the past.

Carolyn's days of waiting for Gyneth to return from school were interrupted occasionally by special treats provided by Martha. Some Thursdays, Martha would take Carolyn along with her on a variety of "off-day" activities. Sometimes they visited Soweto; other times they would go to the stores near the house. There they would walk around, looking into the windows of the stores, buying some sodas at the corner café with even a sticky donut or two for Carolyn to eat. Carolyn felt very grown-up since there were no children around, certainly no black children in the white suburb of Hyde Park, so she pretended that she was a working lady like her mother. She had a serious look on her face as she closely examined the items in the store windows as if she were a quality-control expert. Martha would laugh at her intensity, infuriating Carolyn who saw nothing at all funny about her actions.

It was on one of these days when Carolyn was doing her normal concentrated window-shopping, that Martha was walking slowly along the sidewalk ahead of her. Suddenly they heard the sound of screeching tires. Carolyn looked around and saw a car spinning out of control, careening toward her mother. She started to scream, but the sound choked in her throat. Carolyn watched in horror as the car hit Martha squarely, threw her body high into the air. She landed with a deathly thud on the roof of the car, her shoes and handbag flying. Carolyn stopped breathing. She stood paralyzed, watching helplessly as the car smashed into the storefront, glass shattering and flying everywhere. Her mother lay there, lifeless and twisted, slumping over the side of the car. Then slowly with macabre grace, Martha's body slid to the ground and the blood poured from her shattered face and chest into the crevices on the sidewalk.

Carolyn was unable to move. She stood frozen, her fragile life torn asunder.

The storekeepers ran out as the driver staggered from the car, bruised but otherwise unhurt, and looked in horror at the body of the young woman, so relaxed and happy just a few moments ago. The café owner recognized Martha and Carolyn from their visits to his store, and saw the child standing in terrified shock.

"Who does your mother work for?" he gently asked the dazed child.

"Amron," Carolyn whispered. The café owner nodded. Everyone knew the Amrons. He ran into the store, called the hospital in Hillbrow that took black patients only and asked for an ambulance. He then called Dr. Amron's office and told the secretary what had happened.

So, for the third time in Carolyn's life she observed the death of the person closest to her. Her mind filled with spinning, burning bodies flying into the air, thuds of dead flesh, screams and the sound of crackling, breaking glass. It all ran together in her mind and she closed her eyes only to see it again. She wanted to go to her mother, but her legs would not move. She sank onto the curb of the street, numbed, shocked, waiting for someone to come to her.

And someone did. It was Jacob.

The call came to his office as he was leaving for the hospital. Instead he drove the short distance to the scene of the accident, confirmed with sadness that Martha was dead, and turned to the cowering child.

Jacob pulled her close to him. The little girl looked at him with wide eyes, not understanding, not knowing what would happen next, just gripping his hand tightly. Jacob always seemed to make everything right at home. Maybe it would all come right now, too. She looked up, suddenly hopeful.

Jacob saw the look and knew with regret that it would be his duty to explain to this child that her mother would not be all right.

He led her gently into the car with him.

Austen, the chauffeur, in tears and shaking from the scene he had just observed, took one last look at Martha, and opened the door for Jacob and the shivering little girl.

Jacob sat next to Carolyn on the broad seat.

"Your mother was very badly hurt by that car, Carolyn. She will not get better. I cannot heal her. But she cannot feel any pain now, and she can see you from heaven where she is just arriving to take her rightful place among many good people. She will look after you from there, and will always love you there as much as she did here on earth."

Jacob stopped. Although it was never easy to do, part of his training had been learning how to break the news to families of patients who were terminally ill. But he had never had to tell a child. He was at a loss for words. Carolyn was now furiously sucking her thumb, sobbing and hiccuping. He stopped talking and sat quietly holding her until they arrived home. There the news had already reached the house as Jacob's secretary had called ahead to prepare Estelle. The servants were all waiting at the door, shocked but still hoping for the best. They saw from Jacob's face and Carolyn's distraught condition that there was no hope. With tears flowing, Anna reached out for the shivering child as Jacob wearily handed her over.

For the next few days, Carolyn was overwhelmed by the agony of her loss. Although Armindo and Anna took turns in holding her while she sobbed or lay on her mother's bed silently, there was no reaching the lit-

tle girl. Gyneth came to her bedroom and tentatively
knocked on the door, peeping in to see if Carolyn was
there. Carolyn lay on the bed with her eyes open, staring at the ceiling. Gyneth looked at her friend solemnly.

"I am sorry about . . . you know. Can I help you feel
better? Would you like to have my doll?" Gyneth
pressed her latest birthday present into Carolyn's
hands, a large doll with blue eyes that opened and shut
when she moved. Carolyn lay there listlessly, disinterested in the doll, in conversation, in anything. Gyneth
reached out gently and took her hand.

"I am your friend for always. You are my family.
You can share my mom and dad whenever you want
to," she said earnestly.

The silent tears rolled softly down Carolyn's cheeks.
The pain of her loss was unintentionally made even
sharper by Gyneth's well-meaning words. She nodded
her head and gave Gyneth a weak smile of thanks.
Then she turned away to face the wall and sucked her
thumb, holding on to her blanket and new doll. Gyneth
sat on the small chair in the sparsely furnished room,
unsure of what to do next. After a few moments, she
blew a kiss to Carolyn's back and ran downstairs.

The funeral was held, but Carolyn was not permitted
to attend, being considered to be too young for such
things.

Her eyes lost the sparkle of childhood, and everything Gyneth tried was to no avail. She showered
Carolyn with her favorite toys and books, made David
bake special treats such as the gingerbread men cookies that Carolyn loved so much with their funny candy
eyes and mouths. Gyneth offered to push her on the
swing, promising never to ask for a turn herself. Nothing worked. Carolyn preferred to stay in her room, lying on the bed looking at the ceiling.

Finally after many nights of Carolyn's waking and screaming, Anna told Jacob of the child's agony. He gave her a light sedative. She slept fitfully through the night for the first time, but the next night the terrors started again. Even Armindo's happiest stories could not comfort her in her pain.

Estelle and Jacob were worried. They could see that Carolyn's grief was having an effect on Gyneth, who was now often distraught and clinging more and more to Estelle, as if in fear that she, too, would be snatched away by a terrible accident. They knew of no way to help Carolyn deal with her pain. They talked at length to find a solution.

Finally Jacob made the decision. It was time for Carolyn to go and live in Soweto. Gyneth was to go to an exclusive private girls' school that fall. Since all schools were segregated, Carolyn had to go back to Soweto anyway to start elementary school there. Even though it was still the summer holiday, and they had no doubt that Gyneth would be lonely, it seemed that perhaps the change in environment might do both Carolyn and Gyneth some good. Certainly the child's depression and overwhelming grieving was painful for all of them. Jacob rationalized that Carolyn would be happier in a new place where she would not be constantly reminded of her mother.

Anna was dispatched to Soweto to find a solution to the problem of Carolyn's schooling and housing. After a number of trips, Anna found Alena, a schoolteacher at the very school that Carolyn would attend. She had two grown children. There was no father around, as in many of the families in Soweto.

The Soweto house was clean, Anna observed, having made the long journey by bus and foot to the township to visit Alena on two different occasions. Alena desperately needed to augment her income, and the weekly cash from the Amrons would be welcome.

"There is no need to tell the child that Dr. Amron is supporting her. Let her think that her mother made provision for her. Possibly it will help her in her pain," Anna told Alena.

Finally the time came to tell Carolyn. Anna and Armindo gently entered the room that was now hers alone. They drew the blanket back from the peaked, tearstained face.

"One of your very best wishes has come true," Anna said kindly. "You are going to go to school."

Carolyn sat up. "With Gyneth?" she asked, faint hope in her eyes.

Anna shook her head. "No, of course not, my child. You will go to the big school in Soweto."

Carolyn looked at her with horror. Soweto was very far away. She knew it was two bus rides and took a very long time, since once or twice Martha had taken her there to visit some friends from the "old days." Carolyn had hated it. It was crowded, noisy, and dusty. The coal fire smoke made her cough, and her eyes itched all the time. She knew no one there. While Martha would chat to her friends, Carolyn would look around the meager houses they were visiting for books to read. There were no books to be seen, only a battered old bible in one of the houses.

Carolyn had been very relieved when she had come home to her nice clean room and yard.

This news from Anna seemed to make no sense. Carolyn knew traveling to school in Soweto every day would be very difficult.

"But how will I be able to take so many buses every day—it will take so long, it's very far," she said seriously.

Armindo shook his head. "You will not have to take

any buses," he said. "The school is just a few blocks' walk from where you will be living."

"Living . . . ?" Carolyn repeated, not understanding.

"Yes," Anna said. "I have found the most wonderful home for you. It is with Alena, you remember her? She is an old friend of Ouma and, well, of your mother, too . . . a good lady, very happy to welcome you into her home. Your mother would have been very pleased for you to stay with her. It is probably what she would have arranged for you herself in the fall anyway."

Carolyn shook her head in disbelief. None of it made any sense. This was her home. Confused and afraid, she pulled the cover over her head, squeezing her eyes tightly shut. Maybe when she opened them, Anna and Armindo would have gone, and it would have been a dream. But the darkness brought back the dreadful scenes of agony and death. Carolyn lay under the covers, the tears pouring down her face.

Anna and Armindo looked helplessly at each other. Neither of them wanted the child to leave. They would miss her terribly. But there was no alternative. She had to be schooled, this was the only way. They sat there for a few moments, then left the room.

Carolyn pulled back the cover. They had gone. She tried to tell herself that she had imagined it all. But a voice inside her told her that it was real. There was another knock on the door. It was Gyneth.

Carolyn was pleased to see her. The children hugged.

"Is it really true?" Gyneth said. "Are you really going away?"

Carolyn felt an overwhelming sadness. It had happened after all. "They just told me," she said. "I don't want to go away. This is my home, you're my friend and I don't want to live there with some old lady."

Gyneth held her even tighter, her eyes filling with tears.

"Let's run away together, just you and me," Carolyn pleaded.

Gyneth looked at her with wide eyes. She had not even walked to the end of the driveway on her own, never mind run away. Where would she run to? This was her home.

"I am afraid to do that, Carolyn. Don't run away. Something bad could happen to you."

Carolyn looked at her sadly. Something bad had already happened to her.

Carolyn awoke the next morning to find Anna in her room, packing her possessions into a small bag. She carefully placed a small brown package into the bag.

"These are Martha's clothes for you to keep until you are older—to remember. . . ." Anna turned away, her eyes filled with tears. Clutching the bag, Carolyn followed Anna down the stairs and out to the waiting car. In a daze she submitted to the embraces of the servants, and Gyneth's long hug and whispered promises to see her every weekend.

Then Carolyn was in the car with Anna and driving away from the red brick house that was her home, disbelieving, unable to comprehend what was happening.

Finally, after a silent trip that seemed to take forever, they arrived at Alena's house in Soweto. Carolyn eyed the small room and modest bedroom with a sick feeling in her stomach. It was certainly different from the mansion in Hyde Park. There were no pretty things. The only furniture in the main room was a dilapidated sofa with springs sticking out of it. It had embroidered white doilies on it, but other than that it was unappealing. Carolyn's room had a small dresser at one end and a narrow bed at the other. She would have to share the only bathroom with Alena, who looked kind but smelled of Chlorox bleach. The soap in the bathroom was coarse and cut in big chunks rather than smooth and wrapped in paper like at home. The toilet paper was rough, the floors were cold with only a throw rug, and the whole place was hazy from the wisps of smoke that rose from the stove in the center of the living room.

Carolyn shuddered as memories of another stove and living room not dissimilar from this one came into her mind. Her senses were filled once again with the smell of burning flesh and a spinning banshee. She shook her head, turned to Anna and said, "I don't like it here. I want to go home now." She walked to the door.

Anna yanked her by the arm and whispered angrily, "That is not your home. That is the white people's home. You will live here. This will be your home. Don't be ungrateful. Alena is offering to take care of you. You are a lucky girl to have someone as good as her to live with."

Carolyn's eyes filled with tears. Anna had never yanked her arm so hard before. She wanted her gentle Mama, the one who swayed to the qwela music and sang in harmony with her and Gyneth. What had she done to make everything so bad? She began to sob. Anna felt immediately remorseful. The child was so disoriented. She held Carolyn in her arms.

"You will be fine, child. The pain will pass. Just be good, do your schoolwork, Alena will take care of you." Then Anna gave her a quick hug, and she, too, was gone.

"Mama," Carolyn cried, "please come back, where are you?"

Alena shook her head, pulling the beseeching little hands closer to her, her own tears blurring her vision. She held the child and tried to soothe her pain.

But Carolyn was truly alone. She let out a wail of

anguish. "Mama, Mama, come back, please, Mama, come back!"

Her wailing became a sob, and then Alena said, "Hush, my little one, I will take care of you, hush."

Carolyn looked up at her from between wet lashes and saw the kind face above. She wrapped her thin little arms around her chest and touched the face of the teddy bear on the dress that was one of Gyneth's hand-me-downs.

"I'll be with you, teddy," she said. "Gyneth will come and get us like she always does after school, and soon we will be home again."

She curled herself into a little ball and closed her eyes to block out the sensations of Soweto and to recall the warm arms of her mother and the sweet smells and sensations of the white life she had learned to love. No one could take that away from her no matter what they said or where they dragged her off to. She was sure Gyneth would come for her. After all, they were the best friends in the whole world.

# Chapter 5

It wasn't just her presence that Gyneth missed. Carolyn had liked the same things she did, so playing together had been easy; they'd just flowed from one activity to another. After the black child's departure to Soweto, having the occasional friend over could not fulfill Gyneth in quite the same way. Now her belly laugh, which brought tears of mirth to the eyes of those around her, was rare.

Estelle reached out her arms and pulled Gyneth close to her. The little girl glowed with pleasure at this unaccustomed affection from her mother, who always seemed distracted by one thing or another. She hopped up onto Estelle's bed and gave an extra bounce for good measure.

"Don't move around so much, dear." Estelle grimaced, trying to keep the reproach out of her voice. She wanted so much to connect with Gyneth, yet had difficulty in finding the right words. "I have a wonderful surprise for you," she announced gently.

Gyneth's face glowed with excitement. "Is Carolyn . . . ?"

"You are going to have a new baby brother or sister." Estelle spoke quickly, interrupting Gyneth's oft-repeated request for the return of her playmate.

Gyneth received the news with interest. "How big will it be when it comes out?" she asked, looking at her mother's small stomach with some skepticism as they lay on the bed together.

Estelle laughed. "Big enough to eat, cry, and poop a lot, just like you did!"

"But will it play with me?"

"Eventually. Babies take awhile to learn to walk and talk."

"Well, how long do I have to wait?" Gyneth was insistent on a specific answer. The house was large and empty for her now. She'd broached the subject once or twice that she would prefer Carolyn to return, but then gave up on it when she realized that her mother's frowns were the result.

Gyneth decided to set her new sibling straight on the kinds of games she liked as soon as it arrived. With that matter taken care of, she started to chatter about the school play.

Gyneth loved to act. On stage, she could be as grandiose or dramatic as she desired, and no one, especially her ever-present governess, Emily, could tell her to behave more sedately.

Estelle encouraged her daughter. The child had talent, her acting came naturally with a good singing voice that did not have Carolyn's perfect pitch and instinctive harmony, but was sweet nevertheless.

"It is in your blood," Estelle had whispered to herself while watching Gyneth audition for and obtain the part of the wicked queen in *Alice in Wonderland*. She had not told Gyneth about her own fledgling stage career, a subject full of pain, until one day, while looking through old photographs, Gyneth had come across a picture of a young woman on stage.

"Mummy, is this you? Look how funny your hair was then! You never told me that you were an actress!

Was there a big audience? And how many nights did you do it for?" Gyneth's curiosity was endless, and she pressed her mother for further details. During the tedious weeks of her pregnancy spent lying in bed, Estelle had plenty of time to reminisce. She was filled with pleasure as she remembered the moments of glory as she stood alone on the stage, hearing the applause. As the months went by, Gyneth came home every day with the details of rehearsals, and enabled her mother to relive that part of her life all over again.

And despite stern admonitions from her doctor to stay in bed for the rest of the pregnancy, Estelle was determined to attend the opening night of Gyneth's play.

That morning, however, Estelle awoke with a heavy feeling in her heart, a sort of dreadful premonition of evil. Some days would start like this. It never lasted, just gave her a dreadful sick fear for a few moments, and then it faded again. Estelle breathed in deeply, forcing herself to relax. She had to conserve her strength in order to attend the play. She hoped that Jacob would not have any emergency surgeries. It was so important that he be there for their daughter. And for her.

Their marriage had marked the beginning of a new life for Estelle, but also the end of her dreams of a stage career, as she took a role for which she had never been prepared—the supporting player to Jacob.

Estelle thought back to the years before she'd married. She had studied at the Royal Academy of Dramatic Art in London and had performed in local repertory theater there, as well as in Johannesburg. How wonderful it had felt to be the center of attention. And then the war had started and her father had made the long ocean voyage to England to bring her home.

If she hadn't returned to South Africa on the *Windsor Castle* that very month, ending up with a week's vacation in Durban, she may not have met Jacob.

If she had stayed in London, might she finally have achieved recognition as an actress? Estelle lost herself again in the past, and pulled the covers up over her shoulders.

Jacob had volunteered for service as a navy surgeon prior to meeting her, but when his call-up papers arrived on the night of their wedding, Estelle's father had held them back in order to give the young couple at least one night free of care. When her husband had come home on leave two years later, he was not the same joyous man she had known. In fact he awoke many nights wet with perspiration and trembling with fear, then becoming tense and angry. There were many doctors remaining in South Africa who were building their practices at the expense of those Jewish physicians who had volunteered to fight for freedom. Jacob's infrequent visits home became a morass of confused emotions—relief at having survived, pride in his naval duties, and anger at those who'd stayed on the sidelines.

During the war years, Estelle, now celibate, lived again with her parents. Loneliness created an empty space that she filled with memories of her fleeting moments on stage.

Then one day, it seemed her dream had a chance to survive. Anita Colsen, the woman who had been her drama coach and teacher, called as she was rushing to her volunteer work at the temple.

"Estelle," she said hoarsely, "I am so glad to have caught you. I have to have my tonsils out, of all things, and I will be unable to teach for at least a month. Please, my dear, will you take over from me?"

At last Estelle had a chance to do something creative

and challenging again. She had moved immediately into her new life and found that the natural talents she had submerged in the war effort came rushing forward. She thrived on the newfound independence. Soon she was receiving pupils of her own, and when Mrs. Colsen recovered there was enough work for them both.

Then, miraculously, the war was over.

Jacob came home, they moved into the apartment that had stood vacant for five years, and now life could go on for them.

And it did—but not in the way she had dreamed.

After Jacob had been back three days, she arrived home late from work to find him looking dark and angry.

"Where were you?" he said sharply.

"I was late with one of my lessons," she said. "The poor woman, she's so nervous, auditioning for a part in the Shakespeare festival and . . ." Estelle glanced at Jacob's brooding face.

"This has to stop. Today. Tonight. No wife of mine will work for a living. I do not want people saying that I cannot support my family. You will tell these pupils to go back to Anita Colsen and you will not work again."

Estelle felt red-hot anger rising in her face. "How dare you tell me what to do," she yelled. "I've built this business myself, I'm proud of it and love what I do. I will *not* give it up."

"Then you will have to give *me* up," he yelled back. "I have no practice, no hospital positions, nothing. I will not have a wife who humiliates me, and that's the end of it."

He stalked out of the room and she could hear him putting on his coat and opening the front door.

"Oh please, Jacob, don't go. Let's talk about it."

Jacob paused at the door. "I am fighting to regain the ground I lost. Please don't make me fight you, too. Maybe you will work later when I get established again. But not now, please, my darling."

Estelle pulled him down to her and held him tightly. "We'll talk about it tomorrow," she whispered. "Let's rest now. Come, tell me about your day, tell me everything."

And so the night passed, as did the next one and the one after. Estelle never worked again.

Then it had appeared as if her life were going to be fulfilled after all. After years of struggling, she became pregnant for the first time! Nothing could match the thrill she'd felt nor her excitement. The pain at losing her career faded into a dull ache as the life moved and grew inside her.

The miracle arrived in the form of a little girl, Gyneth. Jacob had longed for a boy, and Estelle saw the flash of disappointment on his face as the screaming little person emerged from her body. The baby was healthy, beautiful, with big blue eyes, perfect in every way, and when nostalgia tugged at her, Estelle tried to push out of her mind all thoughts about what could have been. She tried to derive consolation from the fact that she was fortunate to have a child, and most of the time that worked.

But a small part of her had died with the cessation of her independence, and many times she had looked back and wondered if that same part, dormant, had lain in wait to sabotage her life later.

Estelle leaned against the pillows. She was only five foot three inches and took up little space in the over-size bed even though her second pregnancy was more than six months along. Jacob had left already, of course. His days started at least two hours before hers. The morning seemed to brighten as she ran her hand over the small miraculous swelling in her stomach. The inactivity and time spent resting, trying to safeguard the delicate life that was blossoming inside her, normally caused her fears to multiply as the day wore on. Tonight, however, she was going to attend Gyneth's debut. She pressed the bell on the table next to the bed.

David heard the summons in the kitchen, took the percolating coffee off the stove and poured it into the silver pot that stood on the tray with a delicate vase and a single rose. He added a brioche that was in the warming oven and straightened the matching silver butter and preserve dishes on either side of the Meissen china plate and coffee cup. The madam would not want a single drop spilled, so David ascended the stairs slowly to the master suite, which occupied the entire west wing of the house and comprised a master bedroom and bathroom with his and hers showers, baths, and two separate dressing rooms.

David knocked on the door and entered the bedroom.

"Good morning, madam." He placed the tray so she could reach it easily. Then he drew out his shopping list.

The Amrons' hectic entertainment schedule had developed over the years into a streamlined mixture of obligation and entertainment.

David recited the list of household necessities to be bought. Estelle tried to concentrate on the moment, and when he finally left the room, she leaned back again and sighed. Her early-morning fear had gone, dispelled by the needs of the household. The house was quiet and peaceful. Gyneth was off at school and would return in the afternoon for a short rest, readying herself for the important night ahead.

The dress rehearsal had been the previous day. As

she kissed her mother goodbye, Gyneth's eyes filled
with tears.

"I really miss Carolyn, Mummy. If only she could
see me in this play. Can't she come back to live with
us?"

Estelle had hugged Gyneth, shaking her head briefly
and sidestepping the question. "You'll be late if we
talk about that. Good luck, darling."

Now remembering the conversation, Estelle pressed
one hand over her eyes as the other stroked her stomach as if to protect the unborn child. She felt guilty
about Gyneth's loneliness. She had felt such a sense of
failure at her continuing inability to become pregnant.
No matter how many months she took her temperature
and tried to guess at her date of ovulation, she had
been disappointed again and again. She went from her
menstrual period to two weeks later, tirelessly timing
and organizing for that special day and then lived in an
agony of expectation for another two weeks, waiting
for her menstrual cycle to begin again. On the months
that she was one or two days late, her hopes, despite
her own admonitions to herself, would rise and she
would begin to feel excitement and joy. Then the
bleeding would start and despair would overwhelm
her. The hope of a new month spurred her on as the
whole awful cycle began again. Whenever she had
seen Carolyn playing with Gyneth she had been reminded of what could have been, with a home full of
children. In some ways she was relieved that the child
had gone.

And then finally, her moment came, the delicate
process of creation beat the odds of infertility, and she
was pregnant. Many long months had been spent in
bed, with only short visits to the dressing room or
downstairs to the dining room for the occasional dinner. Amid her joy was fear and panic. Every twinge,

every painful cramp, filled Estelle with dread. She tried not to dream too long of the new life soon to join her family. But the long hours in bed gave her much time to fantasize, to fill her thoughts with hopeful plans.

She sighed. Her thoughts went back to Jacob. How much she loved the charismatic person she lived with, yet how very delicate was his ego that he needed constantly to be the center, the power giver, the generous donor of money, time, and healing talent. Jacob was not only the youngest chief of the surgical staff at the hospital and university, but he was also on the board of the Jewish Home for the Aged, the Jewish Orphanage, the Medical Council of South Africa, and on and on. His time was swallowed up by so many activities that it was difficult for him to give her any of his energy at all.

The lawn mower's sputtering brought Estelle from her musing back to the present. The whole morning had passed away. She moved uncomfortably in the bed. At times she felt as if the longed-for pregnancy would never end. She was nauseated all the time.

Gyneth came bounding through the door, her school uniform awry, her pigtails flying, and landed on Estelle's bed. "I'm home, Mummy, can you believe that tonight is the night for the play?"

Estelle smiled at her, wishing that the school day was longer as she really did not have the stamina to keep up with Gyneth's demands and energy level. Her energy demanded a playmate. It was difficult to replace Carolyn in her life.

Gyneth took the opportunity to give a big jump, and flipped off the bed onto the floor.

"Great, it's early! I still have time to read a bit," she said, grabbing a Nancy Drew mystery.

"So, who do you think is the culprit here, Carolyn?"

Gyneth whispered, discussing the plot as if her friend were still there. "Let's work the whole thing out. We are just as smart as all the characters in the book. Then we'll see if we guessed right!"

Estelle observed the little girl out of the corner of her eye. "Don't mutter, dear. Speak up if you are talking to me."

"I'm not, Mummy, I'm just working it all out as I read along."

Then Estelle felt a sharp twinge in her lower abdomen. Her fear returned. She rubbed her hand on her stomach. The cramp got worse, much worse. There was a rush of warm liquid between her legs. Her probing fingers were covered with blood. Estelle's vision blurred. From far away she heard the bell to the kitchen peal many times as she pressed it with a trembling hand. Estelle was conscious enough to keep Gyneth unaware of her panic. The child looked up in surprise as Anna came running into the room, in answer to Estelle's frenetic ringing. Gyneth smiled happily as she saw Anna, but the older woman did not even look at her. Instead she ran toward Estelle, seeing her white face and noticing with horror the spreading bloodstain on the white lacy comforter. Estelle motioned to Anna to take Gyneth away.

Gyneth looked at her mother, confused.

Anna reached for her but Gyneth was alerted now to her mother's panic. "Is this the time for the baby to come, Mummy?" she asked, pushing Anna's hands away as she tried to pull her from the room.

"You must go with Anna now, darling," Estelle said breathlessly. "I am going to go to the hospital to see how the baby is doing. I will be home very soon. You have to get ready for the play. Bye, darling." Estelle turned away, her hand already reaching for the telephone.

It would be another two hours before anyone could reach Jacob. He was in surgery. His secretary ordered an ambulance and Estelle faced her ordeal alone.

As Estelle awoke from the anesthetic she turned to look for her husband. But he was not there, only the nurse holding her hand and looking kindly into her face.

"Jacob . . . ?" she asked weakly.

"He is still in surgery," the nurse explained. "He really couldn't leave the patient, but he sent a message that he will be down to see you as soon as he can. Now try to sleep a little. You are a strong girl, and there will be plenty more babies for you. We all have at least one of these little setbacks in our lives."

"But, Gyneth . . . not me . . . it's her play, he has to go for her."

Estelle wept. As she was slipping into sleep again she felt warmth between her legs.

Nausea rose in Estelle's throat as she saw moving lights above her, the doors of rooms, the opening and shutting of the elevators and the large round operating-room light looming above her face once again. Dr. Cohen's face was worried and anxious and she tried to ask him why everybody was panicking and where Jacob was, but her teeth were chattering so much, her body couldn't stop shaking and the words wouldn't come out. Then it was all darkness again.

When she awoke, Jacob was there. She thought he was crying. It couldn't be him, she thought as she slipped back into the darkness. She was in so much pain, so much pain.

There would be no more babies for Estelle and Jacob. The damage to her uterus was irreparable and only surgery could stop the bleeding.

Estelle's first days after the hysterectomy were filled with pain, sadness, and loneliness.

Jacob blamed himself for not being there. He tried to keep up a front for Estelle, but his guilt and sadness were evident. They were both so young, with so many hopes for the children unborn to them. Jacob stayed by Estelle's side, stroking her hair as the transfusions dripped slowly into her veins and he wept over her small hand. He would make it up to her. Thank God for Gyneth—at least they had Gyneth. It would be all right.

Gyneth had gone to school that night with the chauffeur.

Pulling on her wig, she ran again for the twentieth time, to the front of the stage and looked in vain for her parents through the small hole in the curtain before the performance. "Where are they?" she muttered to herself. "They're going to be late."

"Come on, Gyneth, your makeup isn't finished yet." The drama teacher hurried her back into the dressing room.

The curtain opened and all Gyneth could see was Emily, alone, sitting grimly in the front row. Everyone else had their whole families there.

Gyneth performed as well as she could, while constantly looking for the familiar faces of those who would cheer her on.

The cast party was an ordeal.

"You were wonderful, Gyneth," the headmistress said, solemnly shaking the little girl's hand and wisely not mentioning the conspicious absence of her family.

"My mother was sick, otherwise she would have been here, too," she said, answering the unasked question.

"Of course, I understand. Please wish her well from me." The headmistress moved on. Gyneth's face was red with fury.

"See you tomorrow," her friends from the cast

chimed as they left the auditorium surrounded by their proud parents.

Austen opened the door of the car and Gyneth slid into the backseat next to Emily.

"Why didn't they come?" she cried, at last letting the tears of anger and disappointment pour out. "I hate them all, especially the new baby. This was my night, why couldn't it have waited one more day to come?"

Emily tried to comfort the child. But warmth was not her strongest quality. "I will tell them how good you were, dear, now pull yourself together. Here's a hanky, blow hard and don't snivel."

"Anna, where are you?" Gyneth ran out of the kitchen door into the dark servants' quarters.

"Anna, is Anna there?" Gyneth was hesitant to go into Anna's room, knowing the staff living area was off bounds to her under all circumstances.

Anna came out, her huge form covered by a mass of pink flannel. "What is it, what's the matter?"

"Anna, no one came to my play, and Emily won't tell me anything. Mummy and Daddy aren't here and I don't know what is happening!" Gyneth's voice rose to a wail. "And Carolyn would have come if they hadn't sent her away."

Gyneth started sobbing uncontrollably. No one seemed to care about her at all, and this was her night of triumph. Her mother was always home but now she was nowhere to be seen. The new baby had taken everyone away.

Anna held the little girl and let her sob. She had not heard from the hospital. But she was prepared for the worst.

"Your mama is still in the hospital, and your father must stay there to take care of her. Of course they wanted to be with you. You know, your mother has spoken of nothing else but your play for months now.

It just wasn't possible. Hush, child, you'll understand when you grow up."

The servants quietly packed up the bassinet, the little baby blankets that Estelle had been knitting, and the crocheted booties and matching hat that Estelle had just finished. Every trace of the baby-to-be was removed from the house. The day Estelle returned by ambulance, Gyneth looked on, not understanding what had happened to the promised playmate.

"Mummy, where is the baby? Is it still in the hospital?"

Estelle turned her face into the pillow and wept silently.

Anna took Gyneth out of the room. "The baby was not well, not properly formed. God had decided to take the baby back to make it better. The Lord will send the baby back one day when the time is right."

Anna's explanation did not really satisfy Gyneth. She tried talking to Jacob.

"Dad, is the baby around somewhere? What happened?"

Jacob turned his face away from Gyneth. "It wasn't really a baby yet, just a little creature trying to become a baby. It hadn't grown properly. There will be no baby, not now, not ever," he said grimly.

Gyneth had a terrible feeling in her heart. She knew that somehow it was because of her that the baby did not come. She'd definitely wanted it, most of the time anyway, because now that Carolyn was not with her, she had been looking forward to having a friend to play with again. Secretly, however, she preferred Carolyn to any baby. In fact, some nights she lay in bed feeling very lonely and would close her eyes tightly and wish that she would wake up and find Carolyn there just like it had always been. Then the night of the school play she had said that she hated the new baby. But she only meant it for the moment. Now she dreaded that all her wishing had made the baby feel unwelcome, so it went away. Gyneth was afraid to tell anyone her secret, so she tried to bury it deep inside her where no one would ever know that it was all her fault.

# Chapter 6

Gyneth stood with Estelle in the large paneled lobby, on her first day in the exclusive private school. The headmistress approached and introduced herself.

"Your first class is in Room Two, over there," she said to Gyneth, pointing toward a classroom where a number of girls in uniform were gathering. "Off you go to join them, my dear."

Without even a glance back at her mother, Gyneth ran off to join her new classmates. Estelle felt a pang of loss. If only she had another child she would not feel so useless now that Gyneth didn't seem to need her as much anymore. The tears welled up in her eyes and she turned away. The older woman saw her discomfort and gave her arm a squeeze.

"There really is no need to worry about Gyneth, Mrs. Amron. She will be fine here with us and in time, I'm sure, you will have other little ones at home."

Estelle swallowed hard, not wanting to explain.

"You know that Gyneth is quite young for this gifted class," the woman continued, "but after we tested your daughter we felt she'd do very well. She is obviously gregarious, well adjusted, and very confident."

Estelle nodded. On the surface, Gyneth was like a

miniature version of Jacob—driven, compulsive, with a voracious mental appetite that was difficult for Estelle to satisfy. But inside was a soft and vulnerable child, longing for approval. Estelle identified with that hidden part of Gyneth, and knew how much she could be hurt.

As soon as the class started, Gyneth's attention was entirely captured by the teacher and she eagerly answered every question loudly. She seemed completely at home, and saw only the approving looks of the teacher, not the faces of her fourteen classmates as they regarded her performance with some irritation.

The teacher handed out classwork, which Gyneth finished in record time. "You do good work, young lady," the teacher said, nodding approvingly as she saw that Gyneth was able to understand a concept immediately and was asking for more to do. She decided to give the child additional tasks that were more challenging.

Gyneth basked in the praise. At recess she examined her classmates carefully and saw only one who looked interesting.

"Hello, what's your name?" She looked admiringly at the beautiful little girl with jet-black hair and almost translucent skin.

"Vanessa," she answered. She was proper and delicate, and paid close attention to her appearance all the time. Gyneth decided she wanted to look like her new friend. School was going to be fun.

There was no doubt about it—it was exactly what Gyneth needed. However, the weekends were still tedious. Gyneth begged in vain to be able to visit Carolyn, but Estelle refused. The children were given permission to correspond, and to the Amrons' surprise, they wrote regularly. Finally, Estelle agreed to a reunion. Of course, it is impossible for Gyneth to visit Soweto.

White people just never went there. So one weekend Anna made the tiresome journey to Soweto and brought Carolyn back.

Carolyn stood at the gate, much as her mother had done many years before. She'd been confused when Anna had arrived, since Gyneth had said nothing in her letters about a visit. Throughout the endless bus ride, she continued to feel apprehensive.

Gyneth looked taller, but the golden hair was the same and her face was glowing with excitement. Carolyn, small and slender, high cheekbones barely visible under the youthful softness, moved forward uncertainly as Gyneth stepped out of the front door and ran to her.

"Carolyn, it's been such ages since I've seen you. Do you know how often I've wished you were here with me? Come on, I have so many things planned for us today." Gyneth could not have been more welcoming. Carolyn slipped back into the sweetness of their friendship as if no time had intervened.

"I've missed you, too. You look so tall now, you're taller than I am!" The girls hugged and giggled, and for the moment Carolyn forgot her anger over her banishment from the Amron house. She let Gyneth lead her by the hand to their favorite place on the swings. Then, gently swaying in the breeze, Gyneth began to excitedly talk about her new school.

"It's so amazing, really, Carolyn, you would love it. There are all sorts of playing fields, swimming pools for both lower and upper schools and as for the gymnasium, you cannot imagine the stuff they have in there. And there is the most incredible drama department and I can't wait to get involved in the upcoming musical. Do you remember all the great times we had singing together, while Dad would play the piano? It's so super to see you again, Carolyn. Did you get all my letters?"

The young black girl nodded, smiling faintly. Gyneth carried on.

"The classrooms are actually smaller than at my other school but really comfortable. Our desks are terrific, with little drawers to keep stuff in. And my homeroom has the most wonderful tree outside. You know how I love trees, so when I get really bored I can look outside and daydream quite easily. There really aren't too many girls there that I like an awful lot, just one, Vanessa. She is so beautiful, I wish I looked like her, black hair and blue eyes. Oh, I have so much to tell you I don't even know where to start."

Gyneth chattered on, but the day suddenly held little joy for Carolyn. She felt her chest tighten with the pain and old anger that Gyneth had never come to bring her home.

Finally Carolyn realized Gyneth was asking her a question. "So tell me about your school. Do you have lots of new friends now? What do you do after school?"

Carolyn was at a loss for words. "It's different . . . very different," she stammered.

"Carolyn, what's the matter? Tell me what it's like in your school. I really want to know. Please . . . ?"

Carolyn took a deep breath.

"We have about fifty children in my class." She paused.

"F-Fifty?" Gyneth was incredulous. There were only three hundred in her whole school.

"There are boys and girls and they are all of different ages."

"How can you get your questions answered like that?" Gyneth was frowning, trying to imagine what it would be like to have so many in the class.

"We don't have too many books and writing pads. Some days I don't even have a piece of paper of my own to write on. I also have to share a desk with someone else. As for playtime, we don't have any playgrounds with fields, trees, gymnasium, and swimming pools. There's an old car tire someone left by the road and we climb on that sometimes. Hopscotch is a good game. We play that almost every day."

Gyneth thought of her normal weekly activities, which included climbing on the jungle gym or tennis, ballet, speech and drama lessons.

Gyneth felt deflated. Carolyn sat silently, swinging beside her. Gyneth took her friend's hand.

"You know, I was in the school play at my last school, I was the queen in *Alice in Wonderland.* You know the story, we read it together. I missed you so much that night, I know you would have loved it." Carolyn now stilled her swing, bitterness in her heart.

Gyneth jumped onto the grass. "I know what we'll do. Let's go upstairs and find a game. How about snakes and ladders? We always loved that one."

Carolyn followed Gyneth into the house. As she walked on the soft Persian rugs and up the elegant spiral staircase to her friend's bedroom, everything she saw was in sharp contrast to the life she was leading. The house was so clean, shiny, with mirrors, woodwork, panels and brass fixtures, spacious rooms and glistening bathrooms. She ached as she thought of the drab colors of Soweto, the dirt and ever-present sand or mud, the cracked mirrors, concrete steps and steel fences. All about the Amron house were soft upholstered sofas, brightly colored fabrics, white bedcovers and of course, the majestic grand piano. Carolyn burned with desire to surround herself with these material things, to sing again as Jacob played the piano, to be safe and secure with her mother just a few steps away, ironing peacefully in the laundry room. But that life was gone. She felt like an interloper.

"What's the matter, Carolyn? You seem so sad." Gyneth sat in front of the game, while Carolyn stood uncertainly at the door.

"It's not the same as this in Soweto. I don't feel good there. I wish we could go back to the way it used to be."

"Well, I certainly asked my parents enough times if you could come back and they wouldn't listen. Now we have a whole day to play. Cheer up, we can still have fun together."

Carolyn struggled to smile. She made the motions required by the game.

When the time came for her to go, she shook Estelle's hand solemnly and gave Gyneth a hug. It would never be the same for her again.

During the long bus ride that took Carolyn back to the township, Anna tried to talk to her, but she had little to say. Anna saw with wise eyes that the child was learning the tough lesson of how it was to be black in South Africa.

Carolyn realized that "friendship" was now to have a different meaning than before. She didn't know the name for the bad feeling she had, but she did know that she didn't want to have it anymore. As Anna was leaving her at the door of Alena's house, Carolyn took her hand and looked at her.

"I cannot visit for a while. I have to stay here on the weekends. Maybe I'll come to visit later. Thank you for coming for me, Anna." With a formal little handshake Carolyn bade Anna farewell, and closed the door of the small house behind her,

Gyneth kept writing, but Carolyn couldn't find it in her heart to reply. She could not bear to hear from

Gyneth about the life that should have been hers, and she resolved not to go back to the Amrons' again.

"Mum, she won't come to visit. Why?" Gyneth was hurt. She could not understand why things had changed between them.

"Your life is so different from hers. Perhaps she is busy with her own school, darling."

"That must be it. Maybe one day I can go and visit her."

Estelle knew that was not an option. She smiled at Gyneth and changed the subject.

After a while Gyneth slipped back into her old way of adapting to the loss of her friend. Carolyn continued to exist in her imagination. She was the one Gyneth spoke to at night, the one with whom she shared her feelings, her constant playmate in her fantasies. As she relaxed after school, Gyneth would share the events of her day with an absent Carolyn who became the empathetic listener in her mind, always saying and doing the right thing, making Gyneth feel better. If someone asked who her best friend was, she still answered, Carolyn—the nonjudgmental, supportive, loving phantom of Carolyn that she had created when the real child went away into another world, without a satisfactory goodbye.

Estelle noticed that Gyneth was fantasizing more about Carolyn, and it worried her.

"Anna, next Saturday, could you bring Carolyn over for the day?"

"It's no good, madam," Anna told her, "Carolyn does not want to come."

But Estelle was adamant and sent Anna one more time to Soweto to speak to Alena in order to encourage Carolyn to make the visit. Her major means of support still came from Jacob Amron. The young girl, however, did not cooperate.

"I will not go. I hate it there," she cried and ran out of the house, looking for a place to hide. But Alena caught up with her.

"Listen to me, child. If the madam wants you to go, you'll go. These people have been very good to you and your late mother, Martha, may she rest in peace," Alena said sharply, holding her thin arm with a tight and painful grip.

Carolyn was subdued but defiant as she traveled back to Hyde Park.

Gyneth was full of excitement about Carolyn's visit. The last week had been their birthday. The fact that the girls were born on the same day was very important to her, making her feel like they were twins.

From her perch on the upstairs landing where she had sat for over an hour in anticipation of her friend's arrival, Gyneth saw Carolyn reluctantly enter the Amron property. She galloped down the stairs, her pinafore dress lifting high above her knees as she jumped three steps at a time, so as to intercept Carolyn before she went into the servants' quarters. Emily glowered at Gyneth as she stampeded by and called after her.

"Young ladies don't make a noise when they walk, slow down!"

But Gyneth was already out the front door, greeting Carolyn with a large hug. Carolyn hugged her back, melting a little when she saw her friend. It was hard to resist Gyneth's affectionate nature, and Carolyn was starved for the love that shone out of Gyneth's eyes. She wished, for the millionth time, that the world could turn back to where it had been when Martha had been alive.

"Carolyn, thanks so much for coming. Mummy told me that you were very busy at your school on the weekends, but I promise you we'll have a great time here." Gyneth looked anxiously at Carolyn to see if she would be as sad as she had been on the last visit.

The young black girl's eyes were glistening with tears. Few people hugged her anymore. She straightened her thin gray cotton dress, pulled the buttons of the sweater together and followed Gyneth, caught up in her excitement, feeling to her surprise, real happiness at seeing her friend again. As they entered Gyneth's room, Carolyn felt her friend push her forward. She stumbled into the room with Gyneth close on her heels, and stared, speechless.

There was a banner hanging the whole length of the room that read "Happy Birthday Carolyn." There were balloons everywhere, and in the middle of the dresser was a big birthday cake with candles on it, and colored plates and forks. There was a huge bowl of red punch with two glasses and on the bed was the largest present Carolyn had ever seen. The brightly colored bow had a big card pinned onto it with her name written in gold.

Carolyn was frozen in disbelief. Her eyes filled with tears. No one had even remembered that it was her birthday. Her mother was no longer there, nor Matthias or Ouma, no one who really cared whether she had been born or not. Except for Gyneth. She turned to her friend and hugged her tightly.

"You are my best friend in the world. I'm so sorry that I did not write to you. It hurts, you see, coming here hurts me so much. It's not your fault, you don't know ... it's my mother and ... living away from here. It's so hard to explain. Anyway, this is wonderful. No one else has ever done this for me. Gyneth, we must be friends forever, no matter what happens."

Carolyn was filled with guilt at having protested so much about the visit. Gyneth could not help the fact that she was white, living in a white world. She was still the only friend Carolyn had.

Oblivious to Carolyn's turmoil, Gyneth was jumping up and down with glee. She absolutely loved surprises and the expression on Carolyn's face was all the thanks she needed.

"Come, let's light the candles on the cake. You blow them out, then we'll eat it and you'll open your present. Then we can go and play outside," Gyneth said, busily organizing everything.

Estelle and Jacob looked into the room. They saw that Gyneth was overjoyed with the success of her surprise. They shook Carolyn's hand, wishing her a happy birthday, and then as she blew out the candles, they all sang happy birthday to her.

It was the loveliest day that Carolyn could remember. She let herself enjoy the luxuries that were again made available to her, swimming briefly in a cold swimming pool, then riding horses and reading excerpts from Gyneth's vast array of books. When Anna took her home, she was just a tired, satisfied young girl who had a wonderful birthday party. She stroked the box containing her present, a set of writing paper an envelopes, a shiny Parker fountain pen and blotter with a bottle of ink, and the candles off her cake. The rest of the cake was wrapped in another box so that she could eat it at home.

It was only when she entered Alena's house that Carolyn felt heavy with sadness at her fate. It seemed that everything was possible when she was in Gyneth's home, whereas her world was one big negative.

Carolyn became a regular visitor at the Amrons' for the next few months, and over time she began to accept with less rancor the contrasts in their lives.

Until it was time for the midterm break.

School vacations were tedious in the township. Carolyn spent long days sitting on the step in front of Alena's house, watching the other children kicking stones around the dusty streets. She longed for a library, but there was none. She counted the days until school began again.

The Amron family vacations, however, were delightful. A short four-day trip was always to the game reserve. This was a special holiday, which Jacob would insist upon every year. It was like going back to the wild, no telephones, no airplanes, just enough civilization so that there were facilities clean enough to please Estelle. More importantly for Gyneth, however, it was the only time she had her parents entirely to herself. On holiday, Jacob was out of reach of his practice, Estelle was removed from her social life and servants, and Gyneth was free of Emily's control.

The afternoon before their game reserve holiday was to begin, Gyneth was packing her small bag and chattering about her upcoming vacation.

"Can I come, too?" Carolyn blurted out.

Gyneth became flustered and concentrated on her packing. Jacob had asked her the same question the week before. But she didn't want to share her parents with anyone, not even Carolyn.

"Well, I don't think so, because there is no place for you in the camp in the game reserve. We have reservations, you see."

Carolyn blushed, embarrassed for asking. Yet deep down, she knew that Gyneth's reason was not logical. She thought she knew the real reason. She was black and black people did not stay in the same places as whites. The bounds of their friendship had been reached.

Gyneth saw the look of futility on Carolyn's face. "My dad doesn't have much time for vacations and he wants to have me and my mom all to himself." Grabbing her hand, Gyneth pulled her friend toward the door. "Should we have a quick horseback ride before Amos feeds them?"

Carolyn shook her head. She could always tell when her friend was lying. She knew that it had to do with her being black.

"I have to go," she said coldly. "You have things to do to get ready for your trip. If I don't leave, it will be dark by the time I get back to Soweto. Bye, Gyneth, have a nice holiday."

Carolyn turned to go and Gyneth, now filled with remorse, tried to give her a hug. Carolyn gave her a perfunctory squeeze and ran off, down the stairs and out to the servants' quarters.

For most of the next week, Carolyn curled herself up in the corner of the broken-down sofa in Alena's house, thinking about Gyneth and her family, enjoying the richness of their country together, while she had no way of going anywhere, or doing anything.

Carolyn did not come to visit for a few months. Gyneth was sure that her selfishness was the reason. Finally she wrote her a note, covered it with hearts and enclosed one of her gold lucky charms, a little poodle. She tried to explain to Carolyn that she had been selfish and had not wanted to share her parents with anyone. The next vacation was in summer, two months' long, and things would be different then.

This time Gyneth had a plan. The Amron summer holiday was the same each year, spent at their home in the Cape of Good Hope.

"Mum, Dad, may Carolyn come with us on our holiday to the Cape this year?" Jacob and Estelle agreed.

In the summer, the Amrons took Anna, Armindo, and David along for the long vacation to care for the family. To Jacob and Estelle, Carolyn's presence would be incidental and hardly noticed. Gyneth, however, was jubilant.

Carolyn entered Gyneth's room, wanting to believe her friend's explanatory note and warmed by the generosity of her gift of a charm, which she knew was Gyneth's favorite. Gyneth jumped off the bed and pulled her onto the sofa.

"Two months from now, you will be joining us on our family holiday in the Cape. Aren't you excited?" Gyneth jumped up and down on the sofa with glee.

Carolyn could hardly believe it.

The next month's visits were filled with planning and excited imaginings as the girls prepared for their holiday.

The summer holiday was the one where the Amrons traveled with another family, the Hillels, to Muizenburg in the Cape for six weeks. Jacob never felt that he could take the entire time away from his practice. So he would come home after three weeks and Estelle and Gyneth would return later.

The Cape was an area larger than the square area of France and was founded in 1652 by Jan Van Riebeeck. It took two long driving days to reach by car.

The preparations started at five in the morning. The families loaded the roofs of their cars with supplies for the road and light baggage. Meantime, the night before, Alena delivered Carolyn to the safekeeping of Armindo, David, and Anna at the railway station, as they loaded the bulky Amron family suitcases and extra luggage into the two train compartments, one for the luggage and one for themselves.

"Anna, when will we leave? Can I open the window? Is there a toilet on the train? Can I see it? Does the sink work?"

Carolyn was more excited than she had ever been. This was her first time on a train, in a station, going out of the city on a holiday. In fact, there were so many firsts that she was filled with wonder as she took everything in. The second-class cabin was crowded, and the suitcases overflowed into the seating space.

Anna grumbled loudly. "Such nonsense, taking all these clothes. Really, all anyone ever wears is a swimming suit and sandals. Phew, it's so warm in here!" She mopped her face with a large pink handkerchief.

"Child, stop jumping up and down so much. David, will you take this bag and put it over there; no, not here, there!" Anna was irritated and perspiring. However, her bad mood soon resolved as the train started moving and the breeze cooled her down.

" 'She'll be coming down the mountain when she comes,' " Carolyn sang in her clear voice, remembering the travel song that Gyneth used to sing with her. The young girl's delight made them all feel in a holiday mood, as they munched on sandwiches that David had thoughtfully prepared. The industrial section of the city slid by and they harmonized with the rhythms of Carolyn's songs, which matched the clackety-clack of the passing railroad tracks.

The Amrons and Hillels drove for two days, in convoy. In the front car were Estelle and Gyneth with the two children of the Hillel family. They were already singing as they left Hyde Park.

The hardest part of the journey was the seemingly endless road through the Karoo, the semidesert area that became a paradise for a short couple of weeks when it received a meager few drops of moisture.

The two families struggled to stay awake as they drove into the breathtaking surroundings of Cape Town and saw the sight that never failed to make them gasp with pleasure—Table Mountain with its "table cloth" of cloud, just reaching condensation point at the rim of the mountain tip. The cloud seemed to float over the flat mountaintop, looking like an ethereal moisture-laden blanket.

They peered out the windows, trying to catch a glimpse of where the Indian and the Atlantic oceans joined, at the very tip of Africa, and they shouted when each one of them said that he or she was first to see the dividing line.

They sped up as they made their way across to Muizenburg where the Amron seaside home nestled at the edge of the beach of golden white sands that stretched far into the warm Indian Ocean. The unpacking was always exciting as Gyneth tore upstairs to see if her room was exactly as she had left it, and indeed it was, even better, since Armindo had carefully placed her favorite pillow brought down from Johannesburg by train with him, right on the center of her bed. She hugged him and he beamed with pleasure as she sped downstairs, eager to find Carolyn.

Carolyn was in heaven. She did not even care that her room was small and stuffy and she had to share it with Anna, who snored loudly. The openness of the beach resort was like a miracle after the drabness and closed-in feeling she had in Soweto.

"Isn't this wonderful?" She spoke softly to Gyneth as they sat in the quietness of the first evening on the sidewalk. "This is a beautiful place. It's so much nicer than Soweto. I would like to come to the seaside every year if I could."

"If you liked it enough, you could even live here when you grow up. When I grow up, I am going to be a famous actress and singing star and so I will definitely have a house at the beach," Gyneth said dreamily.

On the vast expanse of beach, the Amrons and their friends lay sheltered from the wind that sometimes whipped up and around the cabanas. Jacob had designed a little "wind wall," which Armindo staked out in the early morning and set up on cricket stumps as he wove the canvas up and around the best section of beach for their pleasure later on in the day. By the time that Estelle and the Hillels came down to join the children, the beach was neatly sectioned out and the beach chairs arranged within the enclosure. Then at exactly 11:00 A.M., Armindo brought tea on a silver tray and friends, new and old, who were sunbathing at various points along the wide beach, came to visit, joining in the impromptu beach tea party. Over the years this sectioned-off area became known as "The Royal Enclosure" and although Jacob smiled over this, he saw that people liked to be part of it. Each year the section became larger so that more friends could join them.

The first day, Carolyn played aside from the Hillel children, feeling shy when they were around, but Gyneth pulled her into the water and together they jumped in and over the waves. She saw people looking askance at her as she swam and she felt their resentment. Carolyn was the only black person on the beach and although she tried to pretend that was fine, eventually she withdrew under the boardwalk, shivering as her slim body dried in the brisk breezes that swept the sand and stung her skin like little pinpricks.

"Come back into the water, it's so cold over there!" Gyneth called.

Carolyn just waved and tried to look inconspicuous.

Gyneth ran out of the water, shivering, and grabbed her hand. "Come on, silly. Only yesterday you wanted to stay here forever. Now you aren't even in the water!"

Carolyn took her hand, and they ran into the sea and under the waves. She soon forgot her reservations and joined in the delighted squeals of delight of the other children, staying in the water, running in and out of the waves, always eager to catch up to Gyneth again. Then she dived under a wave and came out the other end al-

most under the legs of a heavyset man. He stood tall in
the swirling water, his white hairy legs flexing as his
wet swimsuit flapped around the lower part of his
body. He stared straight at Carolyn, snarling out of the
side of his mouth as he spat out words of venom in a
strong Afrikaans accent. The young girl recoiled from
him, falling back into the surf.

"This is a white beach, pickaninny, go to the beach
where you belong with all the other *kaffirs*."

Carolyn looked around for Gyneth, but she had just
disappeared under a wave. Carolyn ran from the water,
frightened at the hatred in the man's eyes and sobbing
in fear.

The man followed her and stopped menacingly a
few feet away. His shadow fell over her slight form,
and by his presence and words he blocked the sunshine.

"You think you're as good as the white people, hey,
*kaffir*? Well, don't you get any ideas. You belong with
the other *kaffir* over there, waiting on the Baas, not
dirtying up the water with the children. Learn your
place, *kaffir*!"

Carolyn was frozen in terror. The man had motioned
at Armindo, who now was nearing earshot. Instead of
his normal dignified stance, he was cowering slightly,
and seeing that, Carolyn's fear increased.

Gyneth came running up, not understanding the
menacing situation. "Carolyn, what's happening? Are
you looking for my Mum and Dad?" she asked the
man politely.

"Ag no, we were jus' having a nice conversation,
the pickaninny and me. *Totsiens.*" He walked heavily
away.

"What did he want?" Gyneth asked. Carolyn was
now shaking uncontrollably, with fear and the cold
wind.

Armindo appeared with a towel and wrapped it around the quivering child.

Gyneth was insistent. "Armindo, please will someone tell me what is going on?"

Carolyn answered, her voice shaking. "He . . . he told me that I couldn't swim here, 'cause I'm black. He . . . he called me terrible names." Now Carolyn was hiccuping, sniffing, and still shivering. Gyneth put her arms around her friend.

"He's just a crazy man, that's all, he can't do anything to you, you're with me, and Mum and Dad will be here any minute. Look, here they come."

Gyneth pointed to the boardwalk where Anna was lumbering down to the "Royal Enclosure," carrying extra towels and sun hats with Jacob and Estelle not far behind.

Carolyn found her clothes in a little pile at the back of the Amrons' enclosure and she changed hurriedly, hiding herself behind a towel while she sobbed.

"Please, Gyneth," she implored her friend, "don't say anything. I don't want them to think I am causing any trouble. Please, just forget the whole thing."

Uncertain, Gyneth hopped from one foot to the other, trying to keep warm. Armindo, seeing her confusion, said he needed Carolyn's help to serve the tea.

"Gyneth, why don't you go back into the water for a few moments while Carolyn helps me get things ready? There will be a lot of people for morning tea today, and your parents will be here any minute. We must get ready right now." Carolyn nodded to Gyneth indicating that she should do as Armindo suggested, then turned away and started to put out cups and saucers, her hands shaking with unspent emotion.

Armindo's steadying hand on her shoulder helped her compose herself, but the ugliness of raw, irrational hatred would forever stay in her memory.

While going through the motions of helping Armindo, Carolyn kept reliving the incident over and over again, shocked by the expression she had seen on the man's face. Her heart yearned to be in the water, jumping under the waves, as Gyneth and the Hillel children were doing. Then, slowly as the morning stretched interminably on, she began to burn with anger at the injustice of it all. With difficulty she swallowed her feelings and carefully served the tea, English style, offering the sandwiches with care.

Anna heard about the incident that evening, and nodded, knowing the lessons of apartheid were continuing for this young girl, and that nothing needed to be said to confirm the reality.

The next morning, Carolyn said that she preferred not to swim anymore but would help Armindo with the tea. No entreaties by Gyneth would change her mind. She looked on longingly at the children in the waves, and when evening came and there were few people on the beach, she ran into the sea and swam freely, trying to capture the lighthearted feeling she'd had the first day of the holiday. But it did not return.

The holiday came to an end. Carolyn entered the dreary home of Alena once more. But this time she had a tight hard spot inside her heart where a dream was building.

# PART II

# Chapter 7

"Gyneth, are we keeping you up? Perhaps some extra homework would help alleviate the problem?"

The teacher's voice was loud and sarcastic. For most of the lesson, Gyneth had been so bored she could've screamed. Then overcome by a terrible tiredness, she fell soundly asleep, her head on her arms.

Embarrassed and red-faced, she tried to look intelligent and remorseful at the same time, only to be saved by the school bell. Gathering her books into her satchel, she waved to some of her classmates as she made her way listlessly up to the circular driveway where the Amron chauffeur was waiting.

"Only one day to go and then we'll be done with our third year in the Upper School," she called to her friends. "Can you believe in two more years we will graduate from high school? God, what a relief to be out of this place."

Once in her room, Gyneth plopped onto the bed and started reading a new book. She felt a wave of dizziness. Lifting her head from the pillow, she tried to sit up, but the dizziness continued. Gyneth slipped back onto the bed and stayed there.

She felt worse the next day. Her fever rose, she

couldn't read and her skin was sensitive all over. By the afternoon she was seriously ill.

Estelle called Jacob and he raced home from his office with the internist, Alan Salmon, close behind him.

"Does it hurt here, what about here?" Gyneth endured their probing fingers as they examined her and with worried looks embarked on a flurry of activity. Soon specialists were called, and lab technicians arrived to take blood samples.

"Mum, I feel really bad. What's going on? Why do I feel so awful?" Even in semidelirium, Gyneth was insistent.

"We don't know, darling. Just lie still and Daddy will try and find out. You will be fine. Just let them take the blood sample and soon you'll be better."

In between trying to calm Gyneth and answer the specialists' questions about when and how Gyneth had started feeling ill, Estelle stood panic-stricken in the back of the room. The medical drama unfolded around her.

Gyneth began to have hallucinations as her fever rose. Estelle stayed by Gyneth's side, smoothing her forehead with a cool cloth, crooning calming words as fear gripped her heart.

Jacob consulted with the finest pediatricians in the city, then throughout the country, but no one could identify Gyneth's ailment with certainty. Finally, after continuous consultations with a team of six medical specialists, a diagnosis was reached.

"We believe it is a form of juvenile rheumatoid arthritis. There is no cure, but we do have some hope of remission with a new experimental drug, cortisone." The team of doctors were grim-faced as they made their announcement.

"But the side effects of cortisone have not been thoroughly researched," Jacob responded, the worry making him look ten years older.

"We know, my friend, but in truth, we have no option. Gyneth is not responding to any other form of treatment." Alan Salmon put a reassuring hand on Jacob's shoulder. They had been friends for twenty years and had seen each other through many traumas during the tortuous five years in World War II. While Jacob had been captain and chief surgeon of the battleship *Amra,* Alan had been his surgical assistant through thousands of operations.

"We have to try it." Jacob made the decisions for all his colleagues. It would be his responsibility.

And so the routine of injections began, twice a day. First thing in the morning, Gyneth would open her swollen eyes and start sobbing as she saw Jacob approach her with a syringe.

"My darling, I know how uncomfortable this is for you. Believe me, it hurts me to have to do this. But I know that it will make you better, and that's all that counts."

"Daddy, this is so awful and I don't feel better in the least. It hurts all over, and I'm so miserable."

Gyneth tried to hold back her tears and be brave, without much success. On Jacob's return home at night, he would give her the second injection, but she was less vulnerable at night and would only wince and rub her arm to stop the stinging.

After a week her fever started to go down; slowly it appeared the medication was working. Estelle started sleeping through the night again as the fever eventually disappeared.

Gyneth's convalescence was very slow. Her energy level was low and she was in bed all day. But she was improving and the Amrons thanked God for her recovery. However, the medication did have its side effects.

Gyneth stood, on wobbly legs in front of the bathroom mirror. It was the first time in months that she had seen her whole body.

"Oh my God!" Her wail pierced to Estelle's heart. She rushed down the carpeted hallway into Gyneth's bathroom. Emily was supporting her daughter who had her hands over her eyes.

"Mummy, I cannot believe what I look like. I am bloated, like a blimp. Look at my face, it's round, you can't even see my chin anymore. And my arms, they're so puffy. My God, I have a stomach that sticks out when I stand sideways. I look pregnant. I just want to die."

"It will go away, my darling, it's just the medication. The main thing is that you are getting better. That's all that counts. The rest is just cosmetic." Estelle held Gyneth close for a moment.

But cosmetic, to a teenager, is all that matters. And Gyneth knew that she could not show her face to anyone in its present condition.

The injections continued for weeks. No one knew how long to continue the experimental treatment. But Gyneth was definitely getting better.

Meantime the semester had started and while there was no way that Gyneth could deal with the physical demands of going back to school, her intellectual needs continued.

The Amrons arranged for a tutor, one of the teachers from her school, who could cover the classwork she was missing. Gyneth learned so quickly that she had soon absorbed the entire syllabus, and the teacher began to add advanced information. Gyneth soaked it up like a sponge and the hours she spent in private lessons became the high point of her lonely, frustrating day. The rest of the time, she sat in bed surrounded by books and games, and yelled for attention. The meals and snacks that were ferried up to her were a distraction and a pleasure. She thought up all sorts of delectable foods that she could eat and David baked and cooked platters of tempting treats daily.

Life seemed to be always going on downstairs. All Gyneth had was the view outside her bedroom window. She could see the Magaliesberg Mountains in the distance, and watched their changing colors all day. And there was the large oak tree outside her window that moved in the wind and rain. The tree became her link to the outside world, and she watched and talked to it about what it could see outside.

At first Gyneth wanted Carolyn to visit. But during the initial stage of her illness, the Amrons would not allow her to have any visitors until they had the problem under control.

Over the years the girls had seen each other regularly. Gyneth observed the change in her friend as they both became teenagers. There were many times when they sat in silence. Carolyn was much more serious than she had ever been, and instead of singing or laughing with her normal youthful exuberance, on the days she was willing to be communicative, they talked about more serious subjects.

One discussion concerned Carolyn's school friend who had disappeared. He had been a rebel from the very beginning.

"I stayed away from him because to me he just spelled trouble," she explained in an unemotional way to Gyneth.

"But then his mother approached me for help. Apparently he had been playing around with cars, learning to drive every Saturday. One day he didn't come home. Since he was too young to have a driver's license, she was afraid that he'd been arrested."

The girls had been sitting under the tree that day,

listening as the breezes moved lightly through the summer leaves resting on the gazebo that stood on the highest part of the Amron property, with views of the mountains, blue and pink at the end of the valley.

"I found him in the hospital. His spine had been broken. His mother took him home the next day. He could not speak, but the bruises on his face and body made us think that he had been beaten and tortured."

"But by whom? And what for?" Gyneth was appalled.

Carolyn remained silent. Then she looked far away into the distance and answered. "Remember the man in Muizenberg who didn't want me to swim in the sea of the white people? There are lots of men like him in the police. Maybe they didn't want him to drive a car on white streets either."

"Surely not." Carolyn's explanation seemed irrational to Gyneth. "He must have had an accident."

The disparity between the girls' lives had grown greater each year. Yet theirs was a bond of early friendship, and neither of them had been willing to permit the relationship to be affected.

When Carolyn did visit again during Gyneth's convalescence nearly a year later, Gyneth looked at her friend as if seeing her for the first time, realizing suddenly that Carolyn was beautiful. Gyneth closed her eyes, seeing the image of her own bloated body that faced her in the mirror every morning, and anguish engulfed her. Her stomach was inflated out of proportion to her body and hung in folds over her pajama pants. Her face was fat and distorted with bloat. Then there was her hair, thin and listless. She was lumbering in her movements and tired easily.

Carolyn, on the other hand, looked as if she were a taut spring about to uncurl forward with grace. Her slim young body was just filling out into womanhood.

Her short skirt hugged a flat stomach, then opened over long legs, the muscles defined and shapely. Hair framed her head in tight neat curls, and her body was firm all over. She was taller than Gyneth with angular features and brown eyes shaded by long lashes. Even her fingers were slender and tapering, not at all like Gyneth's swollen and pudgy hands.

Carolyn reached for a book, feeling uncomfortable under Gyneth's intense scrutiny. Then, seeing the tears shining in her friend's eyes, Carolyn felt a sudden pang of pity. For the first time, she didn't envy Gyneth. She looked misshapen and depressed. She tried to reach out to her, but Gyneth turned her face away.

"I am really very tired, Carolyn. Perhaps you had better go now. We'll visit again when I feel better. Thanks for coming over." Gyneth closed her eyes, trying to hide her despair. Carolyn hesitated, then not knowing what to say, left the room quietly as Jacob was coming up the stairs. She greeted him politely, making a little courtesy, as Martha had taught her years before. Jacob acknowledged her presence with an absentminded smile.

"How are you, Carolyn?" he asked, noticing that she was now his height.

She was about to continue down the stairs when she suddenly felt the need to say something more. She turned to face him again. "Dr. Amron?" Jacob stood at the top of the stairs, his hand resting on the banister. Carolyn noticed his nails were perfectly manicured, and his hands were powerful and muscular.

"What is wrong with Gyneth?"

Jacob was surprised at Carolyn's sudden self-confidence, not knowing that she trembled inside. "Well, she is recovering from a disease similar to juvenile rheumatoid arthritis," he said.

"What does juvenile rheumatoid arthritis do to her body?" Carolyn asked.

Jacob started to explain in very simple terms what the disease was, but Carolyn kept asking question after question, digging for deeper answers, and her innate intelligence impressed the surgeon.

"You seem very interested in this, Carolyn," Jacob said. "Would you like to read some more about it?" His offer surprised even himself.

Carolyn followed Jacob into his study and as he pulled the book from the shelf, she was already reaching out to grasp it in her hands. *Gray's Anatomy*— Carolyn lightly traced the gold letters on the spine. A chill ran through her. She clasped the book to her chest with a soft murmur of thanks and ran off down the hallway.

Day after tedious day passed by as Gyneth slowly returned to good health. She didn't look at herself often in the mirror. But she knew her face had blown up like a balloon. She didn't mind the injections so much anymore. Her arms were so puffy she hardly felt the needle. She just made herself think of something else and soon it was over. And she always gave herself something wonderful to eat after an injection as a reward.

When her birthday came, Jacob obtained a feature movie for his home movie projector, party favors and cake, all in her bedroom. Gyneth wrote out colored invitations asking her classmates to a party. For the first time in months, she was really excited until she had to decide what to wear.

"Mum, what am I going to wear for the party?" There was nothing in her wardrobe that fit her.

"All my clothes are so small and tight that they look as if they belong to someone else!" Gyneth sat wearily on the bed, her large form covered by a housecoat. Everything physical was such an effort.

Estelle tried to find reassuring words. "Darling, you have been very sick, and you're not quite well yet. So, since you are still in bed, why don't we find a wonderful frilly nightgown and robe and you will be fine." Gyneth grimaced but accepted the inevitable.

Her friends came, dressed in brightly colored dresses. They had presents for Gyneth and were curious to see that she looked really odd.

As soon as the movie was over it was clear that the girls wanted to go outside and were uncomfortable sitting in the bedroom. In truth, Gyneth looked so peculiar that they really didn't want to look at her. She didn't look like Gyneth anymore but sort of like a large, shapeless, sexless person with a round face and small eyes. The girls clattered downstairs, and soon Gyneth was alone again.

"Mom," she yelled. "Mom!" Her voice faltered as tears started to pour down her cheeks. Estelle ran up the stairs one more time, having left the teenage girls giggling behind their hands, relieved to be out of Gyneth's presence.

Estelle's heart went out to her daughter. Teenage girls were so hard on each other. She put her arms around her. "Darling, they will be back again. Please don't feel bad."

But Gyneth felt worse than Estelle could ever imagine. She felt like an outcast, a strange deformed misfit whom no one wanted to look at. The look of repulsion in her classmates' eyes damaged the way she felt about herself irreparably, and as much as she wanted company, she'd rather be alone forever than see that expression again.

In the weeks that followed she began to convalesce, getting up for half the day, spending hours with her private tutor, reading and, of course, eating for comfort, company, and entertainment. Eventually the cortisone treatment stopped.

But Gyneth, who was now about five feet four inches tall, was an immense one hundred and seventy pounds. Gone was the endearing golden-haired child. In her place was a self-conscious teenager, awkward, angry, and precocious.

Estelle tried to put Gyneth on a diet, knowing how much her daughter would suffer, the fatter she was, but when Estelle wasn't looking, Gyneth locked herself in the pantry and consumed large quantities of whatever she could get her hands on, cookies, crackers, candy. She entered into a battle. Estelle tried to control her eating—Gyneth rejected any kind of control. The supervision made her feel like a prisoner in her own home, constantly being watched, her meals controlled, and her size a constant reminder that she was failing.

The first days back at school were torture. The other teenage girls with their thin bodies and critical eyes seemed to look at her as if she were an apparition—the same look from her birthday. And now even girls she did not know stared at her as she waddled along in the short unbecoming school uniform, her brown stockings already torn from trying that morning to pull them over her heavy legs. The uniform had to be made bigger, even though it was the largest size available and Gyneth had suffered through the agony of standing half dressed in the uniform store as the seamstress muttered about her size.

Within a couple of weeks it became obvious that she was far ahead of the class, and this caused even more antagonism from her classmates than her ungainly appearance.

The headmistress of the Upper School called Estelle into her office. "Gyneth is too advanced for this class," she said. "We are going to promote her into the next grade, even though she's very young. You realize that since she started school young, this means that she will matriculate from high school at the end of the year. She will have maturity problems, Mrs. Amron, but she really is so far advanced intellectually that she is disrupting the class. And another thing"—the headmistress adjusted her spectacles uncomfortably—"the child appears to be very unhappy. Have you considered putting her on a diet? She really could lose a few pounds, and I am sure that would make her feel better."

Estelle had tried everything. She spent hours in the kitchen trying to come up with interesting recipes that were low calorie. Then she'd be furious when she found Gyneth sneaking food from the servants, even cajoling Anna to share her *mieliepap* porridge and meat stew, out in the servants' quarters.

"Gyneth, please, I know it's hard for you and you feel hungry, but won't you at least give it a try? I cannot lock you up, it has to come from you. I want to help you. You know how unhappy you are, looking like you do. If you just diet for a few months, it will all be over."

Gyneth sat on the leather chair in her father's study, morose and heavy. "I want to, Mum, but then I get so hungry, and the stuff you give me doesn't fill me up. I want to have all the things that other people eat. Like *mieliepap*, and sandwiches like the other kids have, chocolate cake. You eat all that stuff and you don't get fat, why do I?" Estelle had no answers, just an immense sense of frustration. She felt like shaking Gyneth until her teeth rattled sometimes, then her heart would go out to her ungainly daughter and she would feel her pain.

As for trying to buy clothes for Gyneth, the experience was equally painful for mother and daughter. It was impossible to find anything in Gyneth's size. And every saleswoman looked accusingly at Estelle, as if it were her fault that her daughter was overweight.

Jacob was not much help. He loved to eat and was unwilling to deprive himself of the great pleasure he derived from the gourmet cuisine Estelle prepared for him and their guests. He gave lip service to the need for Gyneth to diet, but did nothing to change his own eating behavior.

"You'll take care of it, darling," he said to his wife when she complained to him that Gyneth was out of control. Estelle was left to weather the problems with Gyneth and her appearance, alone.

In her new class, and now a senior, Gyneth had a chance to begin her school life again. The youngest in the class by far she was painfully insecure and felt huge and unattractive. She avoided undressing in front of the other girls. Alone, in front of the mirror, she trained herself to look only at her face which really was pretty. Some of the moonlike puffiness disappeared and her sea-green eyes appeared large again. Her hair was long and golden brown and she braided it herself into two long cords, not allowing Emily to touch her anymore.

At home the war lines were drawn. Estelle was her nemesis, slim, beautiful, and the beloved of Jacob. Next to her, Gyneth felt ugly, clumsy, and unloved.

Gyneth longed to do the normal things that girls her age did, like go shopping and to the movies with her classmates. Every Monday she would watch the three most popular girls in the senior class, sitting in the quadrangle, swinging their legs nonchalantly.

"Wasn't that movie just peachy? God, did you notice that kiss? Do you think they really kissed?" They giggled.

Then the conversation would turn to the purchases they had made and the fun they had over the weekend.

Gyneth would sit a little to one side, listening avidly to their tales. One day she plucked up her courage.

"Hi, how's it going today?"

The girls looked at her, surprised at the interruption.

"You know, there's a movie I've heard about that's starting at the cinema in Rosebank." Gyneth knew that was the place of their normal Saturday outings. "I can get free passes for four. Do you want to join me?"

The three girls looked at each other and shrugged. They really didn't care if Gyneth came along. Free passes would be great, and well worth the nuisance of having this fatso hanging around them.

Gyneth was stunned that it had worked. Her heart was thumping at the thought that now she would be one of those who chatted lazily next Monday about the last weekend's escapades. It would be worth taking money from her savings box to buy the tickets the day before so the others would think she had free passes.

That Saturday Gyneth met the girls at the arranged time and place. It was two hours before the movie.

"Okay, where are we going for lunch?" Gyneth asked eagerly.

"Lunch?" The girls looked at each other and sniggered. "Oh, we never eat lunch. We want to go shopping."

Gyneth's stomach was grumbling since Estelle had insisted on a low-calorie breakfast, and she had wolfed it down anxious to get out of the house. She was already dreaming about the delicious grilled cheese sandwich and fried potatoes that she would have for lunch. Yet her new "friends" weren't the least bit interested in food.

The first store they went into was having a sale of swimwear. With squeals of excitement, the girls were soon pulling off their clothes and parading swimsuits for each other, prancing in front of the mirrors, turning their slender limbs, smoothing their hands over their flat stomachs and tight buttocks.

"Gosh, don't you just love the way this looks? I absolutely have to have this one."

Gyneth smiled weakly, trying to look absorbed in the prices and styles. But the bile rose in her throat and her face burned with embarrassment as she looked at the expression in the eyes of the saleslady.

"I'm just looking, they really want to buy something," Gyneth stammered, her normal arrogant air failing her. She longed to get out of there. The next store was no better. This time it was dresses. Again the girls pulled numerous styles and samples off their hangers, trying them on for each other.

"Yes, yes, I agree that does look great on you, supergreat, really! I love that color, too."

Gyneth tried to join in with the fun, but soon she became the one handing things back and forth into the dressing rooms as the girls pointed out dresses on the display racks that they wanted her to bring. As time passed, Gyneth longed to eat, now not only for hunger but because she felt miserable. Eating always helped, at least, for the moment. But the long-legged trio were totally absorbed in their shopping expedition.

The more they shopped, the hungrier Gyneth became. She knew that she had to eat before the movie. Otherwise Austen would be there to pick her up as soon as it was over, and she would not have a chance to savor all the wonderful foods she had been promising herself.

Gyneth made a decision. She pressed the tickets into the hand of one of the girls. "I really have a terrible stomach cramp. It's my period, you know how that is, it just started. I just can't sit through the movie. I'm so

upset about it, but feel free to give my ticket to someone else. And you have a good time. I'm going home,
see you Monday."

Before any of them could argue with her, she left.
The three girls looked at one another and giggled. She
was certainly weird. Then they promptly forgot about
her.

Gyneth walked as quickly as she could away from
the boutiques, looking desperately for a restaurant. She
found one. It was not the kind of food that she would
have chosen as her first choice, but she could wait no
longer. The growling monster in her stomach had taken
over her mind, and it needed to be fed.

She ordered sandwiches, two different kinds, lots of
mayonnaise, a chocolate shake, and a giant piece of
coconut cake. She ate voraciously, feeling the pain re-
cede, the agony of not belonging fade.

She never did get used to the teasing. She was the
fattest in the school. Only intellectual challenges, acting the role of an old woman in school plays, and
playing the piano helped. How thin she felt when she
won academic prizes in the class that was two years
more advanced than hers. How beautiful she felt when
she heard the applause after a starring role or piano re-
cital. In those areas of her life, being different was an
asset.

Suddenly, Gyneth realized if she could find a way to
use her intellect and creativity to make people envy
and court her, then she'd be in control, like her father.

That Sunday Gyneth found her father in the study.
He was sipping on a Scotch and water, relaxing in the
early evening with the newspapers.

"Dad, do you think being smart can make people envious?"

Jacob looked up from his reading. "Yes, sometimes.
What are you referring to?"

"You are very good at what you do. You have chosen something that not many people know how to do, so people must show you respect, mustn't they?"

"Yes, that's true." Jacob was still uncertain of the direction of the conversation.

"Well, it doesn't matter if you are fat or thin if you are really good at what you do. Does it?"

Jacob understood. Or he thought he did. "My appearance is not the main thing about me. But I am a man. For a woman it is more important. Because men will only be attracted to a woman who is slim and appealing."

"But if I were a surgeon, people would have to respect me."

Jacob smiled at Gyneth's earnest face. "Yes, if you were a good one. But then men might be scared away by that very fact. Besides, there are no women surgeons in South Africa."

But Gyneth was no longer listening. She had found a way to make her appearance irrelevant. It was so simple. She would become a surgeon. All the giggling schoolgirls would be left behind in the inferior world of women, while she would be part of the superior world of men.

Then a problem arose that couldn't be avoided. Gyneth had to attend her first real party, and since it was at her oldest school friend, Vanessa's house, she had to go. She struggled with the same old dilemma of what to wear and came up with a fairly acceptable dress. Gyneth dressed anxiously and made up her face. She looked good, from the neck up, that was. She pulled her hair loose and let it flow down her back. Oh well, she sighed, maybe they would have a piano at Vanessa's house. That way she could sit and play while the others danced.

Vanessa lived in a nearby suburb where the road led

up to a tall gate and imposing whitewashed wall.
Gyneth had Austen drop her off at the gate.

She was greeted at the door by the maid. "Hello,
Cynthia," she said.

"Good evening, Miss Gyneth. The party is in there."

Gyneth sucked in her stomach and wished for the
hundredth time that day that she were thin and beautiful and eighteen like Vanessa, not sixteen and fat. Still
she held her head up high, pretending confidence.

"Oh, that's a nice dress," Vanessa said, coming to
greet her. Gyneth felt sick. She knew Vanessa was trying to be kind, and she wondered how they must all
laugh at her behind her back.

"Thanks, yours, too," she said.

Vanessa had on a pink satin sheath that molded
tightly to her perfect figure.

Gyneth turned away. What's the point? she thought.
No one will talk to me. I might as well find the piano
right away.

Gyneth wandered into the anteroom where she saw a
piano. She sat down and started to run her fingers over
the keys when all of a sudden out of her peripheral vision she saw a quick movement through the window in
the backyard. Then she heard voices raised and a
woman start screaming, "Don't hit him, *Baas* . . . He
didn't do anything. He's my husband, *Baas,* please
don't hit him."

Gyneth ran to the window and saw a uniformed policeman beating a black man over the head with a
baton, as the blood streamed onto the concrete of the
backyard. Then she saw Cynthia, the maid who had
greeted her at the door, pulling on the policeman's arm,
cowering from the blows, trying to protect her husband, his blood spattering all over her starched white
maid's uniform. Her head scarf lay on the floor with

her wig askew as her desperate pleas for mercy went unheeded.

"Oh, my God." Gyneth gasped for breath as she ran, her heart pounding, back into the party room, where the music had started and couples were swinging to the bop.

"Vanessa, where are you? There's a terrible fight going on."

The group looked at Gyneth in amazement and then everyone ran over to the window and stood gazing down at the scene below. The girls screamed and turned away.

One of the boys laughed and said, "Stupid *kaffir,* he must have been stealing something." Vanessa ran to find her parents and soon they were all outside watching as the policeman dragged the semiconscious man into the "Black Maria," the wagon that the South African police used for apprehending blacks.

"What is the problem? What was he doing?" Vanessa's father stood in the harsh light of the van's headlights.

"He was violating the pass laws, *Meneer,*" the policeman said in this thick accented English. "He doesn't have a pass to be here. Then he tried to resist arrest, so I had to subdue him."

Cynthia sobbed, "But he is my husband and he was visiting me. He will go back tomorrow to Soweto. Please, *Baas,* have mercy."

"There's no mercy for *kaffirs* that don't obey the law." The policeman slammed the door of the wagon. "Now you just go back inside, *Meneer,* we can take care of this disturbance. Sorry to have disturbed your party, *Meneer.*"

They stood silently and watched as the van drew away. Cynthia slumped in a heap on the driveway, sobbing in despair, not knowing if she'd ever see her husband again. Vanessa's mother put her arm around the black woman's shoulders.

The teenagers drew back into the house, the music was turned back on and although rather subdued, the party started up again as White South Africa put on its blinkers and continued with life as usual. This, after all, was not their problem.

Gyneth felt nauseated as she thought of the scene she had observed. She remembered the words of the Afrikaner man who had accosted Carolyn on the beach in the Cape. She thought again about Carolyn's story of her classmate who had been beaten and tortured for no apparent reason. The nether world of black Africa was there all the time, she just couldn't, or wouldn't, see it.

Gyneth knew Cynthia from her fairly frequent visits to Vanessa. But this was the first time she had seen her as a wife, with another life unrelated to her work. Gyneth thought suddenly of Armindo, Anna, Andrew, and the other servants who worked for the Amron household. They had families. Did they have these encounters with the police, too? She shivered as she thought of the door with the wired-back window on the Black Maria van, slamming shut on Cynthia's husband. Why could her husband not visit her? What was a pass? None of it made sense.

Gyneth watched her classmates as they danced and drank, seemingly untouched by what they had seen. Even Vanessa's parents appeared to accept the situation as resolved.

Finally Gyneth could watch no more. She called home and asked for Austen to come and get her. Estelle and Jacob were waiting anxiously at the door. Tears filled her eyes as she related what had happened.

"How could this happen? What would happen if Carolyn was caught visiting me without a pass?"

Jacob looked away. He couldn't explain a system that was fundamentally unjust. He forced himself to look into Gyneth's intelligent, innocent eyes, but faltered as he answered her.

"Gyneth, I don't have a satisfactory answer for you. Yes, this could happen to Carolyn once she is old enough to be considered an adult. The pass laws say that blacks have to obtain a permit to be in a certain area. I think it's a bad law, and the police are vicious in their enforcement. But all we can do is try and make the lives of the people that we touch a little easier."

For the first time, Gyneth saw indecision and discomfort on her father's face. He was always so sure of everything; why wasn't he doing anything about this injustice? She opened her mouth to ask but Jacob turned away and left the room. All of a sudden this place she lived in had a dark side. They were all living a charade, while somewhere in the dark night a van was traveling to John Vorster Square, the central police station, with a bleeding man in the back who had done nothing more than visit his legal wife for the evening meal.

The next day Gyneth joined Anna as she folded bath towels.

"Anna, are you happy living here with us?"

"Yes, of course, child." Anna smiled at Gyneth.

"Wouldn't you rather live with your family?"

Anna's smile faded. "Yes, it would be good, too."

"Do you get angry that you have to be so far away?"

"Hai no, baba, why all these questions?"

"Anna, I want to understand. Don't you want to change things so you can live like we do?"

Anna folded the last towel angrily. "You have your life and I have mine. You are white and I am black. We don't think the same way. You'll grow up, change your life, but I'll be here, a servant, forever. That's enough talk now, I have work to do."

In all their years of loving relationship Anna had never spoken to Gyneth with anger or resentment. As she followed Anna's swaying bulk downstairs, Gyneth realized that she had stepped over a previously undefined boundary. She had considered Anna to be her friend. But friendship was a two-way street—and their positions would never be equal.

Gyneth felt an overpowering desire to find Carolyn and discuss it all. They hadn't seen each other for a few months. Perhaps incidents like this one happened every day in Carolyn's reality, a world entirely different from white South Africa, and one, Gyneth now realized, she'd never understood.

# Chapter 8

"*Nkosi sikelele*, Africa . . ." The children's voices held the note in perfect harmony as they moved in unison with outstretched arms and clenched fists. Some wore school uniforms, though it was vacation time, and their brown uniforms and khaki shirts were dusty with the powdery dirt that was omnipresent in the townships. Some wore ties and laced shoes and socks, and others were barefooted and in shorts. They smiled, clapped their hands and stomped their feet in time to the song of a free South Africa. They ran laughing and playing hide-and-seek behind the adults who were marching, dancing really, as they moved rhythmically from one foot to the other, panting, singing, clapping, stomping, marching as they moved down the sandy road near the town of Springs.

As she padded along the road with the crowd, sixteen-year-old Carolyn felt quite grown-up. She smiled, enjoying the camaraderie of the throng and the beauty of the day. It had only been yesterday that one of her friends had come to visit and the whole adventure had begun.

"My uncle is going to the town of Springs. It's not far away. We have room in the car. Would you like to come with us?"

"May I?" Carolyn had asked Alena. "It is only for a few days. They have a car available and a house to stay in."

Alena saw that there were good people to take care of the children, and so she'd relented. "I suppose it will be fine. Now be sure to behave yourself and do whatever they tell you to," she said, seeing Carolyn's thin face shining with anticipation in a way it rarely did. She was such a serious child, always reading a large volume called *Gray's Anatomy* by the light of a candle.

The car was rickety and it broke down twice. First it was a flat tire. All four of them heaved and pulled at the stubborn wheel, since the jack was not working. The next time the straining engine overheated. So they had to wait by the side of the road until the car cooled down as they nursed it gently with generous doses of water. Even that wasn't too bad because they sat in the stubby brush, sucking on new stalks of grass and looking up at the sky. Cars screamed by with horns blowing as white faces looked disdainfully at their plight. The girls pulled faces at the passing traffic and giggled at everything. The uncle joked and chain-smoked continuously, and it seemed to Carolyn that nothing could spoil the day. Eventually, they arrived at their modest destination and settled in for the night.

Now that the march had started, the festive atmosphere made Carolyn feel a rush of joy as she strolled along at the back and outskirts of the moving throng winding out of the settlement toward the city hall of Springs. These were her people—this was her land, she felt at one with the veldt and the city. It was good to feel free and unfettered by rules, and to just enjoy the day, the peace, the rhythm. . . .

The policeman's voice bellowed out over the loud-speaker. "Stop there. Turn around and go back the way you came. You are not permitted to assemble here. Return to your homes."

The row of khaki-dressed policemen stood with legs apart and guns cocked, preventing the crowd from approaching the city buildings.

"Turn around and go back," The young sergeant was sweating, the rivulets of liquid trickling down the side of his face and into his eyes.

The people in the front of the crowd stopped chanting and slowed to a halt. Then the tense silence erupted into chaos. A rock was thrown, a shot rang out and then the mayhem began. The policemen shot wildly and everywhere the screaming bodies fell, with terrified men, women, and children scrambling over each other, falling bloodied in the dirt, running backward, sideways, into each other.

The panic-stricken police officers let loose their terror on the mass of black people. This was the realization of their nightmares, the black tide that they had learned in school would overwhelm them if not contained by force.

Carolyn first heard the shot, then the screaming. She turned and ran before those in the back of the crowd even realized what had happened. She ran for her life, her chest heaving, her feet flying along the road. She went faster until she saw the outlines of the houses dimly rising on the horizon, and came to the house in which she had spent the night. She slid under the big bed where she had slept so peacefully, cowering and sobbing while outside the sirens began to wail.

After what seemed to be forever, but was about six hours, Carolyn heard footsteps. There was someone in the house. She pulled herself into an even smaller ball under the bed and tried to control her breathing.

"Carolyn? Are you here?" She heard the uncle's

hoarse voice, almost unrecognizable. Slowly she crawled out into the fading sunlight.

The man was covered in dirt streaked with blood. His clothes were torn and ugly swollen bruises distorted his face and almost closed one eye.

"Come," he ordered, with no explanation. Dazed, Carolyn followed him. The road they had happily danced down earlier that day was strewn with moaning, weeping people, some keening over inert bodies, others staggering back toward their homes. Together they went to identify the broken, lifeless bodies of her two school friends. Carolyn felt the bile rise in her throat.

One of her friends lay twisted at an awkward angle. Carolyn reached out and straightened the young girl's legs, pulling her skirt down modestly. The skin felt cool to her touch, and she shuddered.

Their return the next day to Johannesburg was quick and silent. The uncle was angry, grieving. He had seen his niece and his friends buried. He pushed the ailing car back to Soweto, as the bitter tears rolled down his cheeks. Carolyn sat hunched up in the corner of the front seat.

From that time onward Carolyn became silent and wary. She observed everything, the power plays among the new leaders in the township, the clandestine meetings with older freedom fighters. Common criminals took advantage of the lawlessness to prey upon their own people, while others suffered torture for their ideals. The police destroyed whatever they could as they ruthlessly enforced emergency powers. Carolyn learned to fade into the background, realizing slowly that she did not want to live in Soweto, in black South Africa, anymore.

She listened to the stories of camps in the nearby territories—Zambia and even farther north. She even heard that some were going to the Soviet Union to be trained and disciplined—to become true soldiers in the fight for freedom. She heard of the activities of the ANC, the *"Umkhonto we Sizwe"* or "The Spear of the Nation." She had no interest in their activities. Her desire was just to get out.

Carolyn walked as unobtrusively as possible through the streets filled with hulks of burned-out cars and averted her face from the sight. Gangs of vengeful thugs were burning those whom they considered to be collaborators, and nothing and no one was safe. The police were unwilling to enter the township except in heavily armed and protected convoys, so they were normally too late to protect anyone. Charred bodies were all that remained, and ambulances performed the last services for the human remains but left the funeral pyre to smoke and burn.

School was a farce. She yearned for knowledge and the book that Jacob had given her had become her bible. She read it cover to cover, memorizing large portions of it. Every time she felt she should return it, she'd find a reason why she could not, and would read a portion of it again. The book became a lifeline to a world of order and certainty, a world of privilege.

Carolyn rarely left the township. But one day she was desperate for something on which to focus her mind that would take her out of her surroundings. She saw the long barracks of the Baragwanath Hospital and made her way past the gate guard toward one of the long buildings. This was the medical library, and she knew that this was a place where she could read in peace. She slipped through the doorway and took a book off the shelf, sitting down on a wooden chair in the corner of the deserted room. She opened a book on clinical pharmacology. The words meant little to her, but she struggled to make some sense of what she read.

One of the black interns entered the room, and she shrank back, trying to hide herself in the shadow of the bookshelf. He saw her nevertheless and asked her what she was doing there.

"Reading," she answered.

He nodded as if it were perfectly logical for a sixteen-year-old schoolgirl to be reading in a medical library and gave her a textbook on physiology.

"Start with that," he said. "Then we will talk again."

She read. Some of the sections referred to information she had learned in the anatomy book. Slowly it became clear that knowledge was a series of building blocks, and the book Jacob had given her was one of the foundations. She felt the excitement of this discovery as she avidly read one book after another.

Over the next months, Carolyn read everything the intern Jonas Natuli gave to her. Her photographic memory absorbed the diagrams, the pictures of the human body, and the long prosaic descriptions of bodily functions.

Then one day he gave her *A Short Practice of Surgery* by Bailey and Love.

"Infection is the invasion of the body by pathogenic or disease-producing organisms," she read. "A tumor is a new formation of cells of independent growth usually arranged atypically which fulfills no useful function and has no typical termination." Her surroundings faded away from her as the human condition unfurled before her eyes. The body's mechanism was logical, predictable, and safe.

"I want this," a little voice inside her said. "I want to be a doctor."

The next time the intern came into the library Carolyn was waiting for him. "Tell me how you became a doctor," she asked him eagerly.

The young man was tired. He had just come off seventeen hours of emergency room work, and his mind was fuzzy with exhaustion. He had hoped to grab a surgery book to read up about the operation on which he was to assist the professor of surgery the following day, and the last thing he wanted was to talk to Carolyn. But the fire in her eyes drew him to her.

"You have to do well in school in order to apply to the university, to be accepted at medical school. There are few universities you can attend. Johannesburg is one of them. Then you must pray for a scholarship because the fees and books and lodging costs are expensive. Once you have that you will enter medical school and after six years maybe you will qualify as a doctor. Then you become an intern, like me. It's hard work, almost impossible at times, you have to compete with the whites who have had better schooling, have a better life than we do. But it can be done."

His eyes were drooping as he leaned on his hand, supporting his chin, his elbow resting on the table. It was clear that he would soon fall asleep in the warm quiet library, so Carolyn thanked him with a formal handshake.

She closed the book and made her way back through the dark angry streets to her home. All of a sudden, Carolyn knew. She would take control of her life and direct it. A powerful stirring began inside her that she had never felt before. The sensation translated into a surge of sensuality and she burned for a release.

Once home she examined herself in the small bathroom mirror. She saw a tall, slender girl of sixteen with large brown eyes. Her black hair was covered by a scarf, which she took off to gaze at her short stubbly hair. Slowly she removed her blouse to see her high breasts, firm above her slim waist. Turning slightly, she admired her own profile. She looked like a woman.

The stirring she had felt on the way home became a throbbing demand to touch her body, feel her freedom.

Now her body was calling to her. Her hands moved lower, under her underpants to her pubis, and she ran her fingernails through the black curly hair, pausing briefly to touch the inside of the moist pink mouth. She shuddered as the pleasure of her own touch spun through her and all of a sudden she had to feel the sensation again. She slid her fingers deeper into the wet entrance as she found the swollen mound of her clitoris and began rubbing it, massaging as the waves of pleasure made her gasp. She slid down to the floor, her legs bending around the base of the sink as she moved her fingers deeper, grabbing the insides of her thighs with one hand as the other penetrated deep into her body. The orgasm overtook her entire being as she quivered, heart pounding, perspiration pouring down her glistening copper body, subsiding, calming while she sobbed softly in the release of stored emotion. She now knew how to relieve her pain.

The next day Carolyn went to school as usual. Her strong feeling of elation had subsided. Once again she felt the reality of the township around her, and the first trickles of doubt insinuated themselves into her dreams of the night before.

At the end of the day, Carolyn sat in the school yard on the low wall outside the classrooms, looking at the skies, reddened with golden sunsets caused by Johannesburg's mine dust as it caught the sun's last rays. She longed for inspiration, for a sign that would propel her in the right direction. But there was nothing, just the approaching darkness of night and the ever-present smell of the coal fires of the township.

The touch on her shoulder made her jump with fright as she turned around and saw a young man standing close to her, so close that she could smell his musky earthiness. She knew his name was Jonathon and that he was two years older than her. She had seen him with some of the thugs in the back streets of Soweto. She shuddered as she saw his face in the vanishing light, angry and sullen with a raised keloid scar on his upper lip where he had been slashed in a fight with a Nkosa youth from a rival tribe. He was a Zulu, tall and aggressive. Carolyn thought he had something to do with the ANC because he had disappeared for months and then returned, harder and speaking about "the people's rights" and other such jargon. She shuddered.

"What are you doing here so late on your own?" Jonathon asked in a surprisingly soft voice.

Carolyn squirmed off the wall, confused at his solicitude. "What is it to you?" she said, not wanting him to know that his presence disturbed her.

"Nothing really, except that it is late to be wandering around here. There are some gangs that would love to get their hands on you. Come, I'll walk you home. Where do you live?"

Carolyn found herself being propelled into the street and soon they were walking toward Alena's house. Jonathon struck up a conversation with her, and soon she found herself talking about school and the boring teachers. He told her he was working as a messenger, and that he rode a motorbike all day delivering packages around town. Jonathon seemed intelligent and his gentle manner belied his frightening appearance. When they came to the door of Alena's house, Jonathon shook her hand. His hands were strong and his forearms powerful. Carolyn felt the stirring start again in her body, making her feel more confused. This was someone she thought she would hate, yet she found she didn't want him to leave. She watched him walk down the street and found herself looking at his tight but-

tocks and muscular legs rippling under the khaki pants
he wore.

That night Carolyn could not wait to be alone in the
bathroom. Her fingers dug frantically deep into the soft
folds of flesh as she rubbed and caressed, stroked and
penetrated her own body, finally reaching a gasping
orgasm as the perspiration ran down her face and
between her full breasts. It was Jonathon's hand she
had felt, his smell she had inhaled, and his lips she had
imagined on hers.

School continued, wasted days when she seemed to
know more than the teacher. After school Carolyn had
hours to spare. The homework was too easy for her,
and so her afternoons were spent wandering through
the township and then reading in the medical library
when it finally opened at four o'clock. Often she
would pass by a small nursery school on her way to the
library and was drawn to the narrow window with a
sense of yearning, as she listened to the chanted songs
reminiscent of her childhood at the Amrons. She would
stop to listen, then make her lonely way on to the
empty quietness of the library she had learned to love.

One day the nursery school teacher invited her in.
"Do help us, we are so short staffed here, and I see you
so often at the window." Carolyn felt shy and very
young again, but she entered as one little girl came up
to her and clasped her arms around her legs, holding
on tightly. Carolyn bent down and swung the little
toothless angel onto her shoulders, and moved
smoothly into the circle, singing the lullabies in her
clear high voice.

Soon she was a regular part of the closing hour of
the nursery school. Every day the open-faced children
hugged and kissed her. Her voice soared high and full
as she forgot everything when she sang, coming back

to reality when the little hands pulled at hers, begging for a game or another song.

One day as she sang in harmony with the young voices, her eyes caught a familiar profile through the window.

It was Gyneth. A very large, fat Gyneth.

Carolyn was stunned. Few white people ever came into the townships. In fact, she had never seen any except a few members of the clergy, and of course, the police. Her heart filled with dread. It must be something terrible if Gyneth had made this effort.

"What on earth are you doing here?" Carolyn ran out from the schoolroom, not sure whether to hug Gyneth or not. Her friend reached out to her with a big smile and embrace.

"I had to come, Carolyn. When you weren't at Alena's house, I begged Alena to tell me how to find you! I knew I'd never get Austen to drive again to Soweto. You must think I'm crazy to follow you here, but I have so much to talk to you about, I did not know what else to do."

Carolyn looked around desperately for somewhere to sit in privacy. Then she had an idea. She jumped into the car, with Gyneth following.

Soon they were in the medical library in a study cubicle. Gyneth sat on the chair while Carolyn swung onto the desk and sat there expectantly, swinging her legs back and forth. They could see Austen settled comfortably into the front seat of the car, his hat pulled low over his eyes as he dozed, obviously relieved to be out of the township and in the familiar surroundings of a hospital parking lot.

"Please, Carolyn, will you forgive me for sending you away that day when I was in bed and you came to visit? I was so unhappy then, you know, about my weight and being in bed. Were you cross with me?" Gyneth asked in her direct way.

"No, it was not that," Carolyn said awkwardly, not knowing how to explain the anger she felt against the white and privileged world within which Gyneth lived.

"I bet you didn't recognize me 'cause I'm so fat. *'Studla,'* " Gyneth said, using the Basuto word and movement for rotundity.

Carolyn laughed at her gesture. "Our people love women of your size. Our men think that your body looks perfect and mine is too thin!" They laughed together. "Perhaps we should change places!" Gyneth said jokingly.

"That is something I have wished and prayed for all my life," Carolyn said in a way that took the smile off Gyneth's face. "You have everything—the school, the parents, the opportunities I will never have."

Gyneth leaned forward, speaking urgently. "That is why I needed to talk to you, Carolyn. It's as if I'm seeing everything for the first time. We've lived together, been friends all our lives, and yet the most important thing we've never spoken about. Your life, being black, this place, living with all the differences. I never really thought about it before. That must seem awful to you, and indeed it makes me feel ashamed. All the black people I have ever met, like David and Anna, everyone who works for us, no one seems to be unhappy or angry with the way their lives are. Even you—I mean, I knew that you were unhappy about going to Soweto, but I thought it was because you didn't want to leave us. I had no idea how black people were treated until I saw an innocent man beaten with my own eyes. The horrible thing was that although everyone else around me saw it, too, afterward they seemed to forget it, to push it away, in the same way as I have all these years. All I could think of was you, here in this place. . . ." Carolyn sat perfectly still and looked at the floor so that Gyneth couldn't see the tears in her eyes. "I don't know how to change things. I am afraid, really afraid. The police were so cruel, I am scared to speak up."

Carolyn nodded slowly. Then it all began to pour out, much in the way that they used to share their daily escapades with each other. Carolyn told of the massacre at Springs that took the lives of her two friends.

"They mowed us down like we were a herd of animals. The police shot hundreds of people including my school friends. I heard the screaming and knew something terrible was happening. I was one of the lucky ones." The sadness in Carolyn's voice brought tears to Gyneth's eyes and filled her with horror as she realized the truth of what had happened that day. She'd read about the "riot by street thugs and criminals" as it was described, in the newspaper.

"I feel so alone most of the time," Carolyn said haltingly. "The only good parts of my life are the hugs from the nursery children and the medical books that I read on my own at night."

She pulled her legs under her, clasping her arms around her knees. "I have this dream, maybe you will think it is impossible, but I'm determined to make it happen. I am going to become a doctor." Carolyn paused, waiting for Gyneth's reaction. Then before her friend could speak, she slipped her legs out straight again and continued in a firm and steady voice. "I am going to leave South Africa forever."

Gyneth sat silently pondering the momentous announcement. Her own problems of obesity and conflict with Estelle seemed inconsequential in the face of the stark deprivation and heartbreaking losses that her friend told of. Gyneth gripped Carolyn's hand tightly.

"You will achieve your dreams, I just feel it. You've

always been so clever, such a quick study." Gyneth looked sad for a moment, thinking of her own problems. "I understand how studying helps to deal with heartache. It helps me, too." Gyneth hoisted her large frame off the chair.

"After my illness, I decided to become a doctor, a surgeon like my father. That way, I can make being fat and different into a positive for myself. It makes perfect sense for you, too, Carolyn. We are both different from the rest of the world in our own ways, yet in this way we are the same."

"Maybe," Carolyn said thoughtfully. "The fact remains that we live in different worlds, I have left your white life completely, you cannot reach me again. It is not safe for you here in Soweto, nor is it safe for me to travel across the city to see you. I don't have a pass, and I'm supposed to be in school all the time. This whole country is full of sadness for us."

She paused.

"Perhaps one day there will be leaders who will show us the way. There is a man named Nelson Mandela, who it is said, can do this for us—he has to hide and run all the time because the police will kill him if they find him. The people here say that he could lead us into independence for a free South Africa, where we can all be friends and live together in peace. But I think that is just a dream. It could never happen. They will kill him before he can do anything. It is hopeless, hopeless."

Gyneth knew of the man Mandela, but since the massacre that occurred at Sharpeville some years before, he had disappeared and his name was whispered and not even spoken aloud for fear of informers. Gyneth looked quickly around the side of the library alcove to be sure no one had heard them. Carolyn was right, they all lived with fear, and the comfortable easy

life she had in the exclusive northern suburbs was a
fragile web of security, easily shattered by careless
words and actions.

When they heard footsteps, Carolyn slid quietly off
the desk and the two of them stood together, looking
ostensibly at a book. The footsteps stopped. They
looked up. It was Austen.

"Miss Gyneth, we have to get back. The traffic will
be very bad with the rush hour, and there will be trouble for both of us if we are late."

Gyneth looked at her watch. "Damn, I do have to
go. Carolyn, can you come to see me soon? Otherwise
I will come back to see you. I am not going to let this
craziness keep us apart again. I never understood anything until now, but you must know that our friendship
is color-blind."

Carolyn felt a wave of guilt as she bade Gyneth farewell. If her plan worked, she'd soon be far away. "*Sala
Gashle,* farewell, my old friend," she whispered, "who
knows when we'll meet again."

Gyneth's car slipped off into the night air already
thick with the smoke of Soweto hearth fires and the
leftovers of a day's work in the industrial machine of
South Africa.

Carolyn trudged home along the dusty streets. Deep
in thought, she was startled to see Jonathon waiting for
her near Alena's house. It had been weeks since their
last meeting. Carolyn smiled shyly. Jonathon bowed
low.

"Your transportation is waiting for you," he said,
laughing at her and pointing to the motorbike. "Would
you like to go for a ride?" he asked. Carolyn nodded,
slipped onto the seat and clasped her arms around
Jonathon's waist, feeling the dampness of passion begin as her vagina rubbed the hard surface sensuously
and Jonathon's body moved close to hers.

They sped up a hill, away from the city and its noises. Jonathon stopped on a hill that overlooked the row of light-colored sand piles that had been disgorged by the gold-refining process in the mines deep under the city.

Carolyn gasped at the beauty of the sight of the sunset as the skies, red with gold dust, seemed to inflame the city. Jonathon stood quietly by her side.

"This is the country I love," he said haltingly. "Yet it is also the country I hate."

"I love it, too, but I've decided to leave. I don't know how to do it, but I will not live in Soweto anymore. I must find the freedom to choose my destiny. I'm determined to become a doctor."

Carolyn regretted her words the moment they were said. She opened her mouth to joke about them, to make them seem like frivolous statements, but Jonathon had taken her hands in his.

"We have a common cause then because I also want to be free. But I want to stay and claim this place as mine, not allow someone else to take my birthright from me. Stay with me and help me fight for freedom, Carolyn. You are smart and brave. We can do with people like yourself in our youth group."

Carolyn shook her head and pulled her hands away.

"I will not fight or kill or plan for such things. I want to heal people, to have respect because I am good and right, not cruel and strong."

Jonathon nodded. "But you can't obtain your dream with things the way they are. You'll never be free here unless you change everything."

Jonathon pulled her close and they stood together as the sun finally slipped away. Carolyn was distracted by his presence and couldn't think of anything but his hand lightly on her waist, his hard body next to hers and the throbbing in her groin.

Carolyn met with Jonathon regularly. She kept the physical contact between them to a minimum, not trusting her own body to resist him. The last thing she wanted was the fate of so many of her classmates, who were pregnant long before they could graduate from high school.

Yet she knew Jonathon was becoming impatient. Their long kisses and caresses seemed only to frustrate him. Some nights he did not visit her, and Carolyn heard that he joined his friends in drinking the lethal homemade brew *skokian,* and seeking out prostitutes to satisfy his needs.

The dry days of winter brought biting cold winds and Carolyn shivered in the back of the classroom as she heard the droning repetition of verses in poetry class. Wordsworth was so irrelevant to her life! She was chafing with impatience, even more determined to leave South Africa.

Jonathon was the only one she knew who could help her achieve her goal. He had been responsible for sending people out of the country for training, then arranging for their safe return. But she did not want to become part of his group of so-called freedom fighters. She also knew that such a favor would have its price.

That night Carolyn did not greet Jonathon with a kiss. Instead she looked at him solemnly.

"I have to talk to you," she said. "Can we find a private place where we will not be disturbed?"

Jonathon looked longingly at her body. She pulled her arms around herself as she felt the heat emanating from him.

"I'll come for you at ten, tonight," he said. "We can use my house. No one will disturb us then, it will be after the curfew." He looked at her again. The hunger was naked in his eyes.

Carolyn herself was burning with desire, wet with her own unsatisfied needs.

The hours seemed to drag by. Soon Jonathon was at the door and together they were picking their way through the garbage and shanties to his house. Once there Jonathon pulled her into the house. His hard penis was erect and pressed against her soft stomach as he took her skirt off with one hand, and with the other, pulled her panties out of his way. She gasped with surprise, unable to deal with the speed of his movements, and then he was in her, her vagina tight and dry as he forced himself deeper into her body, tearing her apart with his size and strength as she gasped with pain and choked for air, his heavy torso crushing her to the hard floor. Her legs kicked weakly as he ground into her, pounding deeply. And then he was done. Shocked, Carolyn tried to speak. All of a sudden he was next to her again, his cock hard and thrusting between her breasts.

"My God, you kept me waiting so long, girl."

Jonathon brought his cock to her mouth, pushing it into her throat and she gagged. Carolyn pulled away from him and stood up, quivering, as fury overcame her initial shock.

"Are you crazy? Do you think I am just here to be used like one of those prostitutes you hang out with?"

Jonathon looked at her in amazement. Where was the girl who panted under his caresses? "Look, Carolyn, you wanted it as much as I did. Haven't you ever done this before?" he asked her.

"This was my first time and you were so rough. How could you do it to me like that?" She was shaking her arms folded tightly over her body.

Jonathon pulled her down next to him

"Look, I am sorry. I have held myself back for so long, then tonight you told me you wanted to . . ." He mumbled a few more drowsy words of apology—and then he was asleep.

Carolyn sat on the floor next to him, her eyes tightly shut, faint with anger. She felt violated, penetrated. But it was just her body, not her soul. No one could ever have her soul. She curled up into a ball and clasped her knees. She stayed like that until she felt strong enough to stand up. There was blood running down her legs and she burned inside her body.

Jonathon was asleep under a blanket. She went to the bathroom and began to wash herself in the sink. Slowly she massaged every part of her body that she could touch without wincing. She cleaned herself inch by inch until there was no trace of his semen or sweat on her. She pulled on her skirt, then took a blanket off the bed and wrapped it around her body. She sat on the chair and watched Jonathon sleep. Her fury hardened into an inpenetrable resolve. She had paid the price, now she would claim her due. After what seemed like hours, she woke him up.

"We have to talk," she said calmly to him.

"Are you fucking mad?" he muttered. "I want to sleep."

"And I want to talk."

Carolyn slid down onto the floor, and laid her fingers gently on his flaccid penis. It was almost immediately erect again. She caressed him slowly, deliberately. Jonathon groaned as her touch quickened. "You spoke to me of your dream of freedom. I, too, have that dream, and we need to help each other." Now she was massaging his cock, moving up and down with the blanket slipping away from her body as she pulled his foreskin back and forth. "We must plan, you and me, Jonathon, together, like this. . . ." Carolyn's fingers caressed his body. Jonathon writhed with pleasure, his eyes closed, while Carolyn's hands moved faster and faster until, arching with passion, he ejaculated into the blanket.

Carolyn slipped away from his grasp. He grabbed for her but she was too quick for him, and in a flash she was out the door and on her way back to her house, leaving him still partially erect and muggy with sleep, his hunger for her not satisfied. She stumbled into her own house and felt a sense of triumph. She had found the way, and now there was no going back. Her body and Jonathon's need for it would serve as the instrument of her destiny.

Alena saw Carolyn change. She wasn't sure where the change came from, but over a period of weeks it became obvious that this silent young woman was now more forceful, certain and confident. She spoke no more about school, or about her forays to the medical library. She was evasive about her friends and her nightly comings and goings. Alena knew in her heart that Carolyn had started her sexual life; her body filled out and she held herself in a different way. She tried to caution Carolyn about getting pregnant, about the way that men would use her if she let them and about how hard it was to have a baby when you were just a child yourself. Carolyn listened patiently, but discarded the advice. She knew what she was doing, the medical books she read taught her about birth control, and she would not let Jonathon touch her during the fertile time in her menstrual cycle.

Carolyn's newfound confidence excited Jonathon even more. She demanded that he be more patient, gentler. Her ensuing pleasure made him even more solicitous. It was clear to Carolyn that he was falling in love with her. He tried continually to make up for their unfortunate first night together. Although Carolyn enjoyed the attention he gave her, she was determined not to allow an emotional involvement to interfere with her goal.

Finally Jonathon found a way for her escape.

She'd have to learn to fight, using the wooden guns that the group had made so as to teach their followers the right way to handle a real gun when the day of the revolution came. She'd have to learn to hide, to walk silently and unobtrusively in the dark. He would teach her where the resistance cells were within the township. And then he would tell her about the camps outside South Africa. They were her ticket to freedom.

Survival in Soweto was a struggle, a daily battle to avoid detection by the police. Carolyn's life was on the line every time she met the youth group and clasped the fake gun in her arms.

Then one day her chance came. The white population thought that the ANC was dead. Nelson Mandela was in jail, serving a life sentence of hard labor. The other leaders of the ANC were supposedly in hiding with Oliver Tambo, some in Europe and some in Zambia. But in fact the ANC was very much alive, although crippled. Painstakingly, the messages moved back and forth across the secret networks that crisscrossed Africa. A message came through. They were looking for recruits to go to Zambia, to a secret place where they would meet with real soldiers, freedom fighters. Jonathon had received his orders, to create a group of recruits to leave the country clandestinely for guerrilla training.

Carolyn had to pry this information from him. He was reluctant to let her go, especially since he knew that she had no intention of going to the guerrilla training camps, but rather would escape to find her own destiny.

"I know I'll never see you again," Jonathon said forlornly.

Carolyn caressed his face gently with her fingers as they lay in his narrow bed, relaxed after an hour of making love. Jonathon was torn between his own ideals and his need to give her what she wanted.

"You mean a lot to me, more than anyone else in my whole life."

Carolyn said nothing, just continued to caress him.

Finally, knowing that her departure was inevitable, Jonathon rationalized it to himself. If Carolyn were to reach her goals, then together they would have thwarted the system of apartheid in their own way, not just using the methods of the ANC.

Jonathon knew he'd help her.

He manipulated the recruit list so they both would be among those chosen from all over South Africa to train for revolution. Besides Jonathon, Carolyn, and her schoolmate Phineas, there were three from Natal, and three from the Cape. Carolyn's excitement grew as the day neared when they were to slip out quietly during the night to the border.

The plan was to gather at ten, just after the curfew, at Phineas's house. Jonathon's house was unsafe; the police had raided it the week before, tearing the house apart looking for subversive material, but they found nothing and had to be satisfied with beating up Jonathon's two younger brothers, home by themselves. The boys were left bleeding.

Jonathon and Carolyn moved into her house for the days prior to their departure and hardly went out at all. Alena stayed in the background, fearing Jonathon's obvious strength and preferring to ignore what was going on. South Africa's youth had lost patience with the likes of her, those people too passive to resist. In some ways she envied these two their courage in not wanting to settle for less than total freedom. So she stayed silent and turned her head away. And she did not listen to the grunting noises that came from Carolyn's room during the night.

The night they were to leave, Alena was drinking tea with two of her friends. Carolyn and Jonathon waited impatiently for her guests to go home.

When they could wait no more, Carolyn came out of her bedroom. "Alena, don't you think your friends should go? It is after curfew hour now," she said calmly, not wanting them to see her urgency.

The elderly ladies got up slowly, tired after a long day's work washing clothes in the city for white women.

"*Aina,* you are right," one of them groaned. "The day begins again too soon anyway. Thank you, Alena. *Sala gashle!*"

Slowly they said their goodbyes. Carolyn returned impatiently to the bedroom, trying to restrain Jonathon, who was furious at the delay.

"We have to go *now*—it is ten fifteen already. Those stupid old women! Couldn't they choose another night for their get-together!"

"Hush," Carolyn whispered, "they are going and in a few minutes Alena will be in bed. Please, Jonathon, she is just an old lady, and I can't let her know where we are going because the police will torture her and she'll tell them. She's frail and weak. Just be patient for a few more minutes." Jonathon clenched his fist and pulled his string bag tighter.

Finally it was quiet. They slipped out the door and started to run across the deserted streets to Phineas's house. Then they saw a fire and heard the screams as police batons hit flesh. Phineas's house was surrounded by Black Maria vans waiting to swallow the black bodies that were being beaten and dragged out of the house.

"We were set up!" Jonathon's voice was filled with

rage. "Those fucking bastards. They got them all. Oh shit, they got them all." The two of them turned, shaking, and slid further into the shadows. Just a few minutes earlier, and they would have been in the group themselves. Together they slinked back to Carolyn's house.

"I must go," Carolyn said. "I will go alone. We have no choice. You are the only one left and you have to stay to put the next group together. I will wait a few moments and then I am going." Jonathon nodded, his heart breaking as he thought of the young people who were being dragged off, to be ruined by torture.

Carolyn saw his agony. She turned, put her arm around him and touched his leg. He moved closer to her. She began to speak to him softly, telling him that her dream was separate from his, that he was truly needed to further the ANC cause while she was leaving for purely selfish reasons. She stroked his head and told him how proud she was of him, how she would tell the world of people such as him and their other friends who gave up their own dreams to help their people. She kissed him softly. "Farewell, Jonathon, we'll see each other again, in freedom."

Carolyn made him promise to stay in Alena's house where at least he would be safe, and left quickly before he could change his mind. She moved silently through the streets, avoiding the fires and fighting and approached the outskirts of Soweto. As she had been trained, Carolyn faded into the bushes at the side of the road and started to make her way north. She had a long walk ahead of her; it would take days. But she knew where to go for help. There were people all across the country who would aid her and they were alerted to expect a whole group of new recruits

Now it was only her. She felt freer than she ever had before; she had finally found her way. She had to reach the border, and then go beyond it. Only then could she find the route to get away from this whole charade. She wanted to leave Africa. She knew from geography and history, and especially from the medical books, that there was a civilization centuries old in England. There she could find the education she wanted, the peace in the study and the practice of medicine that she longed for. She moved silently through the night.

# Chapter 9

The night air smelled sweet to Carolyn as she padded along the dark side of the road. She felt invisible. The cars rushed by on the highway in mindless anonymity, but she was removed from them, flying in a world of hope. She knew that she was insignificant, unthreatening—no one would imagine that the slender girl would be a terrorist. Carolyn laughed out loud and sang to herself as she loped along. Jonathon had discussed with her the various safe houses along the way where she could get food and shelter for a few hours, never staying longer, constantly moving on. At some points the troupe would be moved by car. In other places, they'd have to walk, always moving farther north. But now it was only Carolyn, and for that she was grateful. Alone she'd attract little attention.

A flickering light in the distance caught her eye and she moved cautiously toward it. Two elderly night watchmen sat around a brazier filled with hot coals, warming their hands. They sang deep and low, in harmony, and Carolyn recognized songs of the veldt, songs of the wild and open land of the old men's youth. Their eyes were closed, hands cupped over the flames as they sat hunched and bundled up in colored blankets. Laying next to the upturned wooden Outspan orange fruit boxes that served as their chairs, each had a gnarled long stick with rounded, hand-polished knobs, their defense against potential robbers. The large dark storage house loomed up in the shadows behind them as they guarded against orange thieves.

Carolyn approached slowly realizing that she was cold. Not wanting to frighten them, she began to join in their song, her high pure voice pitching in perfect harmony with their smooth tones. They opened their eyes, saw her young form and naturally, as if planned in advance, opened their warm circle to admit her closer to the flames.

Carolyn was momentarily comforted by the kinship.

"You are very kind," she said softly, stretching her hands closer to the warmth. Then Carolyn felt a stab of fear grab her heart as she realized that she was leaving her familiar land and home, traveling to places unknown. She pulled away. She had to keep going, pushing to her goal.

"Thank you, *numzaans*," she whispered, addressing them with formal titles of respect, as she turned and continued on her way.

Soon she would have to rest. The adrenaline that had propelled her from the township had ebbed, and she felt sore and tired. Behind a small hut she saw laundry flapping on lines strung between two poles. Embers of a small fire were fading in the dry sand outside the entrance. Carolyn looked inside, where three small children were curled up with an old woman, sleeping on a mattress on the floor. She crept into the warm hut, pulled the blanket that doubled as her knapsack over her head and fell into a deep sleep.

"*Hai, hai,*" the shrill cry awoke her in terror as she felt a dig in her sides. She opened her eyes and saw the old woman trying to sweep her out the door as if she were a big piece of dirt. "Hey, old lady, what do you think you are doing?" she began, reverting to the arrogant ways of the youth group in the township. Then she remembered that these were country folk, so she stood and adopted a humble air.

"Please forgive me, respected *Tante,* I was afraid of the dark and shared your hut to escape the cold. I will leave now, please pardon my presence in your home."

The old lady leaned on her broom and looked suspiciously at Carolyn. The three children stood giggling and hiding behind her skirts. One came gingerly forward and took Carolyn's hand.

"We are going to have some *pap* now. Do you want some?"

Carolyn nodded, standing respectfully with head bowed. She clapped her hands together quickly once and opened them up into a supplicative gesture as she had been taught as a little girl when given food by her grandmother. The old lady's face broke into a large toothless smile.

"Why, you are only a child!" she exclaimed.

The woman was transformed, all motherly concern as she bustled around, readying the modest breakfast. Carolyn ate the sweet porridge hungrily, all the time being watched and mimicked by the three little girls. Every time they saw her looking at them they broke into peals of giggles, then started the hide-and-seek game of "now we see you, now we don't" again.

When it was time for her to move on, Carolyn parted from the group with waves and wishes for a safe journey. She turned one last time to look at the family scene behind her and saw the children laughing, innocent of the adult terrors that would face them. She remembered an earlier time in her life when each day was a new adventure. In the distance, the mountains of gold dust, the mine dumps on the outskirts of Johannesburg, glittered in the sun. Carolyn turned her back on the mining metropolis she never wanted to see again.

The day dragged on into its midday warmth as she tried to follow the main highway, hiding as police vans appeared in the distance, but traveling consistently in an easterly direction. As daylight began to fade again, her legs were aching so fiercely that she longed to rest. But she spurred herself on, knowing she could not be far from her first safe house. Finally she pulled herself atop a small knoll and glimpsed the sparkling lights of Pretoria. She recalled Jonathon's description.

"The first safe house is the ranch of a white family, Jews, friends of the people. We must knock on the door only at dark and say we are lost and need directions. They will house and feed us."

Carolyn waited at the top of the hill for what seemed to be hours. She dozed off and woke stiff and sore with sharp burning sensations in her back and buttocks where she'd been leaning against a rock. She stood up and then started jumping up and down, slapping her thighs and hips with her hands as the red ants that had swarmed out of the innocent-looking rock, actually an anthill, bit furiously at her tender skin. Finally with tears streaming down her face she flipped off the last fiery speck and feeling desperate and frustrated, descended onto the plains, determined to find the safe house.

Looming up in front of her Carolyn saw the flood-lit building that she knew from her history lessons—the Voortrekker Monument, on a hill, illuminated by great floodlights, the Afrikaner monument to the Great Trek of the early settlers in this Southern African land. Each December 16th, Carolyn knew, a shaft of sunlight fell across the monument's altar, as though even the sun commemorated the 1638 anniversary of the Battle of Blood River. The marble and stone edifice symbolized

the victory of the Voortrekkers over the proud Zulus.
The only Zulu Carolyn really knew well was Jonathon.
His glistening body above hers flashed into her mind
and she shook her head to dispel the vision. She had no
time for such indulgence now. Carolyn took a last look
at the monument that symbolized everything about the
white Afrikaner dominance over South Africa, then
moved into the shadows of the brush and focused her
attention on finding the safe house. It was supposed to
be the only ranch in the vicinity of the monument so it
couldn't be far away.

Then Carolyn saw the house. In a few moments she
was knocking at the door. It was opened by a short,
balding man of indeterminate age. "Yes?" he asked in-
quiringly.

Carolyn stammered, now shy and unsure of herself.
"I am l-lost, I need directions," He opened the door
further as though to look for her companions.

"I am alone. There was a traitor and . . ." He quickly
pulled her indoors, indicating she should stay silent.
Ushering her into a warm and comfortable study, the
man quickly closed the curtains and study door.

"You must not speak," he said in a foreign accent.
"You are early. It is only seven thirty, you should not
have come before ten. The servants are still around the
house and we cannot be too careful. Stay here and
don't say a word."

He went out the door, and she sat silently in the
dimly lit room. Carolyn had never seen so many books
in her life. Every conceivable space was covered with
hardbacks, paperbacks, pamphlets, journals. *The Mid-
rash, Talmudic Dissertations, The History of the Dias-
pora, Sephardic Jewry,* and on and on, foreign,
mysterious names and titles that held wonders of
knowledge enough to fill her time for years. Then she
saw *Freud, the Man and his Writings.* She pulled the

book down and opened it with reverence. It was thick and well read.

When the man entered the room again, he saw Carolyn leafing through the book with wonderment. He looked curiously at this child, so vulnerable and innocent with blistered feet and dirty crumpled clothing. What a strange anachronism she was. A terrorist no less. He smiled softly. She could have been one of his very own children, sitting small and relaxed in the large leather chair reading a book in the dim light of the lamp.

What a travesty was this unjust land. Here was a child, running a course that could humble the most hardy adult. How she would ever make it to the border he just did not know. The sound of the closing study door made Carolyn jump.

"Oh, I am so sorry, sir, but I have never seen such wonderful books before. I read a lot, you see, mostly medical books, and I have heard the name of Freud before. He is the master of the art and science of psychology, is he not?"

Joseph Abromowitz could hardly believe his ears. Where on earth did this girl come from?

"Tell me your story, my child," he said and sat down behind the desk. He pulled his glasses down on his nose and peered at her over them. Carolyn began. In fact, she began to talk more freely than she had ever spoken before. Perhaps it was because this man reminded her of Jacob Amron in some way.

She started with the raid, the arrest of the group, and Jonathon, who stayed to rebuild the resistance cell in Soweto.

Joe listened intently. Carolyn told him that she had to leave, to be trained to fight for a free South Africa. She continued on with the well-prepared jargon that she'd heard so many times in the group discussions in

Soweto and that she knew was the only reason that people would help her leave the country. Then Carolyn stopped.

"You want me to help you."

"Yes," she said, "I need to go through the northeastern transvaal to Mozambique."

"Why Mozambique?" he asked. "The people who come through here go through Rhodesia to Zambia where the ANC camps are."

Carolyn took in a deep breath, praying he wouldn't realize she was lying.

"Because they will be expecting me to take the normal route through Rhodesia and I don't want to be anticipated. I'll find my way from Mozambique across to the camp in Zambia later. They may be waiting for us at the border of Rhodesia, but not at the Mozambique border. Will you help me?"

Joe looked curiously at the young black girl. This was not the normal revolutionary that passed through his home on a regular basis. This girl was different. The way she held herself, her intelligence and sophisticated phraseology, her vivid interest in books—she was very different. Joe made up his mind to follow it through.

"It's time you had a bath and some food. My family is alone now. You can come out, bathe and eat and then we'll make a plan."

Joe led her out the room and into the kitchen. There a friendly faced, equally short lady also of intermediate age was ministering to a delicious-smelling brew and assortment of pots and pans on the stove. Two bespectacled young boys sat at the kitchen table, their schoolbooks spread out in front of them.

"Well, hello, hello, my dear," the kindly lady said, also with a foreign accent. "You look like you could do with some homemade chicken soup."

Carolyn realized that she had not eaten since breakfast and felt a pang of hunger.

"Here, sit here."

She was motioned to a small stool next to the large kitchen table and soon she was slurping down delicious noodles, bits of chicken and carrots in the most aromatic broth she'd ever tasted. As soon as she had finished, she was hustled upstairs and put in a tiled bathroom with a fluffy large bath towel and told, "Wash up now, I'll have some clean clothes for you directly."

Carolyn soaked in the deep bathtub, hardly believing that this was happening to her. It felt like the Amron household all over again, except that this time she was in Gyneth's place, in her bathroom, and not outside with the servants. She wrapped the towel around herself and opened the door a crack to see a small pile of work pants and sweater that must have belonged to one of the boys. She put them on gratefully and washed out the bathtub as Martha had taught her. She walked downstairs, gave the towel to the kind lady, then Joe led her back to the study.

"I will help you," he said. "We'll go together. I'll drive you farther north so that you can put some distance between you and your pursuers."

Carolyn's eyes filled with tears. If only white people could all be kind, like this family, like Gyneth. Then she could stay in her country. But her world was not inhabited by people like these, she could never get more than a glimpse of this life, this kindness.

"We must go soon," she said. "They'll be following me. They'll torture the rest of the group and will know I've gone. You'll be in danger, too. We must go now."

Joe opened the garage door, and Carolyn slid into the backseat of the car and lay on the floorboards covered with a blanket. He started the old Volvo and reversed out the driveway. They made their way northeast away from Pretoria on National Road 4.

Joe put his foot down on the accelerator, and they flew along the deserted road. Soon he told Carolyn to crawl onto the backseat and to lie there so they could talk but she would not be seen. She lay on the seat looking up at the roof of the car, seeing the peeling bits of upholstery and then looking beyond to the night stars, away from the reflection of the city lights. The sky seemed to stretch forever, and if she moved her head slightly she could see Orion, his belt, head, and feet. It was exactly as Armindo used to point out to her on the hot nights when they couldn't sleep and sat on the top of the stairs in the servants' wing, softly whispering tales of home and family.

Joe began to speak. "Tell me about your family," he said.

It was as if the memories were on Carolyn's tongue, the feelings were so strong and vivid as if they had happened just yesterday. She spoke first of her grandmother and the fiery inferno that was her final image of the woman who had cared for her. Then, haltingly, she began to tell him about the Amrons. She told of the goodness of that life when she and Gyneth had played and sang and Martha had swayed with them to the music. So many people seemed to love her then. Then, her voice barely audible, she described the day of her mother's death, the sight of her body flying into the air that would never fade in her mind. That day, she told him quietly, her whole life changed, the goodness in it disappeared. She spoke about township life, Alena, and finally of the medical books. Her enthusiasm grew as she described how they thrilled her very being and gave her a feeling of control when she read and absorbed the details about the human body and its intricate mechanisms. Her dream, she confided, was one day to become a doctor.

Joe gripped the wheel tightly. He hardly dared breathe. He had surprised himself at his willingness to drive Carolyn to the border. But now, as he began to glimpse her potential, he knew his instincts were right. This was a person who could make a contribution to humanity. He could not see her become a guerrilla.

To return to South Africa as a subversive would mean her ultimate destruction. He knew of the viciousness of the South African police force. He wore the numbers on his arm of another such group, the SS officers that had ripped his life's blood, his parents, brothers, sisters, and their families, away from him into the jaws of a fiery death. He would not see a people persecuted for the color of their skin—it felt too much like the Holocaust he had survived. And only God knew how he and his wife had survived.

And then there was his beloved Ruth, the soulmate and fellow concentration camp prisoner whom he had loved with a passion so fierce that he had willed her to prevail. On the days when she wanted to give up, he dragged her into a standing position, forced bread and water into her, spoke words of love, demanding that she live. She did. And so did his wife, miraculously, the wife he felt obligated to find after the war. Such an irony it was, that so many had lost everyone, yet he had been spared both of the women he loved. He had to choose one, and with agony in his heart he bade his Ruth farewell, as she found her future in London and he and his wife, broken and frail, began to build a life in South Africa.

Joe listened as Carolyn talked, all the time trying to find a solution. They traveled on, all through the night, past the farming lands of the high veldt, deep into the Eastern Transvaal, until they reached the citrus groves

of the low veldt near Nelspruit. They pulled off to the
side of the road, and Joe got out of the car to stretch.
*"Oi vey,"* said. "I'm getting too old for these night adventures."

Carolyn sat up in the backseat.

"Get down." Joe spun around to warn her, and
Carolyn thought for an old man he moved quickly,
"We have come too far to get caught now."

She did as he bade, and lay down again. Carolyn felt
warm and comfy in the car with this wonderful person.
They had spoken about so many things, her life, his
life since he came from Europe to South Africa, and
then mostly about his books and belief in Judaism.
Carolyn knew little about religion, having rejected the
weekly visit to church that Alena had offered her. The
Amrons were Jewish, but what that meant to her was
that they did not celebrate Christmas. Now she wanted
suddenly to learn more, as this man told her about the
Jewish religion, the Torah and Talmud, which he read
every day because it taught him the laws of ritual and
religion as well as, most importantly, the rites and ob-
ligations of men and women to one another in matters
of conscience.

Joe said that he discussed the Talmud and his own
interpretation of it daily with his children. In the mirror, Carolyn saw his face glow with elation as he described his joy in this process, and she wondered at a
religion that could inspire such intellectual curiosity
and at a family that would ask so many questions of
each other and always have more answers and questions to follow. She imagined herself one of those children and envied the two little boys their golden life
and intellectual opportunities.

There were so few people of whom Carolyn could
ask the fundamental questions of life, the many things
that she had not discussed with anyone, about God and

justice, death and the afterlife Alena believed in, hoped and prayed for every Sunday at church. So now she asked Joe many things, about why, if there were a God, He would create a Hitler and also the injustices she lived with every day in her country. Joe gave her no answers, just more questions with parables and moral examples and stories about people and their interrelationships.

Nor did he tell her when they would part. He just kept driving.

Soon they had passed the southern edge of the Kruger National Park, the vast natural parkland where animals were free to roam and live undisturbed in their portion of this troubled land. All of a sudden they saw the Crocodile Bridge ahead of them, and beyond it Komatieport and finally the safety of Lourenço Marques.

Joe drove the car slowly off the road behind a clump of bushes.

"Come and sit here, my child," he said. "I have an idea, and although you may not agree with me, I want you to listen to what I say and give it your most serious consideration, just as you have done during these long hours that we have spent together. First, you must know my name. I know that puts me in danger, but I want you to be able to contact me again. I am Joe Abromowitz. Next, I did not drop you off earlier because I cannot see you risk your life in this manner. You are a very special person, one who will contribute much to your people and humanity in the future. But you can only contribute if you take a different road from the one you have chosen to follow. You must put this world behind you and move to another world where your mind can grow and flourish, where you can have freedom of the spirit, not just freedom of politics. I know it seems difficult to understand at this point in your life, but believe me you will thank God for this decision and . . ."

She took his hand. He stopped in surprise in midsentence.

"Joe, I mean, sir . . . I do understand." The tears filled her eyes. "You are the one who must understand. I never intended to fight, I wanted only to escape. I, too, feel the mission that I have is more than just to be cannon fodder." She bent her head over his hand and he hugged her close to him.

"Oh God," he prayed, "if there were a meaning to my survival when so many died around me, then perhaps it was to help this child to survive."

"I will help you," he said. "You must go to London, to England. I have a very special friend there, who will take care of you. We can get you a Zambian passport while we are in Lourenço Marques, and with that passport you will be safe and protected while living in London."

He reached into the cubbyhole of the car and took out a pen and a grubby piece of paper. He wrote a name and an address on it and pressed it into Carolyn's hand.

"Take care not to lose that piece of paper—your future could depend on it."

They sat there motionless for a few more minutes, the young and the old, from different worlds and cultures yet joined in their determination and commitment to the realization of their human potential.

Joe sighed. "It is time for us to go," he said. He pulled out a bag from under the seat. In it he had a long black robe with a yarmulke. He dressed himself as a rabbi and piled a number of prayer books on the seat beside him. He pulled out four large cardboard boxes from the boot of the car and dragged them up onto the backseat. Then he pushed Carolyn gently down onto the floor again, covering her with the blankets and more books, strewn all over in a pile. "Can you breathe freely?" he asked her anxiously.

"Yes," she answered in a muffled voice. "I have my nose under the front seat."

Then they were ready. He backed the car out carefully and slowly they approached the border crossing. The guard came up to the driver's window. Joe laboriously rolled it down. The guard peered in and saw the mess of books and Joe's strange appearance.

"What is your business in Mozambique?" he asked.

"Vel, I am a rabbi." He pulled out his identity document and showed the man his picture, with flowing hair and a yarmulke. "I looked good when I was young, ei? Such a looker I vas then. Vel, anyvay, we are heving a convention in the shul of the old city in Lorenzo Marques and since we are a big group, from all over the world no less, ve don't have enough prayer books. So, I have the job of bringing the prayer books for the group. It's such a shlep, a long vay. *Oi vey,* I got the tough job. The other rabbis are flying in from Johannesburg, from all over, but they didn't want the books to go into the hold of the plane, so someone had to drive the books all the way here . . ." He rambled on and on, and the guard motioned him impatiently to get out and open the back of the car. He slowly opened the door and pulled his legs out one by one. "*Oi vey,* am I stiff, such arthritis in the old bones."

As he pushed himself up, the guard said, "Oh, go on, old man" as he laughed with the other policeman. "He is just an old Jew, let him go."

Joe sat thankfully back in the seat.

"Such an effort to move," he said. "You've saved an old man from showing how stiff his bones really are. Goodbye, sir."

Joe revved the engines and made his way deliberately, driving slowly and half stopping and starting as he overrevved the car to climb the approaching hill.

They had made it, she was free!

Papers were obtained easily when they reached their destination. Carolyn was placed aboard a vessel sailing for Southhampton. Joseph told the captain that the young girl was returning to London to her mother, his servant, who was there with his wife and children.

It was time to say goodbye.

Joseph pressed a single rand note in her hand. She looked at it, not understanding.

"Take this with you—do not spend it. When you arrive in Southampton, you must give it to the first needy person you see. It is an old Jewish custom. If you have this mission of charity to fulfill, your journey becomes one with a higher meaning than just your own desires. In that way God will take care of you to ensure you arrive safely and complete the deed of charity I have now committed you to."

"You have saved my life." Carolyn's eyes were wet.

"And the lives of your children," he said quietly, "and for that, I thank God. Use the gifts that you have with care and determination, Carolyn. Don't let foolish pride and ego stand in your way. Live life with verve. I will leave you with a quotation from the Talmud, just as if you were one of my very own children. 'Don't underestimate anybody and consider nothing impossible: every man has his hour, and every object its place. Your moments will come, be ready for them.' "

She nodded and hugged him tightly. She heard his words of encouragement ring in her ears, as they would many times again in the future. He had given her faith and hope again, like the father she never had. He had given her a future.

And then they set sail.

She asked the deckhand what day it was. He told her it was June 2, 1973. She realized with a lump in her throat that the day that she left Southern Africa was the day she became seventeen years old.

# PART III

---

# LONDON 1973

# Chapter 10

The ship slid quietly into its berth. It was cold and drizzling. Carolyn pulled on the sweater and pants that Joe had given her and tied her only scarf around her head. She bade goodbye to the crew, with a hug for the two or three who had shown her especial kindness. She still had a hurdle to overcome, to pass through immigration with the passport that looked as if it had been hers for years. It showed her as a sixteen-year-old citizen of the commonwealth country of Zambia. Joe had assured her she would be granted easy access to England with that status.

Still the uniformed officers at the end of the line looked suspiciously like the South African police, and Carolyn's heart was pounding so loud that when it was her turn, she was sure the man examined her dog-eared book would hear it thumping.

He looked at her, then at the picture, then at her again.

"You come from Lusaka in Zambia?" he asked, looking all the time at her passport.

"Yes, sir," she said in what she had hoped was a strong voice but which came out in a squeak.

"And what are you doing all alone here in England?"

"Oh, I'm not alone," she said in her most confident manner. "I am to join my mother, who's waiting for me in Golders Green. That's where she works and I'm going to join her there."

He looked at her again and then banged the page with a stamp so hard that it made her jump. "There you are, young lady. Welcome to the United Kingdom."

Then she was through the barrier, and with a perfunctory wave by the customs officer as he saw her small sack of possessions, she was in England, safe, free, and almost penniless.

Carolyn stood absolutely still for a moment. She felt disoriented. She had longed for freedom for so long, yet here it was, and she did not know what to feel. She decided to just keep going, to find Ruth. The feeling would come later.

Carolyn asked for the nearest railway station and finding it nearby, saw black, white, and Indian people standing in the lines before the long row of ticket counters. She stood in line, too, wondering at the masses of people rushing by. At the counter she held out her rand notes. "One ticket to Golders Green."

The ticket clerk looked at the notes through his thick spectacles and pushed them back to her saying, "This 'ere money ain't no good. Next in line, please."

Carolyn moved aside. No good? What did he mean? This was a rand note wasn't it? She took a deep breath and closed her eyes. She had to use this money, it was all she had. She opened her eyes again and pushed her way back to the counter. "*Look* here, sir," she said desperately, "you *have* to take this money, it is good, I promise you."

He lowered his glasses. "Now listen 'ere, young lady, whe' I says that this 'ere money ain't no good, tha's wha' I mean. You 'ave to change it into pounds, shillin's and pence, see. So move yourself over to that them bank and change yer money, then come back 'ere an' I'll give you yer ticket. You get that?"

Carolyn looked in the direction in which he had pointed and saw the sign BANK—BUREAU DE CHANGE. She joined that line and waited hopefully till she came to the counter. She held out the notes again, waiting for the man to push them back at her. Instead he took them saying, "Sterling, madam? What denominations?" Carolyn looked at him speechless. "Madam," he had called her! When she didn't answer he flipped out a number of notes with a few coins and counted them faster than her eyes could follow saying "Will this be all right then, madam?" She took the money, nodded and unable to speak stood back in the ticket line. It was all so new, confusing, different. He'd treated her with respect and called her madam. She bought her ticket, listened intently to the instructions she received and found the train that would take her to Victoria Station. She looked carefully into the cars to see if there was one especially for blacks. Then she saw an Indian family and a black man in flowing robes sitting in the same train car as the white people. She realized that this was one of the feelings of freedom she had been looking for, so showing a confidence she didn't feel, she took a window seat.

For the first time since she had felt ground under her feet, Carolyn breathed deeply. She had actually made it. She closed her eyes, letting the clacking of the train lull her into a sleep, curled up in the seat, her worldly possessions clasped on her lap. Her new life had now really begun.

It seemed just a few minutes later the train conductor was shaking her by the shoulder saying, "Ticket, please, young lady, we're almost there, do you have a ticket?" She sleepily held out her ticket that had been tightly clasped in her hand, he punched it and moved on, his money belt jangling.

Carolyn sat up and saw the train slowing at Victoria Station. She gathered her things together, moving out with the rest of the passengers. Carolyn stood still, almost being knocked over by the stream of people who were all moving purposefully forward. She stood to the side and waited for them to pass, then started walking slowly, marveling at the endless rail line and different massive halls with announcements ringing and lights flashing. She saw kiosks and stands with hot and cold food, books and newspapers and she longed to stop and feast on the snacks and books equally. She turned her face away and looked anxiously at all the signs of departing trains. Eventually in desperation she saw a young boy, standing next to the wall, reading a comic.

"How do I find Golders Green?" she asked. He looked up at her, then tucked his book into his pocket.

"You need the tube for that," he said and started talking about the Bakerloo line, the Central line and she got so confused that tears came to her eyes. "Here," he said, seeing that she was quite overcome, "I'll show you."

Carolyn followed him up and down endless escalators packed with people. Then she heard a roaring sound that frightened her.

"That's the train coming," he said, seeing her shrink back against the tiled wall. "Get on and go to Golders Green," he said pushing her toward the opening doors of the arriving train. "Good luck!"

Carolyn felt the rand note in her pocket that Joe had given her. She pulled it out and pressed it into the boy's pocket saying, "Here, thank you for your kindness, for my safety." She left him looking curiously at the bank note, unlike any he had ever seen before as the train slipped slowly out of the station.

Carolyn sat down, breathless, seeing the boy's surprised face moving away. This was how freedom felt. She could jump onto any train she desired. Carolyn longed to share her sudden joy.

She looked around at the people who sat or stood close together, holding on to rubber thongs that were hanging from poles. No one was talking. Then she saw something that made her laugh. A man was reading a newspaper, but he had folded it into a small narrow shape and every time he wanted to read another part, he unfolded it carefully, then closed it up again like a clam. She watched, fascinated by his precision until he looked up at her, obviously discomforted by her unflinching gaze. Carolyn looked down, embarrassed to be caught staring at him.

She saw people of many races around her. Most of them looked drab and were dressed in subdued colors. It was warm in the train and she felt safe.

Carolyn saw a map on the opposite wall of the train and followed its track, counting the stops before Golders Green. Once there, she allowed the movement of people to take her up and out to the subway station. She needed to find High Road Lane. She saw a man dressed in a dark uniform with a tall hat and approached him gingerly, thinking he was a train official.

"Excuse me, sir, do you know where High Road Lane is?" He turned. She realized she was speaking to a London policeman, and she froze. But he was kind and helpful, accompanying her halfway there, saying that it was on his beat anyway. They chatted a little about the weather, Carolyn stammering monosyllabic answers to his small talk, as she slowly understood that she had no need to fear him. He left with a wave, continuing on his evening rounds. Carolyn found the street and paused as she approached the door of the small house. What if Ruth Levy was not there anymore, if she didn't want her, what would she do then?

She knocked. No one answered.

She knocked again. Nothing.

Carolyn sat down on the steps and buried her head in her hands. It was what she had feared. What would she do now? She began to sob, releasing all the emotions she had kept bottled up for so long.

"Now, now, what's all this crying! You have a problem, there's always a solution."

She looked up through her tears. Standing behind her was a chubby little lady with white hair pulled back in a bun, an umbrella in her one hand and a plastic shopping bag in the other.

"Now, it can't be so bad. Here, wipe your nose." She pulled out a tissue and handed it to her. Dutifully, Carolyn blew her nose. She looked at the lady and said in a muffled voice, "Joseph Abromowitz sent me. He said you would help me. Are you Ruth Levy?"

The woman's expression changed completely. Gone was the lighthearted manner with which she had greeted Carolyn. She pulled her up off the front steps and looked closely at her face. "That I am, and Joe is my dearest friend. If he said I'd help you, then indeed I will. Come inside, young lady, you look as if you could do with some hot chocolate."

Ruth entered her home and Carolyn followed, stepping carefully over the threshold, as she slipped quietly into her new life.

# Chapter 11

Ruth Levy was exactly what Carolyn needed. She had seen the worst of the human condition in the concentration camps, but her outlook was undaunted. She knew the fragility of life and, having fought and survived, every day of breath and health was precious. Hers was also a home in which the rules were those of human courtesy, not class or race.

Carolyn observed Ruth carefully. She was solidly predictable and within a few days the young girl felt entirely safe and at home. The house was clean, orderly, logical. Ruth's kitchen was easy to work in, and the library was stacked with books on every conceivable subject. But it was the small music room that fascinated Carolyn most of all. Ruth saw her fingering the records, mouthing the words on their covers in French, Italian, or German.

"Do you like opera?" Ruth asked her gently.

"I don't know what it is," Carolyn answered shyly.

"Aha—we have some learning to do then. Sit down child, we'll listen together."

And so began four hours of the most emotional, lyrical, heartrending music Carolyn had ever heard. As Ruth explained libretto after libretto, the teenager's eyes filled with tears as she suffered the agonies in *La*

*Traviata,* the sorrows of Verdi's *Requiem Mass,* the joys of *Tosca.* Finally, exhausted, she fell asleep, her slight figure wrapped in a warm rug, her arms under her head, still leaning toward the gramophone, the music filling her head.

Ruth gazed at the young woman. She was different, incredibly perceptive, old beyond her years yet unspoiled by western life. She looked as if the African sunlight still shone from her eyes, so keen was her concentration and clear her gaze, yet her story, now unfolding bit by bit, was of amazing fortitude, mature determination and courage. Ruth saw qualities of greatness in the young girl, and tremendous neediness, too. The older woman reached out with a tender heart, aching to give the love she had kept dormant all these years, longing to feel young dependent arms around her neck again. Her tears flowed freely, as she carefully carried the now sleeping traveler in her arms, placing her securely in the bed that would always be hers. She thanked Joe for the gift of love, this special person with whom she could share her talents and life experience.

The first week flew by. After feeding her appropriately and finding suitable clothes for the cold wet climate, Ruth began to make inquiries about the right school for Carolyn.

Carolyn could hardly believe it. It was as if Joe's name had been magic to Ruth's ears and from that moment on, without question, Carolyn became her ward and responsibility, despite the young girl's explanations that she would be no burden and intended to find a job to pay room and board. Ruth nodded her head saying, "Of course you will, and that's just fine. Now eat up like a good girl" as she ladled another enormous helping of brisket and carrot *tsimmes* onto Carolyn's plate.

Carolyn allowed herself to relax, really relax for the first time since she had felt the safe and warm feeling of comfort in the Amrons' house. She listened to music, opera, then symphonies, the music rippling through her mind and body and filling her with great joy. Then, one day as she washed the dishes after another gargantuan meal, she began to sing. Imitating the sopranos she now listened to at every conceivable opportunity, she sang out loudly, capturing the melodies of the most famous arias she had heard. Ruth, doing her accounts in the music room, froze. Unable to believe her ears, she sat quietly, listening to the raw talent, marveling at Carolyn yet again. She could truly have been her very own child, for Ruth taught singing, to young promising students from the local conservatory where she was a professor of music theory. Now here, in her own home, was the greatest talent she had heard in years. She listened until the singing became humming, then stopped altogether. Ruth waited until Carolyn was ready for bed. Then, as she tucked the bedclothes around the slim body, she said softly, "You have a remarkable voice, child. It is a God-given talent and must not be wasted. Do you know how I earn my living?"

Carolyn shook her head.

"I teach singing and music at the conservatory. I also have some private pupils, the most promising students for whom I was preparing monthly statements this evening. Would you like to learn singing techniques from me?"

"I would love it!" Carolyn's eyes shone brightly. "Can we start tomorrow?"

"Well, we will see. First we have to take care of other matters, like school."

The next day, dressed in a new skirt, sweater, and coat, Carolyn nervously accompanied Ruth, who chat-

tered merrily, sloshing along in her galoshes and rain-
coat. As they entered the Hampstead Secondary School
grounds, Carolyn saw many students in twos and
threes walking up the path into the main building. Ruth
entered the administration office, pulling Carolyn behind her, and asked for the secretary to the headmistress.

"I have young Carolyn Ngwizi here. I made an
appointment with the headmistress, I am Mrs. Ruth
Levy," she said in her most official voice. Soon they
were sitting in the headmistress's office and a tall,
scrawny lady with wispy faded blond hair and thick
glasses was sitting straight up like a board behind the
desk. Her presence was enough to inspire terror in
Carolyn.

Ruth explained in her heavy European accent. "She
is clever, very clever. She is now my ward, having
been sent from Zambia to stay with me until she grows
up, to learn and be cultured in the ways of the English." Ruth smiled encouragingly at Carolyn.

"Is she to be legally residing with you then for the
duration of the school year?" said the prim lady disap-
provingly.

"Yes, and not only for this year but all through her
A levels, too. She is planning to become a doctor, a
surgeon."

Ruth looked to see if her listener was suitably
impressed. The headmistress nodded, apparently un-
moved by the piece of shared foresight.

"You will have to fill out some forms in the administration office and then we have to place her in a
class. What grade were you in in Zambia?" she asked
of Carolyn.

Ruth answered quickly.

"The entire grading system was quite different. She
was at a convent, very few girls, they just developed at

their own pace. Now we have no records, but I suggest that after a few weeks in a class you'll be able to plainly see Carolyn's abilities."

The headmistress pursed her thin lips together and looked piercingly at Carolyn. "Yes, indeed," she said, having no doubt that the child would be in remedial classes before long, having had such an unstructured and inadequate schooling.

"Well then, welcome to the Hampstead Secondary School." She stood up and the interview was over. Carolyn had not said a word. She realized that she'd been holding her breath. They filled out the forms and the secretary opened a note placed in the file by the headmistress after the interview and stated, "You will be in O level first year. It is in room fourteen, down the hall."

Carolyn gasped. Today, to actually start today? She had no time to argue since Ruth was already on her way down the hall counting out loud as she passed the rooms until she reached the right one and said with a loud "Aha! There we are." She gave Carolyn a quick hug, pressed a pound note in her pocket telling her to eat a proper lunch, and then she was gone.

Taking a deep breath, Carolyn entered the classroom. All eyes turned to her. The teacher stopped in midsentence.

"I was told to come to this class," she whispered. The teacher looked down her nose and motioned to an empty chair in the front. Carolyn could feel the eyes boring a hole in the back of her head, but she kept her mind focused on what the teacher was saying. It was a geography lesson, a subject at which Carolyn had been especially good at school, since much of it could be learned from books. Soon she was enjoying the lesson enormously, the peace of the room, the focus of the teacher, the lack of interruption from unruly class members. This was what school should be. The students raised their hands to ask and answer questions, and the discipline was superb. The teacher glanced out of the corner of her eyes at the new girl, but didn't ask her to answer any substantive questions since it was her first day.

She did however ask her name. "Carolyn Ngwizi," she said clearly, feeling more comfortable now. "And where were you in school before, Carolyn?" the teacher asked. "In Sou ... Zambia," she stammered, feeling dishonest but realizing that she had to lie.

The class ended and Carolyn turned to get her first real look at the schoolmates with whom she would spend the next few years of her life. They all looked affluent and younger than her. There were dark-skinned people in the class, she noticed with relief. Some looked Indian, some were black and looked as if they came from Africa. Two of the black girls sauntered up to her and eyed her up and down.

"Where do *you* come from, then?" the one said, in a broad London accent.

Carolyn told a half truth.

"I came from South Africa, but through Zambia. I am living here permanently now."

"What about your mum and dad?" They looked at her closely.

"They're dead."

The girls immediately looked sympathetic, and one put her arm through Carolyn's and said, "Well, we'll introduce you to the whole crowd here. There are all sorts of people in the school and a whole bunch of idiots to avoid. We'll give you the whole scene." They went off pointing out the kiosk where chocolate could be bought as well as biscuits, the place to put gym shoes, which Carolyn realized she would need to buy, the library and gymnasium with all sorts of workout equipment such as bars and something called a "horse" that didn't look anything like one. Carolyn was awed. She was now part of Gyneth's privileged world that she had only dreamed about in South Africa. Her head was spinning by the end of the lunch break.

As they went back to class, her new friends shared with Carolyn that ten years ago their families, too, had come from Kenya when the "troubles" started there. Carolyn wasn't quite sure what the "troubles" were but she didn't ask in case she showed herself to be ignorant.

The classes flew by. There was history, chemistry, physical science, mathematics, Latin then English and biology. At three o'clock the bell went for the last time, and Carolyn, her head reeling from the amount of information she had heard, waved goodbye to the two girls who'd befriended her, and walked home. Even the drizzle could not dampen her spirits. She was in a real school. She was sitting in a class, had access to a library, had clean white notebooks, which she had used some of her precious pounds to buy at the school supply desk, and she was flying high.

She ran up the steps and knocked on the front door, impatient to tell Ruth of her exciting day's activities. Ruth saw her glowing face, gave a silent prayer that her first day was a good one, and soon she was chatting away while Ruth listened, laughed, and urged her to enjoy more of the substantial English tea set on the table.

Carolyn could not wait to sit in her room at the narrow desk that she could now call hers and to devour the books and the masses of information she had been introduced to that day.

Her enthusiasm did not fade with time. She was eager to prove herself, more to herself than anyone else, and was anxious for the tests, the papers, and the corrected homework to be handed back with comments. Her grades started off below the class average and she was appalled. She had never obtained less than an A on anything that she had done in Soweto. It spurred her to greater efforts.

Carolyn excelled at geography, mathematics, chemistry and physical science. Biology was a breeze for her since her extensive reading in the medical library had more than adequately prepared her. Her worst subjects were English and history and of course she had no knowledge at all of French, except for a nursery song she vaguely remembered singing with Gyneth called "Frère Jacques." Latin, however, was a source of amazement to her. She found that by memorizing pages of vocabulary, the declensions and conjugations, she could progress very well and get a fairly decent grade.

French, however, remained impossibly difficult. After struggling for three months, in desperation Carolyn approached the teacher, afraid to make herself known to be having difficulties but unwilling to sit frustrated through class, unable to follow or understand what was going on.

"You should probably drop this subject as you will never make the grade in it," the teacher said bluntly, and rather unkindly. Really, she thought, dumping this child in her class after the beginning of term was just a little too much. She would be happy to get rid of her.

"I'll talk to the headmistress," she said.

"Oh no, please don't do that," said Carolyn, panic-stricken that she would be thrown out of the school. "Let me have another try, please."

"No, it really is no good. You are rather hopeless at this subject. I will let you know our decision."

Carolyn was overcome with fear and arrived home without her normal enthusiasm. Ruth, waiting patiently as always, took one look at Carolyn's face and said, "Right now, come in and sit yourself down with a nice cup of tea and let's hear all about it."

Carolyn told all. Ruth hugged the worldly young woman who was so innocent in many ways.

"You know that I will not let anyone bounce you out of school just for not being able to speak silly old French. Now dry your eyes and off you go to finish your homework; we'll go and see that undernourished headmistress tomorrow."

Carolyn went to bed. Although nervous about the morning, nevertheless, for the first time she felt as if she had a family, someone to take care of her, a person she could rely on.

They sat again in the headmistress's office. Ruth bristled, ready for the attack.

The headmistress looked up from Carolyn's file.

Amazingly, she smiled. "She is rather remarkable, you know," she said to Ruth as if Carolyn was not there at all.

Ruth was quite taken back. "You mean you are not going to ask her to leave?"

"Leave? Why not at all, my dear. She is going to turn out one of our more remarkable scholars."

"But what about French?" Carolyn stammered.

"Well, I think it is quite clear that you need to drop French, but in math, science, chemistry, geography, Latin—your grades are among the top in the class. And as for biology,"—she took off her glasses altogether—"Mr. Prince says that in all his years of teaching the subject he has never come across anyone with more aptitude for the course. Now of course your English vocabulary is excellent, but your grammar is still weak. And in history—well, you are coming along, but there is still quite a long way to go. But overall, we are really quite pleased, quite pleased indeed."

Carolyn and Ruth sailed out of the office full of smiles.

The next week, the two Kenyan girls she'd met on her first day at school begged her to come out with them to a new pub in Knightsbridge. Carolyn dressed without much interest, even though Ruth lent her a pair of delicate gold earrings. She threw on a scarf and jacket and met her friends at the tube station. They arrived in Knightsbridge after a couple of changes of train and a brisk run in the drizzle that seemed so much a part of life in London. As they entered the pub, a wave of smoke and noise hit them and they elbowed their way through to the bar. They ordered a couple of pints and sat down gratefully on three tall stools. There were black and white people in the bar, a sight that Carolyn was still unused to seeing, and a sultry singer crooned into the microphone at the small piano.

"Isn't this just too super for words?" her friends whispered and preened themselves for the approving stares they received from a variety of young men around the bar. Carolyn kept her body stiff and looked into her beer.

"Oh come on, cheer up. You look as if you just tripped over yer lip, girl," they said to her, tugging on her scarf. She tried to smile, knowing that she shouldn't have come. A couple of guys sauntered up to them and started chatting up the other two girls. Then there was a flash of light and Carolyn quickly slipped off the stool and took cover under the bar. Surprised, the girls laughed and leaned down to help her up.

"You've hardly had a drink yet and you are already falling off the bar stool. You need to come here more often!" they said teasingly. Carolyn saw a photographer fiddling with his camera and realized that she had just had her picture taken. Her reaction had been to take cover, a remnant of her terrorist training with Jonathon. She felt horribly embarrassed.

Carolyn walked away from the bar and moved over to the piano. The music was West African, mildly reminiscent of South Africa, but with a different beat and melody. She started humming in natural harmony with the singer, who was pleased to have a distraction from the normal eye-streaming boredom of another evening. Soon they were singing together, choosing different songs, laughing and applauding each other's improvizations. Then Carolyn put aside the microphone and began to sing alone, the voice training by Ruth enabling her perfectly pitched tones to ring out powerfully as she remembered the songs of her childhood, that Martha and Anna would sing to her, those loving nights around the warm stove at the Amrons.

Carolyn's friends were completely dumbfounded. Not only did they not know of her tremendous talent, but she seemed so poised, so much older in a way, so confident.

Carolyn was surprised at the applause. The pub was crowded and people were now calling out requests for a variety of songs. Demurring, she gave the microphone back to the singer with a smile and grabbed her coat.

"I'm really tired, so I'm off home now. You were great to bring me along. See you tomorrow!" Then before her friends could argue, she was out the door. The two girls were surprised at her abrupt departure, but being well into their beers by then, they returned to their conversations. They wouldn't miss her.

Carolyn wrapped her arms around herself on the subway and ran the short distance home. Ruth was waiting up for her, just to be sure she was safe, she said, and Carolyn gave her a grateful hug for caring, feeling for a moment like a little girl instead of a young woman.

Over the next few years of intense studying for O levels, then the more difficult A levels, which in South Africa would have been the equivalent of the first year at college, Carolyn constantly reminded herself and Ruth of Joe's words to her: "Consider nothing impossible. . . . Your moments will come, be ready for them."

Carolyn had few friends, by choice. She thought often of how upset Gyneth must have been to have discovered she had left without even a goodbye. Yet Gyneth still had her golden life, was probably now in medical school, the safe, secure pieces of her existence firmly in place. Carolyn had no regrets. She'd had no other option.

Ruth was Carolyn's only companion.

"Were you married before?" Carolyn asked her one evening as they sat in front of the small fire listening to opera.

Ruth rarely spoke about the days before or during Auschwitz.

"My late husband, may he rest in peace, was a surgeon. He studied in Edinburgh before . . . before the war. There were three . . . three children . . . my three babies."

Ruth allowed herself a rare moment of grieving. The pain never went away. She did not allow herself to think much of what could have been had her beloved husband and their children survived, before the animals in the camps sterilized her forever. She missed her family every day, nearly thirty years later, and would for the rest of her life.

Carolyn saw the tears of remembrance pouring down Ruth's face. "Please forgive me, Ruth, I didn't mean to cause you pain. We don't have to talk about it anymore." Carolyn hugged the older woman. Ruth returned the gesture, then motioned Carolyn to sit beside her.

"The time has come for you to know about my life. You are important to me, child. I know you think that you derive all the benefit from our relationship. It is not so." Carolyn's eyes filled with tears. It was a source of endearment to her that regardless of the strange looks they always received, Ruth had seemed immune to the prejudices of others. Nothing could make a dent in her iron will to help Carolyn succeed.

"Joe gave me a precious gift when he dropped you in my lap." Ruth blew her nose into a large handkerchief and patted Carolyn's hand.

"Joe saved my life, not once but again and again. He forced me to stand when I wanted only to fall to the ground and die, he forced a dry piece of black bread into my mouth when I had despaired of ever eating again. Then after the Americans came, he went away, saying he had a wife he had to find, living or dead, and if he couldn't, he'd come back for me and we'd be together."

"I met his wife in South Africa," Carolyn whispered.

"Yes . . . I knew he had moved there with her."

"How long did you wait for him?" Carolyn was sitting on the edge of her chair.

"I moved to England. I was very ill, it took me a long time to regain my health. Then I began to tutor young people in singing."

Ruth had waited a year, hoping always to hear from Joe. Then he wrote, tracing her through the Jewish Agency. She still had the letter. His wife had been in one of the holding refugee camps awaiting resettlement and they were going to South Africa, where his wife had a distant cousin before the war.

They wrote sporadically, but never saw each other again.

"I have made a good life, child," Ruth responded to Carolyn's sad expression, "but you have given me the part I always missed. So you must understand that you are as special to me as I am to you." Carolyn put her arms around the older woman and they held each other. They never talked about the subject again.

There was, however, something that Ruth did not tell Carolyn. Instinctively she felt it was not yet the right time.

One day about a month after Carolyn had arrived, a rather proper Englishman phoned and said, "Mrs. Ruth Levy? Ahem—I am calling to inform you that a bank account has been authorized in your name and a bank draft in the amount of, let me see, two hundred pounds, has arrived for you. This is to be a monthly amount, I believe, so I will be sending you a check to-day, or you can just come in and withdraw the money, as you wish."

Ruth was speechless. "Who is it from?" she asked.

"Well, I am afraid it is an anonymous gift, madam, and all I am authorized to say is the following statement. 'Watch over the children of the poor, for they will bring forth science.' I am afraid I really don't know what that means."

Ruth was overcome with emotion. It was from Joe who'd quoted from the Talmud as he bestowed his generosity on herself and Carolyn. A long moment passed while she struggled for control.

"Er, madam?" said the very proper young man. "How do you wish me to proceed?"

"I'll come in tomorrow and withdraw the money," Ruth said, trying to maintain her composure. "Thank you so much. Goodbye."

She replaced the telephone and allowed herself a

moment of self-indulgence as she wept and laughed, knowing that this was as much a declaration of faith in Carolyn as it was one of loving support for her. She'd do her part in the grooming, education, and launching of the young miracle that had become her family.

A few months before the A level examinations Carolyn filled out the application forms to gain admission to medical school. Ruth kept trying to prepare her for the potential rejection she would receive since she was determined to be accepted at a school in London.

"My dear, you know what an optimist I am. But you do have to be realistic. There are very few places in London medical schools, and it is very much an old boys' network. Of course if your father had been a graduate of Guys or London Hospital, where you seem to have set your heart on going, it would be a lot easier. But it is extremely difficult to beat the system here. Being a woman is bad enough. Being black means you have two strikes against you. All you need is to be Jewish, too!" she said laughingly.

Carolyn looked at her very seriously. "I would want nothing more than to be Jewish. The only people in my life who have shown me kindness and respect have been Jewish. It would be a privilege for me, not a curse." Ruth hugged her with tears in her eyes. There was no way she could protect her from the disappointments that would surely follow.

Carolyn was called for an interview at the various medical schools she had applied to. Three were in London, one in Bristol, and one in Leeds. The interviews were intimidating. She was the only woman at all of them. There was only one other black and he was from Kenya. The last interview was at the London Hospital, which was her first choice. By then she knew what to expect. She decided to be supremely confident while remaining respectful.

"Good morning," she said politely.

The three elderly examiners acknowledged her greeting with equal politeness.

The questioning began.

"You come from Africa, I see from your application. Are you intending to go back?"

"No, I have emigrated to England. My intention is to practice medicine in London, sir." Carolyn answered the bespectacled elderly gentlemen with charm. They looked at the determined, confident young woman. She certainly had fortitude to even apply to their college.

The questioning continued for an hour.

Carolyn's replies were succinct and well phrased. By listening carefully over the past few years to the accents of her wealthier classmates, she had adopted an upper-class English accent.

The interview was soon over.

"You know that the entrance requirements for the London Hospital and medical school are of the highest standard."

"Yes, sir." Carolyn waited.

"These are the requirements. You will be accepted on the condition that you obtain all A's in your A-level examinations."

"Yes, sir, thank you." The men stood. Carolyn shook their hands solemnly and left.

Later, the interviewers had a quiet glass of sherry together in their club and discussed the day's applicants.

"The black girl was intelligent, no doubt about it. It's just too bad that these people have so far to go in catching up, educationally, that is. Quite a charming young lass otherwise. Just doesn't have what it takes to get those kinds of A-level scores, I'm afraid." The conversation turned to one of the other young men, and Carolyn was forgotten.

They knew that their normal exclusionary tactic of

demanding perfection would keep their medical applicants snowy white as they normally were. What Carolyn did not know was that the many applicants that came before her had also been screened but by a different standard. The offers they received, depending on whether the young man's father was an alumnus, or well connected, had varied from requiring four D's to two A's and two B's on the A-level examinations. Only Carolyn had been asked to perform to the highest standard possible.

It was fortunate that she did not know how impossible the task was that she had to perform. She just presumed that those grades were what was required of her to enter medical school. Carolyn wrote her A levels intensely on four separate days over three weeks.

The results were as she expected. She obtained straight A's and won a number of academic prizes at her school.

None of that was important to her. All that mattered was the fact that now, nearly twenty years old, at last the road was clear for medical school and beyond. She proudly sent her letter of acceptance with her grades to the London Hospital, little knowing the disbelief that met it. She was determined to fulfill the predictions that Joe had made.

# Chapter 12

Gyneth's school days were nearing their end and she had to deal with final matriculation exams. She thought often of Carolyn, imagining her also studying for exams, and fantasized how they would finally be together in medical school, at the partially integrated Witwatersrand University.

However, another hurdle lay ahead that to Gyneth seemed far more terrifying than exams—the school dance. Gyneth had to bring an escort. She'd met a couple of young men at the synagogue but shuddered at the thought of having to actually call one of them to invite him to an event as important as her high school dance.

She practiced for hours in front of the mirror, saying over and over in what she hoped was a nonchalant tone, "so, how would you like to go to my school dance with me," or, "ever been to an all-girls school dance before," or, "hi—I need an escort. Once we are there you don't have to stick with me," or, "have you anything to do on Saturday?"

Finally, fed up with the whole thing, she called a boy who was at least tall enough to look presentable on a dance floor.

"Hi, Steve? It's me, Gyneth. How's it going? Look,"

she mentally went through all the approaches and just decided to be honest, "I wondered if you'd like to come with me to my school-leaving dance on Saturday. You'd have to wear a tuxedo, but it should be quite fun." She waited holding her breath, already hearing the refusal she anticipated.

"Well," he said uncertainly.

"It's okay," she said swiftly, ready to hang up, "if you can't come. It's not so important really."

"Hang on a bit," he said. "I never said I can't come. In fact I'd love to come. That's a pretty posh school that you go to and the dance is always a real treat. The only problem is that I don't have a tuxedo."

She could hardly believe what she had heard.

"You'll come?" she said incredulously. "You really will?"

"Sure," he said. "But what am I going to wear?"

She felt faint. "Wear? Oh that's no problem. I'll ask my dad, I'm sure it can be sorted out. I'll find out and call you back."

Her head was spinning. She actually had a date! He was good looking, too, and tall. She could actually go to the dance. Gyneth called her father, begging his secretary to put her through even though he was with a patient. She told her it was an emergency.

"Gyneth, what is the matter?" Jacob asked within a few seconds, visions of broken limbs flashing through his mind.

"Dad—listen, it really is an emergency. He may change his mind or someone else will ask him before I get back to him. It's Steve, he is coming to the dance with me and he doesn't have a tuxedo. What can we do?" she said, ending in an excited squeal.

"Gyneth, really, that's not an emergency at all!" Jacob said crossly.

"It is to me," she said frantically.

"Well, it can be easily resolved. We can rent Steve a tuxedo from my tailor." Gyneth breathed a sigh of relief.

The next few days were a whirlwind of frantic activity as Estelle and Gyneth went from shop to shop desperately looking for a dress for the dance. Eventually, Estelle made the decision.

"We will go to my private couturier and have a gorgeous long dress made for you."

Gyneth gasped. Her mother's dresses were all one of a kind, and she looked stunning in every one. Gyneth prayed for a wonderful flowing fabric that would make her look pretty, too. They found an emerald green silk with a lighter colored billowy chiffon. Gyneth's eyes lit up when she saw it. The couturier and her assistants worked through the night and after four fittings, it was ready.

Gyneth looked at herself in the mirror. Well, she didn't look thin, but at least she looked feminine. She unbraided her hair and let it flow golden and thick, down her back. The fitted dress was covered by the light green chiffon, which was attached to her shoulders and gave a soft look to her body. The chiffon sleeves flattered her arms, and the length and lines of the dress gave her a graceful elegance. She could hardly believe it. She actually looked attractive. Her green eyes sparkled and she looked gratefully at her mother. Estelle said a silent prayer of thanks. It may have cost ten times the price of a shop-bought dress, but it was worth it.

Friday, the final day of school arrived and with it the awards ceremony.

Gyneth pulled her school uniform on for the last time, perspiring as she unrolled the brown stockings toward their garters, which were always slightly short and had to be coaxed up a few more centimeters. She pulled her hair into a braid and vowed to cut it after the dance. She sailed up to the dais as her name was called each time she won an award. She could see her parents in the crowd and they both shone with pride. Gyneth glowed.

Then the ceremony was over and she was aware of the crowd of girls she'd grown up with. She looked longingly as they stood talking together, their long slim legs and slender bodies waving in enthusiasm as they swayed back and forth and said their tearful goodbyes, going on their separate ways. In the past years Gyneth had vowed to outdo her classmates in all her achievements. Nevertheless, at that moment she would have traded every single award that she had won in order to look like them for just one day.

Estelle saw the longing on her face. "Gyneth," she said very gently. "Dad and I have met a new doctor who has just come to town. Apparently he has a diet that really works. Dad thought that he would try it. Would you like to as well?" Estelle steeled herself for the outburst that normally followed.

There was a long pause as Gyneth looked pensive.

"I am ready to try," she said finally with a sigh. "At least now none of the girls can tease me if I fail, as I'll never see them again. I just wish that I could lose it all before the dance tomorrow. The dress really looks quite good, Mum, doesn't it? I don't look too fat in it, do I?" she asked anxiously.

"You look quite wonderful and Steve will think so, too," Estelle said, for once being truthful about Gyneth's appearance.

The night of the dance came. Estelle gave Gyneth some of her special bubble bath and perfume, and Gyneth dressed and made up carefully, paying extra attention to her eyes, which looked huge and greener than usual. She pulled out the painful hair rollers that had hurt her head all afternoon, and the long golden curls unfurled down her back. Anna zipped up the dress and as she let the chiffon fall over the sheath, Gyneth saw the transformation. All of a sudden she was a woman.

She stepped into the hallway and came slowly down the stairs, walking carefully on the high-heeled shoes they had just bought that day. At the bottom of the stairs, Armindo, David, and Andrew all had tears in their eyes as they saw the young woman they had known from birth. They actually applauded, and she bowed low, feeling like someone else.

Then her father came forward with a luxurious white mink and black Karakal fur jacket in his arms.

"This, my little one, is your first mink jacket."

Gyneth caressed the silky fur between her fingers. She could hardly believe it was hers. Then her mother said, "and here is your first pair of real pearl earings." Gyneth put them on carefully and looked at herself in the hall mirror.

Amazingly, she looked like her mother.

The doorbell rang.

Armindo answered it, looking carefully at the young man who entered, to see if he was an appropriate escort for Gyneth. Estelle stepped forward quickly and welcomed the boy, stiff from nerves, into their home.

Within a few minutes, they left in Steve's father's car and Estelle and Jacob looked at each other with relief tinged with sadness, realizing that Gyneth was growing up.

The great school hall was filled and Gyneth held her head high, trying to remember that she was the person she had seen in the mirror and that she looked wonderful, not the way she always saw herself.

Her classmates stared at her. They'd been sure she wouldn't come. She'd said nothing to them all week in

case Steve changed his mind at the last minute, something she had feared right up until he appeared at the
front door of her house.

And they stared at Steve. Where on earth did Gyneth
find him? they whispered to each other. She walked in
confidently, placed her little evening bag down on the
nearest table and then Steve was waltzing her around
the dance floor. She felt light and slim, beautiful and
feminine, and Steve was a fabulous dancer. She could
hardly believe her luck. The only man she had ever
danced with was her father, an excellent dancer, so she
really was not sure what to expect. This was more than
she could ever have hoped. The whole evening was
like a dream come true.

She could feel Steve's eyes on her. Gyneth had
feared that once they arrived he might ignore her. On
the contrary, it was as if he couldn't bear to leave her
side. She felt his body next to hers as they moved
closer for the foxtrot, and it made her shiver with an
unfamiliar thrill. The more she looked at him, the more
attractive he became. Gyneth noticed for the first time
that he had clear gray eyes, with a soft look in them
that made her blush and look away, unaccustomed as
she was to such unwavering, male attention.

They moved outside to cool off from the last dance,
both humming a Beatles song as they walked. The
school was transformed into a fairyland of flowing
dresses and tuxedos, wandering slowly among the
large trees and ivy-covered red brick buildings. For the
first time Gyneth saw her school as it actually was—a
privileged campus for a select few hundred girls from
exclusive white families throughout Southern Africa,
Zambia, Rhodesia, even some from as far north as
Kenya.

As Gyneth proudly showed Steve around, she realized how honored she had been to have attended such

an institution, to have been given such opportunities. Then she thought suddenly of the dramatic contrast between this cultured environment and the overcrowded Soweto schools. Carolyn's brilliance could have been so nurtured, so enhanced with even a small part of what Gyneth had taken for granted all these years.

She shivered. As the breeze shimmered through her thin dress, Steve took off his jacket and put it around her shoulders. He did not take his arm away, and slowly they walked together along the paths over the extensive property. Gyneth knew he was going to kiss her and she closed her eyes, not sure what to expect. Softly his lips met hers and then their pressure increased. All of a sudden, she felt his tongue tip entering her mouth. She froze. She had read about it, heard the other girls talk of it, but this had never happened to her. His tongue became more insistent and pushed more strongly into her mouth, and she tasted his juices. It had a rather pleasant taste, something very intimate, almost familiar in a way. She opened her mouth slightly and received him tentatively. Then she felt his hands moving slowly up from her waist, and she hoped desperately that he could not feel any bulges along the sheath of her dress. Gently and very slowly, he touched the sides of her breasts. Her first reaction was to push his hands away, and then she relaxed. It really felt so good, like a dream unfolding. Gyneth felt a sense of wild abandonment, her nipples became harder and she felt wet between her legs as she pressed closer to him. His breathing became heavier and his tongue bolder as his hands clasped her breasts firmly and started to move down her body.

Suddenly they heard the giggling of another couple and whispering as two people passed them by, and Gyneth realized that she had to stop, gather her thoughts, and look at this person whom she now saw in a completely different light from a few hours ago. She knew that she wanted him. In fact, had they been alone, she would have let herself float with the passion that was carrying her along, the most incredible sensations that she could ever remember feeling.

They straightened their clothes hardly looking at each other, and walked back to the hall. Their dancing was less exhibitionist, more subdued as they drew closer together, feeling each other's heat again.

Then it was time to go and regretfully, Steve's father was waiting for them in the circular driveway. The drive home was uneventful and Steve pecked her on the cheek chastely at her house, because even though his father looked away, Steve was very conscious of his presence. Too soon the dreamlike adventure was over.

Gyneth prayed that he would call, and she knew with certainty that there was a whole series of deep exciting feelings yet to be explored within her own body.

He called two agonizing days later. They went out to the movies, but since they had no transportation, their activities were dependent on his father or her chauffeur and they had little privacy. They parted frustrated, as Steve left for a family vacation at the Cape, from which he would not return for six weeks. Gyneth waited anxiously each day for the mail, and eventually a letter came, and a gentle courtship began, lasting until his return. She wrote funny, loving letters and he answered her with serious long ones.

In the meantime Gyneth began to diet. It seemed easy, her desire for food diminished. She applied the same kind of obsessive discipline to an exercise program as she had to her studies. She cut down on calories, puffed and sweated. Then it started to really come off. She began to see herself in the mirror for the first time. Initially, she was ashamed of what she saw but she made herself look. Then one day she saw someone with a figure that was quite acceptable. It didn't look like her, but it was. She continued on the program and soon she was fitting into the kinds of clothes she had envied on other women.

But something else started to happen and she didn't like it at all. People looked at her differently—especially men. In fact, they seemed to invade her body with their eyes. She had been invisible before, but now just walking down the street would cause men to whistle or stare. Instead of enjoying the attention, she felt uncomfortable, as if she had lost control of her privacy, of her right to walk around verbally unmolested.

She longed for Steve to return so that she could continue to explore what they had started together, but his family extended their vacation another two weeks and she had to be satisfied with infrequent letters.

But the truth was she was stunning. Even she could see it.

Her body was in perfect proportion, with high young breasts, long legs, a small frame, and a delicately boned face with startling green eyes.

Gyneth had reached the point she'd dreamed of for years. It was time to apply for medical school. She had no doubt that she would be accepted. Although her national matriculation results were not yet known, Gyneth was sure she had received honors in every subject, just the way she had throughout her school career. In addition, she knew that her father was chairman of the admissions committee, so her acceptance was assured.

Jacob, however, had other plans. He now saw Gyneth's attractive appearance, and for the first time felt confident that she would marry well. Jacob knew from his own experience that medical school, with its demanding schedule, would preempt any emotional commitments, and he was determined that his only child would not pass up her optimum time for finding a husband. He put off discussions about it until he couldn't bear watching her plan anymore for a future he had no intention of helping her fulfill.

"Gyneth, your mother and I have discussed this subject many times and I have come to a decision. I will not permit you to study medicine."

Jacob's words were like a missile that went straight to Gyneth's heart. She sat in the library chair in shock, unable to comprehend what her father was saying. "Why, why—you can't do that. It is my life—it is what I want!" she cried.

Jacob was adamant. "These are my reasons," he said firmly. "It is no life for a woman. In addition, no one will marry you if you are too smart or too accomplished in a man's profession. As a doctor, and even more as a surgeon, it will be very difficult for you to find someone who will be willing to put up with your hours and the total commitment that you have to give to the profession. I want you to have a happy marriage and children. As a woman you cannot have both a career as a surgeon and also a happy marriage."

"But you have both!" Gyneth cried.

"I am a man," Jacob said. "And it is different for men."

Her father did not understand. She had to become a surgeon. It was the only way she'd ensure that no one would ever laugh at her again. The world would be forced to respect her. If she could not have that, she had nothing, just a body that could not be relied upon. She had worked especially hard at math, science, and Latin so as to have the highest grades possible to guarantee her acceptance to medical school. Now it was all being taken away from her—Jacob didn't understand.

"I'll do it without you," she screamed.

"You will not. I am the chairman of the admissions committee. Your acceptance would have to be subject to a number of reviews. Even though I cannot vote I will recommend against your admission, Gyneth. And no other medical school in the country will take you if ours doesn't. This is best, believe me, I know what's right. You are too young to realize the implications of a bad decision at this stage of your life."

Gyneth looked at her father with hatred. She was powerless to go against his will, his reputation, his power. The odds were stacked against her.

"What am I supposed to do with my life?" she whispered.

"You can study Latin, do a bachelor of arts degree, become a teacher and have your holidays free. There are lots of things you can do, Gyneth." Jacob got up, his signal that the discussion was over.

He knew that she was going to see it his way soon enough. It was a foolish idea for women to work especially if they didn't need to. Soon she'd be dating, would get married, have children, and forget all about this silly dream of hers. He just couldn't see her studying frantically for the next twelve years, going through the abuse suffered by interns and trainee surgeons. He was doing the right thing for her.

In the midst of Gyneth's emotional turmoil, Steve returned. Although she had told him about her weight loss, she was unprepared for his reaction.

"Do you like the way I look?" Gyneth knew she looked wonderful, but in her heart she still felt fat and ugly.

"You look great, but . . . different. Not like the Gyneth I knew. It's hard to explain." Gyneth could see that Steve was shocked and unsure of himself.

"But don't you think I look better than before?"

Steve moved uncomfortably in his seat. "Yes, of course." He was awkward and couldn't stop looking at her.

Gyneth was acutely disappointed. She thought he'd love her new look.

They went to a movie. Gyneth elicited admiring stares from every man she passed and Steve became increasingly ill at ease. As they walked home, Gyneth decided to share with him her frustration with her father.

"He is being totally unreasonable. I'm so furious with him. How can I possibly go to medical school if he is going to oppose me? He has such power in that community, no one will give me the time of day." Gyneth's face was red with anger as she strode along forcefully, causing Steve to half jog in order to keep up.

"Your dad does have a point, you know. Some guys would be intimidated by your being a surgeon. It's not really a life for a woman."

Gyneth was incensed. She could not understand Steve's attitude. He had been so admiring, praising her intellect, impressed by her ambition. Then when she lost weight, it all changed for the worse. He seemed to be intimidated and resent the very things he had admired. The sweet memories of their magical night together faded and the relationship was over. Gyneth plummeted into an agony of despair, feeling out of control, floating, without goals for the first time in her life. She had always thought that being thin would resolve all the problems that could be created in a relationship. Now she was confused.

Estelle was desperate to help her daughter. She convinced her to go to Cape Town, to stay with friends and enjoy the coastal resort. It was there that Gyneth received news of her matriculation results.

"Darling, you got a first class, with distinction in four subjects. You were third in the whole country! We are so very proud of you!" Estelle's voice was excited and filled with emotion. Gyneth heard the news with mixed feelings. Initially she was thrilled. Then the bleakness of an undefined career choice filled her with gloom.

"Automatic acceptance for medical school," she muttered bitterly after hanging up. "That is, if you're not Jacob Amron's daughter."

Listless and disinterested, Gyneth sat morosely on the beach at Clifton, uncomfortably aware of the approving looks of the young men who gathered at Cape Town resorts.

One day as she sunbathed, a shadow fell over her body. She looked up to see who was obscuring the sun and saw a young man with wide shoulders and a broad smile. The man was blond and looked as if he spent every day on the beach. Gyneth was immediately attracted to him, and the familiar tingling feeling she had felt from being close to Steve came strongly back to her. This time, however, she felt reckless, so she sat up and looked at him slowly, sensuously. She wanted anonymity, not to tell him her name or to discover his, but just to touch and feel and explore his body in physical abandon.

All of this had gone through Gyneth's mind before he had said a word. She blushed deeply. He smiled at her and sat down.

"Hi," he said. "I've been watching you. You are very beautiful."

Her eyes opened wide in surprise. It was as if he were speaking about someone else.

"I am Dirk Van Zyl." He held out his hand. She took his firm grip and felt the strength of his fingers as she saw the muscles ripple in his arm. He throbbed with sensuality, and was definitely not Jewish. Gyneth knew that her parents would never approve. That made him even more exciting and she drew her legs up slowly leaning toward him, so that her full breasts brushed lightly against his arm.

The beach was too crowded for easy conversation so they went to sit on the small wall next to the sidewalk. Dirk was a Springbok swimmer who had represented South Africa at a number of international competitions. He was sophisticated, traveled quite extensively, and had the open, pleasant, and agreeable nature of most outstanding athletes. Gyneth found him to be delightful company and incredibly sexy.

She was equally fascinated by his heritage. He told her that he was from an Afrikaner family that could actually trace their heritage back to the beginnings of white South Africa. Gyneth asked him to elaborate. He looked at her to be sure that she was serious and not just teasing him, since, for all his jocularity, his family traditions and historical inheritance was a subject of great sensitivity and pride to him. He was not about to open himself to any kind of belittlement. Gyneth assured him of the sincerity of her interest, so his face became serious and he began to tell her the story of his family.

The Van Zyls descended from a Boer family of Afrikaners who had been early settlers in South Africa. He said, with some pride, that his family could even be traced back to the group of settlers that came on board ship with the Dutch East India Company in 1652 to the Cape and had established a settlement that would provide fresh provisions for the sailors who rounded the Cape and suffered from scurvy.

His great-great-grandfather had been one of the Afrikaners living in the Cape, who had packed all their possessions into ox wagons, the famous *ossewa,* and trekked in the Great Trek north of the Orange River and founded the Republic of the Transvaal. Although the British defeat of the independent republics of the Transvaal and the Orange Free State in the Anglo Boer war of 1902 brought all Afrikaners under British rule, he told a wide-eyed Gyneth, that the Van Zyls maintained their strong sense of nationalism, which continued until South Africa became a Republic in 1963. Gyneth listened, fascinated to actually meet someone who embodied the history she had learned about at school. The separation of peoples in South Africa was legally black from white, but socially English from Afrikaner. The hostilities that dated back to the various wars with the British had faded little and Gyneth, in her private all-girls school, with only English-speaking children and teachers, lived in a world distant from the Afrikaner people.

He saw her staring at him again and so he stopped and squeezed her hand. "I am boring you," he apologized.

"On the contrary," Gyneth said. "You fascinate me. To be honest, I have never met any Afrikaner quite like you. You have such an open manner and are so relaxed."

She decided to go the whole way and test him altogether. "You know, I am Jewish and quite obviously English speaking. My mother was born in England and my grandfather is a cockney from the East End of London. My father's parents were immigrants from Eastern Europe, Lithuania, where they escaped the pogroms of the early part of this century."

She waited for his reaction.

"Yes, I am familiar with such a heritage. I went to the University in Den Haag, The Hague, to study for a few years. I returned just a few months ago. I met a number of Jewish people who had a similar heritage and also many people from the United Kingdom and other countries, too. I am most admiring of what your people have done in Israel and the strong and brave stance they have made in the face of enormous odds."

Gyneth's mouth dropped open. This was a most unusual fellow. He was worldly and had a charm that took her breath away. He became more attractive every minute.

The air grew cooler and Gyneth realized that evening was approaching.

"I'll drive you back to your place. Let's go out for dinner tonight."

Gyneth agreed and as she changed her clothes while he waited in the car, she was breathless with anticipation. He was all wrong for her but he was definitely the most exciting person she had ever met.

They drove along the coast. Dirk put a tape in his car radio and the *Nutcracker Suite* flowed through the speakers. Gyneth closed her eyes and felt as if she were flying. He looked at her out of the corner of his eye and thought how he just wanted to tear off her clothes and take her there in the car. She opened her eyes and he looked ahead, not wanting her to see through his eyes what was in his mind.

Soon they came to a sandy road that turned off the main highway. He turned and they bumped along the road for a while.

"Where are we going?" she said.

"I want to take you to my favorite place," he said, covering her hand with his. "Close your eyes and I will tell you when we are there."

The car slid and jiggled along the road and then he turned sharply again and came to a stop. He told her to keep her eyes closed and he jumped out of the car, placed a rug on the grass and turned to bring her carefully out of the car. He pivoted her around, still with her eyes tightly shut, giggling with expectation, and faced her toward the mountains, cliffs, and the ocean.

Gyneth opened her eyes and gasped with pleasure. The golden sunset was reddening and blazing colors filled the sky. He saw her reaction, and took her in his arms.

Gyneth buried her face in Dirk's chest and felt his muscular arms and torso pressing against her. She felt a wild desire to throw all caution to the winds and indulge in the torrent of passion. As if sensing her need, he pressed himself closer to her and whispered, "It is so difficult to explain, but you have the most unbelievable effect on me, I just want to make love to you now and I can hardly be close to you without losing complete control of myself."

Unbelieving, he heard her say, "I know, I have the same feeling. I want you so much, please, make love to me."

He felt her mouth open under his as he ran his hands over her arms and lightly touched her breasts. She shuddered with pleasure and he could hardly contain himself. He pushed her gently back onto the blanket and slowly, deliciously, began to caress her body. For Gyneth it felt so right, even though she knew it was so wrong, that she refused to think about anything except the spasms of pleasure she felt from his closeness to her. She refused to think of all the rules that existed, that this was their first date, that he was Afrikaans and she could never marry him, that she was no longer going to be a virgin after this experience, that she could actually get pregnant, that he would probably not respect her afterward and would think that she was "easy." These thoughts flashed in and out of her mind, but the wild feelings his tongue was creating obliterated any sane thoughts or self-control.

She gave herself completely to the waves of passion

that made her so excited that she was begging him to go on, deeper, to devour her. She felt a sharp pain and then he pushed strongly into her body. She lifted her hips higher, moving round and up under him as he gasped and buried his body in hers. He started to shake at the same time as she did, and together they sobbed and cried out as the tides of orgasm overwhelmed them. They lay panting in each other's arms, dizzy and sated.

They lay there for some time, in the silence of the mountains, hearing the faint murmur of the sea, which their passion had blocked out.

Gyneth could hardly speak. She closed her eyes and buried her head in the soft area under his arm. He tasted so sweet to her, and his skin was so smooth, she could revel in his body forever. Dirk lay with his arm over his eyes and thought of how passionate Gyneth had been. He lifted himself on his elbow and looked down at her. He saw with dismay that there was blood on the inside of her legs.

"My God, Gyneth, you should have stopped me. You did not tell me that this was your first time. I would have stopped. You should have said something."

Gyneth looked at him. "Did you think that you were just one of many guys I had slept with?" she asked him cynically.

He flushed. "No, not at all, but I did not know that this was your first time. You seemed so sophisticated, I thought that you had been around."

"I am sophisticated, but I have not been around at all," Gyneth said. "I just matriculated from high school, for heavens sakes."

Dirk looked at her in horror. "Come on, you must be joking," he said in dismay.

"Well, I'm not. So does that make any difference to you?" Gyneth said sharply.

"Well, yes it does, actually. I have a sister who is your age, and that is really much too young to do what we are doing."

Gyneth looked at him closely. For all his sophistication he still lived by the rules. She shrugged her shoulders. He had given her what she had wanted from Steve. She felt no guilt, no regret. She had loved it, and in fact would love to do it again, and again and again. This made her feel like a woman, and she loved the way her body excited him, how he'd shuddered and could hardly control himself around her. She reveled in his hot body panting above her and his passion excited her as much as her own.

She snuggled closer to Dirk, feeling very grown up and in control. "Come on, don't be such a stickler for the rules. I am much more mature than most anyway. Let's do it again. Do you have something to, you know, use so that I won't get pregnant?"

He nodded sheepishly and pulled from his wallet a little packet of condoms. They made love again, and this time Gyneth was more adventurous, watching his reaction to her movements and doing things that he showed her gave him pleasure. They satiated each other again, then slept in the open air in each other's arms.

When they woke, the stars were high in the sky, so, slowly, with Tchaikovsky playing on the car stereo, they drove back. Gyneth slipped into the house.

She examined her face carefully in the mirror. She really did not look any different than she had as a virgin. She had half expected a "knowing" look in her eyes. But all she saw was a rather bleary-eyed girl, with burrs and pieces of grass in her hair. She laughed at herself and ran a bath, sinking low into the deep water of the long, spacious tub, running her fingers over her newly discovered body. The slight ache in her lower body was a pleasant reminder of the tumultuous feelings that she had enjoyed for the first time, and she felt a thrill of excitement at the new adventures that would lie ahead of her. For the first time her body became an instrument of pleasure instead of an object to despise.

# Chapter 13

Estelle knew the pain that Jacob had caused Gyneth. She could hear it in her voice as it dampened her daughter's reaction to the news of her matriculation success.

She missed Gyneth's presence. The house was very quiet, no phones or doorbells ringing, just the efficient functioning of the daily routine. Jacob was working hard, too hard. It was as if he was driven to accelerate his life, jamming more into one day than most people did in a week. And although she tried to ignore the tremendous tiredness she felt, there was a terrible ache in her lower abdomen that never went away. Jacob came home late every night, dropped exhausted into bed, and there was little time to discuss her malaise or anything else with him.

One Friday evening they enjoyed a Shabbat dinner alone. Estelle waited until dessert, then decided to address the subject that had troubled her greatly for the past few weeks.

She looked at her husband trying to project a strength she did not feel. "Jacob, we've made a mistake with Gyneth. There has been only one thing that she had wanted in her life—to become exactly like you. You have taken that dream away from her against my wishes. It has broken her spirit. Nothing that can face her in medical school can equal the damage this is causing her. Please reconsider." Estelle took his hand in hers. "It's not too late. She's obtained excellent matriculation results and would make an outstanding surgeon. Think of how proud you will be of her. It is a new generation, my dear, not all men are turned away by a strong competent woman. You cannot still treat her like a child. Let her make some of her own mistakes, find herself and reach her dreams." Estelle thought wistfully of her own hopes for a stage career, dashed so many years before.

Jacob rejected what Estelle said at first. Then he thought of Gyneth's sad face, her erratic behavior. He nodded, not able to speak. He loved his child so much, she was truly the light of his life, but he felt so strongly that what he was doing was for her own good. Could he be wrong? He shook his head and dismissed the idea.

Jacob put his arm lightly around his wife's waist as they left the dining room. He felt her ribs beneath his fingers. When had she become so thin?

"Darling, have you been eating properly?" He stood back and looked at her critically, and then he noticed that she was limping slightly. "Estelle, what is the matter? You seem to be limping."

"I thought it would go away. I have this pain in my lower stomach and groin and it's been there for a couple of weeks. I went to the internist for my regular checkup and he says I'm imagining it, it's in my head. But, Jacob, I'm really hurting and I'm so tired all the time."

Jacob had her lie on the bed as he examined her legs and lower abdomen. She jumped in pain when he palpated her groin. He muttered worriedly, "This could be a kidney problem. Look, Estelle, we have to have this examined. I know that it is not in your head. Monday, we will go to a specialist. I am sure it is something simple and we will have you on antibiotics and better in no time."

But Jacob was worried. Estelle was so active. She rode horses, played tennis, swam, danced—there was no way she was imagining the pain and there had to be something there. He would get to the bottom of it.

Estelle snuggled next to him in bed. It was so wonderful to feel his concern for her. It would all be fine, Jacob would make it all fine again.

The X-ray test was uncomfortable as they injected dye into Estelle's body, but she closed her eyes and thought of Gyneth in her new dress, so proud and beautiful and that gave her the strength to ignore what was being done to her. Finally it was over and the radiologist said that he would let them know the result in the morning. Estelle sat in the back of the car as Austen drove her home. She tried to put it all out of her mind. She had lots to do. They were expecting company for dinner so by the time Jacob came home having done his rounds at the hospital, Estelle was busy, and though limping badly, she was moving around the house, arranging the final touches for the dinner party that was to begin at seven thirty.

The phone rang. Jacob answered. Estelle was in the kitchen tasting the vichyssoise.

Jacob went white. He slammed down the phone and grabbed the intercom. "Estelle," he called frantically. "Sit down—go to the kitchen chair and sit down, then don't move, I'm coming." He bolted down the stairs, his heart pounding painfully and burst into the kitchen to find Estelle standing at the stove, calmly stirring the soup. "Okay, what's the joke?" she said and then as she turned and saw his face she became very afraid. He pulled the kitchen chair over to her and gently made her sit down.

"They saw it on the corner of the IVP X-ray. There is a huge mass at the head of your femur, that is your thigh bone, and the slightest movement could cause a pathological fracture so it is vital that you not move at all."

"But the dinner party, all the people and I have to get dressed!" Estelle stammered, the realization of what this news meant still not registering in her mind.

Jacob looked at her. "My darling," he said quietly, "there will be no dinner party tonight. You are going to be in the hospital for a little while. This tumor has to come out. We don't know what it is, but it cannot stay there." He left her speechless as slowly the awful truth of her condition began to sink in. Jacob had said "tumor."

"Jacob," she whispered, "does that mean cancer?"

A dark shadow swept over his face as his lips trembled.

"Let's pray for the best. It may not be malignant. We will only know when we take it out and do an analysis of it."

The next hour was a rush of confused activity. The ambulance arrived, Estelle was lifted gently into it, and then it sped off to the private hospital where Jacob did most of his surgery. Soon Estelle was in the stark hospital room that was to become her home for many months. She was lifted and moved with the delicate care given to Dresden china.

"Jacob, please, you must call Gyneth. She'll be so afraid if she calls the house and finds out the news," Estelle called out to him as she was wheeled along on the guerney.

"Yes, yes, of course I will. But it has to wait, my

dear. There are more important things to be done now. I'll call her, I promise."

The constant assaults on Estelle's body began. First there were blood tests, then examinations by an orthopedic surgeon, hastily summoned from his dinner by Jacob. Then two nurses started to shave her body, and while she blushed with discomfort they tried to joke with her and help her to relax. She caught only glimpses of Jacob as he bustled about, organizing special nurses, blood, assistant surgeons, and a whole series of details she was unaware of. In fact, all she wanted was for him to come into her room and hold her, but she could hardly speak with him as he flew in and out, popping his head in the room to give her and anyone in there with her encouragement.

Then, too soon, it seemed, she was being given an injection and muggy sleep overcame her and the few remaining hours of the night slipped by. Morning dawned and Estelle was wheeled into the operating room looking desperately around in her drugged state for Jacob. He appeared magically, gowned and capped in his surgical greens to hold her hand for the last few minutes of consciousness. Her last thoughts were that this is what it must feel like to die as she looked up into her husband's eyes and slipped away.

Gyneth lay in Dirk's arms. They had checked into a motel and made love until they were exhausted. Finally he took her back to the apartment. The lights were still on even though it was 4:00 A.M. He drove away as Gyneth opened the door. Pinned on the telephone was a message.

"Call home immediately no matter what time it is."

Her heart racing with fear, Gyneth called. Anna answered.

"Gyneth, your mother is very sick in the hospital

having an operation. Dr. Amron said please to come home on the next flight."

White-faced, hardly able to comprehend the swiftness of events, Gyneth packed, went to the airport and took the first plane home. Only yesterday she had been reveling in the fact that she was back in control of her life, experimenting in a new world of sensuality. Now everything was spinning out of control, and she felt a moment of self-hatred for having been so self-involved while her mother was suffering silently in pain. She arrived in Johannesburg, and took a taxi to the hospital, her heart heavy with fear.

The pain was excruciating. It consumed Estelle and tore her body apart. She felt as if she had heavy weights on her chest and that her lips were glued together as she tried to speak, to tell the blurred figures who seemed to be rushing by her constantly that she was in agony. But all that came out was a croak, and it seemed like hours before a white-figured nurse loomed above her. "Pain, pain," she tried to say but no words came out. She felt desperate panic that maybe she was paralyzed and would never talk again when she saw Jacob above her and she tried to tell him that her body was exploding with pain. He held her hand saying, "Estelle, you are going to be fine. We will give you something for the pain now." Then the blessed relief came as she slipped away again.

The next time she awoke the pain was just as bad but this time she could feel it on both sides of her body. She opened her eyes fully and through the blur of agony she saw that she was in a recovery room with a number of other patients. She croaked again and this time the nurse came over. "Ah yes, Mrs. Amron, you are going to be fine," she said. Estelle felt a rush of frustration through her pain. She didn't care about being "fine." She was in agony now, and why did she have pain on both sides of her body? The tumor was only on one side. She tried to describe what she felt and ask for an explanation, but it was no good since she did not seem able to express herself.

She faded in and out of consciousness, feeling frustration in her agony. Eventually, after what seemed like eons, Jacob was there.

She tried to speak. "Pain ... both ... Why?" He nodded, knowing immediately what she was trying to say.

"We had to take take the healthy bone from your other hip to use in the open spot left when we removed the tumor and the bone that surrounded it. You have had two operative scars, and that is why it hurts on both sides."

She closed her eyes, nodding her thanks to him. Now at least she could pace herself in her pain. The hours passed slowly. The next time she opened her eyes, Gyneth was there.

"Darling, I'm so sorry this spoiled your vacation. I told Dad to tell you not to come home."

"Mum, I wouldn't have stayed. How could I, knowing that you were in the hospital. I'm sorry you have to suffer like this. You must have been in pain for so long."

"Not really, dear. It's all such a shock, so sudden." Estelle struggled to form the words.

Then she remembered. "I haven't seen you since your results. Dad and I are so proud of you, darling, so very proud ..."

Estelle drifted back to sleep. Gyneth leaned down to touch her mother's smooth forehead with her lips in order to hide her tears.

Slowly the days dragged by as Estelle lived from one four-hour interval between her pain shots to another. She was determined as soon as possible to wean

herself off the medication, and every day she tried to
stretch the time to four and a half hours, then five
hours until finally she was able to have pain medication only at night. She was happy to see Gyneth but
unable to converse for more than a few moments. On
one occasion, however, she held Gyneth's hand tightly.

"Darling, please be patient with your father. Try to
understand his point of view. Give him time."

"Mum, will you please stop worrying about this? It
is all over, forgiven, unimportant. The only important
issue is helping you to regain your health."

The rehabilitation started almost immediately. Two
physical therapists came into her room every day to
show her how to learn to walk again and to manipulate
crutches that rubbed and chafed under her arms and
caused her to have welts on her hands.

Estelle was painfully thin. Jacob thought up a whole
series of tempting morsels to feed her, smoked salmon,
caviar, pâté—but she only nibbled at it. Gyneth and
Jacob shared the evening meal with her almost every
night, and slowly she pulled herself into convalescence. Two months later, it was time to go home.
Estelle bolstered herself with the knowledge that the
cancer had been removed and her ordeal was almost
over.

Throughout her mother's hospital stay, Gyneth
longed to speak to Carolyn, but all she could think of
was that Carolyn would be accepted into medical
school while she was studying art and language. Every
time she thought of visiting her, she boiled with anger
at her father, and found a reason not to go. She was
shamed by her weakness, Jacob's power, the irony that
Carolyn had none of her privileges yet she could
achieve what Gyneth could not.

Gyneth turned to the only reliable friend she had
ever found, food. She filled herself with donuts, cream

cakes, chocolates. By the time Estelle returned home from the hospital, Gyneth had regained almost all the weight she'd lost. Jacob found her eating mournfully alone in the kitchen on occasion. She guiltily hid the food as he entered. Since he knew that it was comfort for her, he said nothing. He choked on the words he felt he should say, words of love, acceptance, doubt as to the validity of the decision he'd made about her life. He decided to address the problem and talk to Gyneth once Estelle was healthy, once life returned to normal.

Now Jacob worked more obsessively than before.

A month or two after Estelle's surgery, her team of orthopedic specialists called a conference.

"Jacob, we are pleased with Estelle's results. But we are concerned about the prognosis for this condition. This may be difficult for you to hear. If the tumor returns, and you know the likelihood is high although she is unaware of that eventuality, Estelle has no more bone left to use. The upper third of the femur is all but destroyed. The only solution left will be a hemipelvectomy—a hindquarter amputation. It will be the only option left for her."

Jacob closed his mind to the words but they rang loudly in his ears—a hindquarter amputation—it sounded like something one did to an animal, not to his small and beautiful wife. He shuddered as he thought of how it would look—her body severed from the waist downward on the right side—an empty vacuum where life had once been. He would not accept it—he refused to consider it.

Jacob got up slowly from the chair, thanked the table full of somber-faced surgeons and left the room. He would put the full resources of his energy and intelligence toward finding a solution for his wife, before the tumor returned.

Jacob did not share with Estelle the news that the tumor might recur nor the option that her surgeons had posed to him. He knew that he could not, would not, see that happen.

Estelle's convalescence was slow. Gyneth listlessly completed her second year of college and still Jacob put off discussing her future, rationalizing that to open the subject at that point would be to add stress and tension to an already difficult situation.

One night Gyneth saw Jacob as he returned late from the hospital. His color was strange—he looked blue and she felt a pang of fear.

"Daddy, you look awful. What is the matter?"

"I have a little angina," Jacob said, "nothing to worry about. I'll just take a couple of Angeset tablets and I'll be fine."

But he wasn't and the next morning Gyneth found him dozing in the armchair where she had left him the night before.

"Daddy, why did you stay here all night? My God, you look terrible! Surely you are not going to work that way."

"I have the flu," said Jacob. "Anyway, I have seven surgeries today. These people are all in the hospital waiting for me to help them, I cannot stay home."

Estelle's worried face told Gyneth that she did not accept Jacob's story either.

He operated all day. When he returned he could hardly walk. Estelle was hysterical. "What have you done!" she cried. "You knew you weren't well yet you operated all day." Jacob fell into bed and whispered hoarsely that she should call his internist.

Gyneth sat by her father's bed, and Estelle stood at the door, leaning on her crutches, waiting anxiously for Alan Salmon.

"Daddy, why are you so stubborn," Gyneth whispered softly, almost to herself. Her father's face was contorted with pain and he did not hear her. Soon she heard the footsteps coming up the stairs, two at a time. She was gently pushed aside and behind the closed door as Jacob's good friend and colleague began to examine him. Estelle lay on her bed, Gyneth sitting beside her, as they waited, together.

It was a major heart attack.

Jacob ordered his doctors not to tell the world how sick he was. "My practice is dependent entirely on referrals. If people think I am sick, it will all disappear." Estelle tried to plead with Jacob to go into the hospital.

"You know that if I do that, the whole world will know. No, we'll keep this very quiet. I'll recover at home; the prescription is the same—total bed rest. Right, Alan?"

Jacob winked at his friend, trying to make Estelle relax.

"You had better stop smoking and lose some weight, Jacob, this is no joking matter."

Gyneth felt the anxiety in the house. Jacob's operating room nurse Jenette Malcom moved into the guest suite and the household took up a nervous routine, all hoping and praying for Jacob's recovery.

By the third week of Jacob's enforced bed rest, he was convinced that soon he would be back at work again. In fact he was starting to do some paper work on medical matters in the mornings. He was chairman of the Federal Council of the Association of Surgeons and Medical Practitioners and he was always deeply embroiled in various negotiations with the government, their reimbursement agencies, and the members of the medical profession.

Jacob had decided to tell Gyneth that she was free to pursue her dream, even though it was not what he would wish for her. He would do it on Friday night, at their Shabbat dinner. He told Estelle what he was planning to do. Her thin face lit up. It had taken two years longer than she had hoped, but finally Jacob had seen reason. She did her physical therapy with renewed vigor, relieved to see Jacob's physical progress, and thrilled that her daughter would eventually find happiness.

That night Jacob awoke, shaking, his heart pounding with fear. Since his coronary, he'd had difficulty sleeping through the night. He left the bedroom quietly, not wanting to disturb Estelle, in order to have a cigarette in his private dressing room. He stopped momentarily at the small hall desk to look for his lighter and saw the black velvet case that housed his medals. Jacob didn't know how he'd done it during those war years. It was as if he'd been another person. He'd risked it all, Estelle, his practice, his family. He didn't even think of consequences, he'd just acted. He drifted back into the past, to the hospital ship in the Mediterranean. He'd been involved in every invasion from Dunkirk to Normandy, had performed thousands of surgeries and worked days without sleep. Then one terrifying night, tortured by the screams of dying men in the waters burning with oil around his ship, he'd requisitioned a lifeboat, and dragged man after man from certain death to safety. He'd thought nothing of his hands, damaged by the treacherous inferno, nor his personal safety.

Jacob looked at the fine silk Persian carpet hanging on the wall, one of twelve that were also the product of the war years. He'd purchased them one day from the Governor General of Alexandria when he heard that the man was selling all his goods and moving back to England. Jacob had taken three jeeps and an equal number of sailors, bought the rugs and loaded them onto his ship surrounded by life jackets. They, too, had gone through the invasions and had been the nucleus of the dream house he now lived in.

Jacob lit another forbidden cigarette. It was 2:00 A.M. Normally in four short hours he would be up again preparing for another day in surgery. He inhaled deeply, enjoying the wisps of smoke that lifted aromatically from his fingers, the elegant cigarette case that Estelle's parents had given him, the gold lighter from Dunhill's. He loved to smoke, eat rich foods, and worked long hours, leaving little time for exercise. It was unhealthy but he did enjoy his life. He took his cigarette case and lighter with him and went out to the upstairs hall, to make himself a cup of the strong coffee he always loved. There was the usual coffee tray with cake laid neatly on the upstairs living-room table. He waited for the pot to percolate.

After a few minutes, even though he had been ordered to stay in bed, he walked quietly downstairs and stopped at the door of each room as he looked proudly at the mansion of his dreams and the accumulation of a lifetime. The antique woods of the French and English period furniture mixed richly with the hand-carved pieces of furniture that his father-in-law's craftsmen had made for him and Estelle, a new piece for each of twenty-eight anniversaries. He saw the artwork, a few priceless pieces, some small delicate Rembrandt etchings, and Canaletto paintings in a grouping of four.

Then he paused by the tall French doors and threw them open to the tiled patio that ran the length of the house. The cool night air whispered into the hall as he moved outside to overlook his land. The three levels of waterfalls filled the air with the sound of trickling water. The waterfall had been constructed to flow under artfully designed caves and lily pools disappearing underground only to appear magically and start the cycle all over again at the top of the hill on which the house stood so proudly. He heard the horses whinny softly in the distance as they sniffed his scent in the cool night air. He walked past the olympic-size swimming pool and dressing rooms, the built-in barbecue, playroom, downstairs to the special kitchens for use outdoors, through the herb garden, the format rose garden and toward the summer house with its thatched roof, built by Andrew as his first task when he came to work for the Amrons nineteen years ago. Finally past the paddock, he turned and looked up at the massive structure that belonged to him—his castle, his palace. He breathed a sigh of contentment. He had achieved what he had set out to do, life was indeed good.

He felt the familiar constriction in his chest and walked back to the house, becoming more and more breathless all the time. He staggered up the stairs, grateful that no one was around to see him in his weakness and grasped his pillbox on the table of the upstairs living room. As he slipped two small tablets under his tongue he sat down heavily on the sofa waiting for the pressure to cease. It did, finally, but it took longer than ever before. He turned off the coffee, deciding not to have a cup after all, seeing that it was only a few hours before his day would begin again. He resolved to spend the entire day in bed. He felt frustrated and on edge.

Jacob snuffed out his last cigarette and looked at the time. He had reminisced most of the night away. He started to get up, but felt disoriented. He could not concentrate and his head hurt. Then he felt a sharp pain in his chest and his vision reddened, clouding over, and Jacob realized that he was going to die.

It's too soon, he thought as he saw his parents waiting for him with outstretched arms. I have to tell Gyneth she can go to medical school . . . The long tunnel was rushing by him, filled with light, people. Such a pity, were his last thoughts, I had so little time.

* * *

Gyneth got up at 7:00 A.M. She had an early class that morning. She opened her eyes and felt immediately depressed. She dug around in her sidetable drawer for the rest of the slab of chocolate she had half finished the night before. The sweetness filled her mouth and she felt a little better. She pulled on her robe, opened her door and started down the hallway to the bathroom when she saw that all the lights were still on in the upstairs sitting area. Irritated, she detoured to turn them off before starting with her morning routine.

It was a sight that would stay with her for the rest of her life. Jacob's mouth was half open, slacked and to the side. There was blood in a trickle out of his left ear puddling into a dark stain on the sofa. His legs were splayed open and his pajamas, normally immaculate, twisted and soiled. His eyes were wide open, glassy, lifeless.

Gyneth threw herself face forward against the wall of the landing, bashing her fists against the floor sobbing, "*No,* please, God, no, please, don't let this happen, please, God, *no!*"

Her screams brought Estelle, struggling to move quickly on her crutches, and her father's nurse, who immediately pulled Jacob flat and started pumping his chest as blood spurted out of his nose and ears. Estelle collapsed against the wall as Gyneth continued to sob and beat her face against the floor.

She heard her mother moaning. "It's no good, he's gone, it's no good, let him be." Gyneth's face and hands were bruised and battered as she plead for life, for time, for a reprieve.

But her father was dead and in one short second, the whole world had changed for Gyneth and would never be the same again. She crawled into the corner of the passage as she felt Estelle's hands on her head and they both sobbed together in agony over what could have been.

# Chapter 14

Gyneth stood at the graveside next to Estelle, her shock, disbelief and grief mirrored on the faces of the people filling the cemetery.

As Gyneth had watched the men carry the stretcher with a sheet over its motionless occupant laboriously down the stairs of her home, she tried to think of how her father had looked alive, vibrant, happy. But all she could see in her mind was the sight of him lying in disarray, bloody and uncontrolled. No matter how she tried, Gyneth could not rid herself of that vision. People spoke comfortingly to her, but she was unable to hear them or respond. She just replayed the vision again and again.

The funeral was immense. Estelle, a small, slight figure, stood struggling to balance on her crutches while acknowledging the embraces of weeping friends. Gyneth shuffled from one foot to another, as if to make the whole scene move faster, away into the past. She shrank from people who reached out to hold her, to pour their grief into hers, already overflowing.

Estelle kept whispering, feeling her daughter's horror, "Remember him as he was, my darling, not as he died."

Now Gyneth stood close to her mother, placing an

arm around her as she swayed slightly, then stood erect again, determined to be composed and dignified as she knew her father would have wanted.

Armindo, David, Anna, Andrew, and Austen marched solemnly in the funeral procession, given the honor of being pallbearers along with the rest of the family. They were shocked and frightened, insecure about their future. After more than twenty years with the Amron family, this was the only real home they had known.

Thousands moved slowly by, many of them strangers whose lives Jacob had touched, now present to show their last respects to a great man. The President of South Africa sent an emissary, the newspapers were full of Jacob's life accomplishments. They came from all walks of life, clasped Estelle and Gyneth's hands telling them of how Jacob had helped them. Entire families whose names were unfamiliar to Estelle told how Jacob had supported them, given them free medical care for years, made loans to them, which he later refused to collect.

There were doctors by the hundreds, all ages and specialties; students who told Gyneth of how her father had befriended and guided them through medical school and personal difficulties; how he always found the time to listen intently and offer solid advice. There were young doctors whom he had trained and to whom he had given assistance as they threaded their way through the politics of the medical community— professors and lecturers with whom he had taught, and finally the members of the Jewish community—the chief rabbi of South Africa whose operation was among the seven Jacob had heroically performed on his last day of work, the people from the Jewish Old Age Home and the orphanage to whom he had donated his services for thirty years.

The procession moved on as Estelle and Gyneth saw reflected in the faces of those who passed before them the incredible legacy of the man they now realized they'd hardly known at all.

The weeks that followed were full of decisions for Estelle. Gyneth felt isolated and terribly alone. "Mum, you aren't going to sell the house, are you?" She knew Estelle wanted to sell her beloved home. Gyneth clung to its familiarity and her feeling that any moment she'd hear her father's rapid footsteps coming up the stairs to her room.

Estelle nodded. "It is so big, Gyneth, and the stairs are difficult for me to handle."

"But it's all we have left!"

"We have a lifetime of memories." Estelle's eyes filled with tears, now always close to the surface. Gyneth turned away from her mother. Her own pain was hard enough to deal with.

There was only one person who could understand her grief, knew her father and how she felt about him. But first she had to convince Austen to accompany her to Soweto.

"Please, Austen, it will be quite safe. We know exactly where to find Carolyn, and we'll be out of there long before dark."

"Miss Gyneth, things are very bad in Soweto now," Austen said, but Gyneth was persistent. It had been a year since they had talked and her father's death had thrown her whole life into a different perspective.

Carolyn, however, was nowhere to be found. Austen drove slowly, trying to avoid the largest potholes, stopping for a few moments at the medical library, then the nursery school, and finally Alena's house. Gyneth knocked on the door as children crowded around the Amron car giggling at Austen's wagging finger and admonitions. Groups of teenagers stood sullenly nearby and Gyneth knew she had limited time before Austen would insist on taking her home.

"Yes?" Alena opened the door a crack.

"Alena? I am Gyneth Amron, Carolyn's friend."

Alena's eyes widened in surprise. "Come in, Miss Gyneth, what are you doing here?"

Gyneth sat gingerly on the edge of a chair.

"What time do you expect Carolyn home?"

Alena lowered her eyes to hide her knowledge. "Carolyn disappeared not long after your visit. I don't know where she is." She glanced up again and now her face was devoid of expression.

"Did she start medical school?"

"Medical school?" Alena looked puzzled. "She never even finished her last year at high school. She just left one morning and never came back."

Gyneth felt a small sense of relief, then shame at her reaction, and finally concern. Something very serious must have happened to prevent Carolyn from reaching her goal.

"Please, Alena, my father has died. I need to find Carolyn, it really is urgent."

Alena felt some pity for the large, unhappy young woman. She had heard of Jacob Amron's death and knew that it meant the end of many years of financial support.

"I'll tell you, but only because your father paid for Carolyn's upkeep all these years, and obviously had an interest in her welfare." Gyneth tried not to show her surprise, then anger that Jacob had never mentioned this ongoing communication.

Alena lowered her voice. "She left the country. They were all supposed to leave, but some were caught. She left on her own. They thought I didn't know, but I knew all the time. She never arrived at the camps, instead she went somewhere else." Alena disappeared for a moment, then came back with an old newspaper clipping. The headlines imprinted themselves on Gyneth's mind—SELF-EXILED SOUTH AFRICANS FREQUENT BAR IN KNIGHTSBRIDGE, ENGLAND, she read. "A small bar in Knightsbridge has become the watering hole for a group of former South Africans. They join there to sing old songs and share tales of their homeland, long since left behind." The article went on, obviously watered down by the South African censors, but the meaning was clear. Gyneth's eyes fixed on the startled face of a young woman. It was Carolyn.

Alena's anxious voice pulled her back to the present.

"You must go. This is no place for white people."

In the car on the way back home, Gyneth realized Carolyn must have known she was leaving when they'd met in the library. Even during that moment of closeness, her friend had hidden her secret.

Gyneth entered the house and saw the light on in her father's study. For a brief moment, it seemed as if life were normal again. She pushed the door open.

Estelle sat in her usual place. Gyneth glanced at her father's empty leather chair, then sank into it, feeling the agony of his loss.

Estelle's voice was soft and trembled slightly.

"Gyneth, I'm so glad you're home." Her lips quivered as she struggled to stay calm and composed.

"My darling, I am sad to tell you that I have the same pain again, the one I had before the operation. I met with the surgeon today and he says I must have another procedure. He wants me to go to England to a surgeon who specializes in this kind of tumor."

Gyneth felt faint with fear. Was her mother going to die, too?

"When do we have to go?"

"As soon as possible, maybe in two or three days."

"Two days?" Gyneth was reeling with shock. It seemed as if nothing was stable anymore.

"The surgeon remembers Dad from the Royal College of Surgeons, they trained together in England. He'll take special care of us. There is lots to be done before we leave."

Gyneth tried to be encouraging but the words sounded hollow.

"Mum, you know there is nothing more important in the world to me than you. We'll do it together, you'll be fine."

Estelle pulled herself up onto her crutches and turned away from her daughter in order to hide her despair. The surgeon had refused to describe the operation, saying only that it was more extensive than the first one, and beyond his capabilities.

The next few days were frantic as Estelle, without Gyneth's knowledge, arranged a variety of matters to do with Jacob's estate, including her own will, leaving the travel plans to Gyneth. Estelle had a terrible sense of foreboding about the upcoming surgery and ached with the unfamiliarity of having to deal with the doctors on her own without Jacob's reassuring input and presence. She also knew deep in her heart that they were not being entirely honest. That concern would have to wait until she met Dr. John Charnley, who was to be her surgeon. Then she'd insist on total truthfullness.

After the long plane ride, Gyneth and Estelle checked into the hotel in Manchester and rented a car for the long drive to Wigan. There, after Dr. Charnley examined Estelle, Gyneth joined her in the consultation room for his conclusions.

"I believe that we have a good solution that will enable us to avoid the hemipelvectomy option."

"Hemipelvectomy . . . ?" Estelle grasped Gyneth's hand.

"Yes. I thought the operation was described to you."

Estelle shook her head.

"My dear, I am so sorry." Dr. Charnley took Estelle's hand. "The good news is that I believe that a new surgery, which I've been perfecting, will be a good substitute for the hemipelvectomy. It is a total hip replacement and I have scheduled it for one week from today. We have to make a prosthesis for you in the meantime."

Estelle listened as he drew the planned surgery on a piece of paper, much as Jacob had described to her the former operation. She felt numb with fear. Gyneth sat quietly beside her mother.

Dr. Charnley accompanied Estelle into the hospital leaving Gyneth in the waiting room of the Center for Hip Surgery.

The next week dragged by. The days were bitterly cold and the snow was thick on the ground. Estelle lay in the large hospital bed, pale and sad, submitting patiently to myriads of tests and examinations.

One day as a group of medical students entered her mother's room, Gyneth looked up briefly from her magazine and her eyes widened in shock.

"Carolyn?" The slight figure in a white coat stood motionless.

"Gyneth? Mrs. Amron?" Carolyn could hardly believe it.

"Carolyn?" Gyneth gasped. "Is it really Carolyn?" The students shuffled in as the surgeon began to describe Estelle's case.

Carolyn tried to keep her composure but the shock of seeing her old friend and Estelle was enormous. She tried to appear attentive to the surgeon's words but during the question-and-answer session she could hardly concentrate. Then, thankfully, the group moved on and she remained in the room for a few moments.

"There is so much to tell. I must go with them to the next patient, but I will be back as soon as I can. This is incredible . . . I must go." Carolyn slipped out of the room.

"I heard she was in London, Alena told me," Gyneth said by way of explanation for her mother who seemed to be disoriented and confused by Carolyn's sudden appearance. Estelle squeezed her daughter's hand. She was in too much pain to deal with the situation. She closed her eyes and let the medication overcome her thoughts.

Carolyn's heart was thumping as she went through the motions of ward rounds, longing for it to end so that she could see Gyneth again.

Estelle's case had been an interesting one and she had read up on the condition when she saw it listed on the diagnoses of ward patients that day without even glancing at the patient's name. This was her first experience in a private hospital and she was eagerly absorbing everything about her. The initial semester of medical school had been exhilarating and demanding. The environment was far less forgiving than her high school. Carolyn was the only woman and one of two blacks in the medical school class. She had struggled to cope with the immense amount of new information, unfamiliar faces to recognize, and the fact that she was considered an oddity in the group. She drew on her inner strength to ignore the negative remarks and lack of warmth on the part of her classmates, reminding herself that she was qualified to be a student and replenishing her self-esteem every evening as Ruth welcomed her home with a large hug and a laden table.

Nevertheless, Carolyn's energy was drained by the

demands of her new life and she collapsed into bed late in the night after hours of reading, instantly asleep.

In that first year of medical school, Carolyn had started observing as many operations as she could. An area in which she was particularly interested was orthopedics. An opportunity arose for a London medical school student to spend the winter break with Dr. Charnley in order to assist with some research he was doing. Carolyn grabbed the offer as soon as it was posted. It involved seeing another part of England and since Carolyn had never been out of London, it was very appealing. In addition, she would be working with a surgeon who was becoming a star in his field. Ruth encouraged her to go. Travel expenses were paid as well as board in the doctors' residence at the Center for Hip Surgery. Her fellow students assured her that the position would look good on her résumé when she applied for an internship later. She could never have imagined seeing Gyneth and Estelle in that hospital.

Gyneth was filled with a variety of emotions. Carolyn looked so composed and clinical in her white coat. Gyneth felt old and sad. Her life had collapsed in the past year whereas from the looks of her friend, she had found her dream.

Carolyn returned an hour later, entering the room hesitantly.

"It's been so long, Gyneth." The time was not right for Gyneth to pour out her feelings so she just nodded and squeezed Carolyn's arm. They both turned to Estelle.

"Mrs. Amron, you are in very good hands. Dr. Charnley is the best in the world at total hip replacements. He is the only one to do them in a special operating room and the results are spectacular." Despite her drowsiness, Estelle was impressed by the young woman's composure. Carolyn had a lilting English ac-

cent, with overtones of South Africa. Her strong gaze
was the same, but that was all.

"It is very good to see you, and I know Gyneth is
thrilled to have you here." Estelle winced in pain.

"Is it time for your pain medication yet?" Carolyn
asked politely, seeing the distress on her face.

Just as she spoke, the nurse entered with a syringe.

The young women left the room and found a se-
cluded sitting area.

"Gyneth, is your father operating with Dr. Charnley?
I looked for him in there and could not see him."

The tears flowed down Gyneth's face. Carolyn took
her hands.

"Tell me. What is it?"

"He's gone . . . he's gone, Carolyn."

"Gone . . . ?"

"Just a few months ago. From a coronary; I went to
find you in Soweto. Alena said you'd left South Africa. I need you, Carolyn, I'm so lonely, desperate. He
refused to let me go to medical school, then he died
and now I'm afraid Mum will die, too, she's so frail
and the cancer . . ." Gyneth sobbed silently while
Carolyn held her close, feeling her grief as her own.

That night and for the days thereafter, the two
friends had dinner together in the hospital cafeteria.
They covered the years that had passed and Gyneth listened in awe to Carolyn's narrow escape from Soweto,
her meeting with Joe and passage through the dark to
the ship that carried her to Southhampton and her life
in London. Carolyn nodded understandingly as Gyneth
haltingly described the horror of finding her father's
body, and the frustrations of her thwarted career plans.

All through Estelle's operation and convalescence,
Carolyn was there, consoling, encouraging, caring.

Finally Gyneth began to feel as if there were a future. Estelle was regaining her strength daily and her

positive spirits and determination to become independent again were an inspiration. In addition, observing the change in Carolyn gradually brought Gyneth to the realization that returning to her life in Johannesburg would forever fill her with pain. Maybe leaving South Africa and the past would be her solution, too.

Finally, she sat with Carolyn at the window of the hospital physical therapy department waiting for Estelle to complete her treatment. Carolyn spent every free moment she had with Gyneth, and now they were sharing a brief lunch.

"I don't want to live in London, it's too cold and wet. My parents have friends who live in Los Angeles. They say California is warm, hospitable. And it's the home of the movie industry. Maybe I should go there. What do you think?"

Carolyn smiled at Gyneth, pleased to see a spark of enthusiasm in her eyes. "When we were young girls, you always wanted to be in the movies. Maybe this is your chance!"

Gyneth felt a twinge of excitement. Perhaps she would act, sing, even play the piano to make a living. She had talent, at least everyone had always said so. She had some savings, enough to get by for a while.

"Do you think I could do it?" Gyneth looked anxiously at Carolyn.

"You are the most talented person I know. You can do anything you set your mind to, even medical school if that's what you want."

"I've seen enough of hospitals and doctors to last me the rest of my life," Gyneth said emphatically. They both laughed. Gyneth held her tightly. Carolyn had been everything she could have hoped for in a friend.

Their parting was painful. Both Estelle and Gyneth hugged Carolyn, promising to write often, and waving until they could see her no more as they left in the small car for the airport.

A week later, in Johannesburg, Gyneth and Estelle sat at the dining-room table, laid with silver, china, and linen as Armindo served the dinner, pleased that the semblance of a family was there again.

Gyneth looked at her plate. "Mum, I have decided to go to America, to Los Angeles, in fact. I have some savings, enough to see me through a year or so, and I'll try and make a living using my acting and musical skills. It will be very difficult to leave you, but it's my chance to create my own life."

Estelle sat in the elegant chair, sick with anguish. She bit back her own fears and loneliness and said calmly, "If that is something you must do, I understand. It will be difficult without you here. But I want to tell you something that has been on my mind since, well, before the funeral."

Gyneth nodded, waiting.

"Before he died, your father told me that he was planning to tell you that he'd changed his mind. He was keeping it for that Shabbat, the week it happened." Estelle wiped away the tears that blurred her vision. It was all still so unreal. If only Jacob would just walk through the door.

"He wanted you to go to medical school, to reach your dream. He'd made a mistake, my darling, and he saw how unhappy you were. He wanted to make things right again, but he didn't live to say the words to you, just to me."

Gyneth held her hands tightly over her ears. All her pain, yearning, jealousy of Carolyn, all of it would have been unnecessary, if only her father had said the right words, supported her from the start.

"I don't want to hear this, please, no more." Gyneth

left the room, frustrated and angry, her mother's words resonating in her ears.

Estelle sat at the table for a long time. Jacob had, once again, left the traumatic times for her to handle.

She stood with difficulty, exhausted from the effort of her own convalescence as well as Gyneth's unhappiness. She had given Gyneth as much as she could. It was time for her daughter to lead her own life.

# Chapter 15

Carolyn sipped the foaming mug of beer and listened to the familiar beat of African music. It had been years since she'd visited the bar in Knightsbridge with her schoolmates, but now, after spending time with Gyneth, she yearned for the familiar sounds of her youth, and had searched it out. Carolyn had found it difficult to return to her routine after Estelle and Gyneth left England. Completing the research that she'd been assigned to, Carolyn returned to London and medical school. Back in London for only a week she was still feeling lonely and homesick for the smells and tastes of South Africa. The young woman closed her eyes and sang softly in harmony with the bar's singer.

"You have a wonderful voice!" Carolyn was startled by the familiar accent. She opened her eyes and looked into the strong, smiling face of a very attractive man. He looked and sounded Zulu.

"Thank you. Are you from South Africa?"

"I am Matthew Sibanda. I'm from Johannesburg originally but I have lived in London for many years." He reached out and clasped Carolyn's hand. His touch was warm and his smile friendly.

"What have you been doing here in London?" Carolyn

was momentarily filled with suspicion. Government spies
had been known to infiltrate bars frequented by expatriot
South Africans.

"I came here on a scholarship and attended the London School of Economics. After graduation I stayed on
and got a job."

Carolyn relaxed. He sounded legitimate.

"What about you?" Matthew's steady gaze caused
Carolyn to move uncomfortably on her seat. He
seemed to radiate vibrancy. She still felt the firm pressure of his hand and with it a stirring deep inside her
body. It had been so long since she had been with a
man.

Matthew felt a tingling sensation as he looked at the
poised and beautiful woman next to him. He had not
met anyone remotely like her in all the time he had
spent in London.

The hours passed quickly. Carolyn found herself
laughing freely, for the first time in years, teasing, flirt-
ing, singing along with the music and finally, with
Matthew's urging and spurred on by a couple of
draughts of beer, she stood next to the piano, and,
without a microphone, sang with complete abandon, as
she had done many years before.

Matthew stood in the front of the admiring crowd,
swaying with the rhythm. He could hardly take his
eyes off Carolyn who now felt the throbbing of her
own heart. It was as if the passion she had kept so
tightly controlled was ready to become unleashed and
she felt swept along by its force. As she sat next to him
in the booth, she slowly caressed her bottom lip with
her tongue, feeling Matthew's heat as he pressed his
knee closer to hers and together they laughed and
preened, swaying always nearer to each other like two
mating birds in the spring.

Carolyn was overwhelmed by desire. Matthew's

electric presence had opened up a soft inner vulnerability, an emotional well of need that she had kept submerged for years. She was already quivering, ripe for the physical sensations that now came flooding over her.

Matthew could hardly keep from stroking her silky brown skin with his fingers. Everything about her emitted sensuality, yearning, willingness to be penetrated. Her deep brown eyes drew him in and his groin throbbed in unison with his heart. Carolyn felt his energy and leaned her body into his as their hands touched. They talked about many things—her career in medicine, his in business, and their ambitions for the future. There was so much they could share, so much understood and unsaid in their common heritage.

Needing to be alone, they walked around the exclusive stores of Knightsbridge on the pretense of window-shopping. As they stood pointing at various objects in the window, the temptation of their heated bodies cast all restraint aside. At the same instant they clasped each other wildly, not able to intertwine their bodies sufficiently to satisfy the passion that was whipping them into a frenzy.

"We have to find a room. Come with me, there is a little bed and breakfast just around the corner on one of the side streets here, come." Matthew pulled her along shivering with expectation. They checked into the little inn, saying that their baggage had been lost by the airlines, and then at last they were alone.

Carolyn gave herself up to the unbearably delicious, familiar sensation that had consumed her in the past. She felt Matthew unbuttoning her blouse and skirt even as his clothes fell to the floor. She touched his firm skin as he ran his fingers over her breasts, caressing the nipples gently, then harder as she pressed her body closer. Then, legs intertwined, he slowly moved

his tongue from her breasts to her waist, finally nest-
ling, tantalizing, sucking, licking, tasting the juices
flowing from her innermost being, probing deeper,
penetrating her as his hands fluttered lightly over the
insides of her thighs. She arched her buttocks up to
him and he groaned, losing all control as he moved up
and pushed inside her, pumping harder and faster until
she was screaming for him never to stop. Finally the
quivering began and together they reached the height
of their orgasms as the waves of pleasure overcame
them and they collapsed into each other, glistening
with perspiration, The delicious lethargy of satisfaction
softly filled their bodies as they lay in each other's
arms, hardly able to comprehend the speed with which
their desires overcame them.

"I have been searching for a soul mate all the time
I have lived in London. You are the one." Matthew's
words were soft, but deliberate.

Carolyn pulled away slightly.

"Matthew, you are very exciting and I love the way
you make me feel. But I am committed to my career,
nothing can interfere with that." Carolyn raised herself
up onto her elbows and looked down at the handsome
young man who lay dreamily beside her.

"Hmmm," he murmured, "careers are so unimportant when you have this wonderful feeling. You have
your priorities in the wrong order, my dear."

Carolyn pulled herself into a sitting position. "You
don't understand," she said, "my career is my only pri-
ority. You have to understand or we cannot have a relationship."

Matthew opened one eye. "Oh, relax," he said
gently, "I'm only joking with you. Come here." He
pulled her back and they made love again, this time
slower with more curiosity as they explored each other's bodies with care.

Carolyn's life became more hectic than ever before. She saw Matthew on the weekends and often spent the whole of Saturday and Sunday in bed with him, reveling in the freedom to fulfill her exploding sexual needs.

Ruth knew that Carolyn was seeing someone but since the young woman came home every night, and did not offer any information about her activities, Ruth waited patiently until she was ready to share the secrets of her private life. All that mattered was that Carolyn found fulfillment and happiness. And she had, as Ruth could see from the energy in her step and the glow of her face.

Finally, Ruth could resist no more. As Carolyn prepared to rush out the house early one Saturday morning, she stopped her.

"Is he wonderful?" Ruth's eyes were twinkling with humor.

Carolyn laughed. "Yes, he is. The only problem is that he wants to get too serious. I am not ready for that. I have so much to do before I take on the responsibility of someone else's life and problems."

"Life's timing is not always precise, my dear. Sometimes we have to take the opportunity even if it arrives at the wrong moment."

Carolyn shrugged off the advice. She would not, could not, change the goals she had set out so clearly for herself. Total commitment was required for the next few years of internship, residency, and only then could she consider the distraction of a serious relationship.

Nevertheless, driven by desire, Carolyn immersed herself in the joys of Matthew's body and his love for hers. After a few months she began having difficulty keeping up with her studies. But her obsessional need to satisfy her body was too strong to ignore. Her days were filled with romantic dreams and imaginings. For the first time she was blissfully in love. Matthew's dark beauty enthralled her; the smoothness of his skin and elegant bearing, his long, strong back, the vitality of his expressive, intelligent face. He understood Carolyn's physical needs instinctively. Being with him was like a drug—it sucked her up, drew all her energy, flew her high into the skies and crashed her down in sleepy satisfaction.

She struggled to maintain her studies. Matthew's understanding of her long hours and perpetual exhaustion was limited. It was a source of many arguments.

"I have to spend as many hours on the wards as I can. Book learning is not what medicine is all about," Carolyn tried to explain as Matthew complained that they were now only spending one afternoon a week together.

"Yes, I do understand. But we require some time, too. You can't just breeze in, collapse with exhaustion, sleep, then make love for a few hours and leave. I am not here to service you, Carolyn. You don't make time for the intimacy of life."

Carolyn was torn. Matthew's needs were a directional pull on her universe and although she longed for him, her ambition overrode that need.

"I'll try to find the time." Carolyn kissed Matthew's muscular arm as she lay across him, satiated after an hour of lovemaking, and fell asleep.

# Chapter 16

Gyneth sat in her small Westwood motel room, her head in her hands. The room smelled of cigarette smoke and the plain bed sheets and tattered cover were in sharp contrast to the crisply ironed linens and hand-embroidered coverlets of her room back home. She'd been in America one month, but it seemed like a century. If she had known how difficult moving to Los Angeles would be, she never would have left South Africa. The city sprawled over vast distances and seemed to have no end.

How was she ever going to succeed here? Skip and Elaine, her parents' friends and her only contacts, were in Manhattan, rather than at their home in Beverly Hills, and there was no telling when they would return. She watched the students at UCLA walking across the widespread campus and longed to be one of them, carefree, involved in protests about one thing or another and with responsibilities only to their books and friends. Her time for that was over.

Gyneth was desperate. She had to find a job, find somewhere to live. These were decisions she hadn't been faced with before, and it was frightening to be alone. She felt like she'd been running a race, trying to keep up with ever-increasing bureaucratic demands for identification numbers, credit, or references. Thankfully, she now had transportation, a rented car. She had found her way to the Department of Motor Vehicles, to obtain a California license without which she was unable to function. She'd also opened a bank account, and they'd wanted something called a Social Security number. She didn't have one and so established a nonresident's account. The paperwork was overwhelming. In South Africa all she'd needed was to mention her father or grandfather's name and no more questions were asked to obtain a loan, buy a car, rent anything she wanted. Here only the piece of paper, the license, the credit card was sufficient.

Wearily, Gyneth began going through the help-wanted ads. She was a whiz at Latin, she thought wryly, which was certainly not going to help her much in the job market. She found a couple of opportunities for a receptionist, noted the addresses and consulted her *Thomas Guidebook,* locating the places for the interviews in order to plan the next day geographically. Gyneth had learned the hard way in Los Angeles—the distances were so great that if she didn't plan, she could drive all day and never arrive at her destination. At least the drivers were more polite and disciplined than in Johannesburg, and generally when they indicated they were turning left they did, rather than turning right from the left-hand lane.

Gyneth settled down in front of the television, a novelty not yet available in South Africa. Some of the programs accentuated her loneliness, especially the Johnny Carson talk show since the jokes were topical and the American sense of humor was foreign to her. Gyneth refused to allow the depression that was carping at the corner of her mind to take it over. Instead, she forced herself to observe from television the customs of American life. Then, exhausted and feeling a sense of unreality, she slept fitfully.

The next day, Gyneth had her first interview. It was a disaster. The woman asked for references. Gyneth said she had none. The interviewer requested proof of former experience. Gyneth said she had none of that either. When asked for qualifications, Gyneth told her she was an honors' student at a top university and could certainly work out how to answer the phone and greet people.

The woman looked at her for a long moment. "You are overqualified for the job and have no experience. I am afraid this is not for you."

Gyneth felt the pain of rejection, the same feelings from her school days when she was the fat girl in the class. With her eyes watering with unexpected tears, Gyneth returned to her car and tried to regain her composure.

Come on, she thought to herself crossly. What made you think you'd get the first job you applied for?

The next interview was no better. Her lack of experience and references were like a death knell. When the interviewer heard that Gyneth had never worked before, she developed a glazed look in her eyes and the interview was essentially over.

How was she ever going to get started? An advertisement caught her eye. "Telephone sales—call this number now—no experience needed." The man who answered said the job entailed selling dental equipment over the phone, nationwide, at night, starting at 5:30 in the evening. Gyneth jumped in her rented car and drove to an old warehouse in Venice. The area was depressed and she suddenly realized that she could be putting herself into a risky situation.

She parked the car and gingerly knocked on the door. It opened and an unshaven young man, dressed in jeans and a dirty shirt motioned impatiently for her to come in. Warily, not knowing what to expect, Gyneth entered the warehouse and gasped, her heart pounding as she saw a brightly lit room filled with over fifty people, sitting on rickety chairs at small desks, talking on phones.

"Can you read?" the young man said, picking his teeth with the edge of an envelope. Gyneth looked at him as if he'd lost his mind. Then a wave of depression and hopelessness swept over her. Surely she didn't have to start her life in Los Angeles at this level, with people who were illiterate. Shame overwhelmed her as she thought suddenly of her father, and what he'd think of her working in this environment. Then she was filled with anger. If only her father had taken the time, said the words that would've permitted her to pursue her dreams, she wouldn't be here.

"Read?" she said. "Yes, I can read." She bit her lip to stop saying more. Gyneth really needed the job.

The man looked at her closely. "Some of the folks we get here are not too good at reading. Take this script"—he pointed to a sheet of paper on the desk— "call these numbers"—he pointed to another book full of phone numbers—"and this is what you say. Here, watch me, I'll do one."

He called one of the numbers on the list. "Good evening," he said in an entirely different voice, charming and sickly sweet. "Is Dr. Johnston there?" He waited a few minutes and then presented his pitch about dental equipment and supplies, the discount off the list price, and agreed to send the dentist literature. He ended the call and classified it into one of three categories for salesman followup. "That is all there is to it," he said, and moved aside to offer Gyneth the chair.

Gyneth was somewhat relieved. There didn't seem to be anything dishonest about the activity, although it was slightly demeaning to have to cajole someone into buying. She sat down nervously and started to call hesitantly. The person on the other end was generally abrupt. At the slightest negative sound in the speaker's voice, Gyneth's reaction was to apologize for bothering him and hang up. Gradually she forced herself to stay on the line and persist.

After about an hour, Gyneth realized that none of the recipients of the calls knew or indeed would ever know her, and she could adopt any kind of personality in order to make the sale. So, adopting a whole series of different approaches, Gyneth began to enjoy herself and as the four-hour period ended, she'd made two sales and felt jubilant.

The man who'd hired her smilingly patted her on the back.

"You did real well, sweetie," he said. "Come on back tomorrow night. Payday is on Friday, twice a month."

Gyneth was excited, feeling a sense of accomplishment. She had a job and soon she'd have "experience." Who knows, maybe one day, she'd even have a credit card! She laughed at herself. Just two months ago she would have turned up her nose at the environment she'd just left. In fact, her chauffeur Austen would probably have refused to drive her there.

She stopped at a fast-food restaurant near the motel, feeling guilty. Gyneth knew the greasy high calorie food was not good for her, but rationalized there would be plenty of time to diet when she settled in. Anyway, trips to the supermarket had left her feeling overwhelmed. Everything in America seemed to have sugar in it, even the bread was sweet. And there was so much choice; instead of three or four brands there were twenty or thirty, all presented temptingly, and most were fattening. Besides, Gyneth was lonely, and food had always been her reliable companion.

The next day Gyneth was determined to find somewhere to live. She saw a vacancy sign, off Gayley Avenue, a tree-lined street in Westwood.

A very large lady with powerful arms answered the door. Gyneth almost lost heart. She plucked up her courage and asked politely, "I wonder, do you have a vacancy, by any chance?"

"Yeah." The woman threw open the door. "Joe," she yelled, "a lady wants a room." In the dim light of the foyer, Gyneth saw a man with a snake tattooed on a massive bicep. He wore a vest with hair sprouting wetly out of his underarms and his beer belly bulged over a dirty pair of jeans. Gyneth was temporarily speechless, feeling very crowded in the small entry hall.

"We've got a one-room apartment fully furnished up on the second floor. You can have it tomorrow if you like," he muttered, motioning vaguely upstairs.

"Can I see it?" Gyneth asked.

"Sure." He heaved himself off his chair, grabbed a bunch of keys and started climbing a staircase that seemed tacked precariously onto the outside of the rundown house. Gyneth followed him up. After ten steps he stopped to puff and pointed Gyneth toward the door above. She entered the dingy apartment, furnished in green, her favorite color. However, this was the most depressing shade she had ever seen. There was a bed, sofa, television, a couple of chairs, and worst of all, only one window overlooking an alley.

"I'll take it," Gyneth said, shocking herself. After dealing with the paperwork, she got back in her car and laughed until she cried. If only she could share this with someone—it was so weird and funny.

The next night, after placing a plant in the window,

to cheer her up, Gyneth ate her usual dinner out of styrofoam containers, and thought of the silver and linen that had adorned her table until a few months ago. She yearned for the smooth feeling of the napkin on her lap, the clink of crystal glassware. Later, as she lay satiated with the heavy food, Gyneth wept with homesickness.

Gyneth made sales every night and soon was hailed as the best salesperson of the week and given some cheap wine to drink in celebration.

The other people in the telemarketing operation were from every race and country imaginable. This was where poor immigrants came, she thought, looking around the room, to work in a job in order to obtain the "experience" that was so necessary, and suddenly she realized that she was one of them. Just a few months ago she had been one of the elite.

During the day, Gyneth explored the city. She soon realized that she would have to buy a car since the rental was too expensive. So she started going to second-hand car dealers on Van Nuys Boulevard in the San Fernando Valley. She watched their sales skills with some amusement, having learned about sales techniques from the dental equipment scripts, and practiced going into lots of different showrooms so as not to be intimidated when she actually found something she liked. Finally Gyneth felt ready. She'd negotiated with at least seven car dealers and had managed to knock a healthy percentage off their prices, and for cars that she had no intention of buying.

She found a Ford Mustang. Using her new negotiation skills, she bought it at a good price, feeling proud of her first real purchase.

The world of studies, servants, chauffeur-driven cars, and large rolling estates was like a dream. Gyneth's reality was mundane, modest, and difficult.

She learned for the first time to use a Laundromat, observing the other patrons. Gyneth bought a small iron and found that ironing was actually more intricate than it appeared. She thought about Martha's skill in ironing her father's shirts and a wave of homesickness overcame her as she longed for someone to take care of her. Suddenly she understood how lonely Carolyn must have been, without family, sent away to Soweto, with no real friends or resources. Gyneth realized how privileged her life must have seemed to her friend.

Gyneth had, as yet, made no friends. Everyone seemed to have somewhere to go and someone to visit. She couldn't afford to go to restaurants, had no desire to visit bars and realized that she had to find some companionship, otherwise she'd become as large as the amazon lady or die of loneliness.

Then Gyneth remembered the strangers that Jacob would invite for Friday night dinner if they were in town for Shabbat and attended services at the Great Synagogue, of which the Amrons were founders. She knew how to solve her problem.

The synagogue closest to her was on Pico Boulevard. The rabbi was welcoming and invited her for dinner. Gyneth felt familiarity for the first time since she'd arrived in Los Angeles as she sang the songs from her childhood and said the prayers welcoming the Sabbath with joy. The elderly Rabbi and his wife were pleased to have a young person in their home.

She was soon a familiar face at the temple and volunteered for activities with seniors as well as nursery classes. Her work at night allowed her the daylight hours to be active there. There were many people in Los Angeles, she discovered, who had no family, like herself. Most of them had come from somewhere else, New York, Chicago, Pittsburgh and those from Eastern Europe who had left as had her family and immigrated to America rather than South Africa. They clucked over her, saying that she was "such a lovely refined girl."

Her parents' friends, Skip and Elaine, called to say they were pleased to hear from her but were busy. Gyneth had found that everyone in Los Angeles was busy. They invited her over for dinner and she saw that they lived in Beverly Hills exactly the same way as she had lived in South Africa. They had Spanish-speaking servants, from Mexico and Guatemala, and seemed to have a series of services provided for them— gardening, pool, dog training, and cleaning. They lived well, so well in fact, that they really couldn't appreciate her lifestyle. Gyneth realized that there was a large gap between the haves and have-nots in America. But she knew that she was going to be one of the haves one day—that was what made it different from South Africa, where only certain people could ever be haves and they were all white.

Gyneth met black people at work. They were the first blacks she'd met who were not working for her or her family. She felt awkward, uncomfortable around them, discovering when she told them that she came from South Africa that they immediately imagined that she was a racist.

So she simply started to tell people that she came from England.

One day Gyneth saw a notice on the temple board. "Auditions begin today for *Paint Your Wagon*. Apply at temple office." She remembered the school performances where she'd had the lead in the same show.

The next day Gyneth presented herself at the temple hall and joined the other hopefuls waiting to audition.

She stepped onto the stage and sang her heart out, remembering the moves and gestures that she had used once before in the role, in that other world, so far

away. She reveled in her feeling of lightness, of freedom, of completeness as she pretended to be someone
else, confident and self-assured.

Gyneth got the lead, started rehearsals and cut back
her work hours to fill only the nonrehearsal nights.
It was time to look for a day job. On the application
form she gave herself only a high school education,
the one job experience, and a permanent address in
Westwood.

"Yes, I've been thinking about taking some courses
at night school," she responded to questions about further education. The people interviewing her for the
various jobs were much more comfortable with that
and smiled, encouraging her to study hard.

Gyneth thought wryly of the time and effort she'd
put into her studies only to have to lie about her accomplishments. She chose the position as law firm receptionist.

"We are delighted you have decided to take the job.
Your accent is particularly appealing, an excellent
voice for prospective clients to hear." The administra-
tor of the law firm was pleasant and Gyneth settled
into the work routine, answering the phone and greeting a variety of well-dressed people. That was the easy
part. The harder part was the lawyers. There was only
one woman lawyer and she was very charming, looking politely at Gyneth when she spoke to her. The men
hardly ever bothered to greet her, or treat her like a
person. It was as if she were their servant. Gyneth bristled at times as she was given instructions. With remorse, she thought back to her own imperious ways
and pampered past, wondering if she, too, had treated
the servants in her home with disdain. The young lawyers were the worst. They were arrogant and obnox-
ious. She listened to the other women in the office,
secretaries and paralegals who spoke about the various

associates, and said little. She made herself part of the team, sitting silently in the group of employees who whispered and gossiped the way she and her friends had at school.

"How is your job, darling?" Estelle's voice echoed back to Gyneth on their weekly long-distance call.

"It's fine, Mum. The only part I really can't stand is the internal politics in the firm. The place is filled with interoffice jealousies, and they make me feel sick to my stomach."

Gyneth hated the way the partners considered themselves to be superior while the associates groveled, struggling to win favors. She was appalled at the hours the young lawyers kept. The firm specialized in litigation.

"Well, they did a couple of all-night sessions again this weekend," she overheard the paralegals grumbling one Monday morning. "Did you see my desk? It'll take me all week to catch up!"

Gyneth knew that the only way the young attorneys could be noticed and given the opportunity to try a case was to give their lives to the firm.

The justice system seemed to be overwhelmed by procedure. Gyneth saw huge amounts of paper being shuffled around.

"We have to drown the opposition in paper," she heard often as the young associates prepared new cases. "The approach is to destroy their case as soon as possible. In the depositions we have to annihilate their key witnesses. We have a couple of questions that will just rip them apart." She abhorred their adversarial approach, like tigers ready to attack, or vultures preparing to rip their prey to shreds once having pinned them down in a vulnerable position. They pitted weak against strong, shrewd against naive. And not once did she hear the words "justice," "fairness," "right" or "wrong."

In her lunch hour Gyneth sometimes sat in the law library, richly furnished with the same kind of upholstered furniture that her grandfather sold in his chain of retail stores. Gyneth felt comfortable there and amused herself by reading the various law books she saw on the shelves. It reminded her of how Carolyn had gained inspiration from the medical library.

The volumes that fascinated her most were the ones on immigration law and procedure. Gyneth knew she had to get a green card to stay in America. At lunch every day, she took her little brown bag with her to the library and opened the volumes. Immigration law was very complicated, lots of information about visa numbers, quotas, and relationships.

While Gyneth studied the law books someone was studying her. Harrison Jaffe, a young associate, had observed her fascination with the large volumes of procedural law.

Then he understood. Obviously Gyneth was an illegal. He was intrigued. The next time Gyneth sat quietly in the library reading and eating lunch, he sat next to her.

"Hi," he said. "I don't think that we have actually spoken before, I am Harrison Jaffe." He held out his hand and she took it feeling an unexpected thrill as his warm hand enveloped hers. Gyneth had seen the tall young man who entered the firm with the newest group of associates and noticed his charm and poise.

"I was interested to see you reading about immigration law. Any special reason?"

"I'd like to sort out my visa situation. It looks rather complicated, I'm afraid."

"Well, perhaps I can help you," he said. "I'm certainly no expert but I have worked with the IRS and other agencies of the Federal government and this cannot be much different. Why don't you tell me the problem?"

Gyneth longed to talk freely to Harrison, to trust him. He seemed so empathetic, so charming. But she was learning to be cautious, self-protective. Finally, she decided to go on her instinct and discuss her problem with him.

"I came here as a visitor and now want to stay permanently. I've read enough to see that I have to petition for a work permit, and find something to make me so special that no American could be found to do my job. It seems quite hopeless. The only other option is to marry someone, and I've no plans at present." She smiled shyly.

Harrison listened carefully. "Let me think about it. I'll make some calls to one of my friends who is active in this area."

Gyneth looked at him intently, wondering at why he'd offered to help her. He couldn't possibly be interested in her as a woman, she was too fat. He must have something else in mind.

"Well, I had better get back to work. Thanks for the input. See you later." Gyneth took her little brown bag and returned to the front reception. He watched her go, wondering what he had said to make her withdraw.

Gyneth intrigued him and her beautiful face seemed alight with intelligence and enthusiasm. He just knew there was more to this young woman than met the eye. She had a kind of stature, a poise, holding herself with pride and walking as if she knew she was desirable. He liked that. Her body was voluptuous, inviting, and when she started to talk, her quick wit and charisma made her even more attractive.

The next day Harrison found her in the coffee room. "Gyneth, here is the name that I promised you." He was courteous and distant. She took the folded note he gave her. It contained the name of an immigration attorney.

"Thanks a lot." Gyneth continued preparing her coffee, thinking wistfully how she longed to invite the attractive young man to the synagogue play, where he would see her in an entirely different light.

"By the way, when you have a moment, could you please come into my office?"

Gyneth followed him curiously. He closed the door and smiled.

"You know what a gossip factory it is out there. I didn't want to embarrass you in front of everyone. However, I'd like to invite you to come out with me for a drink and dinner after work, any day you are free."

Gyneth was thrilled, despite her earlier determination to be cautious. She smiled at him. "I'd love to. How about tomorrow night at Harry's, eight thirty?"

The next night was a mad rush. Gyneth grabbed a change of clothes as she left in the morning and hurried through the day, anxious to go to her rehearsal, then meet Harrison for dinner. The rehearsal dragged on—it was as if she could get nothing right and the director finally told her to take off the night and get some rest, her mind was obviously on other things. She nodded and scrambled to change into her most flattering outfit, longing to be thirty pounds lighter. She focused her attention on her face. At least that was one part of her that was always reliably attractive.

Gyneth arrived breathless and late at Harry's restaurant and saw Harrison sitting patiently at the bar. He looked at her, intrigued. Could this be the same person who sat, docile and passive, behind the telephones at the office? She was vibrant, elegantly dressed with expensive understated jewelry, self-assured.

"You look wonderful," he said, clasping his warm hands around hers. As soon as they had ordered dinner, Harrison began to tell Gyneth about his background.

"We didn't live in a very fancy house, just a modest Brooklyn home, but a traditional Jewish one, lots of love and too much food. I was the youngest by ten years of four brothers and sisters, an afterthought, in fact." Harrison laughed. "I went to Harvard, and then got a master's degree in international studies at the Johns Hopkins University. Finally I received my law degree at UCLA, passed the California bar examination, and have, as you know, just joined the law firm as an associate."

Harrison paused as the wine was poured, and he realized with some surprise that Gyneth understood and appreciated the vintage and flavor.

"You know, I really don't like practicing law at all," he blurted out suddenly. "Litigators are like a bunch of piranas feeding upon each other. I'd prefer to be in the entertainment field, that's where one can be creative, proactive. But it's difficult to change firms now, I have to stay in this job at least two years so as to appear solid."

What he was saying reflected her sentiment exactly. She was so pleased that he didn't fit the traditional aggressive type who seemed to succeed in litigation. The fact that he was interested in the creative arts excited her even more.

"Tell me about yourself. What was life like in England?" Harrison knew only the story Gyneth had told everyone about coming from London. She hesitated and then decided to tell him the truth. He was certainly more sophisticated than most of the people she'd met and she did not want to have to live a lie.

"I actually come from South Africa. My family was very wealthy, established, renowned. My grandfather was an industrialist, and founded the furniture industry there, and my father was a famous surgeon. I lived in an enormous home, fourteen thousand square feet on three acres of land. We had horses, six servants, an English nanny, all the accoutrements of wealth and status. I attended the university where I majored in classics, then my father died, and I decided to leave and come here." She noticed Harrison's amazement.

"The expression on your face is the reason I made up the story I did. People either think I am exaggerating my background or brand me as a racist, which I'm not."

"Why on earth are you working as a receptionist?" he asked.

"Because I have to earn a living," Gyneth said simply, "and that was the only job I could get without contacts in this country."

He held her hand. "You must be frustrated beyond belief in that job."

"Yes, at times I am," Gyneth answered. "But I've tried to rationalize it all, and whenever I feel like walking out or demanding respect, I tell myself that this is a great opportunity for me to see how the system operates."

Harrison looked at Gyneth with new respect, seeing an elegant, mature woman with obvious breeding and intelligence. Her struggles were similar to the way he was biding his time until he could practice the kind of law that really excited him.

"It's getting late, and I really should go." Gyneth took a deep breath. "Would you like to come to a musical I am appearing in at a temple nearby? The opening night is in ten days, on a Saturday."

Harrison looked uncomfortable. "Actually I already have a date on that evening. Could ... perhaps we could both come?"

Gyneth swallowed her sharp feeling of disappointment and said airily, "No problem, I'll leave two tickets and the address for you at the office."

She withdrew a little, feeling fat and unattractive all of a sudden. The meal was over, and after a few rather awkward moments, Harrison offered to take her home, not wanting the evening to end. But for Gyneth the magic had gone. There were many thin, attractive women in Los Angeles, one of whom Harrison was already probably dating the next week. Then Gyneth pictured him in her ugly little apartment. It was all wrong and not the way she wanted her life to be. She refused, saying that she had her own car and would see him in the morning.

Harrison looked into her eyes and put his finger beneath her chin, tilting her lips up to meet his.

"Good night, Gyneth," he said quietly. "Thank you for a magical evening."

She felt his lips gently touch hers and then he was gone. She drove home dreamily, thinking of how warm his lips felt and how gentle he had been.

The next week, Gyneth was so busy and excited that she hardly ate, realizing that she had lost six pounds without trying. Opening night came. As Gyneth walked on for her first scene, she became another person and swept through the evening, carrying the show. The applause was wildly enthusiastic. She felt the waves of audience appreciation wash over her.

Then it was over and the cast gathered around, hugging and kissing her as they all congratulated each other.

Gyneth enjoyed the praise but her eyes anxiously sought out Harrison. She saw him, standing in the wings among the people celebrating on the stage. She was about to run to greet him when her heart dropped. She saw his date, a young woman with a sleek and slender look and long dark hair. Gyneth tried to turn away, feeling the greasepaint on her face, the tightness of her costume. But it was too late. Harrison was striding toward her, smiling his congratulations. The young slender woman stayed close to him.

"Thank you so much for coming. Did you enjoy the show?" Gyneth said politely, hiding her discomfort with a welcoming smile.

Harrison took her hand and said, "It is difficult to say how much your performance thrilled me. You have a remarkable talent, you know." He looked deeply into her eyes and for that second there was no one else on the stage but the two of them. She pulled away from his gaze and flushed slightly, his praise meaning more to her than anyone else's that evening.

The dark-haired woman took his arm possessively and said sweetly, "Yes, indeed. We thought you were wonderful."

Gyneth withdrew, feeling her hostility, noticing the subtle message that Harrison was already taken. Feeling desperate, Gyneth searched for words to hide her sense of loss as she realized that she had misinterpreted Harrison's interest in her. He was obviously deeply involved with this woman.

"It was quite good of you to come. I know there are lots of other things you could have done this evening and the temple really appreciates your support of our modest production. Here let me introduce you to our marvelous rabbi." Thankfully she'd seen the rabbi and his wife coming toward her with great smiles of pleasure at her success. She turned into their warm embrace and took the opportunity to slip away, blending into the throng of her new friends. The next time she looked, Harrison was gone.

She reflected on the life she was building. Slowly, slowly she was beginning to belong. She had a momentary pang of guilt, as she thought of her mother, now alone. She'd share some of her experiences with her that weekend on their regular call.

Estelle was lonelier than she had ever been. She had put off having the X-ray. She really didn't need confirmation of what she'd known for months, that the tumor had recurred. What she didn't know was the extent to which the cancer had spread.

The specialist tried to be helpful but his words were discouraging.

"I told Jacob that an amputation from the waist down on the right side was the only solution for you. At least you had a year or so with the total hip replacement."

Estelle was unable to speak. She tried to accept what the stern-faced doctor had told her. It was difficult to think past the fact of the deforming operation.

His words rang in her ears as her chauffeur drove her home to the new house she'd moved into just a few weeks ago. It was a country cottage set among aromatic roses and protective oaks. Estelle was pleased that for the first time in her life, she had a home chosen with only her taste in mind. It had a feminine softness, an open feeling of sunshine, and was filled with color and lace. Even though she spent many hours alone in her new environment, nevertheless it was hers, and with a feeling of defiance she had filled it with new things, discarding the old with the lifestyle that had definitely ended on Jacob's death.

It was the middle of the night when the phone rang. Gyneth answered groggy with sleep.

"How are you, darling?" Estelle said.

"Mum, it is three A.M. in Los Angeles, even though it's noon where you are. Can I phone you back later?"

Estelle tried to keep her voice calm and even in the

face of Gyneth's irritability. "I'm sorry to call so late, darling, but I have some disturbing news. I ... I've been having pain again." Gyneth felt the bile rise in her throat. She knew what was coming.

Estelle continued in a wavering voice. "I had an X-ray this morning and the cancer is back. It has spread all over the prosthesis. They've told me"— Estelle's voice faded into a whisper—"that the only solution is a hemipelvectomy, an amputation from my waist on the one side. I'm going to London on Monday. Dr. Charnley has referred me to a surgeon there."

Gyneth sat up in bed. Her hands were quivering.

"Mum, I'll fly to London tomorrow and be there to meet you. What time is your plane coming in?" Gyneth took down all the details of the flights. When she hung up she felt sick. Her mother would be deformed. She pounded her fists into the bed covers. It was all going to go down the drain—her job, her apartment, her life. She suddenly thought of the musical with three more nights to play. She had no option, the operation couldn't wait, she couldn't let Estelle face it alone.

The next day Gyneth broke the news to the white-faced director and her understudy, and called one of the women from work, saying that she had no idea when she would return. She thought fleetingly of sending a special message to Harrison, but then discarded the idea, remembering the possessive way the young woman had held his arm. Gyneth paid her rent for three more months, then took a cab to the airport and boarded the evening flight to London.

Only when Gyneth was sitting in the plane with the metropolis of Los Angles growing smaller and smaller beneath her, did she allow depression to overcome her. The only consolation was that she would see Carolyn again. They had not communicated for the past year, but she knew they would pick up their relationship from where they had left off. Their friendship had borne the test of time.

# Chapter 17

Alone and bereft of hope, Estelle wept silently, her body shaking with great wracking sobs, as she hid herself under the South African Airways blanket on the long journey to London. A million thoughts were speeding through her mind. She wished that Jacob were with her and still spoke to him continually, as if he were. The times that hurt the most were at the end of the day when she yearned for someone with whom to share the day's events. Her bed was so empty, so cold. She filled it with pillows on one side so that it wouldn't seem so large, but nothing could take away the void in her existence.

And sometimes in the late-night hours, Estelle burned with fury at him. Her mind was reeling with unanswered questions. How could he have continued to work, knowing how ill he was? Why did he value his life so little and the lives of others so much?

Why did this happen to her? Her own death now confronted her. Was she going to die by inches, her body dying in pieces while her mind stayed healthy? She contemplated whether she actually wanted to live at all. She couldn't imagine herself without any body from the waist on one side. Would the world see her as a freak? She finally fell asleep, her slight frame curled up like a small child in the seat, as the African continent swept by thousands of feet below.

Gyneth was waiting at the Pan Am terminal, and as she caught sight of Estelle, burning tears blurred her vision. Her mother was pale, thin, hardly filling the narrow wheelchair.

"Everything is going to be all right, Mum. We have each other and we'll fight this together." Gyneth's words rang hollow in her ears, but she hoped that they were reassuring to her mother.

"I know, thank you for coming to be with me, darling. I'm so sorry, this is terribly disruptive to your new life in Los Angeles." Estelle tried to be matter-of-fact, but her grieving was too close to the surface and the tears flowed down her face.

They clung to each other for a moment, Estelle trying to stem the sobs that rose in her throat as she struggled for composure. As Gyneth felt her mother's rigid self-control collapsing, she controlled her own deep wrenching emotion, kissed her lightly on the cheek and deftly wheeled her out to a waiting car.

Once at the hospital, Estelle was admitted to the operative ward. Nurses held her hand with cheery greetings. The efficient wheels of the hospital started turning, and Gyneth went, exhausted, to the nearest hotel. She sat on the small bed gazing out at the never-ending drizzle. The bleakness of the weather matched the despair in her heart. Now that Estelle was being cared for, Gyneth allowed herself to feel a rush of pain and loss. She was so devastatingly alone. She called the number Carolyn had given her.

"Is Carolyn Ngwizi there?"

An older lady answered. "She is out and will not be back until rather late. May I tell her who is calling?"

Gyneth left her name and number.

"Are you her friend from . . . from childhood?"

"Yes, I am. You must be Ruth."

"I am indeed. Carolyn has spoken often of you, child. She will be pleased to know you are in London. I will leave the message on her pillow to be sure she gets it."

Ruth sounded motherly, concerned, and protective. Gyneth felt even lonelier.

She went down to the drafty dining room and ordered a meal, which provided little solace. It felt as though her world were on hold. She slept fitfully, seeing visions of her father in his last seconds of life and her mother, curled up like a child in the hospital bed.

The day of Estelle's operation, it snowed. Gyneth sat in the bleak and bland room outside the operating wing. Family members of other patients sat reading, knitting, playing, crying. And as the time passed excruciatingly slowly, doctors and nurses in surgical scrubs and white uniforms flew by, but no one had word on her mother's condition.

Finally her mother's surgeon walked through the swinging doors, his green outfit creased and his face tired. Amputating a limb was the ugliest of all orthopedic operations, especially on one so young and beautiful as Estelle.

"Everything went well," he said with an optimistic smile. "Your mother is fine and soon she'll be on her way home again." Gyneth wept tears of relief, then she thought of the enormous adjustment that was to take place. She had to share her relief with someone—anyone. So she turned to a family waiting for their mother who was in surgery.

"She is going to be fine. Isn't that wonderful?"

They nodded and smiled at her, then continued their vigil.

Before she'd lost consciousness, Estelle thought groggily how much easier it would be if she died under the anesthetic. But reluctantly hours later, she rose through the drug-induced mist to awareness. Haltingly, she moved her hand to feel the leg that still throbbed. There was nothing there. Yet she still felt the pain. Estelle slept again, telling herself she was confused.

In the next few days, Gyneth was at Estelle's side all the time, talking and reading to her.

"You are going to be fine," Gyneth whispered to her mother, stroking her forehead lightly as she wafted in and out of consciousness the first few days after the operation.

"So much pain, in the same place as before." Estelle's face was drawn and reflected the enormous struggle that she was enduring.

"Your mum is a real trouper," the nurses would say, "a real lady. She's one of our best patients, no trouble at all." Gyneth was grateful for the support. Carolyn had called but couldn't come by until the weekend since her schedule was crammed, so Gyneth had spent long hours alone in the hospital or hotel.

On the third day Estelle told Gyneth to go out of the room.

"Why?" Gyneth wanted to know.

"I want to be alone," Estelle said.

Gyneth understood.

Estelle dragged herself up onto her elbows, pulled back the blankets and looked down at the space where her body had been. She felt dizzy and sick. It was unreal, it could not be her this was happening to. She pulled back the outer dressings until she could see herself properly. She shuddered at her body and wept. She would never show this body to anyone else—she would hide it from the world. She had prided herself on her body, now she belonged in the circus sideshow. For a moment she was almost glad that Jacob would never see her disfigurement. She wept uncontrollably until one of the nurses came in and covered her up, holding her until she cried herself to sleep. She awoke to see the surgeon next to her bed.

"You're going to do very well," he said. "The amputation has taken away the entire right side of your pelvis. All your organs are intact and you still have a waist. With a well-fitted artificial limb you will look as right as rain." He patted her hand and moved on, his entourage of young healthy students following him.

Estelle felt the agonizing solitude of her plight. Who would attend to the part of her that was screaming inside with fury? And to make things worse, no one on the medical staff seemed to understand that the excruciating pain was still there, that the promised freedom from its dominance was still eluding her.

That Saturday, Carolyn peeked her head around the door. Gyneth jumped up with joy and threw her arms around her friend.

"I am so glad to see you. The days have dragged by since we spoke on Monday."

Estelle managed a welcoming smile. Carolyn returned Gyneth's hug and stood next to Estelle, her face filled with sympathy.

"You have been through a really tough time, Mrs. Amron. I'm so sorry that you've had to suffer like this. But the prognosis looks really good, I spoke to the nurses on the way in."

Estelle could not help smiling. Carolyn was very British and professional. It was difficult to reconcile the poised young woman with the trembling, bereft child who had left the Amron estate so many years before.

"Thank you, my dear. Gyneth, why don't you two go and have fun somewhere. I need to rest, and Gyneth you've been here so much, you need a break." Gyneth's eyes lit up, and Carolyn took her hand.

"I know a great place, we can have a couple of beers and catch up on the past year."

"Mum, I'll be in first thing in the morning to see you."

"Sleep in darling, I'm not going anywhere. Have fun."

The pub was small and quiet. They ordered two beers and settled into the dark booth.

"I have moved to Los Angeles," Gyneth announced.

"You have? How super! When did you do it?" Carolyn was thrilled and surprised. She thought Gyneth would never leave the comfort of her lifestyle behind her.

"I have been there almost a year, I left soon after we returned from Mum's last operation. It's been grim. Trying to make it there is really difficult, but things were looking better, that was, before I had to drop it all to come here."

"You'll pick it up again as soon as you return." Carolyn was encouraging.

Gyneth thought for a moment of Harrison, the play, her job, and shrugged. She did it once, and could do it again. She felt some real satisfaction, knowing she was a survivor.

"Well, I have some news, too." Carolyn had been longing to speak to someone about Matthew and the internal conflict about her desire to be with him and her commitment to her career.

"Is he tall, dark, and handsome?"

Carolyn laughed. "As a matter-of-fact he is! His name is Matthew Sibanda, a Zulu from Johannesburg."

"My God, Carolyn, how did you find him!" Gyneth had never seen her friend so dreamy-eyed.

Carolyn told Gyneth how they met.

"The real problem is that he wants me to get married, and I have no intention of doing that now."

Gyneth felt a twinge of envy. She'd relish that sort of caring relationship at this point in her life.

"We had a massive row last night. He wants me to move in with him, says it's easier, but that means a commitment, and I don't want it yet. He told me that I have to give him an answer by tomorrow. Oh, Gyneth, I've never felt like this about anyone. I ache for him during the week, but after the weekend I want to escape from his emotional demands. If only I could have the physical without the rest of the stuff that goes with it."

Gyneth thought of her brief dalliance with Dirk. "Are you prepared to lose him? Because that sounds like the kind of ultimatum he's given you."

Carolyn thought for a moment.

"I don't want to live without him, but I also don't want the commitment he's demanding." She paused. "If he cannot see how important medicine is to me, then it probably wouldn't work anyway."

Gyneth listened and said nothing. There was no advice she could give. Carolyn was already close to making a decision and the subject was best left alone.

Estelle recovered quickly from the surgery, which was ironically less complicated than her other operations, and since she was already adept on crutches, soon it was time to be discharged from the hospital and start rehabilitation. Unbelievably, Estelle could now not only feel the pain in her leg, but could wiggle her nonexistent toes. Her absent foot felt itchy, she had pins and needles in her thigh, and the pain had not lessened at all. Estelle thought she was losing her mind. She tried to talk herself out of what she felt, but couldn't. Instead she left the hospital, ten days later, feeling disoriented, longing for Jacob's presence to help her deal with the confusion.

Gyneth gladly left the little bed and breakfast and

drove Estelle slowly to the Dorchester Hotel where she thought she'd be more comfortable, knowing that months of grueling effort lay ahead to achieve her mother's physical rehabilitation.

Once in her room, Gyneth luxuriated in the bath, wrapped herself in a soft robe, and entered her mother's room. Estelle was balancing on her crutches, naked, and she cried out trying to clasp a towel over her body.

"Mum, I am so sorry, I did not mean to alarm you." Gyneth came closer. "Please don't be embarrassed, I'm your daughter and I love you no matter how your body is." Estelle stood there unable to hold the towel and walk with the crutches at the same time, and sobbed. Gyneth brought a chair behind her and she sat down gingerly.

"Mother, it really doesn't look as bad as you think. You still have a beautiful body, Mummy, please it will be fine." Gyneth tried to find the words to reassure her mother as her stomach heaved from the shock of seeing the swollen stump, only one slim leg and the scars from previous surgeries across her mother's delicate body.

At that moment Gyneth knew the challenge that lay ahead. Together they would have to find strength in each other.

The struggle began the next day. The Roehampton Rehabilitation Center had been created for amputees, veterans of the Royal British forces. Estelle began the slow, painful process of being fitted for and learning to walk with an artificial limb.

Many times Estelle wondered why she had not chosen the easy way out of overdosing on her pain shots, ending everything quickly. But when she saw her daughter bustling around the hospital, fussing about Estelle's various appointments with the physical therapists, she realized that her reason to live was Gyneth, who had put her life on hold to care for her. They went everywhere together, physical therapy, swimming, exercises. Gyneth helped her bathe, dress, even gave her pain shots when necessary. Estelle knew that to give up would be to betray her child, making her tremendous sacrifice all for naught.

Estelle forced herself onward. She had never done anything harder in her whole life. She used Gyneth's love to bolster her courage and raise her tolerance of the pain, the rubbing, chafing, pressure and uncertainty. At times it was all too much to bear, and she would lose hope, sobbing silently into her pillow late at night while Gyneth slept in the next room.

One day, as she tried to conceal the sharp burning pain that shot through her absent limb with red-hot precision, one of the therapists saw her grimace.

"Is it the pain you had before the amputation?" she asked knowingly. Estelle nodded, praying that the woman would believe her. The therapist took her hand comfortingly. "It's quite common. It's called phantom limb syndrome, caused by the nerves in the brain that remember the part of the body as if it were still there. Over time, it will fade." Estelle felt an enormous sense of relief. She was not crazy after all.

Gyneth and Carolyn met for drinks a couple of times a week. One evening Gyneth arrived to find Carolyn with a tall, elegant black man.

"Gyneth, I was worried you wouldn't come. Matthew wanted to meet you and I didn't have time to call in advance."

"Well, I am certainly pleased to meet you, Matthew. Carolyn has told me lots about you!"

"All good things, I hope," Matthew responded, smiling. Gyneth could see his appeal. His elegant charm was magnetic.

The conversation was lively. They spoke about South Africa and then in answer to Matthew's inquiries, Gyneth told of her life in Los Angeles.

Throughout the conversation, Carolyn seemed distracted. Finally she got up.

"I have to go, but you two can stay. Tomorrow there are two operations that I want to observe and I have to read up all about them. In fact I've already stayed here too long. See you on Saturday, Matthew, and Gyneth I'll see you the day after tomorrow." Carolyn had offered Gyneth the opportunity to join her in classes for part of her day. They'd set aside a time to meet two days later when Estelle did not go for rehabilitation. With a hasty peck on the cheek for both of them, Carolyn left.

"She's so driven. Life is just passing her by and she isn't even aware of it." Matthew sighed.

"It is her way," Gyneth explained. "She has been that way ever since we were kids. She was always serious, determined. That's what enabled her to make it so far."

"So she tells me." Matthew grinned and ordered another round of beers.

Gyneth felt light-headed, free and relaxed. She rarely had more than one beer and was on her third. Matthew made her feel at home, his familiar accent reminding her of the safe, secure days of her past.

"Look, why don't we meet for a drink on Friday at this time. I finish work by five and we could meet here at five thirty. I'll tell Carolyn, and if she wants to join us she can. I doubt that she will."

"Sounds super to me. Time for bed. See you then." She giggled at her own juxtaposition of words as Matthew helped her into a taxi.

The next day, Gyneth, slightly hung over, drove her mother, as usual, to Roehampton. It was clear that being at the rehabilitation center had become a source of inspiration to Estelle. Her strength was magnified daily as she met people much worse off than herself, children, paraplegics, adults with no legs at all. Their presence spurred Estelle on. She became determined not to let her disability beat down her spirits. Every day at 10:00 A.M., Estelle would stand between parallel bars, and pull herself upright. Then, laboriously she would flip her artificial limb forward and transfer her upper body weight into the cup that housed her stump. The pain would pierce through her as she moved forward, but each step was accompanied by cheering and applause from the three wheelchair-bound young men who were waiting their turns on the "Rack," as they affectionately named the walking bars. With perspiration pouring off her face, Estelle would finally reach the end after five or six agonizing steps, then turn around and start again. To the world she was determined, positive, and uncomplaining. If she gave up in despair alone at night in her bed, Estelle did it where no one else could see her.

The following morning, Gyneth stood outside the London Hospital, suddenly feeling shy and inadequate. Carolyn was late. Finally after half an hour, she stopped a young man.

"Excuse me, sir, I am looking for a friend, a medical student. Carolyn Ngwizi. Do you know her?"

He looked around him. "Certainly I do," he said. "You must mean the black girl."

"Where can I find her?"

"Well, let me see," he said. "We've just finished our physiology lab and she may still be in there concluding her experiment. It's around the corner, third door on your left."

Gyneth hurried down the hall. Next to a long table

with petri dishes on it was Carolyn. She glanced up, saw Gyneth and motioned to her to wait a moment.

Gyneth smiled tremulously, feeling awkward.

Within a few moments, Carolyn came over. "I'm really sorry. I got caught up and forgot the time. Were you waiting long?"

"About half an hour," Gyneth said irritably.

"Well, cheer up, we have the rest of the day."

Carolyn put her arm around Gyneth and they proceeded to her next class. With some envy, Gyneth watched the slender self-assured young woman, so familiar yet so alien, as she bantered confidently with fellow students, and concentrated intently on the class material. She seemed to fill the room with her presence. Yet Gyneth could see why Matthew was frustrated. Carolyn was totally self-involved. She glowed in the medical environment whereas she was impatient and short-tempered when Matthew was present.

"I've had enough of the nagging," Carolyn announced as they sat together in a small restaurant. "I think we should separate and go our own ways. I'm going to tell him this weekend."

Gyneth was silent. Matthew had arranged to see her that night. Knowing Carolyn's decision, she would feel uncomfortable. The meeting would have to be canceled.

Carolyn asked after Estelle. As Gyneth spoke of her mother, the pain of her present confused situation was clear, although Carolyn could not know that her own exalted place among the medical students made Gyneth's sense of failure more intense. Across the table, they clasped hands tightly.

"Mum wants you to visit. You'll be the first person outside of the center who will see her dressed and without a leg and she's very nervous about it. Will you come tomorrow?"

The next day Carolyn finished at the hospital and met Gyneth in the lobby of the Dorchester Hotel. From there, she found herself propelled upstairs to see Estelle.

Sitting in the chair, waiting for the two young women, Estelle piled small pillows in the space where her leg should have been, trying to disguise the void. Finally in frustration, she draped the small foot blanket over the cushions, decided it looked ridiculous, and started to rearrange it all again, half laughing and crying at the foolishness of the situation.

This is good practice, she thought grimly to herself, for what I have to face when I return home. I had better develop some cushion-arranging skills, and a good sense of humor. Estelle composed herself and waited expectantly to see the young black girl who had grown into a woman of ambition.

Carolyn entered the room with some hesitancy but Estelle warmly reached out to grasp her hands and took control of the situation, using her considerable social skills to overcome any discomfort. She would have to make people feel comfortable around her—it was the only way.

"Carolyn, Gyneth told me all about your day together at classes. You have done wonderfully well. Come in and sit down, let's hear all about it!"

Carolyn smiled shyly and sat down.

"Well," said Gyneth, "all we now need is Emily to tell me to take my feet off this chair."

"More likely she'd tell you that young ladies sit down quietly!" Carolyn added. The two young women started to giggle.

"How about her rules against picking up food with your fingers?" said Estelle. "Even at a barbecue!"

Gyneth looked at her mother with surprise. "Mom, you mean you didn't think Emily was perfect?"

"Perfect? My dear child, she frightened me half to death. I tried to keep out of her way in case she told me to behave, too. The only one she had any respect for was your father and even he had to watch his manners!" Soon they were all telling stories about the early days in the Amron household.

"Do you remember how cross David was when we hid in the pantry and put our fingers in his chocolate cake!" Carolyn recalled.

They laughed together as memories flooded back. Estelle took Carolyn's hand and squeezed it, and the young woman's eyes filled with tears at the unexpected gesture. She had only seen Estelle vulnerable, in hospital. Now, dressed and composed, she more closely resembled the Estelle Amron of Hyde Park.

The following Monday, Gyneth found a message from Matthew when she returned from rehabilitation with Estelle.

"Meet me at the same place at five thirty."

Gyneth found Matthew in a booth, a large pitcher of beer in front of him.

"How are things?" she asked carefully, knowing that Carolyn had planned to end their relationship the previous weekend.

"You probably know already. I had a feeling she'd do this, especially after you canceled our engagement last week."

Gyneth blushed but said nothing.

"Is it so much to ask, to want more than a few hours a week?"

Gyneth nodded understandingly. There was little that she could say. In her opinion, Carolyn was making a big mistake. Matthew was madly in love with her and they were perfectly suited. She patted his hand sympathetically.

They sat there for several hours. Gyneth spoke about

her unrequited relationships and although her stories were amusing and the conversation lighthearted, Matthew could not help seeing the deep need she had for the very intimacy that Carolyn had rejected.

Finally Gyneth knew if she drank any more she'd not be able to stand up.

Matthew hailed a taxi and they both stumbled into it.

"We'll go to my place. Let me make you some coffee before you go back to your hotel. Your mother will have a fit if she sees you like that."

Gyneth agreed and giggled. Matthew's apartment was neat and clean with a small bedroom and a large living area with a kitchenette in the corner. She sat on a chair as Matthew brewed coffee and turned on the heat.

The coffee was strong and Gyneth hiccuped, feeling nauseated.

Matthew took off his jacket and loosened his tie.

Gyneth hiccuped again. "I don't feel very well," she whispered.

"Here, lie down for a few moments." Matthew led her to the sofa.

Gyneth felt his strong arms lower her onto the cushions. She ran her hands over his chest. He had a wonderful physique. Feeling a relaxed abandon, she undid the top button of Matthew's shirt.

He looked at her, surprised.

"I'd love to see what you look like. I've never seen a black man's body."

Matthew laughed. "Here, I'll take it all off." He pulled all the buttons off his shirt as he opened it wide to show his muscles and flat stomach.

"See, just the same as white men, and underneath the blood is the same color as yours."

Gyneth blushed.

"So how about your chest?" Matthew gently pulled

Gyneth closer to him. She closed her eyes. All the taboos of the past came rushing into her consciousness, so that even her state of inebriation could not dispel the warning bells that told her that it was wrong to have sex with a black man, regardless of the fact that he was her best friend's lover.

Yet neither the taboos nor the betrayal could stop her now. It had been so long since she had felt a man's hands on her, especially one so confident and skillful as Matthew. So she kept her eyes closed tightly and lost herself in the sensations that filled her body.

Matthew penetrated her quickly and deeply.

"Yes, yes, more, more, don't stop, don't ever stop," she panted. Then Gyneth moaned in disappointment as she felt him withdraw.

"Please, come back to me, I need more." Gyneth looked through bleary eyes as Matthew left the sofa briefly to take off his clothes. She sighed gratefully as he slipped inside her again, and she gave herself entirely to the mounting waves of erotic pleasure that filled her as never before. Gyneth sobbed with the release of years of pent-up desire as Matthew held her quietly. He was filled with sadness. No one could give him what he wanted but Carolyn. He longed to feel her in his arms again.

Sick with remorse, he pulled himself up and sat on the edge of the sofa. Just then the front door opened. Carolyn stood poised on the threshold, frozen in shock.

"Oh my God, Carolyn . . ." Matthew was faint with disbelief.

"Gyneth, is that you? I can't believe it . . . Matthew? No, I won't believe it. No, it can't be true . . ."

"It's not what you think. We drank too much. Please, Carolyn, it's not what it looks like." Matthew was on his feet, reaching for Carolyn. "Please, let me explain!"

Gyneth tried to focus, arising from the bleariness brought about by too many beers and total physical satiation. "Is that Carolyn? Where am I? What's happening?"

The door slammed as Carolyn left.

"Oh my God, this can't be happening." Matthew pulled on his shorts and ran out of the door. But Carolyn had already jumped into a taxi and was gone.

Matthew held his head in his hands and, despite his attempts at self-control, he began to sob, dry, heaving, racking sobs. How could he ever win Carolyn back? It was the ultimate betrayal.

"Matthew, it was all my fault, I'll tell her, please, I started it. Oh my God, I can't believe she came in. Oh my God . . ." Gyneth tried to sober up, to comprehend the enormity of what had happened.

Finally, Matthew sat up, his face full of anguish.

"I cannot blame her if she never speaks to us both again. What on earth were we thinking of?"

Gyneth was filled with guilt and remorse. What had seemed to be an amusing adventure a few hours ago now had become an irretrievable mistake.

Gently, wordlessly, Matthew helped Gyneth dress and placed her in a taxi. Back at the hotel, she fell into bed in her clothes. The next morning she fought through a piercing headache and was sickened with guilt at her betrayal of her friend. She had to explain that it was her fault.

She called Carolyn's number. Ruth answered.

"Carolyn is not home. She had to stay at the hospital last night. I'll tell her you called."

Gyneth called every day, late at night, early in the morning. Carolyn never took her call.

Finally a letter from Carolyn was delivered to the hotel.

"I cannot forgive what you did. There are no explanations that are good enough. I never want to see you again. Carolyn."

On their last night in London, Estelle ordered room service and she and Gyneth ate together. Gyneth was in agony, knowing she could never give her mother the whole story, but that she had to talk about it or she'd break in two.

"Carolyn and I have had a falling out."

Estelle looked concerned. "I knew something was the matter. You have been so distracted the past few days. What was it about?"

"I can't really say, but I've done something that hurt her a lot and I've no real excuse for it. I don't think she will ever speak to me again."

"The only way to resolve anything is to talk about it, and soon. The longer you leave things like that, the worse they get."

"She won't see or talk to me." Gyneth picked at her food despondently.

"Perhaps you can write to her when you get home, darling."

Gyneth forced herself out of her misery. Her mother was leaving the following day, a lifetime of physical struggle ahead of her.

"I feel so guilty not coming back with you," Gyneth said.

Estelle squeezed her hand. She had reached a depth of love with Gyneth that she hadn't ever dared hope for. It was the treasure she would take with her as she tried to readjust to the life that awaited her.

"You have been away from your new world in Los Angeles long enough," Estelle said. "My life must also go on. I have friends and I'll be fine." Estelle did not really believe her own words but it was important that Gyneth hear them.

Slowly, for the last time, Estelle walked across the

therapy room to the applause of the staff and patients at Roehampton. Dressed in a pantsuit she looked almost whole, and that was her goal. It was difficult to think of herself as disabled. At times the whole nightmare seemed unreal, until she felt the pain in the limb that was not there, and saw the space where her slim shapely leg had been.

The next day at the airport, choking with tears, Gyneth embraced her mother, then watched as Estelle, in a wheelchair, was pushed slowly down the ramp to the waiting plane. She was so alone. Gyneth turned and walked to her boarding gate.

She was still berating herself for her behavior with Matthew. She had not called Carolyn after receiving the letter because whatever the depth of her friend's anger, it was justified.

How could she ever put it right again?

# PART IV

# Chapter 18

"You always look so elegant and glamorous, Gyneth, where did you get that outfit? What a gorgeous shade of green!" The woman was herself fashionably attired, and Gyneth knew from seeing her at a variety of social events that she was acutely aware of new trends. Her envy was a compliment to be cherished.

"Mara Bollen does all my shopping for me. She found it in Milan this season." Gyneth fingered the delicate pale lime fabric and remembered how she had once loathed the color green. After Estelle's amputation three years earlier she had returned to Los Angeles and the hideous green paint in her apartment. This was combined with the smell of rotting food that assailed her as she opened the door, exhausted and lonely. She hadn't cleaned out the fridge before her hasty departure and gagged as she threw out remnants of moldy leftovers. Now the memories of those years flooded back as she bade farewell to her client and strolled down Rodeo Drive looking in the windows.

On her return from London, Gyneth had called the law firm but, of course, her job had been filled. Her visit to the temple was also disconcerting. There was a new secretary there who didn't know her but when she saw the rabbi, he was friendly and concerned about her

mother. She told him a little about the months that had
passed and then he was busily on his way, too. She
sighed. Everyone in Los Angeles was so very busy all
the time. Gyneth pushed away a sudden intense feeling
of isolation, determined this time not to allow it to
overtake her.

Her car felt unfamiliar, and, having nothing else to
do, she kept driving up into the hills behind the west
side of Los Angeles. The day was crisp and clear and
the mountains ranges in the distance threw purple
shadows across the valley stretching out grandly before
Gyneth's eyes. Driving down Coldwater Canyon, she
marveled at the houses on stilts that dotted the hillside.
Gyneth preferred the valley side of the hill with its expanse and view of the mountains that reminded her of
the Magaliesberg not far from her Johannesburg home.

She noticed a number of small clubs along Ventura
Boulevard in Studio City on the way toward Universal
Studios. On impulse she stopped at one small jazz club
she'd visited before.

"Is the owner here?" she asked, speaking to one of
the Latino cleaning crew, in what she called "Span-
talian," an amalgam of Spanish, the second most com-
monly spoken language in Los Angeles, and Italian,
which she had learned at college.

He shook his head and pointed to the telephone at
the bar. There a number was scrawled in pencil above
the phone. "Emergencia," it said. The man who answered when she called was less than polite.

"Yeah?" he answered. Gyneth explained that she
was at the club and wanted a singing job.

"Come back later, at ten or so," he said and hung up.

With a spurt of energy, Gyneth drove to the Universal Hotel where there was a piano bar. Gyneth found
the courage to ask the manager for a job playing the piano and singing.

"My show is a little different from most. I come from South Africa, and show music has influenced me greatly." Gyneth sat down at the piano and started to play "Summertime," singing with energy and emotion. The manager, who had been on the point of telling her that he already had a pianist, was intrigued. Gyneth thought quickly. She closed her eyes and remembered the days she'd jazzed up the classics and made her Aunt Essie wring her hands in dismay. She had taken a number of jazz lessons thereafter on the insistence of her father who told her that if she wanted to play contemporary music then she'd better learn some of the basics. Now Gyneth said a little prayer and swung into some passable Rodgers and Hammerstein, songs from Judy Garland movies, moving into "Red Sails in the Sunset," her father's theme tune from his nightclub band, which financed his college education, and finally "South of the Border." The manager was impressed.

"We get an older crowd here," he said, "and a whole bunch of tourists. They may really go for some of that stuff. Okay, we'll give you a try. You can play three times a week. We have another pianist in here for the other nights already. Maybe there will be more if you go over well. I'll pay sixty-five dollars for a six-hour night. You start in the bar at six, in the dining room for a couple of hours, then back in the bar again till midnight. The tips are yours. You have one drink a night on the house. Don't be late." He turned and walked away.

Gyneth felt a surge of pride—she had done it! Then she started to panic. She had no sheet music, piano to practice on nor a real show to offer. Then thankfully, she thought of the temple nursery schoolroom with its small rickety but still functional piano.

Gyneth returned to the jazz club still hoping to get a job there, too. She waited until 10 P.M., napping on the front seat of the car, sprawled out and locked in until an insistent knocking at the door awoke her. The police officer was beckoning her to roll down the window. Her heart was thumping with terror as she did so.

"Are you ill?" he asked.

"No," she said tremulously.

"Then move your car, you're blocking the driveway." Gyneth looked at the entrance to the parking lot, realized she was halfway across it and breathed a sigh of relief. A leftover remnant of her life in South Africa was that she was still afraid of the police.

She looked at her watch. It was 9:30 P.M. She hastily moved the car, then went into the club. It was still deserted, since the jazz crowd only came at 11:30 or later. She approached the owner.

"Hi, I'm Gyneth Amron. I called about a job . . ." Before she could finish her sentence he snapped gruffly at her, "No jobs here, we're full up, come back in three months." Gyneth recoiled from his words and without a word of response, returned to the car, her eyes filling with tears as she told herself that rejection was part of the business.

So her lopsided life in America began again, busy nights and empty days. Gyneth discovered a large population in Los Angeles that worked only at night and an array of stores that stayed open all night long. In Los Angeles, the unusual was the norm. Still her income was barely enough and she was determined to get another job during the day.

She kept thinking about her skills and what she was good at.

"I'm really good at eating," she said, chatting with the barman one evening during a break. "I wish I could make a living doing that." He chuckled, but her thoughts stayed on the lavish parties her parents gave, often with the theme and food of different countries.

One annual event was the most memorable; Jacob's Christmas party, which he gave at their home each year for over five hundred members of the nursing and medical staff, beginning in the morning and lasting all day and night.

Soon many parties sprang to Gyneth's memory; their menus, chocolate logs filled to the brim with zabaglione, tureens overflowing with caviar in silver serving bowls placed atop antique tables on the front lawn while Armindo and David prepared blini for those who preferred it. Oh, how Gyneth yearned for the exotic smells wafting from the dining room, such as the aroma of Coquilles St. Jacques, prepared in shells collected on exotic beaches, each one an original creation of nature. Certainly she knew the ingredients of a great party, the food, ambiance, and entertainment. The glimmer of childhood memories suddenly crystallized into a clear idea—Gyneth would cater parties in this glorious city, lavish, star-studded parties!

The first company she called was run by a woman named Helga Adamson. Gyneth shuddered as she heard her coarse voice and aggressive manner. She tried to explain what she could do but the woman was in a hurry to end the conversation. Impatiently she told Gyneth to come in for an interview the following day.

The interview was perfunctory. There was no secretarial position open. She smirked at Gyneth's résumé and asked about her family and when she realized that Gyneth had no connections and little experience she practically threw her out. The other caterers she called were equally negative, and no one else would give her an interview.

Gyneth continued to play and sing, and by now she had also obtained the job at the small jazz club where she met other musicians who were friendly and welcoming. As she entered the room each night, there was a smattering of applause.

"Hi there, Gyneth! Are you going to play my favorites tonight or do I have to buy you a drink?" Gyneth laughed at the four old men who whistled and stomped their feet every time she played their requests. Her small audiences were appreciative. And in addition to the regulars, the managers at both locations were pleased with her performance.

One day there was a message on her home phone from a photographer who often worked for temple members at family events. Gyneth returned the call immediately.

"I have a gig for you. The band that was to provide the entertainment for this party that I am photographing has split up at the last minute, refusing to play together. The party is at a client in Holmby Hills. Two adolescents are throwing a surprise anniversary party for their parents and they don't know anyone who can play the kinds of songs that their parents would enjoy. Can you help?"

Gyneth was thrilled. She quickly organized Danny Sells, her favorite drummer and percussionist from the jazz club, and a bass player who played with her often at the hotel, and begged them to give her a few hours of their time for rehearsals.

"Danny, there is a real opportunity here. I just feel it. Can we put something snappy together as a theme to lead in and close with?" Gyneth's enthusiasm was contagious and Danny and the other musician agreed to spend a number of hours creating a program of upbeat, jazz, dance, and blues numbers. Gyneth was energized and excitedly told the photographer that she had it covered, quoting a price with an override for herself. Amazingly the children who were hosting the party agreed and gave her the assignment.

The night arrived and Gyneth, elegant in the flattering green dress that she'd worn for her school dance many years ago, admired her image in the mirror. The gown had a classical line, appropriate for a black tie ball and she felt alive, exhilarated.

She arrived with the other members of the group and for the first time in Los Angeles she saw a house comparable to those of her youth. It was a large estate, placed well back from the street on rolling lawns, with a tennis court and pool concealed by thick foliage. The flowerbeds were manicured and the driveway long and flowing. Gyneth felt a twinge of anger at being peremptorily waved off to the tradesman's entrance but then reminded herself that this would be just a temporary role, and one that signified the beginning to a future where she would be in control.

The party was lavish with champagne and caviar flowing liberally. As dancers twirled to the group's music, Gyneth's poise and relaxed familiarity with the microphone made more than a few people in the assemblage look at her curiously. Some asked for a business card, which she didn't have, but she gave them her name and number. Tired but glowing with satisfaction, Gyneth finished the evening with a medley that included her father's favorite, "Tico Tico."

The news spread by word by mouth.

"Danny, I can hardly believe it." Gyneth was on the phone to the drummer almost daily. "We are booked solid for the next few months. We'll need more backup musicians, and a couple of new arrangements."

Gyneth obtained referral letters from all her clients and soon she was so busy that she was unable to play at the hotel. She went out of her way to include her friends from the various jazz clubs she frequented, and soon many musicians were calling, asking to be remembered for the next job.

She sent out an introductory letter on newly printed stationery to all the caterers and temples on the West Side of town. She donated her services for senior citizens programs at lunches during the weeks, and through her activities, became familiar with the various charity organizations in the Jewish community.

Gyneth's temple activities brought her in contact with many leaders in industry, real estate tycoons, lawyers, and doctors. She expanded her network continually.

"Yes, we are hiring now. A personal assistant for Ms. Amron, these are the skills we need . . ." Gyneth heard her secretary speaking to the personnel agency. She waved to the bookkeeper who had started the week before.

"Is this fun or what?" The young woman laughed. Gyneth was always so upbeat. And she had every reason to be. Business was booming.

"Janice," Gyneth called to her secretary, "can you pop over to the new apartment and check on the movers? I have so many calls to make!" Gyneth was still working out of her home and was moving to a larger apartment in Westwood. She knew that before long she would have to find an office.

Her secretary came early and left late. Soon the newly hired assistant followed Gyneth everywhere, taking notes, following up on a thousand little tasks that went into the coordination of events.

Eventually the caterers were calling her for leads. She laughed to herself as she remembered how she had begged Helga to take notice of her. Now Helga was on the phone continuously, her attitude obsequious, and she had all the time in the world to talk.

Money and success were great leverage. Gyneth was becoming someone to notice and her presence and poise made her stand out among those who had money but no breeding. She advised on atmosphere, style, what to do to make a party unique.

She spoke to Estelle weekly. Her mother was coping, with great effort. Some of the Amrons' friends found it so difficult to accept Estelle's disability that they saw her less and less, and their rejection caused even more pain than the cancer. Even though others were there for her, Estelle's expansive life had reduced to a sadder, lonelier existence.

Whenever she spoke to her mother, Gyneth felt overwhelming guilt at the thought of not being home, close to Estelle. She vowed that as soon as she could afford it she would go and visit her, but in fact it was an empty vow since she had no real desire to leave.

"I'll try and come to see you soon, Mum," she said on their regular weekly call. "It's just that things are really busy here and it's not a good time."

"Gyneth, I'm so pleased things are better. The last thing I want is for you to drop everything. It really is fine to live your life without feeling guilty that I am here and you are not. We will see each other when the time is right."

One of Gyneth's favorite clients was the owner of a women's dress store. Gyneth enjoyed planning Mara Bollen's son's bar mitzvah because the two women had a similar sense of style, and they became friends. Gyneth loved Mara's taste in clothes and finally asked if there were anything in the store that would fit her.

Mara clasped her hands. "I am so relieved that you asked me that. You really do need some help in that area. Maybe we can do a trade of services, yours for mine. Would you let me help you?"

Gyneth nodded hesitantly, memories of dreadful shopping days with her mother making her shudder with self-hatred.

The next day they went to the store. After trying on

a few outfits, Mara knew Gyneth's size. From that moment onward, she brought out only clothes that fit. Gyneth could hardly believe it. She'd never gone into a store where everything she tried on fit. Mara dressed her with excitement, whipping out accessories, bags and scarves, jewelry and shoes. Each outfit came together like a work of art and all throughout the experience, Gyneth marveled at her evolving appearance. She could actually look attractive if dressed well. There was no need for her to delay buying clothes until that elusive day when she had lost weight, to constantly be berating the way she looked now and yearning for the future when she would be thin and able to start living as an attractive woman.

Gyneth held herself with new confidence and the image she protrayed drew admiring looks from both men and women. She miraculously discovered her sex appeal again even though she'd not lost one single ounce. Her new feelings made her look and feel twenty pounds thinner.

Gyneth started to date again. The first few times out were uncomfortable. It was as if she'd lost the knack of light conversation and teasing flirtation. She'd talked about business, profit and loss, marketing, promotion and money for so long that she'd forgotten how to relax.

The phone continued to ring. Some of the men who called backed off when they learned of her six-figure income. Many of them had already been married and had deep emotional problems. She wondered if the city attracted people who were emotionally unstable or if it made them that way. Others were so boring that she could hardly wait to end the evening.

However, one man in particular amused her. His name was Alex Dreyfus, a senior executive in a public relations firm. He represented one of Gyneth's clients

and arranged to meet with her to coordinate the press
coverage of the event she was arranging. His voice was
deep and appealing on the phone and Gyneth was intrigued to see that he looked as elegant as he sounded.
They settled into the best outdoor table at the Bistro
Gardens restaurant in Beverly Hills.

"You have a wonderful reputation, Ms. Amron, I am
truly pleased to meet you." Alex looked at Gyneth approvingly. She was wearing a yellow and black jacket
that flattered her figure and drew attention to her green
eyes.

"The admiration is mutual, Mr. Dreyfus. And please
call me Gyneth. Shall we order first and then do business after?'

Gyneth was pleased to see that Alex's manners were
more European than American as he asked her prefer-
ence.

"The lady will have the poached salmon, and I will
have the steamed mussels. And perhaps one chocolate
soufflé for dessert?" Gyneth laughed and agreed.

"And two glasses of your house Chardonnay."

Suddenly Gyneth felt feminine and attractive. It was
obvious that Alex had accomplished social skills. She
relaxed in his presence. The conversation flowed easily. He was outgoing and positive in his attitude and
made her laugh.

"The most important piece of information I always
give my clients, but they never seem to remember it, is
not to believe their own press." Alex sighed. "But self-
adulation is just too tempting, I'm afraid."

Gyneth laughed. Alex was refreshingly honest, a
rare quality in Tinseltown. For once, Gyneth slowed
down, allowing their time together to move easily from
business to personal and back to business again. Alex
could become a real friend.

They met regularly, first to plan the mutual client's

event and then to talk. Alex seemed to understand her and in his courteous way he made no physical advances toward her. Perhaps that was why she enjoyed being with him—he didn't intrude past the external appearance that she now was so expert at creating. She looked and felt great, but as soon as she took her clothes off, she saw the hated body that couldn't be hidden. It was safe to joke, laugh, and maybe kiss a little. But that was enough. She needed to keep her body inviolate. And with Alex, Gyneth was free to show her considerable intellect, hide her despised body under elegant and flattering clothes, and keep her outer persona intact. For Gyneth, it was a perfect arrangement.

# Chapter 19

Carolyn threw herself back into medical school. It gave her stability, without emotion, letting her follow a frantic pace. Yet the vision of a sleepy Gyneth, breasts bare, sitting up beside Matthew's naked hard body was imprinted on her mind forever and their betrayal brought tears of fury to her eyes.

She silenced the needs in her body with her tried-and-true method, dismal as it seemed to her now, and immersed herself in her studies. Carolyn would not let the prophesy that she saw in the eyes of all her professors when they saw her race and sex be fulfilled—she would succeed beyond all expectations.

The young woman's brilliance and strength of will was unparalleled by any of her classmates. At first, her professors,with barely concealed bigotry, presumed her lack of ability. But soon they were amazed, even grudgingly pleased, at her astute judgment and avaricious approach to learning. With unwavering concentration, she took every opportunity for learning, whether it be in the labs, wards, or library. Each new slate of professors patronized the slender black girl sitting in the class but she knew that after one or two of her answers they would smirk no more. Her admirers grew; she gained a reputation among the faculty as a marvel.

Carolyn continued to feel like an outsider at school but not at home for Ruth was always there, a loving and stalwart ally. The older woman led a solitary life, participating in only one annual community activity, on Yom Kippur, the Jewish day of Atonement when Carolyn would accompany her to a small orthodox shul in the East End of London. Carolyn ignored the odd looks they received as she stood holding Ruth while the older woman allowed herself to mourn for the family she'd lost to the Holocaust.

Carolyn spent every spare moment in the hospital, observing operations, reading up on procedures and following the patients' progress on the wards. She immersed herself in the protective environment of her profession.

Her constant presence was noticed by a young consultant who saw the slender black girl on the surgical wards almost daily. She appeared to be well liked by the nurses and her obvious commitment was intriguing to him. She reminded him of his earlier days when the excitement of his role absorbed his every waking moment.

One Saturday morning, he stood next to her as she read the bed chart of one of his postsurgical patients.

"Hello there. I'm Jeff Kramer. I see you have an interest in Mr. Johnston."

Carolyn closed the chart quickly and politely held out her hand. "I do hope you don't mind. I am fascinated by the diagnosis. I really should have asked your permission to review his chart since he is your patient."

"Not at all. Perhaps you can give me your evaluation of his case."

Carolyn smiled. She had been reading up on the man's condition.

Jeff watched her while she described her readings. He liked especially the way she stood, confident and still, her energy focused on the matter at hand.

"Let's go into the doctors' tea room and discuss this further." Jeff led the way.

Carolyn was professional in her manner and distant. Their conversation concerned medical topics only.

"I have a very interesting case that will be checking in tonight for surgery in a couple of days. Would you like to work on it with me? It is a carcinoma similar to Mr. Johnston's but with some significant differences."

"I'd love to." Carolyn's eyes sparkled.

Jeff felt a tingle of anticipation. Carolyn was a mystery to him. Her accent had a twang that was decidedly different. Black women were a rarity as physicians.

Carolyn could see the appreciative look in his eyes. He was an attractive, tall man with glasses and a ready smile. She guessed he was about thirty-five, ten years older than herself. Some of her classmates had developed mentor relationships with their professors and she had seen their knowledge and confidence progress dramatically. Over the next few weeks Carolyn spent a lot of time making sure that she excelled in whatever Jeff Kramer asked her to do. He seemed willing to spend the time to teach her, and she was determined to prove to him that his faith was well placed.

Although after their first year, most of the students had taken a room closer to the hospital, Carolyn could not afford to. She took the subway from Golders Green, passing the shul Ruth attended annually on her daily walk from the station to the hospital.

Every morning and night old men gathered to pray and they made Carolyn think of Joe and the conversation they'd shared about the Talmud and Judaism.

One Saturday, on her way to the library, she walked, as always, through the grimy East End of London where Jewish immigrants from Poland and Lithuania had built the community. Now the new immigrants were from Bangladesh and Pakistan. Carolyn passed Ruth's shul as usual. This time, however, she stopped. The old man at its door eyed her with suspicion.

"Yes, young lady, you vant something?"

She gave a little curtsy, reverting back to her youth and the ways she had been taught to show respect.

"I had a teacher once, he told me about Judaism and the Talmud. I was curious."

"You vant come in? Come, cover your head like this." He handed her a fragile piece of lace with a hair clip. "You can sit with the ladies."

Carolyn followed him into the dark cool interior of the small synagogue and he motioned to the side where the women sat together behind a white lace curtain. At the front of the room was a raised dais supporting a wood-paneled cabinet decorated with carvings. Here the rabbi stood dressed in his flowing robes.

She slipped behind the curtain as the man pulled one of the young women forward. She wore a hat and sensible shoes.

"You can explain to her about everything—she wants to understand. Don't disturb the others." He moved away.

Some of the women had been whispering, catching up on the week's gossip, while others muttered and sang softly as they prayed along with the service. They all stopped what they were doing when Carolyn entered, and stared. Soon they began to whisper and giggle among themselves.

Carolyn suddenly had a strong desire to leave.

"Don't mind them," the young woman said softly, moving to her side. "They gossip about everyone, including me. Come, I'll explain everything." She squeezed Carolyn's arm reassuringly seeing her discomfort.

She began to explain. "In front is the Ark of the Covenant. That is where we keep the five books of Moses, you know it as the Old Testament. We call it the Torah."

Carolyn nodded. Joe had told her about the Torah.

"We're now chanting the morning service. We believe that Friday at sundown until Saturday at sundown is the Sabbath, we don't work in any way on the Sabbath. We don't cook, clean or study anything but Torah and Talmud on that day, in family unity. Sometimes on Friday we make a dish called cholent, sort of a pot roast, for the Saturday meals. We don't even turn the lights on and off on the Sabbath—we just contemplate the intellectual and spiritual parts of our lives and renew our spirits for the week that lies ahead."

Carolyn nodded again and began to relax. How wonderful it would be to have the luxury of a Sabbath, a place and time to renew herself and share in questioning the universe for a whole twenty-four hours! The young woman looked at Carolyn, her intelligent gaze steady. This black girl was strange, different. She seemed to be very comfortable in the shul.

"What is your name?" she asked.

"Carolyn Ngwizi. What's yours?"

"Rachel Cohen. I'm the rabbi's daughter. He's the one you see over there with the robes on. He is the spiritual guide of the congregation, listening to everyone's questions. He doesn't have the answers, but he asks you questions that help you find your own answers. He's a wonderful father."

Carolyn looked at the short, bearded man. Rachel looked like him. She had his round face and friendly eyes.

"Would you like to go outside, then we can talk a little more?" The other women were casting disapproving looks and Rachel saw that her mother was about to come over and scold them for whispering. Rachel did not want Carolyn to be embarrassed.

They found a quiet place in the ladies' room.

"Do you live around here?" Rachel asked curiously.

"No, in Golders Green. I'm a medical student at the London Hospital," Carolyn announced.

Rachel's eyes widened. "How wonderful," she said, looking at Carolyn with new respect. She knew there was something unusual about this young woman.

"I come from South Africa. A Jewish man there was instrumental in helping me to escape persecution. I'm living with a wonderful woman who is also Jewish—a Holocaust survivor. Her name is Ruth Levy. You might have seen me with her, we come here every Yom Kippur."

Carolyn paused, her words tumbling out awkwardly.

"I am intrigued by your faith," she stammered softly. "Your people seem to understand the evils of discrimination, and empathize with people of color." Carolyn found herself speaking in staccato sentences, trying to both explain and understand her own feelings at the same time. "I grew up with a Jewish girl, we were close friends." She felt a sudden longing to hear Gyneth's giggle, feel the excitement of her enthusiasm and ebullient energy. It was as though her life had been devoid of fun since she and Gyneth had been apart.

"Look, I have to get back to the service, otherwise my mother will be after me. I have an idea," Rachel said, in a burst of friendship, "why don't you come to my home for lunch tomorrow and we can continue our conversation?"

Carolyn was touched. "Thank you—but don't you

think that you had better ask your parents first? They might not like the idea of having me."

"Nonsense!" said Rachel. "I'll see you here at one o'clock. We'll walk home together."

Carolyn left and went to the library where she studied all day. She stopped by the surgical ward on her way home to see Jeff Kramer's patients. She learned more from her time with him and his patients than from her classes. When she got home that night, she told Ruth about her meeting with Rachel.

"They sound like lovely people." Ruth gave Carolyn a warm glass of milk as she went up to bed. "Tomorrow we will speak of your lunch with them."

After Carolyn was in bed, Ruth went to her library and turned on the light. She had some researching to do. It had been many years since she had read a book on Jewish tradition. Carolyn had to know how to behave with the rabbi's family the next day. She would explain some of the rules of Kashruth, the Jewish dietary laws.

"There will be prayers before and after the meal. Here"—Ruth pulled out the old prayer book she had searched for the previous night—"they will sing these ones."

They were simple songs that Carolyn easily learned. Ruth sat at the little desk and phonetically wrote out the words so that Carolyn could join in the songs. Within a few moments Carolyn had photographed in her memory the words of the blessing on the bread and sang with Ruth in her clear voice. Ruth was filled with pleasure when she heard Carolyn chanting the words and notes of her youth. She added more words of advice.

"Watch the rabbi and his wife. You'll see that he'll defer to her out of the corner of his eye even though she'll seem to let him make all the decisions. Also, we must buy some flowers. You should never go empty-handed to someone's home for a meal. Always bring a small gift."

On Sunday, Rachel met Carolyn at the shul and together they walked through the streets to a very modest house filled with smells of cooking, delicious enough to make a strong man wilt with hunger.

Carolyn handed her flowers shyly to the large woman with the smiling face who greeted her at the door.

"Come in, come in. We are almost ready to eat. You must be starving. Rachel has told me all about you. A medical student! Isn't that wonderful! A doctor no less, and all the way from South Africa. Come, sit, sit, soon we eat." She swept back into the kitchen as the young women sat down in the overstuffed chairs.

"Where is your father?" Carolyn whispered, a little nervous about breaking bread with a rabbi.

"Oh, he's taking a short walk with one of the community members who needed some advice. He likes to walk when he can because he sits a lot. This way he says he gives advice and exercises at the same time!"

Rachel laughed. Carolyn joined in, feeling warm and welcome in this comfortable home.

Soon the rabbi arrived, a little out of breath.

"A pleasure to meet you," he said. "Sit, sit, we have much to talk about. You must tell me all about yourself."

Carolyn felt a little shy, but his intelligent gaze reminded her of Joe, and so she relaxed and started to tell them about her escape. When she got to the part about Joe dressing up like a rabbi and crossing the border with Carolyn lying quietly under a pile of prayer books for a fictional rabbis' convention, they started laughing so hard that the tears were running down the rabbi's face. "This is a man I must meet," he said emphatically. "When he comes here you must bring him over for Shabbat dinner."

They went into the dining room to a table laden with good things. Carolyn noted that it was a dairy meal. Ruth had taught her that the dietary laws did not permit dairy and meat products to be eaten together.

They began with the blessings for the food. Carolyn joined in and began to sing the blessing for the bread. She completely lost herself in the music as she always did and when she looked up, the family were staring at her, speechless.

"Where did you learn to sing that?" the rabbi asked, the question on all of their minds. Carolyn told them about Ruth, her love for her evident. The rabbi nodded, understanding. A very unusual young woman, like none other he had ever met. He had been worried about her influence on his daughter, who was a naive and impressionable twenty-year-old, but not anymore.

The meal was filled with surprises. The more they talked, the more Carolyn added her little remembrances of the Talmud into the conversation, those fragments from her brief but memorable talk with Joe, and Rachel's mother's brows shot up so many times it seemed as if finally they would disappear into her hairline.

Then it came time to part and she and Rachel hugged as she promised to come again the next Sunday.

From that day on, Sunday lunch with the rabbi became part of Carolyn's routine after she did ward rounds with Jeff Kramer.

"Where are you off to today?" he asked one Sunday. "How about a spot of lunch?"

"I have plans, unfortunately, but thanks anyway." Carolyn suddenly felt the need to confide in this man who had shown such an interest in her career.

"I have met the most wonderful people—Rabbi Co-hen and his family, they are part of the Jewish community not far from here."

Jeff's eyes widened in surprise. He was a member of Rabbi Cohen's shul but attended services only on the rare occasions that his parents implored him to join them.

"I know the community well. My family belongs there. How ... er ... where ... are you a member there?" He found himself at a loss for words.

Carolyn laughed.

"I'm not Jewish, if that is what you are trying to say. I guessed that you were or I wouldn't have said anything about the Cohens. There aren't too many Jewish doctors here, are there?"

"No, not too many. You must tell me more, Carolyn, how very interesting!"

"I'd be happy to, but not now or I'll be late for lunch."

"Well how about joining me for dinner Wednesday after surgery?"

"Sounds fine, where?"

"There's a little Italian restaurant, Posto, about two blocks from here. At seven o'clock?"

"I know it well, I walk past it every day. See you there!"

Carolyn half ran down the stairs, feeling lighthearted and excited. Then she calmed herself down. What on earth was she thinking of? Dr. Kramer was probably married, with kids, a house, and a dog and she was acting like a schoolgirl on her first date, when all he'd done was ask her to have dinner together. They had a nice, respectful professional relationship and that was exactly where it would stay.

On that Wednesday, Carolyn checked her appearance in the cloakroom mirror, standing on her toes to try and

see if her skirt was straight. Shopping for clothes was
low on her list of things to do, but Ruth had given her
a colorful shawl to throw over a dress that had seen
better days, and after applying a slight touch of lip-
stick, she was not displeased with the result.

Her own lack of pleasure with her appearance, however, was not reflected in Jeff's eyes as he saw her enter
the restaurant. Suddenly he felt a rush of desire as he
looked at her shapely legs and taut breasts, barely visible
beneath the folds of the shawl. Her eyes were huge and
accented the delicacy of her features.

"You look wonderful in those colors," he said softly.
Carolyn heard his voice change from the businesslike
professionalism of their normal exchanges and felt a
shiver of anticipation.

"Thank you." She sank into the deep sofalike chair.
"This is a welcome change from the cafeteria!"
Carolyn tried to sound matter-of-fact, but the intimacy
of the environment had instantaneously changed the
nature of their relationship.

"I enjoy working with you enormously," Jeff continued. His words were professional but his voice soft as
he looked reflectively at her. He had always thought
Carolyn attractive, but now he found her sensual and
enormously erotic. Perhaps it had been a mistake to
meet her here. It had deepened his attraction to her.

"Tell me about yourself. Where do you come from,
how did you land up in our wet and dreary town?"

"It's a long story."

"I have all evening, and you have my fullest attention."

Carolyn felt his voice caress her and yearned to lean
toward him, to touch him. Horrified at her reaction she
pulled the shawl tightly around her and began to speak,
hesitantly at first, then after the dinner was ordered and
served, more boldly. He deserved to know. After all,

the amount of time Jeff had spent coaching her showed his trust and confidence, and the least she could do was to be honest with him about her past.

Finally, hours later, as they sipped cognacs together, the low murmur of conversations from other booths in the restaurant soothing and unobtrusive, Carolyn ended her tale.

"You are even more remarkable than I had suspected." Jeff was mesmerized by Carolyn's story. His desire for her had grown throughout the evening, and he realized that if he were to touch her, it would mean stepping over the invisible boundary of mentorship forever.

Carolyn, too, felt the closeness and longed to curl up into his arms. He was serious, strong, and intuitive. Despite the enormous differences in their backgrounds, they shared the same passion for medicine, and it was very comfortable for her to be able to be herself, ambitious and driven.

The evening ended with a handshake. Feeling frustrated and pensive, Carolyn sat on the swinging subway. On a number of occasions she had looked up into Jeff's eyes and was sure she had seen her own desire reflected in them. But he had made no move in that direction and she could not be sure. She realized he had told her little about himself, and that she did not even know if he were married.

They greeted each other with polite professionalism the next day.

Jeff agonized over his next move.

Carolyn was so much of what he wanted in a woman, intelligent, moral, ambitious. But their racial and religious differences could not be ignored. He decided to back off and give himself time to consider his attraction to her, and whether she was, in fact, the one he had been waiting for.

Carolyn felt Jeff return to the pleasant easygoing relationship they had shared before their only evening out, and she pushed any other ideas she might have had out of her mind. It was clear to her that he was not interested.

Over the next few months, Carolyn noticed Ruth resting a lot in the evenings when she had always been out at concerts or operas of which she was an avid fan. Now she seldom went anywhere. Carolyn looked at her with a clinical eye.

"Ruth, you look very tried. I want you to come to the hospital for an examination and blood workup with one of my professors, a very gentle man." Carolyn knew of Ruth's anxiety around doctors. She had been experimented upon in the extermination camps by the Germans, sterilized, and tortured beyond all human endurance. White coats and examining rooms made her shake with fear. But, to Carolyn's surprise and considerable consternation, Ruth agreed readily.

The school's professor of internal medicine agreed to see Ruth in his office without his white coat. Carolyn draped a colorful blanket that Ruth had crocheted over the end of the examining room table so that there would be something familiar in the room when she entered. Understanding Ruth's background, the professor agreed to try and make the atmosphere for Ruth's examination as nonmedical as possible.

Carolyn stayed with Ruth throughout the physical, the X-rays that caused her to quake in terror, and the blood tests. She took her home in a taxi and made a strong cup of tea. Ruth looked at her with tears in her eyes. In Carolyn she saw the children she'd lost to the Nazis. The young woman had enriched her life beyond her greatest expectations. Carolyn fussed around her, thinking the same thing.

"I do love you," Carolyn whispered as she hugged

Ruth. "Here, why don't you take this sedative that Professor Seymour-Jones prescribed for you, and have a good rest."

Carolyn didn't feel right about the situation. The next day she rushed to the lab and hand-carried the blood test results back to Professor Seymour-Jones. Together they looked at the X-rays and results.

"I am afraid it is not good, my dear," Seymour-Jones said. "I can see secondaries in her lungs, confirmed by the blood work. The primary tumor could be any one of these," he said, pointing to shadows in the lower portion of her abdomen. "It looks as if it's inoperable. She doesn't have more than a few months to live. I am so sorry. I do know how close you are to her. Would you like her to come in and I'll tell her—or taking into account her fears, would you prefer to tell her at home where she feels safer?"

Carolyn felt sick with grief. Ruth had been like a mother, her only family. Why hadn't she noticed sooner that she was ailing. Carolyn beat her fist into her leg, frustrated and grieving.

Seymour-Jones saw her agony. "This is a very quick-growing tumor. She'd had a great deal of radiation in the past and it destroyed her ability to withstand something like this. It's a malignancy of an aggressive nature and there was nothing you could have done about it, even if somehow you'd known about it on the day it started. It grows very fast. Look, here is the reference to the tumor, go and read up about it. You must accept that this is not your fault, Miss Ngwizi. Carolyn," he said softly. Not one to use students' first names, he searched for a way to comfort her. "You are learning one of the sad truths about medicine—we are very humble in the face of many of the diseases that kill mankind. At times there is little we can do but try and make the patient feel comfortable during their last days. We must learn to accept our limitations as physicians. Now, if there is anything more I can do for you, please let me know. I think Mrs. Levy should be admitted to hospital only when she becomes uncomfortable and we will administer analgesia to make her last days bearable."

Carolyn left the hospital in a daze. Bereft, she wandered down the street, wondering how she was going to find strength and words. She found herself at the shul, went inside; no one was there so she sat in a pew and tried to gain some serenity from the place. None came to her. She realized that this was not something she could put off. It had to be handled, and as soon as possible.

All too soon she was at the door of her house. She heard the piano notes gently accompany Ruth's voice as she sang an aria from *La Boheme*. Carolyn entered the house and saw Ruth looking energetic and youthful as she lost herself in the music. For a moment Carolyn felt the wild hope that maybe this had been a horrible dream and everything would be all right. Then her scientific training made her face reality. She knew that together they would make the next months as bearable as possible but she would not lie.

Ruth finished the final trill with a flourish and turned to Carolyn with arms outstretched. They held each other for a long time. Then together they sat on the sofa, its well-worn cushions comforting and familiar. Ruth took Carolyn's hands in hers.

"Nu, Mein Kindela," she said, using the loving diminutive she often used for Carolyn when the girl had sat up night after night studying. "It is not good news, is it?"

Carolyn shook her head, unable to speak.

"How long then?"

"Two, three months, maybe more." Carolyn choked

on the words and then the sobs came. She buried her head in Ruth's hands, the pain and grief of her future loss beginning to engulf her. Ironically, Ruth comforted her.

"Ah yes," she said, sighing, "it is the living who must suffer the pain of the dying. I only regret I will not see you marry and have children, nor will I be able to *kvell* at your graduation. So very, very much I will miss of your life, my child. But God has blessed us with each other for these short years and that"—she kissed Carolyn softly on the head—"no one can take away from us. It has been so good, so very good. You are the child I lost and the one I never had and you came to me like a miracle from the second man I ever loved. Did I ever tell you that Joe and I were in love?" Carolyn blew her nose like a small child, sniffling, as Ruth held her close.

"I do not know how he could have loved me then, I was ugly, disfigured from the experiments. He whispered in my ear every day that we must live, that only in life there was hope. He said it so fiercely that nothing they could do to me mattered as long as I was alive. *Live, he said, live to tell the world.* Then, when we survived I was so afraid of everything, I couldn't bear to be alone. After we were liberated from the camps, Joe had to leave me. His first loyalty was to his wife. But I have never stopped loving him. Isn't that silly, an old lady like me?"

She was quiet for a moment, rocking herself back and forth, remembering. Carolyn looked into Ruth's expressive eyes, and saw that they were filled with love and peace.

"And one day he sent me his love in the most wonderful gift he could ever have given me—you, my dearest child. In you, he gave me the happiest years of my life.

"And something else. I know that he would want you to know. Joe has sent me money for your support ever since you arrived here. Together, in that way, we have shared in the miracle of your success. My child, you are a wonder, and will go on to fulfill the destiny that God has chosen for you. You have given me true happiness and love. So there must be no more grieving. We must revel in the life that is still left to us together. While I can breathe, we will sing and play music, walk and inhale the cool air, see the trees and sky, the bustling life around us. We will laugh together and cry a little, remembering all the times we've shared. Come, we've not a moment to waste. Sing with me, my child. I still have lots to teach you about that lovely voice of yours."

Ruth pulled Carolyn over to sit beside her on the piano stool and together they played and sang as if they had forever ahead of them.

Soon Ruth was tired and Carolyn helped her to bed. Then she began to think of what else she had to do. While Ruth slept, Carolyn dug around in the study looking frantically for the records that must exist with Joe's address. Finally she found a small bundle of letters, spaced over a number of years, from Joe to Ruth. Carolyn began to read one and then stopped. They were too personal. She carefully tied up the bundle after noting the address, remembering, all of a sudden, the small house with manicured garden that lay quietly in the shadow of the Voortrekker Monument in that country so very far away that she had once called home. She called the overseas operator and placed the call. Her heart started to thump loudly and her ears were ringing as a young man answered. Carolyn asked for Joseph Abramowitz in her best English accent.

"Hello?"

"Joe?" she said in a shaky voice.

"Yes?" he said guardedly.

"I'm calling for Ruth Levy. She is very ill and I know she would want to see you before it's too late. I am . . . a very dear friend of hers, someone she befriended. I'm a medical student and I've been living with her for the last eight years. She does not have many more months to live. It would be a wonderful surprise for her to see you again. I, too, would appreciate it. Can you come?"

Carolyn avoided mentioning her own name, cautioned by her old fear of the South African police causing repercussions for Joe or, even years later, tracking her down. She knew from the excitement in Joe's voice, as he promised to come the very next Monday on the South African Airways daily flight to London, that he knew it was her. Trembling, she quietly replaced the phone. It was the right thing to do. Ruth would have him with her for the last few good weeks of her life; in fact, they would be like a family, three people who fell into one another's lives through the hatred and evil of others and nevertheless found something beautiful and good to live for.

The next week sped by. Ruth rested much of the day so as to spend the evenings with Carolyn alert and reminiscing. Her few friends came over, the house was filled with talk, music, and fond memories. Carolyn struggled to keep up with her studies, rising before dawn to study so that she could spend as many hours as possible with Ruth at night.

Finally the day came. Carolyn prepared the extra room and told Ruth that she was expecting a guest, a friend of hers from South Africa who was going to spend a few days with them. Ruth accepted the news, pleased as always when Carolyn invited her few friends to the house. The rabbi's family had become frequent guests, and now they brought support and sustenance, chicken soup, freshly baked cakes and cookies, and warm affection for both Ruth and Carolyn.

Monday evening Carolyn went to the airport. As she anxiously waited for the arriving passengers to clear the customs hall, she saw him, as roly-poly as she remembered. He seemed somewhat helpless, his little bald pate shining as he puffed over the luggage cart and looked anxiously around for a familiar face. His demeanor belied the couragous and dangerous life he had chosen for himself. Carolyn smiled broadly and then he saw her.

"Joe?" she said and he nodded. He would not have recognized the tall slender young woman if not for her wonderful smile. Carolyn wanted to hug him but suddenly feeling quite shy and awkward she went quickly to him, heaved his bag off the cart and started down the escalator to the subway. Joe followed and soon they had dispensed with the tickets and were seated in the train.

"You look so wonderful, Carolyn, you've grown into a beautiful woman. Tell me how it has been, please, from the beginning. I have thought of you often and wondered how you've been doing. When I heard your voice it was such a wonderful gift for me, though your news is so sad about my sweet Ruth. Tell me about her. Start at the beginning, we have a long train ride and much to talk about."

Joe was much older than Carolyn had remembered. He seemed such a little man now, but his intelligent eyes were still the same. There was so much she had to tell him about the past eight years. Carolyn took a deep breath and began.

Soon they were at Ruth's door. Carolyn warned Joe that she knew nothing of his visit, in case he'd been prevented from coming. Ruth was sleeping on the sofa. She opened her eyes and saw the two of them standing there. She closed her eyes again and muttered, "Such a dream, such a dream."

Joe sat down gently beside her and touched her hair, still brown among the gray, saying her name softly. She opened her eyes wide. "It is really you? How can this be?" Ruth started to cry and Carolyn slipped quietly out of the room and left them alone.

Soon she heard the crying stop and the laughing begin, and they called for her to join them. When she returned they were smiling like two proud parents. They sat, touching each other, laughing and crying at the same time. The hours flew by, until, exhausted, they collapsed into the bed Carolyn had prepared in the guest room. Although she had not known if they would sleep together, she had taken care to arrange the room for privacy. The next few weeks of borrowed time would be precious and fleeting.

The days flew by and Carolyn stayed close to home and slowly, sadly, Ruth became more and more frail. Eventually she was unable to go out anymore. But she could still sing, and so Carolyn and Joe played and sang in concert with her every night.

As the pain grew worse and Ruth took more and more medication, all of those around her knew that the time had come for her to go into the hospital.

"I will miss you so much," Carolyn whispered as she held the frail hand in hers. "Who will be there for me?" The tears poured down her cheeks until she could see no more.

"You have fought my battles, but this one is yours and I cannot help you."

Small and shrunken in the large hospital bed, Ruth drifted in and out of sleep.

Joe held Carolyn as she sobbed and slowly they watched as Ruth faded peacefully into a twilight world while they sat vigil at her bedside. Then with Joe holding one hand and Carolyn the other, one moment suspended in eternity, Ruth's eyelids fluttered and she was gone.

Joe led Carolyn through the burial and shiva. The friends and community that were Ruth's life moved through her home to pay respects. The Cohens took over the management of the household, preparing food for the mourners and twice-daily prayers for those present. In response to Carolyn's sobs of grief, Joe whispered words of consolation and understanding, affirming that it was important to mourn. As he prepared to leave, he explained to Carolyn that Judaism wisely set out a pattern to help the bereft. The next thirty days she was to mourn but return to work. The following eleven months would be the extended period of mourning and thereafter, life must go on. Only on the date of Ruth's death should she light a candle and say the prayers of remembrance. Otherwise Carolyn had to throw herself wholeheartedly back into the joys and trials of living.

Carolyn heard his words but knew that her life would never be the same. She was again as alone as she'd been those many years ago in Soweto.

On the day of Joe's departure, they agreed to write. Carolyn would use Ruth's surname as Carolyn Levy since Joe's mail was opened and his telephone calls were tapped. Carolyn hugged him, grateful for his presence and help.

"Her last weeks were her happiest, because you were here," she said.

"No, my dear," he said, "it was because *we* were with her."

Carolyn nodded silently as she grasped his hand. "Thank you for my life, Joe, for Ruth. She gave me a future, both of you did."

Then he was gone, a small man with a heavy suitcase traveling back to a land where he risked his life and that of his family every day for those denied freedom because of the color of their skin.

Carolyn heard the contents of Ruth's will with a mixture of sorrow and gratitude. The house, which was unencumbered, and everything in it, was now hers. As she walked through the rooms she saw them with new eyes. This was the first time she had owned anything of value and it gave her the secure feeling of being a real part of England, a person with a home. She fingered the beloved crocheted blankets that Ruth had made over the years to cover the worn sofa cushions. She was determined to learn to appreciate the significance of everything there—the small Persian rug, silver candlesticks, classical music and books. She decided to learn cooking in accordance withe the dietary laws of *kashruth,* in order to invite the rabbi and his family to her home. She belonged somewhere now and she could hardly believe it.

In addition to this good fortune she was given a sealed letter from the solicitor's file, with the mandate, "To be opened upon the death of Ruth Levy." It was from Joe.

"Now that Ruth is not there to care for you, I have left a sum of money to help you pursue your dreams. From Joe."

Five thousand rand lay in the envelope. It was enough to support her for the rest of the year until graduation, and Carolyn sent a silent message of thanks to her paternal benefactor.

Together, Ruth and Joe had joined their love to assure Carolyn her future. She would make them proud.

# Chapter 20

"I absolutely have to have the final bid for the rentals by today at four!" Gyneth smiled as she passed through her busy offices and heard her assistant's voice demanding the details for one of the many events booked for that month.

"I am so glad that you are doing that, Janice. You have such a way about you!" Gyneth giggled as Janice grimaced and continued with her call.

Gyneth dropped her bag and briefcase with a large thump onto her desk.

"Amron Events" now had a team of thirty people. Gyneth had taken an office in a small two-story office building in South Beverly Hills. She painted it white and rented antique furniture. Every month she would buy another piece of furniture and slowly replaced the rented items with her own. The best move she'd made a year ago was to hire Alex Dreyfus, her platonic companion, to provide public relations expertise for her growing company. It was important that she was seen at the right places and was asked to bid on *the* events and although she had a finger on all major social activities, it was much harder to develop that kind of awareness in the corporate world. So Alex became her director of corporate communications.

"Yes, indeed. We provide a complete service from flowers to caterers, entertainers, themes, masters of ceremonies, and even the planning of the script for the entire event if necessary." Alex was speaking to the reporter from the *Los Angeles Times* who had just called in response to his press package. He gesticulated for Gyneth to join him in his office, opposite hers.

"Our themes are very 'Hollywood' and Gyneth Amron oversees the execution of every event with the precision of an executive producer." Alex looked admiringly at Gyneth as he spoke. Working for her was like being on a whirlwind of perpetual motion. The reporter promised to come by with a photographer.

"What you have accomplished in the past few years is remarkable. Gyneth." Alex gave a sigh of satisfaction. He had been trying to get the reporter to come over for months.

Gyneth relaxed on the antique sofa in Alex's office and thought back to her first "gig" in a luxury Holmby Hills home. Now she entered the front entrance of those same mansions and discovered that many of her clients wanted to confide in her.

"It still amuses me how this city works, Alex. It's so important for each client to know what everyone else is doing here in terms of entertainment. No one wants to be like anyone else but everyone wants to be doing the 'in' thing rather than anything 'passe.' "

"You feed into that obsession so well, Gyneth, and that's the secret of great public relations. Knowledge and the 'inside track' brings the kind of power that even a large amount of money cannot ensure."

"Well, we certainly do spend a lot of time with these people. The Simon event took over eight months to arrange and by the end of it I felt like the resident psychiatrist. I must have heard every member of the family voice their innermost fears." She laughed.

"Do you remember the fight they had over the budget?" Alex laughed.

"It was a good thing you were with me on that one, Alex. I thought he was going to knife me with the letter opener when he saw the final figure." They chuckled together.

Gyneth had learned a lot about American society in the past year. Teenagers had a definite code of what was and was not acceptable at a party and their parents paid excessively to match up to the others in their social set. Charities fought to raise huge sums of money, and to attract large donors, overspent on lavish parties. For the couples who were the most unhappy together, anniversaries and birthdays were an easy way of proving to the world that all was well, and assuaging their guilt while continuing an illicit affair.

With each new client, Gyneth gathered verbal currency, filing it away as she counseled, sympathized, empathized, and fumed for the benefit of each new "friend" who confided in her. She kept their confidences and for that they were grateful to her, and it was Gyneth they called when there was something else to celebrate.

And though she sometimes felt ambivalent about the social set into which she was absorbed, the need to succeed drove her on.

"Why don't you take off a day or two, Gyneth. You have been at it seven days a week for months without a break." Alex could see that Gyneth was exhausted. "Business is doing great and you have good people to watch the store."

"I'm too busy, Alex, maybe later on in the year."

Gyneth knew that Alex could never understand her constant fear that the world she was building for herself would vanish, since she had not made the kind of success that really counted. She changed the subject.

"It took me ages to get through to my mother last night. The telephone circuits to South Africa were busy for hours. I could hear in her voice that she really needs to see me. Maybe I should go back there for a few weeks."

Gyneth thought suddenly about her illegal immigration status. It would have to be settled. That night she dug around in the pile of papers that she had kept from her days as a law firm receptionist until she found what she was looking for, "From the desk of Harrison Jaffe" and the name of his friend, an immigration attorney. Gyneth smiled wistfully as she remembered the wonderful evening they had spent together. He was probably married now.

The next day she called and made an appointment to see the attorney. He was delighted to help, had heard of her company and agreed that with her present business activities there would be some sort of plan that could be made to change her legal status.

"We have to do an intercompany transfer. You will have to set up a company in South Africa and then become it's chief executive. Then we will obtain a visa that will be available in a few weeks to transfer you from that company to this one here in Los Angeles. This will give you nonpermanent residence status in Los Angeles, but a status that can be adjusted to permanent residence once you are here." Gyneth listened carefully, vaguely remembering some of the concepts she had read in the law books.

Gyneth decided to defer the problem. She was just too busy to deal with it and threw herself into her work with more energy than ever before.

Alex observed Gyneth drag herself into the office, often late in the morning, having collapsed into bed the night before around one after supervising the wrap-up of all the current event's details.

"Susan is going to close up from now on. You really have to delegate more, Gyneth, otherwise you will collapse." Alex had ordered a light lunch and they ate together.

"You're right. I'm exhausted all the time. How do you keep so energetic, Alex, your hours are almost as long as mine?"

"I work out at the gym. You should join me, Gyneth."

"It's hard enough to see myself in gym clothes, I'd hate for you to see me like that."

Alex caught a quick glimpse of the insecurity Gyneth hid so well. In the past year he had thought often of asking her to join him for a purely social evening but Gyneth had made it clear that she had no interest in more than a business relationship. Now, however, she looked sad and vulnerable, and for a brief moment he longed to wrap her in his arms. To him, she was the most vibrant, attractive, and exciting woman he knew.

"That may be how you feel," he began hesitantly, "but you are a beautiful woman, Gyneth, truly beautiful."

"Well, I won't be beautiful if I don't complete the Sanchez proposal by two. They are coming by to discuss the final details." Gyneth deflected Alex's compliment and swept up the last remnants of their hasty lunch, while pulling out the data sheets from the various caterers. Alex, intensely frustrated, paused for a moment before returning to his office. But Gyneth was oblivious to his presence, deep in concentration, comparing bids.

Gyneth did begin the painful process of exercising her body, neglected for years. One night, a couple of months later, sitting in her apartment overlooking the twinkling lights of the city that lay beneath her, she realized that she longed for the intense excitement of a new relationship. Despite her thriving business, her life was lonely.

Gyneth approached the problem as she did everything else in her life—with efficiency and focus.

"Alex, I've decided to join a number of charity boards. It means that we will have to donate some of our services, and it may be a good idea to get some press on that fact. It's time for me to get my new body out there, into the meat market, so to speak." Gyneth laughed at herself not noticing the surprise on Alex's face.

"It's time for me to stop acting like a nun, Alex. And I guess the only way to do that is to tell people I'm ready to date, don't you think?"

Alex turned away. Gyneth was like a hammer looking for a nail. Everything in her life was given the same treatment—businesslike, efficient, and arranged.

Thank heavens, Gyneth thought, for Alex. She felt no chemistry between them just friendship. He had told her he was recovering from a bad marriage and was not about to jump into another painful relationship and that made him safe and an easy companion. She felt good about herself and her decision to start dating. The right man was surely just around the corner.

The next day Alex brought up an idea he had been researching.

"I have been studying a new area of opportunity for us—the legal community. Changes in the ethics rules for lawyer advertising and the increasing competition among West Coast firms mean that even the most respected firms will begin to solicit clients. I think we can enter that market with ease. But we have to move now."

"Great idea. Let's do it."

"I have made an appointment with the managing partner of a major law firm. This is my suggestion. We should propose a number of carefully staged events over the period of a year. The events could include luncheons, seminars, elegant dinners at one of the partner's homes and a tasteful black tie event for VIP clients and prospects."

"I love it!" Gyneth's eyes sparkled. Alex was a genius at seeing opportunities and had a flair for the unusual. The firm he had chosen was renowned in the entertainment field but also had an active securities and corporate law division. Gyneth had met the managing partner, John Silver, at a client's wedding, which her company arranged and had included his name in their database of prospects.

Gyneth and Alex arrived early.

"Come in, can we get you some coffee?" Silver welcomed them into his spacious office and Gyneth looked approvingly at the wood panelings and antique desk. The artwork was impressive and she saw a number of modern pieces intermingled with traditional renaissance lithographs and nodded appreciatively.

"You have a beautiful office," she said as she settled down in the deep armchair at the side of the comfortable living room area.

"Thank you—from you that is high praise. I am aware of your exquisite taste, Ms. Amron." Gyneth blushed slightly. Then she began to present her proposal. He was impressed.

"This is a very interesting idea," he said. "You know, I would like to have you present this to the executive committee of the partners in the firm. You can do a far better sales job to them than I can. Let me see who is available and if they are not able to meet you today, we can set it up for another time."

He called his secretary and while she attempted to organize the other partners, he asked Gyneth to elaborate on some of her ideas. Within a few minutes the secretary announced that all the partners were available and, after finishing phone calls, they would join the meeting.

One by one the four partners arrived. Gyneth and Alex were introduced. The last partner smiled broadly as he took Gyneth's hand in both of his.

"It is a great pleasure to see you again, Gyneth. The last time we met, you were also the star of the gathering."

Gyneth felt light-headed as she looked into the clear gray eyes of Harrison Jaffe.

"Harrison . . ." She felt the warm touch of his hands. "It has been a long time. You . . . you look very well." Gyneth felt herself flushing as she greeted him warmly. Only four years ago he'd been a new associate at another law firm. Now he was not only part of a more prestigious firm, but he also sat on the partners' executive committee, an honor that usually took at least ten years to achieve. Gyneth resolved to find out the real story behind his meteoric rise.

Alex saw the electricity pass between Gyneth and the good-looking young lawyer. He felt a flash of hot jealousy at the softness in her voice and her momentary slight confusion.

Harrison observed Gyneth with admiration. She was as poised as ever but now she was elegantly and expensively dressed. She appeared supremely confident and was obviously very good at her business. She was voluptuous and incredibly sexy. He couldn't take his eyes off her.

Gyneth's presentation caused much discussion.

"It is a bold move for a firm as conservative as ours."

"Your budget is remarkably high, Ms. Amron."

"It is," Gyneth answered confidently. "You will pay

for the best in the city and that is precisely what you will get from Amron Events. Frankly, you would do more damage to your sterling reputation by creating a mediocre event than you would by doing nothing at all. The decision is yours, gentlemen."

The idea was brilliant and appealing. At the exquisitely correct moment, Gyneth rose to leave, knowing that a decision would necessitate a major policy change for the law firm. She felt Harrison's eyes on her as she and Alex said goodbyes to all present, wondering after she left whether she'd imagined the increased pressure of his fingers in her palm as she shook his hand last.

In the elevator going down from the twenty-seventh floor her knees were trembling. Alex looked at her closely. She ignored his inquiring look and said, "I think it went well. Let's hope they go for it. Would you do a meeting summary, Alex, noting the questions they asked? Be sure that we have covered every base. And by the way we need a really good legal agreement with them. These guys won't hesitate to sue if they feel things didn't go their way."

Alex scribbled her instructions as she gave them quickly, feeling a sharp twinge of annoyance at the way Gyneth was rapidly firing orders at him. The softness she'd shown toward the good-looking young lawyer had disappeared. Alex felt like shaking her; and longed to hold her. Suddenly he realized that it was not only Gyneth's imperious attitude that was disturbing, but his own jealousy.

The next few days were very hectic. There were three events back to back and Gyneth hardly had time to think of anything else.

Then, her secretary buzzed her at the end of a frantic day as she was about to begin her working night at two events being staged simultaneously. "It's Mr. Jaffe calling."

Harrison's voice made her heart flutter and she crossly reprimanded herself for acting like a teenager. After all they'd only had one date over four years ago.

"Gyneth, I wanted to say how much I enjoyed seeing you the other day. You're remarkable and you've become so successful in such a short time."

"Well, so have you," Gyneth said admiringly. "It is quite an achievement to be a member of the executive committee of James, Cooper, and Silver!"

"It really is rather a long story," he said, pausing for a moment. "You look different, Gyneth, yet I can still see you sitting in the law library quietly eating your lunch and reading. I've never forgotten you." Gyneth listened to his words and closed her eyes as a wave of desire filled her body.

"I have also never forgotten you," she said softly. For a moment they were silent, remembering, anticipating.

"Gyneth, when can we meet? What about dinner?"

With trembling fingers, Gyneth looked at her calendar. She had events booked through the rest of the week.

"I can do it on Saturday if we make it late because I have to at least make an appearance at two events first."

He paused. "It would be easier for me during the week. How about tonight?"

Gyneth stammered slightly. "Well, I guess I could. I have to stop in at a couple of events first. I could meet you at about nine o'clock at Harry's Bar." She laughed. He did, too.

"Fine," he said. "I like continuity. See you there."

Gyneth hung up and felt like a young girl on her first date. The sexual excitement she'd felt when she saw Harrison again had unleashed long dormant feelings in her body. Could this be the man she had been waiting for, hoping for? She was filled with longing for all the soft, sweet languorous feelings she'd felt with Dirk, the lazy exploration of her body, the explosion of desire, the comfort of lying in the arms of another. Gyneth leaned her head back for a moment against her executive chair and closed her eyes. It was time for her to feel these things again, she was ready for a relationship.

Gyneth rushed through the details of the two events with her staff. Her major concern was making the host and hostess feel that she was not neglecting them. She made herself very visible until she was sure that they were well into the swing of the party and all was going well. She arrived at Harry's before 9:00 P.M., remembering that Harrison was always on time and she had been late the last time they went to dinner.

He was there early, too. They both laughed and felt the warm glow of anticipation as they settled down into a corner table and began to talk softly, their eyes only on each other. Harrison wanted to know all about her business. Gyneth happily chatted away, proud of her progress and certain that he was not a man to be intimidated by her. She reveled in the admiration she saw in his eyes and yearned to feel his arms around her. She couldn't stop looking at the curve of his mouth as she remembered their one elusive kiss and the soft warmth of his lips. Finally, turning away so that he would not see the raw longing in her eyes, Gyneth insisted that Harrison tell her about himself.

He told about how he hadn't been able to stay at the firm at which they'd met. The atmosphere was destructive and the firm was like a revolving door with associates leaving daily and backbiting among the partners. A post had come up at his present firm and he took it.

It was a step backward since he'd become a first-year associate again but the move was worth it.

Harrison then blushed slightly and explained that the young lady who'd accompanied him to see Gyneth perform in the temple play was in fact the daughter of the managing partner of the new firm, John Silver. He paused. Gyneth waited for him to continue. When he didn't she suddenly felt cold, knowing instinctively that the next words out of his mouth would hurt her. She clenched her hands together under the table.

Harrison swallowed hard. "She is now my wife."

Gyneth felt cheated and exposed. Why hadn't he told her this in the beginning? He just let her go chattering on about herself while he was probably laughing at her. She should have known; a man as smart as Harrison would easily attract the boss's daughter. Certainly it had advanced his career.

Harrison leaned forward, seeing her distress. "You are going to think that I am crazy to say this," he said. "Gyneth, the moment I laid eyes on you I knew that we were meant to be together. I cursed myself a thousand times that I didn't pursue you years ago when we first met. Then I heard that you had gone to London. Gyneth, if I'd known you were back here, I would have found you."

He looked deeply into her eyes. "Darlene has been very good for me. She was the one who convinced me that there was no merit in staying in a job that made me so unhappy. She opened up the opportunity for me and then once I was in her father's firm, she saw to it that I was brought in on some of the more important cases and introduced to some of the largest clients. It just went on from there. Her father introduced me into society here and basically launched my career. It seemed like the right thing to do, to become engaged to Darlene. I had difficulty in finally making the deci-

sion. It took me three years. It seemed the longer I
waited to marry her the more she pushed her father and
the more promotions I received. I gave in last year. I
felt as if I were exploiting her, and was obliged to balance the scales by getting married."

Harrison paused, longing to hold Gyneth's hand,
which now crunched the linen napkin into a tight ball.
Her face was white and her eyes filled with tears. He
forced himself to continue.

"The wedding was at the Hillcrest Country Club.
Darlene's father has also arranged for me to become a
member there. My whole life is tied up with theirs
now."

Gyneth sat in stunned silence. She was on the outside once more. The agonizing feeling was familiar.
For a moment all her accomplishments seemed worth-
less. And she would have given it all up for one day of
life as Harrison's wife.

She looked at the desirable man across from her. He
should have been hers. He felt it, too. But it was too
late now.

"Why are you having dinner with me?" Gyneth
asked sadly.

He looked deep into her eyes. "Because I fell in love
with you four years ago and nothing has changed."

"How can you be in love with me? You are married
to someone else!" Gyneth cried out, her chest tight
with pain.

"I cannot help the way I feel. I also can't change the
way things are. Gyneth, I did not plan it this way. It
just happened."

Gyneth rose. "I want to go home now," she said. She
took her purse, and trying to regain her composure, left
the restaurant. Harrison motioned to the maître d'hotel
to put the check on his monthly bill and ran after her.

"I am taking you home, you're too upset to drive.

Tomorrow you can pick up your car." He called the valet, explained that Gyneth was ill and put her in his car. She sat staring dully out the window the whole ride home.

Once there, Harrison accompanied her to the door. Gyneth turned to shake his hand, but with one look at her sad face, he drew her into his arms, and would have lingered had she not moved away.

"Good night, my Gyneth, thank you for a magical evening," he whispered as he had years ago.

Tears ran down her face as she turned from him and went inside.

Early the next morning, Gyneth awoke with swollen eyes and a renewed resolve that she must not have an affair with Harrison. She wanted him completely or not at all.

She took little pleasure in the business of that day or those thereafter. She avoided Harrison's calls and although they obtained the contract from the law firm, Gyneth seemed unable to develop a plan or put the creative energy into the project that it needed.

Alex was concerned and frustrated. He came into her office and closed the door.

"I'm really overwhelmed, Alex, I haven't even gone through half my mail. Can this wait?"

"Gyneth, we must talk. I have been making most of the business decisions for the past few weeks. It never seems to be the right time to talk with you."

"It isn't the right time now either."

"Nevertheless, we are going to talk." Gyneth looked up from the piles of correspondence, surprised at Alex's voice, hard and commanding.

"You have become a different person since about the time we made the presentation to the Silver law firm." Alex was convinced that the change in Gyneth had something to do with the young lawyer in the meeting.

He felt her slipping away from him, the long discussions they had over the business, the camaraderie they'd shared had all faded. She was unavailable.

"I am essentially running the business."

"You are, Alex, and you do it so efficiently. I am grateful to you." Gyneth realized that he was furious. "I am having some personal problems, Alex, nothing to do with you or the business."

Alex clenched his fists. He was sure his suspicions were valid. It must be Harrison Jaffe.

"I've decided to take off a few days. You were right. I've been overdoing it, so that even the smallest things are difficult to cope with. Can you control things until the weekend, I'll be fine next week again." Gyneth barely stopped to hear Alex's reply as she grabbed her bag and left through the back door, so that her employees would not see her tears. Perhaps the time alone would help her.

It was a mistake. The isolation intensified her pain and she found herself replaying Harrison's voice over and over again on her answering machine. She threw the tape across the room. Even his voice moved her.

Her feeling of failure was overwhelming. There was only one solution.

Food.

She binged on every fast food that she could find— donuts, hot dogs, french fries. She felt bloated and nauseous.

Alex called and said that he was coming by for her to sign some checks. He missed her continually, needing to feel her energy and enthusiasm near him. He knew she was in pain and he resolved to tell her how he felt.

The door chimes clanged loudly and Gyneth listlessly opened the door.

It was Harrison.

"Gyneth, please, I need to talk to you."

She shrank back and tried to close the door in his face. He put his foot in the way and stepped firmly inside.

"You must listen to me, let me explain."

Gyneth didn't have the strength to resist him, so, reluctantly, feeling fat and ugly, she let him in. Harrison closed the door, and pulled her close to him. She sobbed until she thought her heart would break. She had dreamed of his arms around her.

"I look such a mess, how could you even want to be with me," she sniffled as she cuddled closer to him, burying her face in the warmth of his chest.

"You are the most beautiful woman in the world and to see you vulnerable like this only makes me want you more. Come let me help you, you don't have to hurt like this." He held her and stroked her hair. The door chimed again.

"Oh God, that must be Alex. He mustn't see you here. Go into the bedroom, I'll deal with him."

Gyneth walked to the door. "Alex, is that you?"

"It most certainly is," he called. "Can I come in?"

"Alex, I feel absolutely awful and I think that I have the worst stomach flu. I have been throwing up and I only now managed to keep some medication down and I am just destroyed. Could you leave all the paperwork in the mailbox and I'll deal with it tomorrow? I hate to have you see me like this."

Alex stood close to the door, his arms full of papers. It was so unlike Gyneth not to want to attend to the financial details of the business as soon as they were presented to her.

"Are you sure you are all right? I really couldn't care how you look, let me come in and take care of you, please."

"No, I'll be fine. You know how I like to look my

best. Please understand. I do appreciate your friendship. I'll call you in the morning. Good night, my dear, and thank you."

Gyneth heard him stacking the papers outside of the door and with a sigh of relief, went to the bedroom.

Harrison was standing at the window looking at the view.

"I've never seen the lights so bright before. Come to me." She went to his side and then his arms were around her and they were touching, kissing, holding as if there was no one else in the whole world but them. Gyneth had never made love that way. Harrison wanted to touch every part of her body, to love it, hold it. He marveled at her rounded thighs, her warm, soft breasts, her inviting lips. He spoke constantly, telling her how he loved the feel of her skin, the touch of her lips, the caress of her fingers. His tongue explored her innermost being from the soft pliant sides of her vagina to her mouth and ears. She felt absorbed, consumed by him. She drifted in the waves of passion and the loving exploration by the man who was meant to be hers. The feel of his body was so familiar that even though it was their first time together, it was as if they'd loved each other a thousand times before.

"We must have known each other in another life," he whispered. "I feel it, too. We were meant to be together, it is not just our imaginations." They grew more and more demanding of each other's bodies until finally they joined in passion that sent them both into a shuddering release. Afterward they lay quietly in each other's arms, each unwilling to move or break the spell.

"I always knew you were meant to be mine," Harrison whispered. Those were the last words Gyneth heard before she slept. She awoke suddenly, feeling chilled. Harrison was getting dressed.

"Where are you going?" she asked dreamily.

"You know I have to go. I will see you tomorrow evening at five thirty. Can you meet me here?"

Gyneth pulled herself up and drew the covers around her. She felt sick and empty again.

"Harrison, this is crazy. I don't want to have an affair. I either want you totally or not at all. Please, we have to stop this. You must not come to me again."

Harrison bent over and silenced her with a soft kiss. She held his hand tightly not wanting him to go.

After he left, Gyneth looked out over the city. To her the romance had gone from the lights. Now all she could see was a house with a happy woman waiting for her husband. Darlene, slender, established, knowing that all her needs were taken care of by the two men in her life, her husband and her father. Between them, they would satisfy her every whim. Maybe her husband didn't love her, but he'd still come home every night. He'd be there when she reached for him in bed, felt ill, or was afraid. Gyneth knew now that she would always be the outsider, the one Harrison made love to, then left.

Gyneth shook her head. She could not live that way—she would not.

She slept holding the pillow in her arms, dreaming of a home, with Harrison as her husband. But every time she reached for him he disappeared again.

Alex had felt foolish waiting in his car outside Gyneth's building. His instincts told him that someone was in her apartment and he was determined to know who it was.

Finally, he heard the snarl of a Porsche as it revved into action. He sat up quickly, just in time to see the fine features of Harrison Jaffe as he looked for traffic, then reversed into the street. At the same time, the lights went off in Gyneth's apartment.

Alex was filled with anguish. His foolish reluctance to push Gyneth, to risk their working relationship, which he so valued, had caused him to be aced out. Gyneth was taken, he'd lost.

The next day Gyneth pulled herself together, washed her hair and dressed carefully. She had much damage to correct. For a week now she had neglected her business. She signed all the papers that Alex had left for her and went to work. Everyone was relieved to see her back, but Alex looked at the dark rings under her eyes. "Are you well enough to come back to work?" he asked, his tone distant.

"I feel fine, a little weak but fine. How are we doing on the Silver law firm account?"

"The contract has been signed, we are now waiting for a budget and final proposal of events for the year. They agreed to all our terms and added a restriction preventing us from doing work for competitors concurrent with the contract and then for another six months thereafter." Alex was controlled and professional. Inside, he burned to tell Gyneth that he knew why she was so intensely interested in that project above all the others.

Gyneth sped through the day, noting that there was now a list of two or three events every weekend night for the next twelve months. For the first time she could actually do some cash flow forecasting. She didn't have a husband or father, she thought wryly, but she did own a viable business, something of her own that could be relied upon.

Throughout the day she told herself that she was not going to be at her apartment at 5:30. She would not be available when Harrison happened to be around. She had a life, too. But as the day wore on she found herself speeding things along, clearing her calendar so that at 5:30 she was free.

Gyneth arrived at her apartment at the same time as Harrison. She felt swept along by an unstoppable force. They fell into each other's arms, not able to undress fast enough to satisfy their desperate need for each other.

"I thought of nothing else but you all day. You were in my mouth, my arms, on my tongue. I could taste you and feel you and I couldn't concentrate on anything." He spoke softly, passion punctuating his words as he caressed her. Gyneth was breathless with desire, a desperate need for Harrison overwhelming her resolve. They tore at each other's clothes and sank into the deep rug in the entrance to her apartment. His skin was smooth and his tongue searching, and Gyneth enveloped him in her breasts pulling him as close as possible to her by wrapping her legs around his. He entered her quickly, deeply thrusting into her innermost being. Gyneth moaned with pleasure. She could not get enough of him and clasped him tighter, arching her hips to meet his, grinding around and under him as they both groaned in ecstasy. Then he drove even harder into her and her dreams joined with his as together they came within moments of each other and lay sobbing in each other's arms until the waves of pleasure subsided. Then Harrison held Gyneth close, talking softly about how he loved her body, her skin, every part of herself that she had loathed and that he now caressed. Gyneth absorbed his words like life-giving nectar. He wanted the body she hated so much. He refused to let her cover herself and hide from him. He wanted to look at her, admire her, caress her constantly. Could it be that she really was attractive to him?

They met every day.

Gyneth told her office that she had a personal exercise trainer and was working out at her home and that nothing could interfere with her schedule. Certainly everyone could see the change in her figure. She was eating less and the sexual exercise was burning up some calories. She laughed at the fact that the only time in her life that food had been unimportant, she couldn't tell anyone her wonderful secret.

Alex could see the signs that no one else could recognize. Gyneth was in love, and it was not with him. He started dating aggressively. Every night there was a different woman in his bed, blondes, brunettes, those he met in bars, through friends, at clubs. But no matter how hard he tried, it was Gyneth's intelligence and sparkle that he missed, and her body he wanted to hold.

When Harrison left every night and Gyneth dressed to go out to the one or two obligatory events, she wondered how long they could continue this way.

The contract for the law firm was in full swing and the partners were already seeing positive results. The time had come to organize one of the formal dinners.

When Gyneth had finally come up with a strategy for the firm, she had suggested that two or three dinners at the partners' homes would make prospective clients feel a familial camaraderie as part of the firm's valued inner circle. Now Gyneth realized that she had strategized herself into a trap. John Silver suggested that the first intimate dinner be at Harrison's home.

Gyneth threw Harrison a desperate look.

He flushed. "Well, I am not sure that we are quite ready. You know, Darlene is still decorating and won't be done for a number of months yet. We really are not ready," he stammered.

"Nonsense!" John announced. "Why, just the other day Darlene was telling me how things are coming along. And anyway it will be a wonderful opportunity for you to show off your lovely new home on North Alpine."

Suddenly Gyneth felt a wave of paranoia. Did he suspect something? Was this a test of some sort?

John turned to Gyneth. "We will have the first dinner at Harrison's home. I will tell Darlene to expect your call."

Gyneth smiled weakly and excused herself. Harrison just had to stop it some way or another. She just could not deal with his wife. Alex kept a stony expression on his face throughout the meeting and all the way back to the office. He felt a twinge of hope. Perhaps Gyneth would see reason once she was faced with the reality of the deception her lover was practicing.

That night Gyneth was furious. "What is wrong with you, why can't you stand up to that man? It is your house—tell him that you are not going to do it and that is that. You cannot do this to me, Harrison, you cannot humiliate me this way."

"You don't understand," he groaned. "Darlene wants to do it. She sees it as a wonderful coming-out party for the house, that she doesn't have to do any of the work while it is bankrolled by the firm. There is no point in trying to stand up John when Darlene is on his side."

Gyneth looked at him with a moment of insight. He was so dependent on what they were doing for him that he was unable to be his own person. The flash of perception soon faded as he caressed her. The passions that Gyneth had kept dormant for so many years now raged within her to the extent that all Harrison had to do was touch her and she was aching for him, wet, ready and panting, pleading for him to take and possess her.

The next day Gyneth made the decision to go forward.

"Alex, would you please call Mrs. Silver and make an appointment for us to meet her to discuss the dinners. I am available on Tuesday or Wednesday."

Alex drew in his breath. Perhaps he had a chance after all. He knew Gyneth. Her need to be on top of every situation would make her role in this triangle untenable. He would be around to pick up the pieces.

Gyneth told Harrison that she did not want him to be there and that she would meet Darlene on her own. She took Alex and her personal assistant, Ann, with her. Alex understood Gyneth's need to bring along people to a first meeting for what was one of their simpler events although Ann was surprised.

"These must be VIP clients, Gyneth. Who are they?" Ann was curious. They had become so busy lately that every staff member had a full schedule.

Gyneth gave a perfunctory explanation. "It is the boss's daughter, we have to impress her."

However, even with strength in numbers, Gyneth was intimidated.

Darlene greeted them at the door, looked curiously at Gyneth and then said, "Oh yes—I remember your play. You were quite marvelous. Harrison tells me that you have a very successful business. Well, do come in, I'm looking forward to this event so much." Darlene led the way into an elegantly furnished house with marble floors, and a finely carved circular staircase gently lit by crystal chandeliers. Gyneth looked around her. Harrison and his wife had it all, the power, prestige, the home, and privilege. And in addition, Darlene was elegant, charming, and still slender. Gyneth felt like the help. She gritted her teeth together and smiled sweetly.

"How kind of you to remember me. Well, here we are. Ann will look at your facilities while Alex and I will explain the procedure."

Darlene showed them the kitchen and listened to their ideas. She interjected only to request that the rentals be Waterford and Sterling.

By the time the meeting was over, instead of feeling triumphant, Alex was aching to comfort Gyneth. He could see the agony in her eyes and knew that she could hardly wait to leave.

Gyneth regarded Harrison quite differently that night. He wasn't quite as strong and forceful as he'd first appeared. He may have professed love for her but he had every comfort a man could desire, living with Darlene; every one that was, except love. And his wife was feminine, longing to please, elegant and sophisticated. Most of all, she had the key to his livelihood— her father and the family contacts that were his as long as they were together. Harrison had traded his soul for a lifestyle and Gyneth was not part of that bargain.

The dinner went off without a hitch. Darlene sat at one end of the table and Harrison at the other. Gyneth made an appearance at the beginning of the evening and checked all the final details. She left the execution to her head chief and coordinator. Darlene was the perfect hostess, gracious, hospitable, her conversation intelligent and solicitous. One look at Harrison told Gyneth his embarrassment, even discomfort at her presence. Finally she could take it no longer. She slipped out the tradesmen's entrance and drove home, banging her fist onto the steering wheel.

"Goddammit, how could I have allowed myself to get into this situation! I'm as weak as Harrison, I should have canceled the contract; not even taken it on! Why did I humiliate myself this way? What's wrong with me? I'm no longer the fat, ugly teenager, watching others try on the clothes I want to wear, I own my own business; I've made a life for myself. It's time to get back into control." Gyneth was yelling at the top of her lungs, sobbing with rage and humiliation.

But then she was racked with indecision and confusion. Harrison had made her feel both sexual and loved. And those feelings were liberating.

The next night as Harrison arrived at her apartment, Gyneth came to the point.

"I want you to divorce her," she said firmly. "I have a good business and you're a competent lawyer. Forget about the membership in the club and the Silvers' friends. I am a survivor and you can be, too." Then Gyneth's resolve faltered as tears came to her eyes and she took his hands in hers. "Harrison, please, I cannot continue this way. For I have been hiding and lying, sneaking around, never able to go out, just meeting here in my apartment. We can never spend a night together, you are always dressing and leaving me to sleep alone. I want a family, children, a home, and a husband who is proud of me and whom I can be proud of. The social position is not important. We can find happiness together."

He listened to her in silence. Finally he answered.

"I have thought the same for months now. But it won't happen the way you think. They have a lot of power in this city—you'll find that they can destroy your business, Gyneth. This is a very small town, you know. Everyone knows who is 'in' and who is 'out.' If you are seen as the 'other' woman you'll lose a lot of credibility, and many of your clients would rather use one of your competitors than incur the ire of John Silver. He raises a great deal of money for good causes in this city and sits on many boards. They will destroy you and me, Gyneth. Don't underestimate their power."

Gyneth knew instinctively that he was right. So much of her business depended on goodwill. Was her business more important to her than her life with him? She was not sure. Anyway it was not her decision alone. It was clear to her that Harrison was unwilling to risk his future that way. She could not assail him for being spineless and weak—she herself was unsure of the best thing to do. They were not foolish teenagers anymore, they had both invested so much into their careers. It was not easy to throw it up in the name of love.

Harrison saw Gyneth's indecision. He also knew how he would never give up what he had. He reveled in the social acceptance, mingling with the rich and influential, the early days of struggling to be noticed far behind him. Nothing and no one was worth going back to that again.

"It is over," he said. "You've been the best thing that has ever happened to me, Gyneth, and I truly believe that we were together before and will be together some way, somehow, again. But that time is not now and I cannot give you the life you want." Harrison looked at her steadily although his heart ached.

Gyneth stared at him for a long time. Her eyes filled with tears. She had known by forcing a confrontation that this might happen. She could not argue with his decision. He had been quite clear with her from the beginning. Even if she were willing to risk Darlene's father's ire, societal gossip, and the struggle to start over again, she could not create his willingness to risk everything for her.

There were no more words to say. Harrison held Gyneth briefly one last time, feeling her body stiffen as she tried to keep her composure. He left her for what they both knew was the last time. Gyneth wept again the whole night but now the tears were cleansing. She had no need to hide, there would be no more sneaking around and lying.

She thought wryly that every situation had its upside. She'd lost a lover but gained a new figure.

The next morning dawned fresh and crisp, one of those days that made Los Angelenos grateful for living in a paradise, and guilty for polluting it. Gyneth felt ten years older, wiser and completely focused. She could now devote her life to her business. She felt whole again. The right man would come along for her now, and for the first time she was ready for him.

Alex knew it was over.

"How about lunch at the Bistro today?"

Gyneth was trying to read the computer printouts that were strewn all over her office. "Alex, I really don't think I have the time."

"Sure you do. Let's go." Alex picked up her purse and grabbed her hand.

"It's good to see you laugh. You haven't done much of that lately." Alex probed gently, trying to get Gyneth to share some of her obvious grief with him. He knew what it was like to lose someone you loved. And that was clearly what had happened.

Gyneth's eyes filled with tears. "This is so silly, just a brief romance, nothing important, and it's over anyway." She tried to be nonchalant.

Alex took her hand. "Losing a relationship no matter how inconsequential, is still a loss. It takes time and is painful. I am here for you. You mean a lot to me, Gyneth. Please let me be there for you."

Gyneth squeezed his hand, but did not notice the look in his eyes. She was too wrapped up in her own loss. It was as if a part of her had been truncated. Suddenly, she felt a deeper understanding for her mother.

Alex could see that Gyneth was not sleeping well and remembered the lonely hours of the night after his wife left with another man and how he would ache physically, yearning for her soft body next to his.

Alex knew that that time had come for him to make his move. The next week, the moment presented itself.

They were working together trying to complete proposals to be made to five new potential clients. Gyneth laid her head in her hands and sighed.

"I am so tired, Alex, I never seem to have enough hours in the day." She looked up. "You spend entirely too much time here at the office. Don't you want to leave earlier, have a life for yourself, go out, date, take a break?"

Alex realized Gyneth had no idea how he felt. To tell her, he had to risk their friendship. He'd lived the pain of rejection before. When his wife had left him suddenly, while he'd been on a business trip and unaware of the torrid affair that she had enjoyed for months in their matrimonial bed. She said he was uncaring, unaware of her needs, a workaholic. And now he'd found someone with his same obsession for business, but she was the one who was unaware, uncaring. He bit down on his lip.

"You are probably right. But you know how much I care for the business and of course for you, my dear," he said lightly, "and this really cannot be left undone. I have plenty of time on the weekends for dating and relaxation."

"What do you do to relax, Alex?" Gyneth asked, curious.

"Well," he said cautiously, "you know I like to play tennis."

"No, I didn't know," Gyneth said, surprised. "Where do you play?"

"I play at some friends' homes in Brentwood. Do you play, too?" Alex asked, knowing full well that Gyneth played a good strong game.

"I certainly do," she said delighted to have found a tennis partner. "Why don't we set up a game together!"

Alex's heart leapt with joy. He answered nonchalantly enough, however. "I actually was planning to play this Saturday but my regular partner has the flu. Would you like to play instead?"

"I'd love it," said Gyneth, immediately thinking of her heavy thighs in the short tennis skirt. How frustrating this all was. Other people just accepted such invitations thinking only of fun while her first thought was how awful she would look in the particular outfit required for the event. She sighed. It was, after all, only Alex. That was a relief. She could just be herself.

Saturday turned out to be enormous fun. Alex was an excellent player and beat her 6—1, 6—2, 6—0. Finally she puffed her way through the last rally.

"Alex, we have to play every week. It's the only way I can redeem my ego!"

"My dear, your ego is so large, we had better play every day!" They laughed and teased each other and Gyneth realized that it had been a long time since she had relaxed and really enjoyed herself. Alex also seemed younger and looser. Gyneth caught herself looking at him as if for the first time, and finding him immensely attractive.

They went out for an early dinner and Gyneth felt Alex's eyes on her, not quick glances as was normal for him, but longer, more lingering looks. She felt a shiver of anticipation, then anxiety. They were simply friends, the only safe relationship she had. Romance would just spoil it all and she would be alone again. Nervously, not willing to acknowledge the chemistry that was beginning to flow across the table, Gyneth began talking about business.

"The new projects coming up in the week ahead are really terrific. Have you noticed that the quality of our clients just seems to get better every year?"

Alex became silent and tense, losing some of his en

thusiasm. Gyneth felt sad to have destroyed the spontaneity of the day, but she knew no other way to cut off the growing dynamic between them. The possibility of another lost relationship terrified her.

Later, Alex sat alone in his apartment on Sunset Plaza Drive, struggling to sort out his feelings. Gyneth was the woman he'd been searching for. But he wanted to be her lover, not her employee. It was time to make Gyneth become aware of him. That night Alex reached a painful decision.

The next week was taken up with frantic meetings regarding proposals to two major companies, a consulting firm, and an accounting practice. Gyneth had expected approvals on both but a lower-priced competitor at the last moment had entered the bidding process and to Gyneth's dismay, her company was rejected in favor of his. She realized that her success had educated the competition so well that they were winning at her game. Even though she told herself that imitation was flattering, the reality was that a sizable amount of potential revenue had been lost, and a new approach to the business was called for. She resolved to spend that weekend discussing her concerns with Alex.

On Friday evening when everyone had left, Gyneth and Alex sat together finalizing the details of a new proposal.

Alex took a deep breath and prayed for courage. "I have something to tell you," he started.

Gyneth saw the serious expression on Alex's face and anxiety again gripped her. Was he going to say something personal? She quickly interjected a flippant remark, hoping to defuse his tension.

"Don't tell me that you're flaking out on our tennis game tomorrow 'cause you know I'm going to beat you!"

"No, it's rather more complicated than that." Alex

swallowed painfully. "I want to submit my resignation."

Gyneth went white. She looked at him in shocked disbelief.

"Why, Alex, what's the matter? Are you ill? Please tell me the problem, it cannot be that bad. What is it?"

"I need to have my own space, Gyneth. I've been working for you for three years now and really don't want to be someone's employee anymore. I need a long holiday, time to think, I've had enough of working at this pace. What you said the other night is very true. I do not give myself enough leisure time. I want a fuller life, a relationship, maybe even a wife and children."

Gyneth was frantic, feeling the stability of her business slipping away. "Alex, please let's discuss this. You can take as long a sabbatical as you want to. Take a vacation, one month, two months, six months, for heaven's sakes, but don't leave altogether. I really need you here. You are the only person I really trust, I'll make you a partner in the business if that is what you want. Please reconsider, please."

Gyneth looked like a little girl, pleading, distraught, no longer in control. Alex caught himself as he longed to comfort and hold her in his arms. But he held himself back. She had to know what it felt like to be without him, really without him, not just for a few months, but potentially forever. His resolve strengthened.

"Gyneth, I must do this. You'll be fine. I have put enough systems into this organization so that with your leadership, it can run itself. You have a number of bright young people here who would just love to have my job. Just go with your instinct, my dear."

Alex took her hands in his.

"You will be greatly in my thoughts, Gyneth. Take care of yourself. Get some rest—you also need it."

Alex walked to his office, only to leave it a few moments later, taking one box filled with his personal possessions. Gyneth ran to his office. It was pristine and bare. He'd packed everything earlier and now it showed no trace of his ever having been there. Weak with disbelief, she watched as the door closed. Then white-hot anger burned through her. Furious, she lifted the delicate antique chair in Alex's office, and threw it across the hall to shatter the mirrored wall on the other side of the reception room. Then she collapsed onto the floor, and wept. Was there no one she could trust?

# Chapter 21

Upon graduation Carolyn had won the Chancellor's prize for the most outstanding student and, more importantly, obtained the best internship at the London Hospital.

"I am so proud of you, Carolyn," Jeff had said. "What do you have in mind for the future?"

"I want to do surgery. That way, I can have the best chance of saving lives with quick action. I am frustrated by long, lingering diseases treatable only by medication."

"A wise decision. Of course, it's one I took, so I'm biased." They laughed, feeling the camaraderie that had developed over the many months they had worked together.

In the two years that followed that conversation, Carolyn made a momentous decision. She had, with the help of Rabbi Cohen and his family, converted to Judaism.

The conversion process was arduous with oral and written examinations. She would never forget the final interview with the Council of Rabbis. After a few moments of nervousness Carolyn had regained her normal confidence and responded thoughtfully to their Talmudic questions as the repartee accelerated with more parables and further probing until she saw Rabbi Cohen smiling into his long beard and the other members of the council charmed by her energy and intellectual agility. When they'd asked her why she wanted to convert, she had answered with care.

"I was a fugitive, running to freedom and away from oppression, not very different from the Jews as they fled from Egypt into the desert searching for the promised land."

Rabbi Cohen told her later of the argument that had ensued after she had left the room. "Unfortunately there will always be those who will disapprove of your conversion," he said, then repeated the objections of his colleagues. "They asked why a black girl would want to be Jewish? You must encounter enough discrimination as a black, why this, too? And then," he paused, his eyes flashing with anger, "one of them wanted to know if any of the others would want his son to marry a Jewish woman who was black."

Carolyn sat silently, knowing how the comment must have upset her good friend.

"I came to your defense," Rabbi Cohen said, his long beard quivering with indignation. "You would have enjoyed my response! I told them that they were as prejudiced as those they accused of anti-Semitism. If you were white, would they even hesitate after the magnificent performance they'd just witnessed? How could your responses have been improved upon? Since when had they seen or heard a scholar of theirs who could argue the Talmud, understand the interpretations or *duven* like you? They would be *kvelling,* bursting with pride, if this were their daughter, their son. 'Examine your own consciences, my colleagues,' I told them, 'it is your honesty that is at stake here, not hers.' " His face was flushed and perspiring with the depth of his feelings.

He explained that after his speech, they had cast
their vote. It was unanimous in her favor. Carolyn had
become a Jew.

Now she was completing her surgical residency. She
had a particular interest in breast diseases and during
the arduous years in training, had developed a concept
for a surgical instrument for lumpectomies that caught
the eye of a representative of a local medical products
manufacturer. To Carolyn's surprise, the company
bought the idea from her, agreeing to pay her a royalty
for life. Now with that promise of income and the be-
quests from Ruth, Carolyn's life was financially more
secure than ever before. The Cohens were like an extended family yet Carolyn still felt a sense of ennui
and deep loneliness. She couldn't understand the
yearning that filled her with sadness, a sense of dislo-
cation that continued to grow. She gradually realized
that she was homesick, yearning for something she
could not define.

Feeling lonely one evening after finishing her ward
rounds, on the off chance of finding Jeff, she stopped
by the operating room.

"Is Dr. Kramer around?" she asked the scrub nurse
who was standing in the nurses' lounge.

"I certainly am. What are you doing here so late?"
Jeff stood in the doorway, in surgical greens. He
looked tired, and Carolyn's heart jumped as she saw
him.

"I haven't seen you for a while, and just popped by
to say hello."

"Well, I'm glad you did. I was going to track you
down in the next few days anyway." Jeff sat down in
the nurses' lounge and leaned back in the easy chair,
looking approvingly at Carolyn. He had planned to ac-
cidentally bump into her the very next day.

"I . . . er . . . I just happen to have two tickets to

Covent Garden and the opera, *Don Carlos;* would you care to join me on Saturday night?" His tone was non-committal and friendly. Nevertheless, Carolyn felt a thrill of anticipation. They spoke often about their mutual love for opera, and live performances never ceased to thrill her.

"It's my favorite opera. I'd love to. Should I meet you at Covent Garden?"

"No need. If you're coming straight from the hospital we can travel on the subway together."

As she dressed that Saturday, Carolyn felt feminine, attractive, and nervous all at once and realized that she was reacting to Jeff as she had the night they had dinner at Posto. It was the first time since then that he had moved out of the boundaries of their mentor-pupil relationship. Suddenly she really wanted to be with him as a woman, not a colleague.

The music soared through the air and she floated in ecstasy. It had been so long since Carolyn had sung—although at times she allowed herself the luxury of trying to sing along with the arias on the records she played. Her voice needed practice and had certainly never had a long period of extended training, just the few hours Ruth had given her. Still Carolyn felt inspired again to sing as they left the theater.

"How about a coffee and cognac?" Jeff held his arm gently around Carolyn's waist as he guided her across the street to hail a cab. He could feel her firm body under her coat and he wanted to pull her close to him. He had waited so long for her, knowing how focused she had been on becoming a surgeon. Now that she had achieved her goal, the way was clear for him to make a move.

"Look, I live in Golders Green and I'd love to have you over to my place. You've never seen my home," Carolyn said. "I even have a great cheesecake."

Jeff laughed, holding her close with one arm while catching the eye of a passing taxi with the other. Carolyn had told him of her conversion to Judaism the previous year and he had been stunned, then enormously pleased. It was one more thing they had in common.

"You're as bad as my mother, trying to feed me all the time."

"Well, she knows what's good, I like her already!"

They chattered happily about the evening's entertainment all the way to her house.

"Don't you feel the music in your body when it's full of emotion? I almost ache with the sounds." Carolyn sang up and down an octave as they walked into the entry hall. Jeff closed his eyes for a moment.

"Stop, let me hold your hand . . . yes, there, I felt the notes. Wonderful!" They laughed and she closed the door behind them.

"I'll put the coffee on, make yourself at home."

Jeff looked at all the pictures on the piano.

"This is Ruth, and Joe, the last few weeks, we sang so much together then."

Jeff picked up a photograph of a young blond woman.

"That's Gyneth in London. She was my best friend. We grew up together and shared a lot. I lived with her family when we were children. Her father was a surgeon, Jacob Amron."

Carolyn told Jeff a little of the story of her past and the role the Amrons had played in it. Despite her light tone, it was obvious that the subject saddened her greatly and Jeff noticed it.

"Gyneth and I have lost touch," Carolyn said quietly. "There was an incident, many years ago, but I can't forget it." Carolyn thought suddenly of the wildness of her lovemaking with Matthew and felt a pang of longing.

Carolyn could sense Jeff's attraction to her. She hadn't wanted to be close to anyone for so long. It was not the same passionate, magnetic sensation that she had with Matthew, which sucked her up and left her breathless, but rather the strong desire to have him hold and caress her, keep her forever in his arms.

"You are the most remarkable woman I've ever met," Jeff said softly, fingering the delicate coffee cup. "Of course you must know that already."

"No . . . well, yes, sort of. Not exactly. It really is so difficult to explain. I feel different from other people. Perhaps I lived in South Africa too long where black people are unacceptable to the white world. But with you, it just feels like being with a friend. You could be green for all I care."

"I wasn't even referring to that. It's that you are so determined and serious, so talented. I miss talking to you when weeks pass by without our seeing each other in the halls. I want to see more of you, Carolyn, to do many things together, concerts, opera, plays."

Carolyn couldn't speak for a few moments, she was afraid her voice would sound too eager, too vulnerable.

"I'd like that, too."

Jeff stretched his long legs straight out in front of him.

"Well, that took care of that. Now will you sing for me?" Carolyn laughed. Then she put on a record by Miriam Makeba.

"She's a great South African singer who went to America. She captures the voice of my country." Carolyn began to sing in harmony with Miriam's voice. Jeff sat and listened, spellbound. This was his dream woman—they had so much in common. He was

falling in love and there was nothing he could do about
it.

"Carolyn ... Carolyn ..." Jeff whispered as she
concluded the last haunting notes of the song. "Come
here, come to me." Then his arms were strongly
around her and she closed her eyes, feeling his lips as
they explored her neck. She wanted him closer, inside
her, all over her. She could feel him hard and thrusting
and she threw all caution to the winds. It had been so
long, and she was moist, ready, wanting. Jeff felt her
breasts, round and hard underneath him as they slid to
the floor and he pulled her dress down, over her thighs,
ripping the fragile fabric. But nothing could stop them
now and his tongue met hers and then traveled down
her body, tasting, caressing, as she whimpered and
pulled him into her, crying out as she felt him and reveled in his hardness, his thrusting, throbbing rhythm.
Finally, together, they reached a panting, groaning climax.

"I've been waiting so long for you, God knows how
I ever held myself back for so many years, I've wanted
you since the very first day I saw you in the wards,
Carolyn. I will never let you go, you know that, don't
you? We are going to be together forever, forever."

Carolyn heard his words and for a moment was
filled with the desire to run away, to escape into solitude. Then she felt the comfort of his arms and looked
up into the gentleness of his eyes. It was Jeff, her
friend, mentor, confidant, and now her lover. She could
be safe with him. Carolyn snuggled closer to his body.
He felt so good, and she had been alone too long.

Their courtship consisted of long days together in
surgery and the occasional evening at the opera or theater. Eventually the moment came for Jeff to introduce
Carolyn to the Kramer family. He was an only child
and had a close relationship with his parents.

He told them that his girlfriend was an orthodox Jewess and insisted on keeping a kosher home.

They had been ecstatic.

He said she was a surgeon with a senior registrar position at the London Hospital and that within the month she would set up practice, as he already had, in Harley Street.

Finally he announced he was going to marry her. His parents could not have been happier. Jeff had arranged to bring Carolyn to the next Shabbat dinner.

The night before, he went alone to see them.

"Mother, Dad, Carolyn is, well . . . she's very special." Jeff looked at their expectant smiling faces. "She's black."

"She's what?" both his parents said in unison.

"It's almost incidental, in a strange way. You'll see when you get to know her. She is the most remarkable person I've ever met. Carolyn converted to Judaism long before we started dating and our values are very similar." Jeff paused, knowing how he had shocked his parents. "Mom, Dad, I am going to marry her. I do hope you will learn to love her as much as I do."

His parents sat very still. They considered themselves liberal, and believed prejudice to be evil. They had brought Jeff up to believe that, too. But now it was in their own family.

The next night Carolyn had been very nervous, wanting the Kramers' approval.

They all shook hands and as soon as the formalities were over and the drinks poured, sat down on the chairs facing the fireplace. Carolyn gently lifted her hand to indicate that she had something to say, as the Kramers were both speaking at once, dreadfully tense and ill at ease.

Everyone looked up, startled.

Carolyn spoke with deep emotion. "I would like to

say something that I know is very un-English, and that
is to talk about the issue that is uppermost in all of our
minds, but will probably remain unstated all evening."
She paused. "I am sure that you would have wished for
another kind of wife for Jeff. My blackness must be a
shock to you."

The Kramers reddened and looked away.

"I love Jeff tremendously. I know that there will be
many problems ahead that are directly related to our
difference in color. We feel that our love is strong
enough to withstand them. But the one thing I will not
do is to cause the destruction of the family closeness
you share. I would hope and pray that you can learn to
love me as I will you, and see beyond our difference in
color as Jeff and I have done. But if it is too difficult,
despite my love for Jeff, I will not stay."

The Kramers looked at Carolyn in amazement. Jeff
felt the tears rise to his eyes, his heart full of pride at
Carolyn's courage, and he loved her all the more for it.
His parents were visibly touched by her words. He was
confident that together they could face any problems
that lay ahead.

Jeff's practice was well established in Harley Street
and he wanted to get married as soon as possible.
Carolyn, however, had just launched her private practice and it was growing well. The research she'd done
while in training on new, less disfiguring, surgical techniques for breast cancer, had helped her develop a good
reputation. She was reluctant to focus on wedding plans
and promised to discuss the date after about six months.
Besides, in the weeks that followed Jeff's proposal, she
continued to feel a deep loneliness. Her struggle to become a surgeon was over, and an emptiness of purpose
took its place. She could not understand her feelings of
isolation. The Kramers had welcomed her into the family and being with Jeff was comfortable. He was tender

and they made love with sweetness, occasional passion, and gentle consideration. But there was no spark to their closeness, and no matter how much she tried to rationalize it, she knew that something was lacking. The time she'd spent with Matthew had left her invigorated while at the same time spent with passion. She never felt that way with Jeff.

Could she be making a horrible mistake?

Carolyn found her thoughts returning to South Africa and memories of Hyde Park and Soweto. Waves of homesickness filled her moments alone. She started to track the news about her former homeland, seeing that the blacks there were beginning to ascend to power and realizing that she was frustrated not to be part of that coming of age. With growing insight Carolyn began to understand that in her heart, she was still the young, angry girl who tiptoed out of the township and ran through the night to freedom.

Patients came to Carolyn's practice by referral from other physicians who knew of her reputation in breast research. The vast majority of her patients were women, but one day, soon after she began surgical practice, her secretary closed her office door and approached her desk, whispering conspiratorially.

"There is a . . . well, it's a *man* in the waiting room."

Carolyn laughed at the way the nurse said it, as if a *man* were such an unusual happening.

"I do treat men as well as women," she said, smiling.

Carolyn opened the door to greet the new patient and realized what the secretary meant to say was, "there's a *black* man in the waiting room."

Carolyn sighed. It was the little things that grated on her. In the past, she wouldn't have even bothered to note such a remark.

He was facing away from her, looking out of the

window. Carolyn smiled and greeted the man with outstretched hand. When he turned, she saw that it was
Matthew Sibanda.

"Matthew," she said, for a moment at a loss for
words. He was a little heavier, more dignified, but still
achingly familiar. "This is ... I mean ... is this a social visit, or are you sick, is it a medical visit?" Memories of the painful scene with Gyneth pierced her
suddenly.

"Yes, it's medical, but I have wanted to see you
again so we can do both, if you agree," Matthew answered.

Carolyn tried to regain her composure. She led the
way into the examining room away from her secretary's curious gaze and settled down to take a full history.

Matthew gazed at her, remembering. "You look
wonderful, Carolyn, prosperous, as beautiful as ever."

Carolyn flushed and felt self-conscious. She struggled to appear calm although her pulse was racing. She
ignored his compliment. "What appears to be the problem?"

Matthew understood Carolyn's need to be in control.
But this time he was not going to let her get away from
him. It had been coincidental that his doctor had mentioned her name, almost in passing, since her specialty
was breast surgery. But Matthew had suddenly been
transported back to intense nights of lovemaking,
steaming hot bodies blending together frantically as
two young people never tired of each other. He had
been in agony after his foolish coupling with Gyneth.
Furious at one time and inconsolate at another, he had
ranted and raved at the walls of his room, leaving message after message for Carolyn, wanting to explain.
But she was obdurate once resolved, and there was no
negotiating with her. He knew that she would not

yield. So eventually the pain subsided to a dull ache, and the void in his life was filled partially with other less satisfying relationships.

Carolyn went through the history taking and clinical examination of the lump on his chest with apparent impersonal and objective thoroughness.

"Do get dressed and then come into my office and we can talk further," she said and quickly left the room.

"I have good news for you, Matthew," she said. "The fatty lump appears quite harmless. Now, we can go one of two ways. If you are concerned, and there is the smallest of chances that this might be something more than I consider it to be, we can excise it. It would be a local anesthetic, take about half an hour and cause you little or no discomfort. We will obviously send it off for a pathological analysis, but I feel quite sure that it will be benign. Or, we can watch it for a while. Either way I do not believe that it is anything to worry about."

Matthew did not want the visit to end. He knew the moment he saw Carolyn again that he had to have her. He had noticed her brief moment of softening, a yearning—and then it was gone again. He knew exactly how to bring it back, make her scream for him.

Carolyn felt his eyes on her. He was so attractive, sensual. He seemed to fill the whole room. She would never forget how he'd made her feel and seeing him again was unsettling. Carolyn wanted to know about his life, whether he was married, and what had become of him.

But the visit was over. She had no medical reason to prolong it.

"Think it over, Matthew. I am certainly not in favor of surgery just for the sake of it, but there is your peace of mind. If this continues to be of concern, you might want to consider the excision. It's a very minor procedure." Carolyn held out her hand, remaining outwardly professional while inwardly trembling with remembrance as she felt his warm touch. "It certainly has been a long time. Goodbye, Matthew."

Matthew found himself in the lobby and on his way down the stairs to the street. He had not even had an opportunity to talk about the last time they had seen each other. It would have to wait.

He laughed to himself. He had done a few things in his life that were crazy. But this was the craziest. He was actually going to subject himself to surgery to claim Carolyn as his prize. The challenge was irresistible. He swung into his Jaguar XJS and turned the music up loud. His erection stayed with him most of the way home.

His wife, Inga, was waiting. He could see she was already on her fourth or fifth drink. The marriage was a mistake, she was someone he had grabbed on the rebound, a friend of one of his colleagues from the London School of Economics. His job in international banking took him away a lot, so he didn't have to deal with her lack of intelligence and increasing bouts of drinking. She had been very attractive, of Swedish origin, and he had been lonely. Now after seeing Carolyn, he knew he could not stay with her another moment.

Carolyn, feeling restless and confused, closed the office and went home.

She felt a flush of guilt as she found Jeff waiting. Here she'd been mentally reliving her months with Matthew, while Jeff was waiting, faithful, loving, dependable. Carolyn was filled with confusion. She gave him a quick hug and together they hastily prepared a meal. She pushed all thought of Matthew from her mind.

# Chapter 22

Carolyn turned on the television, anxious to see the latest news about Nelson Mandela, released from prison a short time before. She watched Mandela as he mesmerized the press and public in his first appearances. He made black people all over the world stand together and shout their pride in acknowledging him as one of theirs. Treated like a head of state, he was unwavering in his attitudes and commitment to the cause of the ANC. Whenever Carolyn saw Mandela, she felt like a traitor to the heritage of her people. There were moments when she wanted to stand up, chant, cry, and raise her hands to the cry of *"Amandhla!"* with the others she saw on television. But hers was the white, constrained, British life, without raw overt emotions, the life that she had chosen for self-protection.

Jeff was concerned that Carolyn was withdrawn. At first he had thought it was because of the many decisions that were being demanded of her regarding the wedding plans. But now he realized it was more than that. Carolyn seemed obsessed with watching every television broadcast she could about South Africa, grasping eagerly for every newspaper, magazine and article about that country.

Matthew's surgery was to be performed the following week in the outpatient center of the London Hospital. Carolyn was well liked there by nurses who'd known her since her student days. Matthew watched the respect with which she was treated. He was almost oblivious to the sting of the injection of local anesthetic or the numb probing that pushed and pulled as Carolyn cut away the small lump. Then it was over and she deftly dressed the wound and prescribed some pain tablets for that evening when the anesthesia would wear off. That night Carolyn fantasized about Matthew's arms around her, his hard body penetrating hers. She awoke and, seeing Jeff's sleeping form next to her, slipped quietly out of the bed. She went downstairs to the study, the memory of Matthew's body still uppermost in her mind, and masturbated on the sofa until she reached a shuddering climax and tears of frustration poured down her face.

Ten days later, Matthew came to see Carolyn to have the stitches removed. He made sure to be the last patient of the day.

After she finished the delicate work and dressed the wound lightly again, he looked directly at her and smiled with the full force of his sensual charm.

"I know that this is a strange request and probably one that few of your patients ask for, but would you join me for a cocktail?"

He had caught her completely off guard.

"Well . . . I really don't think so. But . . . thank you anyway."

Now he took her hand in his. "All I want is to talk. There is a subject that hangs between us and it must be resolved." He paused and touched her face lightly, "If you prefer, we can just stay here in your office."

Carolyn felt as if Matthew had looked right into her and had seen the loneliness and the passion she felt nightly for him.

"Well, all right. But not for long, I must get home to my fiancée." She felt safer as she said that. It was just a drink with an old friend—that was it, no more.

The local pub was crowded with the usual after-five patrons and Matthew chose a booth, not far from the back exit, but away from the standing crowd. To Carolyn, it seemed time had regressed fifteen years into the dark pub in Knightsbridge where they'd first met. Their intimacy was immediate.

"That night with Gyneth was a horrible mistake," he began.

"You don't need to talk about it," Carolyn answered quickly.

"But I do," Matthew insisted. "I don't think you know how much I loved you then." Carolyn closed her eyes briefly as they filled with tears.

"When you left, I was bereft. It was such a terrible mistake. I had spent hours talking about you that evening to Gyneth, hearing about the years you spent together, finding out more about your life. Gyneth drank too much and as we got up to leave, she practically passed out. I was pretty drunk myself and Gyneth kept going on and on about how she couldn't return to the hotel drunk in case her mother saw her that way. I took her to the apartment to sober up and then it . . . that . . . happened. It was stupid, meaningless, and I have regretted it for years. Then, you wouldn't answer my calls." He touched her face gently, as he had a thousand times before. "I have never stopped loving you, Carolyn, please forgive me."

Carolyn swayed gently toward him.

"Talk to me, tell me about your life," Matthew said softly as he looked deeply into her eyes, feeling his body heat growing as he yearned to rip off her clothes and claim her as his own.

She felt the same yearning as, surprisingly, she

found the words tumbling out about her sense of isolation, the feeling that she had turned her back on her heritage and past.

Carolyn stopped, embarrassed at the depth of her honesty with Matthew.

"It's your turn now. What happened after I left?"

Matthew started slowly. It was difficult to encapsulate the years into a few moments.

"I was determined to succeed in the London business world but it was difficult, very difficult." He paused. "I obtained a job in international banking— lots of travel and long hours. I married a Swedish woman but it didn't work out. We separated a few weeks ago."

Carolyn stayed silent.

Matthew omitted the fact that the loss of Carolyn had fueled his ambition. Speaking softly, he leaned close to her, establishing more intimacy. "Nothing and no one could ever make me feel the way you did"—he paused and lightly brushed his lips across her palm— "and still do."

Carolyn shivered. It was as if her whole body was on edge waiting for his next touch. She felt wonderful, alive, and powerful.

The hours passed.

Suddenly Carolyn realized that it was past dinnertime, and any reasonable lateness that could be explained. Matthew saw her face change as she looked at her watch.

"My God, it's so late," he exclaimed. "I had no idea. I am so sorry. Have I ruined your evening? I do apologize, the time just flew by. How about meeting me for lunch tomorrow? Can you spare an hour? I was so enjoying our conversation—this is the first time I have shared these kinds of reminiscences with anyone in so long."

Carolyn nodded. She needed to be with him.

"At one o'clock then, here?"

She agreed.

Carolyn half ran to the door, waved goodbye and was gone.

They met for lunch again the next day. Then for a drink the next. Matthew immediately picked up the nuances that often slid by Jeff when he was too tired to be sensitive to Carolyn's subtleties. They seemed to be exactly on the same wavelength, even more in tune than they had been many years before. Finally they sat close together, Matthew's body touching Carolyn's, and she was filled with desire.

They met one afternoon in the lobby of the Hartford Hotel. Soon they were in the bedroom and Carolyn felt the groan of passion deep in her throat as Matthew removed her clothes and pressed hard against her soft stomach. Then he was on her, in her, and before she could breathe her excitement, he lost control and thrashed into a frenzy of passion. At the moment of tearing climax, Carolyn looked into his face and the moment of joining pierced her with the clarity that had eluded her for years. Matthew was her soul mate. Carolyn shuddered as her own climax fluttered away. The sobs began to pour from her heart as she realized that her life would never be the same again. Jeff, her practice, none of it seemed to fit her anymore, but this did. Matthew was part of what she had been looking for; the belonging she felt in his arms gave her some of that which she'd lacked.

"You are so beautiful, so sensual, Carolyn," Matthew murmured as he reached to touch her again. "I feel like you are part of me."

Matthew had seen her look in the moment of climax and knew that she'd realized what he already knew. They were meant to be together. It would take time, but Matthew was patient. He was going to have her even if it took the rest of his life.

Carolyn vacillated from distraught guilt to elation then depression. She struggled with herself, refusing to admit the needs that raged within her. "The present is the moment that counts," Carolyn repeated constantly as she forced herself through the demands of the following day. "Stop dwelling in the past—it is over and can only hurt you now. You made your choices, leaving South Africa, walking away from Matthew. Forget it all—you have your fiancé. You belong with Jeff."

Yet the yearning was still there. She stopped that evening on the way to the subway and watched the children playing in the street. Many of them were black, Indian, Asian. She remembered a windy day in dusty Soweto when she was one of those children—she was the one who carved out the squares in the sand and shouted to the other children to skip and hop their way to victory or failure. Those were the days before the riot in Springs—she was a child who sang a lot then, who laughed at small things, who cried for the friend who hadn't come for her.

The next Saturday Carolyn was walking slowly from the subway to the hospital to do ward rounds, when she decided to detour through the shopping streets normally patronized by North and East African emigrants. Her eye was caught by a store window featuring multicolored swatches of cloth draped over a model. It reminded her of the fabric worn by Sotho women, in Basotuland, where her mother had lived. The bell clanged her arrival as she entered. The only other person in the store was a young woman with heavy makeup, polishing her nails. Carolyn felt stifled, even the musty smell was cloying, and was about to leave when she saw a swath of cloth in red and blue, exactly like the ones she remembered from her youth. She picked it up and shivered as the softness of the fabric caressed her. Twisting it with stiff fingers, unused to the intricate folding pattern that her mother had shown her more than thirty years before, she arranged it on her head and turned slowly to look at herself in the mirror.

Carolyn gasped at her reflection—and then she began to sob. The store assistant jumped up from her chair, now nervous and suspicious that the potential customer who didn't look like a lunatic was now behaving like one.

"Are you all right, miss? You aren't going to do anything crazylike, are you?" Carolyn tried desperately to compose herself, but it was as if years of stored-up emotion were now pouring out.

"No, no, of course not. Thank you, I'm so sorry, really, it's fine." She held out some money and bought the cloth.

The next evening, Jeff walked into the bedroom and gasped.

Carolyn stood in front of the mirror putting the finishing touches to her outfit. A turban framed her face, the dress flowed freely over her slim body and bangles shone and glittered.

Jeff had one of his more frustrating days. Although he was used to death and the devastating effects of cancer on the human body, it was always especially hard to see it in a child. That morning one of his favorite pediatric patients had died.

As Carolyn moved toward him, her limbs seemed to flow underneath the diaphanous fabric. She seemed to be floating. Her eyes were bright and the colors in the draped turban and robes contrasted with her glowing skin. She was tribal, primeval, pure—and she was African.

Jeff felt a sense of disbelief as though he had found

himself in a play that was his life. His fiancée had become a stranger. He wanted to touch her—but she seemed inviolate, not part of him at all. Carolyn did not look like the sophisticated British surgeon who moved efficiently through the hospital. She looked exotic, mysterious, unfamiliar.

"Carolyn? Is something happening tonight, a costume party?" Jeff asked, disturbed by her appearance.

Carolyn turned to face him. Her eyes were glittering and her face serious. "No. This is the way I want to dress from now on."

Jeff looked at her incredulously.

"Look, there is obviously something going on here that I don't understand. I need a fiancée, a lover, a friend. And lately, you have been none of those things. And now, this." He pointed at her outfit. Jeff sat on the edge of the bed and waited. "Tell me about it," he said.

She was at a loss for words. The moments moved with agonizing slowness as she struggled to express the feelings that tore her heart.

"I cannot express it. I—I feel so alone. I am what you see, yet I have been someone else ever since I walked across the border of South Africa into this new world that I call home. I want to go back to being me. I want to be black again. You cannot possibly understand what I mean, Jeff. I've been trying to be like you, Ruth, Joe, even like Gyneth and her family. But I am not—and now I don't really know who I am anymore. All I do know is that I want to be proud of what I am—and that is first and foremost black—and I don't know how to do that."

Carolyn felt the hot tears welling up in her eyes. God, she had not cried so much in years, since Ruth died, yet now she couldn't stop. All of a sudden she saw Jeff as a stranger—a white man, a beloved one, but different, not like her. She was terrified by the feeling. She sobbed while Jeff tried to find words to help her. She was so distant from him.

Carolyn met Matthew the following Monday after work at the pub. He could see the strain on her face.

"Talk to me," he said, taking her hand in his. Carolyn's eyes filled with tears. She felt so vulnerable, for the first time in many years.

"It's as if I have to find my way back into the past in order to find peace in the present. And then there is Jeff. He is such a good man, Matthew, he's been there as a friend and mentor for a long time. I don't want to hurt him."

Matthew listened silently, stroking her forearm lightly with his fingers.

"Sometimes our hearts are telling us the way, but we have trained our minds so well that we cannot hear the words anymore," he said softly. "Happiness is not always a logical decision, Carolyn. Jeff would rather have you willingly than because you felt you owed him."

Carolyn nodded miserably. Yet she had given him her commitment. And that was the most important gift she could bestow on anyone. But now her very presence with Matthew was proof itself of her betrayal of that trust.

"I will love you always. There is no reason to hurry your decision." Matthew pulled her face toward his and kissed her softly. Then her lips parted and the flame that ignited whenever they touched was there again. They left and went to Matthew's apartment, a furnished rental he had recently taken when he had left his wife. Their lovemaking was urgent, and Carolyn lifted her body to meet his strong thrustings as he called her name and together they shuddered to climax.

Carolyn lay spent in Matthew's arms.

"We will work it out together, my love. I am a patient man," he whispered.

Carolyn tried not to think of Jeff awaiting her return. She had said she'd be late, but he had said he would wait. Maybe her very absence would tell him what she dreaded saying. She shuddered and buried herself in Matthew's comforting embrace.

# Chapter 23

The Monday after Alex resigned, Gyneth went to the office early and called the janitorial service so that the mess she'd made in anger would be cleaned up before the staff came in. She pulled off the rest of the broken mirror until there was nothing in its place but the ugly wall behind. Then she called for a replacement, offering to pay an inordinate amount to have it installed that morning, and she bought another chair, a reproduction of the one she had destroyed. By midday the office looked as if nothing had happened.

At that point, Gyneth called a staff meeting.

"Alex is no longer with this company. If he calls, no one is to speak with him except me, and you are to give him no information. I want the locks on the doors changed today and everyone who had a key before will get a new one."

She turned to the young bespectacled man who had acted as Alex's assistant. He sat on the edge of his chair, his eyes wide with shock at the fast-moving events.

"John, you are to undertake the responsibilities of direction of corporate communications with regard to the following accounts—all law firms, stockbrokers, and banks. Lori, you will perform those responsibilities for all the rest of the clients. Any new client that comes in will be assigned by myself to one or the other of you. I alone will make that decision."

Gyneth sat at the head of the conference table in the small meeting room, scene of many brainstorming sessions. Some of her staff sat on chairs, the rest on the floor while others stood. The room was crowded but no one spoke. Gyneth was impeccably dressed, her Italian suit and contrasting scarf carefully chosen. She was determined to present herself in control.

"Lori and John will both accompany me on all presentations until they get the flow of it, starting today. Jennifer, you will take over Lori's tasks and Diane will take over John's. We will be hiring a new person who will be trained to undertake Jennifer and Diane's activities. There will be salary adjustments for all of you with changed responsibilities."

She paused and took a deep breath.

"The reason Alex left was entirely a personal one. It had nothing to do with me or with any of you. I am sorry that he felt he had to do it in this way and at this time. However, our company depends on each one of you and we will continue to build it as a team in order to grow and benefit together. Are there are any questions? If not, thank you."

There was silence, then as Gyneth left the room there was a burst of speculation about the broken glass and chair, new locks on the doors, and Gyneth's obvious fury at what Alex had done. Gossip was rife, everything from embezzlement to a lover's quarrel, but the subject was clearly closed for Gyneth, so gradually everyone returned to work.

Gyneth felt utterly abandoned. Her personal life was desolate, her business was facing external threats, and her staff were disturbed and distracted by the management reshuffle. Even though she resolved not to think about Alex at all, she was obsessed with him and his actions. Desolate, she had no one to turn to.

In this city of winners and losers, people had little patience with the latter. Her fear and frustration would be like an evil eye to them, and they'd avoid her in case she was on her way to becoming a loser and by association that malaise might infect them too. Gyneth couldn't confide in anyone.

The next day she dragged herself out of bed and the day after that as she worked frantically during the day and ate her way into oblivion at night. Several weeks passed and somehow she got through it as she bloated up and lost interest in her appearance.

One day, Mara Bollen dropped into the office. Gyneth had been a regular customer at her store and although she had left numerous messages Gyneth had returned none of them, not wanting Mara to see her fat and ugly state.

Mara was appalled. "Gyneth, I've been so worried. You don't return my calls, I haven't seen you at the store, something must be going on. What is the problem?"

Gyneth looked at her with shame. Even though she thought she was hiding her agony, the whole world could see it. Her life had become a struggle for emotional survival. The loneliness at work without Alex, the silence of her apartment, the feeling of sliding into failure was obvious in every pound that she had gained.

Mara saw Gyneth's unhappy pale face, without makeup and loose, unstructured clothing that made her look even larger than she was. Something in her life had gone seriously awry.

"I want you to go and see my therapist." Mara saw Gyneth's grimace. "Yes, I know that you think that therapists are just a Los Angeles thing, but really it cannot hurt you. You are obviously so unhappy already, nothing could make it worse. She'll listen and maybe even help. And she won't tell anyone what you tell her—it's confidential. Here's her number. I am going to call her *now* and tell her to expect to hear from you."

Mara called her therapist, then forced Gyneth to accompany her to Elizabeth Arden's for a massage.

That moment was a turning point for Gyneth. Someone actually cared about her. It was a small step, but with it came a glimmer of hope for a future.

Alex arrived in Maui carrying only one suitcase and a heavy heart. Gyneth's enthusiastic energy had been a stimulus that created a never-ending series of crises that needed his attention. Without her presence, the hours dragged by and the days seemed empty. He re-evaluated his finances and, by moving some of his inheritance from his father into a variety of accounts, Alex created a decent stream of income and a means to support himself without working for an indefinite period of time.

The soft warm breezes of the island lifted his mood slightly, so he drove along the street in Lahaina looking for a rental. The first house he saw was ideally located. Alex made the appropriate arrangements and within a few days, moved in. Then the silence enfolded him again. He missed Gyneth very much. He found himself beginning to develop strategies for her business, ways to beat her competitors, then, frustrated with his inability to disentangle himself from her life, he began playing tennis every day, smashing the ball over the net with such force that even his young opponent, the local tennis pro, was hard-pressed to return it. He jogged daily, sprinting through the thronging tourists in the business district, forcing himself not to think of Gyneth.

Gyneth heard from a mutual friend that Alex had gone to Hawaii and had dropped out of the frenetic rush that was Los Angeles society. She was relieved not to have to bump into him at events. Gyneth tried, unsuccessfully, to force him into the recesses of her mind.

Her energy was also directed into staying on top of her business. She longed for an alter ego as she rushed around trying to bolster the presentations that her staff were making while using her charismatic personality to woo existing and prospective clients. But her inattention to details meant that many of her brilliant ideas were not executed and within a few months, Gyneth was struggling to maintain her lead in the industry. She needed Alex.

She constantly longed for his relaxed, nonjudgmental presence, his humor, the way he teased her during tennis and ordered for her in restaurants. As tactfully as possible, Gyneth began to make inquiries. Alex was last heard of in Maui. She decided to take a much-needed vacation, though the thought of having to squeeze herself into a swimsuit made her shudder. One of her friends had a villa in Maui where she could have complete privacy and, maybe, develop the courage to look for Alex.

Gyneth left over a long weekend. On the flight to the islands, heavy turbulence prevented the flight attendants from leaving their seats and Gyneth was terrified. She held onto the seatbelt until her hands were aching and thought of all the things she still had to do in her life. One of them, she realized with intense clarity, was to be close to Alex again. She had missed him more than she could ever have imagined. And despite her anger at his sudden departure, she was filled with remorse at the way she had taken him for granted. Alex had left her because she'd become unbearable to work with.

Within an hour of her arrival, Gyneth located Alex's name in the telephone book. He lived in Lahaina. She drove to his address feeling breathless with anticipation.

Alex came to the door, looking young, tanned, and relaxed. Gyneth ached with the desire to bury herself in his arms. His torso was firm and muscular from weeks of tennis and jogging and his shorts were tight over a lean and contoured body. Recognizing instantaneously how attractive he was, Gyneth realized that Alex was everything she could have wished for, yet she hadn't seen it before. His face revealed how stunned he was to see her.

"Alex, may I come in? I should have called . . ." Gyneth stood uncertainly at the door.

Alex stood aside silently. A number of people lounged on the deck of the house. Alex introduced her.

"This is Gyneth Amron, a friend from the mainland."

The other guests acknowledged Gyneth but she was uncomfortable. She tried to make small talk, but she was so distressed by Alex's physical presence that soon the conversation dwindled.

Alex sat with his sunglasses on looking at Gyneth. She was pale, with dark rings under her eyes. He had heard of her fit of temper and the broken mirror and chair from one of her employees. He also heard from the same source about her struggle to maintain the business and that without his skills and help, she was losing the battle. He had hoped, longed, for her to contact him. But the fact that she was now sitting in his house was shocking to him. Seeing the results of his actions appalled him. He had almost destroyed the woman he loved because she wouldn't give him what he wanted. He was as bad as she was.

Soon the other guests sensed their need to be alone and one by one they took their leave.

Gyneth began to talk. "Alex, so much has happened even though it has been a few months. I've changed. I must have been awful, selfish, and insensitive. Can you ever forgive me for the way I treated you? You were always there for me and your support was a large part of our success as we grew, and I never acknowledged it."

Emotion filled Alex so that for a moment he could not look at Gyneth but turned his head away, concealing his feelings behind the dark sunglasses.

"I'm so afraid, Alex. I don't know if I can pull it together. The business is in a tailspin and I'm getting desperate."

Gyneth held her face in her hands. She had messed it all up, how could she explain how much she'd missed him. It wasn't just the business.

"It's more than that, Alex. It's . . . it's you I miss, the time we spent together, the way . . . how you made me feel." Gyneth stammered. He seemed so distant, sitting immobile, half turned away from her, looking out over the ocean. Perhaps she had made a terrible mistake and he didn't care about her at all. Gyneth couldn't stop now, she had to say it all.

"I want you to come back with me, Alex, be my partner in the business, be with m-me again." She stopped.

Alex felt the pain in his chest increasing as he tasted the victory he had fantasized about for months. It was a bitter taste, because the sad woman in front of him was no longer charismatic or desirable.

He turned slowly to face her. Reaching forward, he took Gyneth's hands in his. She felt his warmth and smelled the familiar scent of his after-shave. A wave of longing swept over her.

"It's not only you, Gyneth, I'm equally to blame, walking out without any warning, wanting to hurt you." Alex paused and Gyneth held her breath.

"I was furious because you didn't seem to care about whether I was there or not, and I left in the most abrupt way I could in order to injure where it would cause you the most damage, in the business. You see, I only resigned because I thought that after a few weeks you'd realize your love for me, the way I'd always loved you. It was a stupid move in my part."

Gyneth gripped Alex's hands tightly, hearing his words of love. It was more than she could have wished for. Instead of humiliation he was giving her love. For a few moments she couldn't talk. Then softly, slowly, she responded.

"Alex, I never knew, not really for sure. If only I'd known, then so much could have been different. Maybe I wasn't ready for you, but I am now."

Alex drew his arms around Gyneth and held her gently. She breathed in his smell, and felt the roughness of the hair on his chest against her cheek. His skin was smooth, and she felt his lips touch hers for the first time. Gyneth could hardly believe it was happening. She looked at his face above hers, his eyes closed and his fingers tracing her forehead and she realized how much she had yearned for such tenderness, the feeling of real love. Slowly, they began to explore each other. This was not the Alex she had thought she'd known for so many years. He was stronger, in control, and passionate. She let him lead her through the house to the bedroom and closed her eyes as he undressed her. She opened herself up to him, embarrassed that she felt so ugly but slowly coming to realize that he was touching her with tenderness and pleasure, and that she could relish the beauty of that feeling.

The night faded into daylight and they lay intertwined, awakening to love each other again. Gyneth began to feel like a woman. Gone were her fears about the business, money, status. She unfolded like the hibiscus that bloomed in abundance outside the little house.

# *Chapter 24*

"I'm leaving for London tomorrow. My mother called and it's not good news. The doctors in Johannesburg don't want to operate on the tumor and her surgeon in London feels that radiation and chemotherapy is the only solution. Alex will take care of everything while I'm gone. I thank you all for your support and friendship. Your wishes will keep me going. I really don't know how long I will be gone, but it could be weeks." Gyneth tried to retain her composure as she ended her short speech to her key management team of six employees, most of whom had been with her since she started the company that she and Alex now owned together.

Estelle was in hospital in London, suffering through yet another series of cancer treatments in a frantic struggle to beat the disease that was consuming her. Gyneth was torn, desperately wanting to share the last days of her mother's life with her, but now that she had discovered Alex and was reveling in their physical and emotional closeness, she could hardly bear to be without him.

Gyneth boarded the plane and sank down in the first-class seat. She was so depressed, and desperately wanted to stay in Los Angeles. London held so many unhappy memories for her. In almost every phone call over the past few months Estelle had asked her about Carolyn. Eventually, in frustration, Gyneth told her mother that her disagreement with Carolyn was still unresolved and they'd had no contact. Estelle made a last plea to her daughter to come to peace with the situation, then dropped the subject.

When Gyneth arrived at the hospital, Estelle was sitting up in bed, her face unusually flushed. She looked excited. Gyneth became afraid.

"Mother, what is the matter, did something new happen?" she said anxiously.

"Yes and I could hardly wait for you to come. I have very good news. In fact it is something of a miracle. I can't believe the coincidence."

Gyneth was filled with hope. Perhaps some last-minute mistake or cure had been found. Then seeing Estelle's heightened nervousness she thought for a moment that the medication had made her mother confused. It had done so on a couple of previous occasions. She made soothing noises and started to fuss over the blankets.

"Oh, for heaven's sakes, Gyneth, stop fussing. Listen to me." Estelle's voice was authoritative and demanding.

Gyneth was stunned into silence.

"I've discovered that Carolyn is a surgical consultant right here in this very hospital."

Gyneth felt her heart jump.

"Isn't it wonderful?" Estelle was insistent.

Gyneth put her arms around her mother.

"Yes, Mother, it is."

"So you two can make up your silly fight and go back to being friends again. I don't want you to be alone, so . . ." Estelle's voice dropped to a whisper and her eyes filled with tears.

A knock on the door interrupted them.

"That must be them now. Come in!" Estelle sat up in bed.

Carolyn and Jeff entered together.

"Gyneth, this is Jeff Kramer, he is my oncologist and one of the surgeons caring for me. And here is his fianceé, Carolyn!" Estelle announced their arrival with emphasis.

Gyneth was speechless. Carolyn, engaged to a Jewish surgeon! Her face flushed as she remembered the last time they had seen each other.

She held out her hand. "Dr. Kramer, I am pleased to meet you. C-Carolyn . . ." Gyneth looked beseechingly at her friend, and whispered, "Can you forgive me, please, will you? It was a terrible mistake, and all my fault; please, will you let me explain?"

There was a brief moment of awkwardness but then Carolyn reached out her hand. Gyneth took it and pulled her friend close. The two young women held each other tightly. Now all that mattered was that they were together and Estelle had made it happen. The same thought in both of their minds, they turned to the bedside and held the frail woman in their arms. No more needed to be said, and quietly Jeff left them alone.

Estelle seemed drained of energy. Her treatment was discontinued when the doctors conferred the next day. It was becoming obvious that further efforts were futile and the unanimous decision of her medical team was that her quality of life was what mattered for the short time she had left. Carolyn stayed with Gyneth at her mother's bedside for the next thirty hours.

Estelle deteriorated rapidly. It was as if she kept herself going long enough to reunite the children she'd watched play together in their youth. Then, as Gyneth dozed with her head on her mother's hand, sitting, as she had for days, at the side of the bed, Carolyn saw the slight flutter of her eyes, the movement of her lips and knew, with the clinical experience of years of life and death, that Estelle was gone.

"Gyneth, my dear, Gyneth, wake up. She's gone." Gyneth felt her friend's warm hand on her shoulder as she lifted her face from her mother's lifeless fingers.

"Oh no, Mummy, please, no." Gyneth felt the sobs start, and could not stop.

"She was in so much pain, and struggled so many years, it was time for her to go in peace, Gyneth. I am here for you, I'll always be here for you."

No matter how ill Estelle had been she had seemed invincible, always fighting back and surviving. Gyneth couldn't believe that she'd never hear her voice again, see her loving face, seek her counsel.

Estelle had wanted to be buried next to Jacob in Johannesburg. Gyneth forced herself to make the decisions necessary to return her mother's body to South Africa. Carolyn met her at the hotel the night after Estelle's death.

"I would like to come with you to be at the funeral. You have no one there, Gyneth."

Tears filled Gyneth's eyes. She was dreading the whole experience. Memories of her father's burial had kept her up most of the night before as she alternated between missing Alex and grief. She and Alex had spoken long distance for over an hour and she longed to feel his arms around her. She insisted that he not travel to Johannesburg for the funeral since she had to stay at least a month to clear up her mother's affairs. Reluctantly he had agreed, and she immediately regretted being so insistent.

Carolyn's decision was very welcome and she hugged her friend gratefully.

Matthew had received the news with a calm under-standing.

"It is your opportunity to bring the strands of your life together, to dispel the myths about the past and free yourself to go forward. All I ask is that you are very aware and careful of whom you talk to and where you go. Your survival instincts have been long dor-mant, and it is still a dangerous place for people like us. Please call me often, or I will worry." He held her close as they spent a few hours together.

Jeff had nodded glumly when Carolyn gave him the news of her upcoming journey. It had been a week since their last discussion and Carolyn had been un-available almost every evening. He was despondent and tried to be supportive.

"This will be a good time for you to think about our future. I'll miss you so much, Carolyn. Perhaps this trip will help sort things out, and we can go back to the way we were. I'll be waiting." Jeff kissed her chastely on the cheek at the airport.

Carolyn and Gyneth boarded the plane together, each silent with their own thoughts. This was not the way they'd left South Africa, with drama and intrigue on excited adventures into the future. Now they were both afraid and apprehensive of the days that lay ahead.

# Chapter 25

Despite her composed exterior, Carolyn was shaking with apprehension as the British Airways plane rolled to a stop in the land they called New South Africa. Gyneth was aware of Carolyn's discomfort and squeezed her hand briefly. But her own grieving and painful knowledge that she wouldn't see her mother's welcoming face at the airport, was all-consuming.

Carolyn traveled on a British passport, stating her place of birth as Mozambique. Her refined English accent, deliberately polished throughout the years at medical school, gave no trace of her origin. Nevertheless, now entering the environment she had gladly fled so many years ago, the tightness in her stomach belied her calm, expressionless face as the passport and customs officials examined her documents with exaggerated deliberateness while Gyneth, already done with the process, waited patiently.

Eventually they were outside in the cool winter air, gazing at the clear blue skies and puffy clouds that were the trademark of the Transvaal.

"It looks the same, doesn't it?" Gyneth said. "Yet it isn't, and nor are we." She sighed deeply. "I'm dreading tomorrow. I'm going to have to deal with the funeral arrangements and meet the lawyers and accountants."

"It will soon be over." Carolyn tried to comfort her friend. "Perhaps while you are busy, I'll take a trip back to Soweto, see if anyone I know is still there."

"It's not safe, Carolyn, please be careful; if something happened to you I couldn't bear it." Gyneth's eyes filled with tears again.

"I'll be fine, don't worry." Carolyn sounded more confident than she actually felt.

The taxi ride was silent as most of the plane trip had been. Gyneth was filled with sadness and Carolyn with anticipation. They sped through endless new housing developments and industrial parks on the way to the exclusive northern suburbs of Johannesburg. Now Carolyn began to feel disoriented, afraid of what she'd discover.

"I called Anna and Andrew. They are expecting us." Gyneth was tense, dreading seeing her mother's home, without the warmth of her presence.

The driveway was long and winding, and aromatic flowers spread along its length in waves of undulating color.

Gyneth stepped out onto the flagstone and rang the doorbell. Andrew opened the door with Anna by his side, her face stained with tears. Silently she drew Gyneth into her large embrace.

Carolyn hurriedly paid the driver, then, plucking up her courage, stood hesitantly in the driveway, waiting for the right moment.

"Carolyn? Is it really you? You are such a young lady now! You look just like your mother, the face is the same." Anna came toward her, arms outstretched.

Carolyn felt the tears begin to trickle down her cheeks. It had been so long since she'd seen anyone who'd known her mother. She realized suddenly how

desperately she had longed for this familiarity, a sense
of her own history.

Andrew shook Gyneth's hand, then greeted Carolyn
shyly, intimidated slightly by her bearing and sophisticated appearance.

"It is so wonderful to see you both again," Carolyn
whispered. They both laughed as they heard her English accent.

"Gyneth tells me you are a doctor, like Dr. Amron."
Anna's eyes were bright with tears. Who would have
thought the little girl who cried to be able to swim with
her friend, would achieve such greatness?

"I am," Carolyn said softly. "I have so much to tell
you both, and there are many questions I want to ask."

"There will be time. Come inside, child, it's good to
have you home again."

Andrew placed Carolyn's bag on the bed in the guest
room. Gyneth would sleep in the adjoining room. Together the two young women walked silently through
the house, seeing and feeling Estelle everywhere. They
hugged briefly, and even though it was early evening,
Gyneth was suddenly exhausted. Needing to be alone
to give vent to her grief, she bade Carolyn good night.

Anna fussed around for a few moments, making sure
Carolyn was comfortable, and seemed unwilling to enter into any real conversation until the morning.

Carolyn turned on the television in her room. There
had been none when she'd left. Now the familiar yet
jarring language of Afrikaans, and the clipped nasal
South African accent, made her shudder. The sounds
and words brought back the memories of the worst of
her past even though her environment was luxurious,
belonging to the world she had just left. She felt suddenly lonely, and for the hundredth time, wondered if
she had done the right thing.

She sat up on the bed feeling flat, disoriented. It was

now twilight, and reason told her to sleep off the trip, save her strength for the next day. Instead, Carolyn threw off her traveling clothes, choosing a modest skirt and blouse, flat tennis shoes and a scarf to cover her hair. She removed her makeup, and put her purse away after taking out some money. It was time to explore.

She walked through the tree-lined streets of the residential suburb until she came to a main road. After a few moments, a taxi cruised by. He dropped her off downtown. Carolyn walked slowly through the congested area, unrecognizable to her. She remembered the streets filled with white shoppers, and European-type clothing in the stores aimed primarily at wealthy upper-class whites. Now store promotions were to the black population and the city was unkempt, dirty. Minivan taxis overflowing with black workers filled the roads, and smoke from industry darkened the skies over the area. In the late twilight, Carolyn could glimpse the yellow tops of the mine dumps, last seen from the road she had taken on her flight to freedom. A pang of fear gripped her and she clenched her fists. She remembered the exhilaration she'd felt as she threw off the shackles of township life. How would it look, so many years later?

The night came suddenly in the city. Tall buildings and the elongated city blocks rapidly emptied of people. Carolyn's sense of alienation increased. People were fearful. She could feel it in the glances of those who were hurrying to quit the downtown area before nightfall. Small groups of young men loitered on street corners leering at her. No police were visible, either on foot or in cars. The streets slid into darkness. Carolyn was walking faster, looking warily behind her, to the left and right, trying to retrace her steps back to the well-lit street of the main shopping area and international hotels. She breathed a sigh of relief as she saw the tall modern structures no more than a few blocks away, and slowed her pace. She felt rather foolish for being so fearful.

She was almost knocked over as she rounded the corner. Stumbling from the encounter, Carolyn looked up and saw a youthful face. He couldn't have been more than thirteen.

"Gosh, I am sorry, I really didn't see you."

"Ag, it's okay." He smiled as he pressed the gun in her side. "Jus' give me your money, and you can pretend you still didn't see me." Carolyn's eyes widened in surprise and shock. The youth mistook her hesitation for reluctance and dug the gun deeper into her side, bruising her ribs.

"You will bleed here, sissie, and I'll get your money anyway. So hand it over or die." He leered at her. Carolyn dug her hand in her pocket and emptied it, pushing the rand notes into his hand.

"Go, leave me alone. It's all I have, take it." She was trembling with fear and disbelief. This could not be happening to her.

With an extra dig in the ribs for good measure, the young black teenager pushed her harshly against the wall. Carolyn landed on her knees, bruising her forehead against the side of the building. When she turned to look for her attacker, he was nowhere to be seen. The streets were almost deserted, and those, both black and white, who saw her kneeling on the sidewalk, her head bleeding, turned their eyes the other way and hurried past.

Carolyn stood up shakily, dusting herself off. She felt the contusion on her head with trembling fingers. It was not too bad, but she'd have a bad headache for a few days. Trying to calm herself, she leaned against the building. The young man who had accosted her had not been born when she had left. He was from a different world from the one she had lived in, one full of chaos and hatred. None of that reasoning made her feel any better. She staggered to the entrance of the nearest hotel. The doorman looked at her with suspicion.

"Yes, what do you want?"

"I am Dr. Ngwizi. I was attacked. Please can you call me a taxi, I am staying with friends in the northern suburbs." Her British accent convinced him. Carolyn slumped into the backseat of the taxi with relief. He dropped her off at the end of the driveway and she crept silently into the house. Only when she was in her room, did she allow herself to give in to the shock and relief. She had come so far, only to almost have it all taken away from her in a crazy, meaningless moment. Finally she examined her head, saw that no stitches were needed, and retrieving some ice from the freezer in the well-stocked kitchen, she packed it into a towel, took a Valium and tried to calm her confused feelings. She was thankful that since Anna and Andrew lived in the servants' quarters that they had not seen either her exit or confused return. Exhausted and in pain, eventually she fell into a troubled sleep.

The next day Carolyn awoke early before anyone in the household was up. She left a short note for Gyneth.

"I'm doing fine and hope you got some rest. I'm going out now but I'll be back later around five."

The taxi driver was reluctant to go to Soweto, but she paid him double. Carolyn stood holding on tightly to the seats while the driver jammed on his brakes every now and then, cramming person after sweaty person into the van. The journey retraced her lighthearted steps to freedom many years before, but Carolyn was less confident now of her ability to take care of herself than she had been that day, buoyed then by the confidence of youthful ignorance and ambition. A number of times she almost told the driver to take her back to the house.

But it was too late. The driver screeched to a halt, unwilling to stop for more than a few seconds at the entrance to the township, in case marauding gangs assaulted him and stole his van, killing him carelessly for being in the way. He almost threw her out and then was off in a cloud of throat-closing dust. Carolyn felt completely alone, destitute, sixteen years old again, a pickaninny in a black township. Bending her head low, she walked as unobtrusively as she could, making her way across the dusty streets, habit taking her toward Alena's house, past the preschool, which now stood empty, blackened by fire. She walked slowly, each painful step taking her back in years.

Through Carolyn's adult eyes, Alena's house now looked shabby and even smaller. Hesitantly she knocked at the door. There was no reply. She looked in the window, covered with iron bars. Amazingly the inside looked the way it had always been. There was a different sofa but the crocheted doilies were still there, the small table in the corner. No one was inside. Carolyn suddenly felt an overwhelming wave of exhaustion, nausea, and depression. She shouldn't have come. It was all too long ago, her life was so good and this life had been so hard, there was nothing here to discover. She leaned against the dirty wall and closed her eyes. She should go back to Estelle's house. She was acting like a foolish child, anxious to return but not using any of her adult skills of reason to plan her actions.

Carolyn wearily started walking back to the main road. Silently, before she was aware of it, she was surrounded. The four young men with old eyes grabbed her arms, forcing her back against the wall of one of the houses. A knife, not dissimilar to the very one she had obtained from Phineas, was pointed at her throat.

"Give me your money, bitch," the one boy hissed. "Quick or I'll cut your throat." Carolyn fumbled in her pocket, pulling out another few rand notes, which fluttered into the dust.

"Hey, look at all this, man." The boys crowed with excitement. "Where else do you have this stuff stored?" The one boy put his hand under the front of her skirt, and pulled on her underwear, tearing it off. Carolyn felt the icy anger that had once been part of her life, but had faded into the past with everything else. Now it was there again, and with it her instincts for self-preservation slid into place.

"You touch me and you are dead," she hissed, grasping for words that would shock the young animals now panting over her. "You'll be skinned and your balls will be cut into small pieces if you touch me." The leader hesitated, reacting to the tone of her voice but the others forced her into the dust, even as she kicked them. "Ag, man," the leader said, "let's go, she's just an old bitch anyway." He stuffed the notes into his pocket and cuffed one of his friends who was unzipping his fly. Laughing and making lewd signs and comments, they sauntered away, unhurried, unafraid of pursuit or apprehension.

Carolyn's reaction was far different than it had been the night before. She was furious, coldly determined to gain control of herself and her environment. The old rules had changed. Now anyone was fair game, the hunters and their prey. Race was no longer the issue, violence was simply the law of the land.

She forced herself to walk with confidence, determinedly striding across the wasteland of the township, scarred with the factional warring between the rival political forces, Inkatha and ANC. Avoiding the

burned-out hulks of cars and shacks, she crossed the
main highway and passed the familiar barracks of
Baragwanath Hospital. Carolyn felt no nostalgia now.
She stopped the next minivan, instructing him to take
her to Estelle's house. The route he took was along
Louis Botha Avenue, formerly a main thoroughfare
from the Amrons' to the downtown area. However now
few, if any, private cars used the road that had been
given over almost exclusively to taxi minivans driving
erratically from one side of the road to another, drop-
ping off or picking up fares at random. The driver
drove past the shopping center where her mother had
died. She felt tears in her eyes and nauseated at the
memory as, for the first time in many years, she again
heard the thumb of dead flesh as her mother's life
ebbed away in front of her.

Gyneth was in her room.

"It's been the most awful day, Carolyn. The funeral
cannot be until Monday because of some Jewish holiday. I just want it all to be over, the pain is so unbearable."

Carolyn held Gyneth's hand for a moment. Her
friend looked closely at her face.

"What on earth happened to you? You look terrible."

Carolyn felt the trembling start in her hands.

"I thought that maybe I wouldn't remember, how to
protect myself, I mean. But I do. Things aren't good
here, Gyneth, I went to Soweto and it's even grimmer
than I recall. I was mugged a couple of times."

"God, are you all right?"

"I am now."

"This is not the way I thought it would be, Carolyn.
Everything is so difficult, the phone system is dreadful,
people are narrow-minded. I'm so relieved we don't
live here anymore."

"I know what you mean," Carolyn said grimly.

"There is so much that is unresolved here. When I am in Los Angeles sometimes for months I don't think about my father. Here he is all around me. And I keep expecting my mother to walk in any minute."

"Do you want to go back to the old house in Hyde Park?" Carolyn was hesitant.

"Let's do it tomorrow. I have to find some way to pass the time until Monday. And this place just makes me depressed. Also, I need to meet with Anna and Andrew. I have hardly had time to talk to them and their futures are in limbo. I must do it tonight."

That evening Anna and Andrew sat patiently around the kitchen table waiting for Gyneth to speak.

"My mother left a pension for each of you. If you save it carefully, there will be enough for your later years. After all the legal affairs are concluded, the lawyer will give you a check. We will have to sell the house and there will be lots of furniture that I know my mother would want you to have. Over the next few weeks we can start going through everything. I'll be going back to Los Angeles soon and Carolyn will be returning to London. The funeral is on Monday." Gyneth felt as if she were living in a nightmare.

Carolyn watched carefully as Anna's face hardened slightly. Gyneth saw it, too. The room was filled with tension.

"Anna, can we talk? I mean a real talk, between equals. We are no longer employer and servant, just people who have known each other a lifetime. You and Andrew are all both Carolyn and I have left in the world since Armindo and David died and the rest of the servants went to other jobs. Don't you think it is time to be really honest with each other?"

"What is there to talk about? Your mother is dead, your life will go on in America, and we will continue here as always. Some of us don't have the chance to move."

Carolyn could hear the bitterness in Anna's voice. Andrew sat with downcast eyes.

"Life could be different here in the future," Carolyn started, but Anna interrupted her.

"You don't know what you are talking about. This is the *new* South Africa now, blacks live wherever they can afford. So the rich blacks, they live in Hyde Park and in Houghton and the poor people like us still work for them. For us, nothing has changed."

Gyneth took Anna's hand in hers.

"You know how important you've been to me. You loved me so much. Thank you for that."

Anna's eyes filled with tears and the bitterness disappeared.

"Yes, but you left anyway. It was just us with Mrs. Amron. And after a lifetime of work what do I have? A pension, but no place to go." Anna's large frame shook with wracking silent sobs.

Carolyn and Gyneth encircled her with their arms while Andrew kept saying, "Mama, Mama, don't be so sad. Things will be better soon." He pulled out his tattered bible and started reading silently from it. The familiarity of the words calmed him as he rocked back and forth gently.

"We have all lost something, Anna," Carolyn said softly. "We may have new lives, but we have no past to show our husbands, our friends. And we are torn all the time between the past and the present." Carolyn thought sadly of the decisions that still awaited her as Jeff's glum face flashed into her mind.

"At least you have each other," Anna said, blowing her nose hard into a large handkerchief.

Carolyn grasped Gyneth's hand. They had nearly lost each other, too. How foolish they'd been to allow a moment's misjudgment to destroy the only continuity that still existed in their lives. It must never happen again.

That night before bed, Carolyn sat pensively next to the telephone for a few moments. Then she dialed Joe Abromowitz's number. It was listed in the directory and had been quite easy to find. Carolyn noticed with amazement the hundreds of names of black South Africans now living in the white suburbs, with private phones, none of which had been possible just a few years before.

The woman who answered sounded frail.

"Is Joe there?" Carolyn asked hesitantly. Her question was greeted by silence. Then the woman asked with quavering tones, "Who is asking for him?"

"I am Carolyn Ngwizi. He helped me once, a long time ago, I live in London now, I am a surgeon there," she added unnecessarily.

"Ah yes, Carolyn," she said sadly, "he was so proud of you. Such a success you made, he spoke of you often." She paused.

"My dear, Joe passed away five months ago, may he rest in peace. I wish I had gone first but it was not to be. He was happy that he'd helped you. Goodbye, my dear." Carolyn's eyes filled with tears. His last letter to her seemed to have been just a few months before and it had been full of good advice as always. She should have called him then, and she would have heard his voice one more time.

"I am so sorry," Carolyn murmured as she gently replaced the phone. She wept until the first wave of shock and grief was spent. It was another ending, marking a milestone to her maturity.

The next day they went to Hyde Park. The Amrons' stately home was still the grandest house on the street, but seemed smaller, less imposing. Gyneth and Carolyn stood for a moment at the front door, hesitating. Then Gyneth pressed the bell. It's familiar chimes brought Carolyn memories of sitting on the kitchen stool, watching David prepare trays of smoked salmon and miniature sausage rolls for the guests whose arrivals were being announced. The door opened and a white woman with graying hair looked suspiciously at the two women, one tall and blond and the other black, slender, and elegantly dressed.

"Yes?"

"I'm Gyneth Amron. We used to live here and now live in London. I wonder if we might look around the house for a few moments?"

"What about you?" she said, eyeing Carolyn and opening the door another inch. "You didn't live here."

Carolyn smiled encouragingly, and swallowed hard. She introduced herself using her best upper-class British accent.

"I was the daughter of the maid," she said, biting down hard on her lip. They had discussed how to handle this situation and decided that pretending humility would be the best approach. After all, they wanted to see the house again.

"We have a lot of crime around here, you can't be too careful," the woman grumbled and finally the door was opened. They stepped inside and back into the past. With adult eyes Carolyn saw and really appreciated the fine wooden paneling and beveled glass, the expanse of wooden floors leading to the elegant French doors that opened to the vista of the rolling lawns and gardens below. She touched the brass banister on the sweeping staircase where Jacob had first noticed her interest in medicine and walked slowly throughout the house, the woman following her closely with suspicion. This life seemed so much more real to her now than it had seemed when she lived in Soweto. She was comfortable here now. This environment was where she belonged.

The owners had sold off the bottom acre and stables and moved the swimming pool, destroying the herb garden. Martha's room was tiny but still light and airy. The maid occupying it regarded Carolyn with suspicion and she sensed her resentment. Carolyn struggled with the unfamiliar Sotho words as she tried to be friendly, but it was clear that her presence was neither welcome to the present owner nor her maid.

After a brief visit to the tree where Gyneth's dog had been buried, the two women hurriedly left.

"It makes me want to weep. Did you see how the owner looked at us when she realized that you would be visiting the house with me? I thought I'd be nostalgic, but all I wanted to do was get out of there as soon as possible." Gyneth had taken a few photos, but her heart was not really in it. All the old anger she felt at her father came rushing back.

Carolyn was filled with mixed emotions.

"Leaving this house was one of the hardest things I ever did," she burst out. "Nothing in my life felt right after that. Even now, I feel resentment at your parents for pushing me out. They knew how awful Soweto was."

"My dad did support you until you ran away, Carolyn, he sent Alena money every month, she told me."

"He did . . . ?" Carolyn felt dizzy at discovering that Jacob had been her secret benefactor while she had been living in the depths of despair.

Gyneth continued. "I only realized just before my father died that he wasn't as perfect as I'd thought. The decisions he made were not always easy to accept. I wanted so badly to be like him, to do what you have done. Both of us lost something we thought we wanted, but maybe we are different people for it."

Suddenly, Carolyn realized that she had created in London a replica of the world in South Africa from which she had been excluded. In that moment of clarity, Carolyn understood. Jeff represented Jacob, Gyneth, Estelle, this life. Yet there was still the other part of her, the part that Matthew touched.

Gyneth drove slowly into the Hillbrow district. "This was such a fun place when I was growing up."

"I never even knew it existed." Carolyn looked across at her friend. "We were living in entirely different worlds; how could you have known the difficulties of life in Soweto when all you did was have fun?"

"Carolyn, don't be angry with me now. It's all in the past. You can't hold me responsible for the sins of all those who oppressed you."

Carolyn nodded and massaged her neck, aching with the tensions of the morning.

"You're right. Being in this place brings back all the old feelings, puts me at loggerheads with the world."

They passed the entrance to the main hospital in Hillbrow. Carolyn had never been inside.

"Gyneth, can we stop? I would love to see this hospital."

"I really have had enough of hospitals in the past few years. I'll wait in the car."

Carolyn entered the main lobby and, forcing herself to appear confident, walked the corridors, observing with her medically trained eye, the deterioration of medical care. The hospital was dreary, the wards filled to overflowing. The nurses were resentful, angry. The environment certainly did not give the same impression of the crisp London hospitals she was used to. She watched a nurse pass a bedpan full of urine over the bed of another patient, sloshing it slightly onto the clean bedclothes, and was appalled that an RN would behave in such a way. Finally a guard stopped her.

"Where do you think you're going?" He spoke with a strong Afrikaans accent. Carolyn flashed back to a beach many years before and felt the return of white-hot anger at that memory.

"I'm a surgeon in practice in London," she said in her clipped English accent. "I am observing some of the clinical practices in your country. Do you have a problem with that?" The guard mumbled gruffly and stepped out of her path.

Carolyn left the hospital soon after and made her way to the parking garage. Suddenly she heard a voice, calling for help, and the laughter of children. Turning in the direction of the sounds, she was horrified to see a group of children in tattered clothing, accosting an elderly woman with a shopping bag. A small boy with encrusted dirt on his face, shoeless and brandishing a long knobkerrie stick, was beating the woman on the arm, unable even to reach her head, since he stood only as high as her thigh. He could not have been more than ten years old. The others spat in their victim's face, while one tripped her. The woman fell to the ground as the children finally got control of her purse.

"Stop that," Carolyn yelled as she moved to help the woman. The little boy turned and saw her. He threw back his head and laughed, giving the woman one last kick as he sauntered off.

"Let me help you," Carolyn said, as the woman lay sobbing on the sidewalk, her glasses broken as she held her one arm cradled in the other. With practiced fingers, Carolyn quickly examined her.

"I think you're all right, my dear. Come, we'll walk together." They walked slowly back into the hospital so the elderly woman could sit down.

"Where do these children come from? Why are they

doing this?" Carolyn asked her, not knowing who else to talk to to express her frustration.

"They're called the twilight children, black street kids who live around here in gangs. Their parents threw them out, no money, no jobs, no room for any more mouths to feed. They're a menace I can tell you, there are at least two or three muggings a day. I shouldn't have been so foolish as to walk around alone here. It's too dangerous."

"But they are children," Carolyn said, "one or two could not have been more than ten years old."

"They are criminals, that's what they are." The woman felt the bruise on her arm.

Carolyn sat for a few more moments on the hard hospital bench. The waste of human potential appalled her. What had happened to the children's parents? How long could they survive on the street, in the garbage of a big city, feeding off unwary passersby. Bidding the older woman goodbye, she walked slowly back to join Gyneth.

Carolyn sat silently as they continued their tour of the city. The homes in the Houghton area were surrounded by tall walls with pointed pieces of broken glass and elaborate security systems.

"The world here has changed greatly," Carolyn finally said. Gyneth, lost in her own thoughts, looked up and agreed.

"I am emotionally so drained by what I have seen in the past few days. I've understood that my life in London is the realization of the dream I had as a little girl, but I am living on borrowed time in the white world. Although that world is mine, there is unfinished business here for me. I have to find a way to resolve the yearning, the need to give something back to my past, but not lose my future in the process." Carolyn sighed.

Images flashed through her mind. She told Gyneth about the twilight children.

"I cannot stop thinking of them. What can be done? They are lost to society, and a menace to themselves and others."

Gyneth continued to drive slowly through the suburbs. "It is a problem throughout the country now. The accountant was telling me that there is over thirty percent unemployment among the blacks, so it's no wonder they cannot afford to care for their children. There are some relief groups, but they change little."

Suddenly Carolyn had the answer. She could have been one of those children, a waif, stealing, running, hiding, ultimately dying in the street, with no family who cared to find and nurture her. Now she knew how to create a legacy for her country.

"Gyneth, there is something I have to do. I want to help those children. Money alone won't do it." Slowly the idea began to crystallize in her mind. "We could create a foundation, the Carolyn Ngwizi and Gyneth Amron Foundation for Homeless Children."

Gyneth became caught up in her friend's excitement.

"When my inheritance comes through I can make a donation to get things going."

"And I will fund it initially from the income I have been receiving for a new surgical instrument I designed and sold to a medical products manufacturer a couple of years ago. The sales of the product are beginning to improve and I receive a royalty check every three months. I can donate that directly into our foundation since the income from my medical practice is more than enough to support me. Then," Carolyn clapped her hands together in excitement, "we can raise money all over the world for these children. We will house, educate them, give them role models, opportunity. Gyneth, it can be done. We will need someone who knows the system, understands the New South Africa. We are anachronisms here, we don't belong anymore. But this way we'll give back in a way that will create a better future in a real sense for hundreds of children."

Carolyn and Gyneth could hardly contain their excitement. Gyneth started to think of names of people in the community who could serve on the board and help organize such a program and together they created a plan of action late into the night.

Finally the day for the funeral arrived.

Gyneth and Carolyn held each other as the clods of earth fell heavily onto Estelle's grave. There were hundreds who came to pay their last respects, Estelle was widely respected as a woman of great courage.

That night Carolyn helped Gyneth go through her mother's personal belongings. Amid tears and laughter they relived their lives together, feeling as if time had stood still.

"What are you going to do about Jeff?" Gyneth asked gently, knowing that Carolyn had been struggling with herself for weeks.

"Things are not so good between us." She paused and closed her eyes. She had told no one of her betrayal of him.

"I have seen Matthew again."

Gyneth gasped and her face reddened. "Carolyn, we have never really spoken about that awful night. Please, let me explain . . ."

Carolyn took her hand. "There is no need. Matthew went through it all already. Let's leave it in the past." She sighed deeply. "I shouldn't have left him, Gyneth, the way he makes me feel is like nothing else. But now I have another whole life and he's not part of it. It's all such a mess." Carolyn put her face in her hands and dry sobs racked her body. Gyneth moved to her side.

"Years ago, I thought a married man, Harrison Jaffe, was the love of my life. Then I saw him for what he was, weak, selfish, and materialistic. Maybe I have some of those same qualities myself, but I certainly didn't want them in a husband."

She patted Carolyn on the back, calming her.

"Maybe Matthew is that part of your past that you need to close off, to finish properly, for the same reasons that you came here. You need to find out the right person for you from this moment forward."

Carolyn listened to Gyneth. What she said was painfully true. But the players were reversed. It was Jeff who had been the one who had helped her finish the circle of belonging to the world of the Amrons.

Carolyn felt the tense internal conflict that had been with her for many years begin to soften and resolve. Joe had said it to her as he had wished her well in her journey through life. She had a destiny to fulfill, her mother had started the journey, opening the way to the city for her, and the Amrons, Joe, Ruth, and now Jeff, all of them were parts in the puzzle of her life that was now finally falling into place.

Matthew.

He was the future.

"Gyneth, finally I know what I want. God, I hope it's not too late." Carolyn grabbed the phone and dialed London frantically.

"Yes?" Matthew's voice was gruff, sleepy.

"God, I'm sorry, I forgot what the time was. Matthew, it's Carolyn. Please wait for me, I need you. It's taken me forever to understand everything. I'll be home within a week. Will you . . . will you be there for me?"

"Yes, I will be there." Matthew's voice was stronger. "I have always been there." He hung up.

Carolyn hugged Gyneth.

"I must have been crazy calling him at this hour. But he said he'd always been there. It's going to work out, Gyneth, it's going to happen." Gyneth laughed. Carolyn had gone from abject misery to joy in a few minutes.

"You are crazy. And so am I. And nothing in our lives has ever been straightforward or conventional. But I understand you so well, my friend, as you do me."

"Let's get out of this place, Gyneth. Your mother's accountants will set up the foundation, we can raise money in London and Los Angeles, and go on with our lives."

Gyneth signed a power of attorney to enable her mother's estate to be settled and the house sold. Anna and Andrew left with moving vans full of furniture and the belongings of a lifetime. The remainder was to be shipped to America.

They stood together the next week at the airport. Gyneth threw back her long blond hair and sighed with relief. "Thank God it's over. Alex, here I come!"

Carolyn laughed. "It's just beginning," she said, thinking of Matthew's strong arms around her.

"We must speak every week, arrange to see each other often. If only we lived closer to each other," Gyneth said, clasping her friend's hand in hers.

"Who knows what the future might bring! We have a lifetime ahead of us. Maybe one day we will live in the same city, be neighbors, have families together. Nothing is forever, we both know that. And anyway, don't you feel that our friendship has withstood so much that being separated by two continents still cannot diminish its strength?" Carolyn saw the tears fill her friend's eyes as she agreed. Now that the moment had come to part, both women realized it could be months, even years, until they were together again.

Their flights, one to New York and the other to London, were called within minutes of each other.

They linked arms and walked together into the international departure lounge.

Despite the turmoil of emotions they felt at leaving each other, South Africa and the past behind them, it was finally clear where they belonged. Gyneth and Carolyn were going home.

The Author welcomes your letters to:

Larraine Segil
123 North San Vicente Blvd.
Beverly Hills, CA 90211